Y0-BQS-268

# LOVE

*and*

# EMPIRE

# LOVE
## *and*
# EMPIRE

Erik Orsenna

Translated by Jeremy Leggatt

Cornelia & Michael Bessie Books
*An Imprint of* HarperCollins*Publishers*

This work was first published in France in 1988 under the title *L'Exposition coloniale*. Copyright © Septembre 1988, Éditions du Seuil.



FIRST EDITION

*Designed by Irving Perkins*

Library of Congress Cataloging-in-Publication Data

Orsenna, Erik, 1947–
[Exposition coloniale. English]
Love and empire / Erik Orsenna: translated by Jeremy Leggatt.—1st ed.
p. cm.
Translation of: L'exposition coloniale.
"A Cornelia and Michael Bessie book."
ISBN 0-06-039103-0
I. Title.
PQ2675.R7E9713 1991
843'.914—dc20 90-55574

91 92 93 94 95 CC/HC 10 9 8 7 6 5 4 3 2 1

*For Catherine C.*

*Perhaps, nearing the end of his days, the man who invented Tristan and Isolde passed by a house with closed shutters—and turned his eyes away. . . .*

—Louis Aragon

# *Contents*

## PART THREE

# *Prologue*

IN THE BEGINNING was the bookstore.

I speak of a time when books still counted. A remote period of our history separated from us by two worldwide conflicts, by several attempts at genocide, by the erection (most dampening) of the Eiffel Tower, and by other less momentous events.

In the beginning, then, was the bookstore. It is there I was conceived, in a setting favorable to the footloose, among travel books, mariners' charts, manuals of tropical medicine. My parents had not been long acquainted, and their passion for one another was violent. My father, who lived with his mother, could not receive visitors. And since he detested the countryside and his betrothed rejected carriage rides and rooms rented by the day, the bookstore was all they had.

"The act to which you owe life was too brief," he confided to me many years later. "Had I lasted a little longer, perhaps you might be less small. . . . But I plead mitigating circumstances: the store shutters had not been lowered, a customer might have appeared at any moment. . . . Forgive me."

Apologies accepted. So much for stature. Enough said.

In the beginning was the bookstore. It was from there when the hour came that Louis, my father, left for the hospital. All around us, nuns hurried up and down, patted cheeks, quieted clamors, called for boiled water, handed out feeding bottles, gave thanks to God at every turn—just what you would expect in a maternity ward. Oblivious to the din, Louis leaned over my cradle, put his mouth close to my ear, and spoke to me.

"You should let that child sleep," said a nun.

"I do hope you haven't a cold," said another nun.

"Monsieur, if you please! You are tiring that child out," said the first nun.

But the child was not tired. He was still floating; he had exchanged one bubble for another, that was all. The warmth of the maternal womb had given place to the sweetness of the paternal discourse. And the new, different sensations were no less sweet: those two small orifices, the seats of hearing, can give the soul fully as much pleasure as the entire skin. It was a truth the passage of time would progressively confirm.

The nuns feared for my health. They said again to my father, "Monsieur! I beseech you, monsieur; the newborn need peace and quiet."

What did they know?

Since the speaker scorned even to notice their presence, they called on two orderlies for help. The men dragged Louis, still talking, from the ward. Not far from there, the newborn's mother slept.

The same newborn's mother must have taken for herself all the slumber available in the Paris region, for when Louis reached his home he was so wide awake he was unable even to blink. I have a son, I have a son: this refrain warmed his heart like sunshine. In the middle of the night, immersed once again in Christopher Columbus's *Memoirs* and asking himself what made a man happier, having a son or discovering America, he was startled by a knocking at the bookstore doors downstairs.

"Monsieur! Monsieur!"

The bigger of the orderlies who had so brutally thrown him out was shouting through the door.

"Come quick, come quick!"

Louis dashed downstairs.

"Your son is screaming his head off; the doctors think his life may be in danger."

"How long has this been going on?"

"Since you left."

They raced to the hospital. The nuns were waiting out in the corridors, knobby boxwood rosaries intertwined in their fingers.

"Come quick, oh, Jesus, Mary, and Joseph, come quick!"

Scarcely was Louis seated, scarcely had he resumed his stories, than his young listener lapsed into the most absolute calm, with a curve of the lips and a retraction of the corners of the mouth which the nuns present unanimously declared to be a first smile. From then on, not another word about asking the lecturer to leave. He was duly issued a cot and a regulation nightshirt: long, flowing, white, with a red Sacred Heart emblem on the left-hand side. In order to slip it on, my father was obliged to break off his discourse for a second. My roars at once rose heavenward again.

To give us privacy, they surrounded us with black screens of the kind generally used to shield the dying from the outside world. Requiems and prayers for the dead rose all around us in the big communal ward. Naturally this accompaniment in no way diminished the happiness of our little trio: myself the newborn Gabriel, Louis the raconteur, and the newborn's mother, who had meanwhile wakened and whose gaze was riveted on her spouse's face. Nuns kept crowding in and out of our little stall on the pretext of seeing to our comfort ("Is everything all right, madame; monsieur, is there anything you need?"). In truth, though, they came to seek the answer to a theological question: to wit, was this a miracle, my ceasing to scream the instant my father began to speak into my ear? Some were ready to grant this and were already thanking the Most High for choosing their humble community to show Himself in all His beneficence. But most of the nuns favored a slightly less exalted explanation which for want of a better name might be called love.

There, amid the sisters of St. Vincent de Paul, I lived my finest hours, as Louis would remind me until the end of his days. The nuns showered him with kindnesses, with endless attentions, with devotion even (since the possibility of a miracle was still not wholly to be discounted and perhaps too because he was handsome and so young, not yet eighteen). They indulged his every whim, lest he leave and my roars begin again. And Louis took advantage of the situation. As soon as it was light, still telling stories to his son, he would complain of multiple ailments, and God knows his imagination was a fertile source of worries. He claimed to be suffering from a terrible pain in the ribs, then from goose bumps on his left arm, then from spots before the eyes, and then, at around 9 A.M., from loose stools. Each time the relevant specialist was summoned in an effort to reassure him.

"No, monsieur, you are in perfect health."

"Swear it," said Louis.

"By God, I swear it."

Whereupon the wave of hypochondria would ebb, leaving my father in peace for another few hours.

Early in the morning of our second day, people began to appear at the porter's lodge outside the emergency ward.

"Is this the place for travel books?"

"No, monsieur, this is a hospital."

"But they told me this is where I would find the bookseller: Ambroise Paré pavilion, Velpeau wing, second floor."

While getting his things together that dramatic night, Louis had found time to pin his new whereabouts on the bookstore door.

"Most decidedly you go too far, monsieur," the hospital director told him.

"And how can I make my living if I am unable to sell anything?"

Once again, the authorities had to give in. The green-painted corridors of the maternity wing witnessed the march-past of Louis's usual clientele: blushing adolescents avid for salacious illustrations, academics in search of background facts on the empire of Mali (1240–1599), travelers reluctant to roam the central Sahara on camelback for two years without maps, and finally the last species, the bookseller's favorite, couples on the eve of departure for a tour of colonial duty and seeking counsel on health matters, on clothing, on mosquito netting, on cannibals.

For such was my father's profession: a bookseller who specialized in travel books.

Alas, it was time for us to be discharged. A full moon nine months earlier, in 1882, must have quickened Parisian energies. A parturient throng crowded into the hospital. Louis rose most reluctantly, and not indeed without vertigo as a result of lying supine for so long, his mouth open, endlessly talking. He called, but without response. The nuns scurried about, snipped cords, sewed up torn perineums, sponged slimy creatures, hailed doctors: another breech over here!

The newborn's mother was ready first. She pushed through the glass-paned door behind which Louis, not flagging for an instant in his recital of the stories so needful to me, had removed the nightshirt decorated on the left breast with the Sacred Heart and had begun to shave. The mother cradled her empty abdomen.

"I am leaving, Louis. I can no longer live either with you or with your mother, Louis. You must forgive me, Louis. We are all so young. No one will suffer. Goodbye, Louis."

In those days married women rarely left. But in her slumber my mother had forged the steeliest of resolves. Having myself (much later) come to know some of my father's little ways, I can only condone her decision. Yet the fact remains that I have no recollection of the kiss she must have planted on my forehead, nor any memory of the chill when she closed the glass-paned door and left our green-hued room forever to embark on a destiny of which I remain to this day wholly ignorant. Perhaps she is one of those old women walking eternally by the sea at Cannes or Nice, moving, as age dulls them, at an ever slower pace. There are so many old people of all nationalities in that part of France that you have every chance of coming across long-lost relatives there.

So we left alone, the two of us, Louis bearing Gabriel and speaking into his ear. Goodbye, the nuns said, too busy even to glance up at us as they stooped over bellies, heads between spread legs, on the brink of the gulf into which they seemed tempted to plunge in order to join the fetuses. But in that case why had they kept on those gigantic headdresses, those great white birds, so cumbersome for such a crossing? Yes, why?

I have many other questions concerning these beginnings, and foremost among them is this: What stories was my father telling me? He always maintained that he talked about women. Such complex beings, Gabriel; it's never too soon to start wondering. But how to be certain? My father had no knowledge of stable relationships. At all events, from that day to this I have been afflicted with a curious deafness to anything not concerning women. For love stories, for the rustle of dresses or of stockings, my hearing is exceptional, miraculous. For anything else, I have to strain my ears; all the other noises in creation are indistinct, as if reaching me from afar.

Onward, onward; the story moves on and I have so much to tell. Of Brazil, rubber, the two sisters, Indochina, Vienna, Clermont-Ferrand, the Winter Velodrome—so many episodes you will need to know, so much information essential for my trial.

# PART

# ONE

# 1
# *The Call of Empire*

## I

My name is Gabriel, son of the bookseller Louis, grandson of the bookseller Marguerite, and like all booksellers we waged war on books.

Despite his tender years, Gabriel played his part in this war as best he could. He was much too frightened of being returned to his nanny, an inhuman woman who never told stories and placidly ignored the most strident of childish screams thanks to the balls of wax she thrust deep inside her ears, all the way into her inhuman skull.

The bookshop was packed to overflowing, and still the flood rolled in. Worse, since the establishment of the Republic—a regime notoriously in favor of educating the masses through reading—the flood seemed to have swollen.

Gabriel strove to make himself useful, helping undo the packages and handing the volumes across one by one as Louis sang out their titles.

"Victor Cherbuliez: *Count Ghislain's Calling;* Louis-Joseph Hanoteau: *Tamachek Grammar;* Francis Garnier: *Journey of Exploration in Indochina* (new edition, 3 volumes; why not 8?); Paul d'Ivoi: *Across France's Colonies with Sergeant Simplet;* Édouard Foa: *My Hunting Expeditions in Central Africa.*"

"And here I was thinking they never sent us anything on Mondays," Marguerite murmured. "How many inches today?"

"Seventeen," answered Louis, measuring the spines with a dressmaker's tape. "We'll never manage it."

"Squeeze harder," Marguerite suggested in a tentative voice. "I don't know what else to do. Squeeze them in tighter."

"Listen, already they're not shelves but hydraulic springs. One more page and the whole house will be blown to smithereens."

"But this is impossible! There must be some trick to it. Let's ask other booksellers. All businesses have their trade secrets. Revolving bookshelves perhaps?"

So our days passed. Gabriel had quickly noticed that once night falls it is the best behaved and quietest of children who stay up longest. So he would lie quite still on the living room rug, hidden by an armchair and half roasted by the fire on the hearth.

"No doubt about it, books make for cramped living, just like marriage," my father would say.

"What do you know about marriage?"

Neither of them had any experience of it. They would embark on meaningless comparisons. Was married life more cramped than single life? Little by little I would doze off. Later the cold roused me. The fire had gone out on the hearth but the family discussion went on apace.

"Books are even more cunning and reproduce even faster than rats. One day we're going to have to de-rat the place," said my father.

"Come now, Louis!"

But Marguerite's cry of horror was feigned. These last words of his reassured her.

"How dreadful it would be, Louis my son, if you became attached to books!"

"No chance of that!"

"You would not have wanted to leave. They are so heavy, such a hindrance. Swear to me, Louis, that leaving for the colonies is still your heart's desire."

He swore.

I remember the evening always ended with a solemn exchange of promises between mother and son.

"We forgot to put him to bed!" one of them would cry.

And to give myself courage before the long slide into blackness I thought very hard of the Empire, where it was always hot the way it is hot in front of a fireplace and where there was always room to store all one's books. Later, Louis would come up to kiss me good night, rousing me, murmuring into my ear.

"Grow up quickly, Gabriel. I need you. It's not easy taking Marguerite on single-handed; come and help me, Gabriel. I'm scarcely older than you and I'm waiting for you to catch up."

But we must not equate these understandable spasms of exasperation—when the need for shelf space was truly pressing—with an aversion to storytelling. On the contrary. The good habits begun in the hospital persisted, with the help now of books. Almost every day the two booksellers Louis and Marguerite would ferret through their labyrinthine warren of books, and—"Hello," they would say as they returned, "just listen to this story I found you!" And Gabriel would listen, would listen so intently, would so muster his energies for listening that for a long while he neglected to learn how to speak.

"Once upon a time," Marguerite began. Immediately she would break off to warn her listener, "Remember, these are not fairy tales, Gabriel, they are true stories."

For Gabriel was not allowed fairies, or dragons, or magic carpets, or Tom Thumbs.

"A child must first of all learn about reality," Marguerite would say. "To grow, a child must have solid ground beneath his feet."

Gabriel can recall only a few of the innumerable true stories of that period. But he offers the following as an example. It was among his favorites. He asked for it month after month.

"If you are good," Marguerite would reply. . . .

"Once upon a time there was a young man whose first name was Jones, hardly any older than you. He had but one wish in his whole life—to get into Buckingham Palace and see Queen Victoria. At fifteen he disguised himself as a chimney sweep and spent three whole days in the huge palace. He hid under beds and fed on leftovers. He sat on the throne, spied for hours on end on the queen's daily doings, then left, without anyone saying a word to him. Two years later he scaled a garden wall, climbed in through an open window, and crawled beneath a capacious sofa where important visitors were seated. From this position he witnessed several meetings, heard the infant princess royal crying, and glimpsed the queen's shoes (and nothing else, Gabriel, for queens have very long dresses).

"But alas, a footman caught him. He was sentenced to three months in a reformatory. He was so well behaved there that on the day of his release the warden said to him, 'Good luck, Mr. Jones, we consider you completely rehabilitated.' But the very next day he was discovered outside the palace. The warden was most disappointed to see him return, flanked by two policemen. Other treatments were attempted, but to no avail. No sooner was he released than Mr. Jones would return to Buckingham Palace.

"By now reporters had started to dog his footsteps, and all his approaches to the palace drew crowds. The owners of music halls (huge rooms, Gabriel, filled with smoke and untrue stories) approached him with requests to tell the queen's secrets. But as you might imagine, he refused. The authorities were most embarrassed, you see. First of all, Mr. Jones was doing no harm. Perhaps he was even setting an example; perhaps the true love of a subject for his queen was exactly that. After much deliberation, the authorities decided to ship him out on HMS *Warspite,* a vessel that rarely put into English waters. It was hoped that the sight of the ocean might rid him of his obsession. But no sooner did he reach Portsmouth after a year at sea than he rushed for the London train. They had to forbid him ever to set foot on dry land.

"One night in 1844 he fell into the sea between Tunis and Algiers. (One day you will read *The Times,* Gabriel; it is the best newspaper in the world.) The officer who fished young Jones out of the water reported the interview: 'Why did you throw yourself into the water, Mr. Jones?' 'To see the buoy light burning.'

"Can you imagine that, Gabriel? 'To see the buoy light burning.' Perhaps one day you too will love queens, Gabriel, and their light."

That was how all Marguerite's stories ended: Perhaps one day you too will be like General Bugeaud. Or La Pérouse. Or Magellan, or Alexander. Christopher Columbus. Hernando Cortés. Or their lieutenants. There is no shame, Gabriel, in entering the service of men of genius.

So many destinies make one dizzy. Before my eyes were other Gabriels, every conceivable kind of Gabriel, a delectable catalogue of Gabriels riffled as if by the wind. It was perhaps at that precise moment that my rate of growth slowed, in order to permit the postponement of so crucial a choice. And then, of course, such profusion of choice engenders hesitation, militates against the development of what people call character. From this standpoint Marguerite's educational efforts on my behalf were perhaps not wholly successful.

* * *

The only place not overrun by books was the sideboard, our reliquary; there, so loftily perched that Gabriel had to jump to catch a glimpse of them, were the three most important members (not counting the living) of the Orsenna family.

Let us begin with my namesake, my grandfather Gabriel, baptized Gabriel the First so as not to get us mixed up, an authentic Hidalgo to judge by the daguerrotype, with somber eye and gaunt cheek, in mourning or formal attire, solemn, arms folded before the depressing spectacle of the world, at first sight a decidedly gloomy character. But he was the only love of Marguerite's life, and so short-lived: one week.

She met him in Paris one August day in 1865 as she fled the summer heat and set off unchaperoned aboard a river pleasure boat.

There he stood, foursquare at the prow, so sad in his black suit that the nineteen-year-old girl just in from Lyon to round off her education was at once intrigued. Next day she put off her turnkey of a guardian uncle (with a fabrication about charity work or a visit to the poor wards at the Hôtel-Dieu hospital) and went back. The Hidalgo was still at his post, gazing into the sepia water without so much as a glance at the wonders gliding past him: the Louvre, the Academy, the Conciergerie, the Hôtel de Ville. Seeing him so disdainful of those glories the whole world envies us, Marguerite grew angry. And her anger did not abate in two or three hours of its own accord, like a normal burst of anger, but took up residence in the girl, beneath her blouse somewhere between her stomach and her ribs, little glowing embers that by night kept her awake and by day drove everything else from her mind—so much so that by the end of her fifth afternoon on the pleasure boat she took the plunge, so to speak, approached the figure in the prow, and muttered in tones so severe they made him start, "Clearly the gentleman does not like our city?"

Sadness and an understandable concern for family privacy prevent me from offering more than an abridged version of what happened next.

The Hidalgo rose and introduced himself: Señor Orsenna, exile ("Oh, I'm sorry," said the girl), a native of Vera Cruz. A member of President Miramón's staff. Driven like him from Mexico by the usurper Juárez. And he begged her to take a seat where he was standing, went and found her a stool, and began to explain his country's hopelessly entangled situation to her. Marguerite's heart beat fast. She felt that the pleasure craft was taking her forever from Lyon and childhood to enter adult worlds, adult wars, adult lives. As they rounded the eastern tip of the Île de la Cité, the Hidalgo outlined Napoleon III's plan: to cool the ambitions of the United States by creating a vast Catholic empire in Mexico, with the Austrian archduke Maximilian as emperor. "That is why my country's fate rests in France's hands; do you understand, mademoiselle?"

The boat put in to shore, and the Hidalgo said farewell. All night long, with not a thought for sleep, Marguerite recited those names she had never heard before: Miramón, Juárez, Maximilian. She got up, wrote down all those outlandish syllables on a piece of paper, so as to remember them and not seem too ignorant next day, went back to bed, and finally found slumber in the sadness of the Hidalgo's gaze.

Of course she went back. He was there, in the same place but in improved spirits, all smiles (or very nearly) at seeing her. And day after day he launched himself into a long recital of his plans for after the civil war. "You will come and live with me in Mexico, in a big cool house where the children will have no fear of the dark. . . ." And as he spoke, Señor Orsenna, who had recovered a vitality more worthy of the tropics, brought his hand closer and closer to hers. So much so, and soon with such intimacy, that the captain of the pleasure boat (after carefully weighing the risk of losing such good customers against that of being closed down for indecency as a vulgar floating brothel), begged the lovers to observe a little more decorum. Marguerite blushed as a girl from Lyon could blush in those days, turning scarlet from one second to the next. But the intense shame she felt was but as wind fanning the flames within her. When the Hidalgo told her he was leaving next day, she said, "Come with me." And Louis was conceived.

Later, when her son or others asked why she had never sought to love again, Marguerite always gave the same answer. He had been everything to her: sadness and gaiety, turquoise sea and dusty highways, hatred of American bandits and respect for the French Academy, war and cool houses, the need for Empire, the love of ships. He was a hand and a body. "I have lived in the Noah's ark of love; now, after the Flood, why would you have me go in search of a fragment of feeling here, another fragment there?"

That is why I am called Gabriel, like the Hidalgo. As for the Mexican name Orsenna, I still wonder how Marguerite managed to appropriate it for herself. There was no wedding ceremony between her and the exile. Yet my papers are in order: Orsenna, Gabriel; son of Orsenna, Louis; grandson of Orsenna, Marguerite. As we shall see, my grandmother was a peerless wager of wars against officialdom. And she won them, every one.

Half a year after the last of those seven days of love, the sad, sad letter arrived at the end of a bizarre itinerary, the heavy itinerary of sadness: Puebla (Mexico); Mexico City (Mexico); Bordeaux (France); Paris (France); Compiègne (France), where Napoleon III held court; Lyon (France), where Marguerite had returned to make ready her trousseau (and to prepare her family for the news). For a whole month she lived beside this tropical letter which had been opened several times by various censors, and which she kept sealed. When the month was up, without taking the time to read the whole letter *(Alas, mademoiselle, my brother often spoke to me of you; alas, in the course of the siege . . .),* she knew she no longer possessed anything in the world, neither love nor husband nor marriage nor father for the child she was expecting, the fruit of those seven days.

Gabriel the First did not reign alone on the sideboard. At his right sat the fallen emperor Napoleon, third of that name. Even on sunny days he eyed me suspiciously.

"Emperors are like that," Marguerite explained. "They see the world and its other side at the same time, you know. . . ."

Which was not at all reassuring.

According to Marguerite, Napoleon III was most concerned about my appetite.

"Eat, or he'll be upset."

I immediately stuffed an extra spoonful of food into my mouth, with resultant distension of my cheeks. For beneath that inquisitorial stare it was impossible to swallow anything. Because of the fallen emperor I hoarded entire meals in my mouth: tapioca soup, chicken, red-hot roast potatoes, ricotta cubes (unable to find Mexican cheese in the stores, Marguerite considered ricotta an excellent interim substitute), as well as testicle-like dried apricots (a comparison that entered Gabriel's universe via elementary school). And little by little my face grew rounder and rounder. It is to Napoleon III that I owe the heaviest cross I bear, that of not possessing a gaunt visage like Don Quixote or like El Greco's subjects.

"My knight of the round face," Louis would say with a smile of his son Gabriel, intending no disparagement.

On the emperor's other side, bolt upright and not one whit intimidated, stood Eduardo G. Orsenna, the Hidalgo's father, the only souvenir of Mexico her departing love had left Marguerite, a small man crowned with a straw hat and squinting, probably because of the tropical sun.

"With a face like that he couldn't have been interested in anything but the wholesale fish business," Louis would say.

"What's the wholesale fish business?" asked Gabriel.

"The same thing as religion," Louis replied.

"Louis, please!" cried Marguerite.

And for a few days no one would refer to Eduardo G. Orsenna, the Mexican ancestor no one had ever really known, and who must have been very surprised to find himself here in the bosom of a foreign family in the misty village of Levallois, so far from the Caribbean.

## II

Marguerite loved her town.

She would describe its heroic beginnings, when the *champ Perret* was not yet Champerret but simply waste ground, a kind of encampment at the gates of Paris, outside the city's fortifications.

First there was mud, even in summer. Then came the streets. Then the market. There was the battle over the school; some wanted it to be religious, others didn't. They were always taking up a collection, one day for the church, next day for the fire engine. They did not install gas lighting until after that; it was safer that way. "Would you like to build a city, Gabriel?" Yes, he replied. Levallois is not big, so they often stopped at the same places. Many people greeted them. "Good morning, Madame Orsenna, how is your son?" For Gabriel it was a sweet feeling: a turn around his small estate, a sense of kingship.

In the evenings Louis would ask, "You're sure these walks are good for the child's health?"

Marguerite was impervious to everything. She was sheltered by her memories. But Louis was right; the Levallois air was laden with every conceivable stench, with the most variegated pungencies. Given the right wind, we probably scented Neuilly. If you had known Levallois then you would find its atmosphere today empty, sanitized, the most arid of elements.

First of all was manure. Levallois was all cowsheds and stables. A good many Paris carriage drivers stabled their horses there. This was understandable; with rents within the city walls as high as they were, where else could they have lodged their quadrupeds? Horses of all kinds, Arabs, Barbs, Percherons; I won't name them all. I could tell them by ear alone, just by their hoofbeats. Whatever the color of their coats, chestnut or dappled, roan or bay, they would piss away with gusto at first light, followed almost immediately by the dairy cows that had also ended up in Levallois. The plop-plop of cow patties usually sounded next, whence that powerful animal smell that struck you every morning when you opened the door or unlatched the window.

"No doubt about it," said Louis. "Gabriel is better provided for than the baby Jesus. All this livestock standing guard over him. The manger at Bethlehem was nothing compared to ours."

"Louis, please!" answered Marguerite.

She would dress me hurriedly and we would leave.

Our first call was always at the quinine factory on the rue Voltaire. Marguerite wanted to be sure its production continued unabated. "As long as I can see that smoke rising I don't have to worry about our Empire," she said; it was proof that French settlers were colonizing new lands. Gabriel did not share her enthusiasm for that particular smoke, with its odor of cooking endives and of nux vomica. You sympathized with tropical microbes; one whiff of that acrid smell and you packed your bags and left. Our next ports of call were no more appetizing: the Laming factory (ammonia and ammonium sulfate), which made your nostrils prickle; then the Corbière-Esnault disinfectant plant, where just walking past its walls turned you into fresh-scrubbed floor tiles for the rest of the day; then the Holstein candleworks, with their disturbing musty odor, or the Gautier-Bouchard establishment, whose dyes and varnishes, like onions, made you weep.

From time to time Esun Guy, the Bonapartist letter carrier, would emerge from behind a layer cake of houses, satchel on his back. A conversation would be struck up.

"Do you remember when the place de Châteaudun used to be called place de la Reine-Hortense? I've a good mind to return today's letters to their senders: 'Address unknown.' What do you think?"

This Bonapartist plotting never lasted long, because of the demands of his job ("By noon sharp I'm supposed to have delivered all the mail").

And then Marguerite too had things to do. She would question guards and doormen.

"Are you hiring today?"

She pretended to believe that her Hidalgo would arrive in Levallois one fine day seeking work. It was one of her ways of feeling less alone.

Gabriel would tug at her sleeve, pulling her toward his favorite attraction, the Bribant cookhouses, where they boiled cows' and sheep's heads. You never saw these things arrive. It was probably at night, so as not to shock people. Next morning they would leave again by the cartload, exuding a grayish liquid, some with eyes, others not. Pallid gelatinous heaps pursued by cats, crows, and yapping dogs, they set off in the direction of Paris and its epicures.

Every evening after these excursions Marguerite scrubbed Gabriel's cheeks and neck with a small strongly scented mauve briquette, the latest brainchild of the Oriza perfume factory.

"Now your father won't be able to say Levallois smells bad."

As soon as he came through the door Louis sniffed, smiled, and spoke of other things. He always went along with make-believe.

But worst of all was the Seine. From it rose the most tenacious of effluvia, an illusion of coolness mingled with decay, like the dank air of a cellar with all its composite smells. Frequent fogs reinforced this impression of inhabiting a basement. From October to March you rarely saw the sky. You pictured buildings soaring high above Levallois, another city, noble sunlit stories. On foggy days, days of heavy fog, Louis went mad, shutting the house up tight, forbidding anyone to go out. The nearness of the river terrified him. To get to the bookstore he took his compass along, first outlining all the safer cardinal points on its dial in blue greasepaint: northeast, east, southeast, south. The others he underlined in red.

So the Orsenna family ventured near the water only in the finest weather. Marguerite explained the direction of the current to her grandson: That way is the sea. Then we would set out along the towpath to the Cavé yards, divided into two sections, the boilerworks (a contemptible trade, a trade without odors, a trade based on noise, the din of hammers on metal plates) and the boatyards, with their smell of charred oak. The shipwrights bent the ribs of their vessels into shape one by one, over the flames. All kinds of craft lay around on the grass, waiting for the right tide to set them afloat.

Levallois stank, all right. And in summer or in windless spells it stank to high heaven. They say the place smells much better these days. A pity. In my day, there was in the air such a conflict between animal flatulence and chemical wastes, such a hesitation between the sweetness of Oriza perfumes and the bitterness of quinine, such intoxication, such a mania to invent things nonstop (and who cared how bad they smelled?), such industrial and olfactory prodigality that I raise my hat in salute. And mourn its passing.

Yes, in his childhood Gabriel inhaled the very stench of the nineteenth century. But this stench fed him. Don't expect him to disown it.

I remember other walks.

On exceptionally fine days we left Levallois and struck out for the cemeteries: Auteuil, Montmartre, even Père-Lachaise when the sky was truly cloudless. We strolled among the graves. I had just learned to read.

"Look at the first names," Marguerite said to me. "Your eyes are better than mine; tell me if you see a Gabriel."

I watched her out of the corner of my eye, trotting to keep up with me, suddenly wrinkled, with no particular goal, moving from plot to plot at random, hands pushed into her pockets, face and blue gaze hidden beneath her hat, dressed in deepest black. How old she is, I said to myself. Why does she get so old in cemeteries? There was nothing left to her of her Hidalgo. I believe she would willingly have exchanged a true grave of Gabriel the First, a real grave, for the slender hope that he might still be alive.

On the way back (licorice or coconut balls every half mile), she would tell me her ideas about death.

"Of course he's not there, Gabriel, but the dead are not like us, they travel so much more. And I'm going to tell you a secret"—she lowered her voice—"every cemetery in the world communicates with every other. Never forget that—all cemeteries communicate."

## III

And every Monday, Marguerite would go back to the Colonial Ministry, in those days just a semblance of a ministry relegated to a handful of gloomy offices on loan from the Navy, on the place de la Concorde.

"To treat our Empire this way, what a dreadful shame," she said whenever she stopped by. It made them like her.

"Yes indeed, madame," the pallid attaché assigned to the information desk would sigh.

This lightning exchange was the abridged version of a conversation originally much longer but gradually whittled down by dint of repetition.

To give you a better understanding of Marguerite Orsenna's concerns, I offer the fuller version:

"Well now, I am eager for my son Louis to participate in our country's expansion."

"A most creditable impulse, madame."

"Do we possess such a thing as a Colonial School?"

"Yes, madame, the former Cambodian School."

"How does one enroll?"

"You need the permission of the Under-Secretary of State for the Colonies. Please fill in this form and come back in a month."

When the month was up Marguerite returned.

"Madame, I shall be frank." With these words, the attaché blinked his lashes and lowered his voice. "Madame, you haven't a chance. Your family is listed as Bonapartist."

Violent anger on Marguerite's part. "I don't think much of an empire that tramples its emperors underfoot!"

The officials present cast a long all-encompassing look around the encircling walls of sepia folders with their exotic titles (Bingerville, Porto-Novo, Niamey), made sure there was no one there to denounce them, reaffirmed their Republican convictions, but acknowledged that, yes, there certainly seemed to be a contradiction there.

"Good, so when can we expect a Republican School, that is—if I have correctly understood the Republic—a school with an exacting and anonymous entrance exam?"

"Soon, madame, doubtless very soon. The Under-Secretary of State is very keen on the idea."

Inevitably, she had become more than just a regular visitor; she was a supporting player, one of the cast, a member of the family. They invited her to their receptions, and God knows receptions came thick and fast in those days. A reception to celebrate the attaché's promotion (henceforth I shall have an office to receive you in, dear Madame Orsenna). A reception to salute the entry of Laos into the Empire. And receptions for the creation of French Guinea and the Ivory Coast. A reception to mark the marriage of the former attaché, who throughout the cordial occasion ("I thought it better not to invite my spouse; she would have known nobody here, but she asks me to send you all her greetings") stood close to Marguerite and begged her to continue her visits even after the school opened, which would not be long now. And the wine went on flowing at these receptions, four of them in less than a year. One to celebrate the defeat of the cruel monarch of Dahomey, one to mark the transformation of the State Secretariat into a full-fledged Ministry of the Colonies. ("Now that we have attained this plateau of responsibility," the new Minister announced, "you will understand that we must cut down our little celebrations. The eyes of France and the world are upon us.")

But it had become a habit. There was no way of cutting back the receptions. They were very careful, though, to close the windows and draw the curtains, for patriots had begun to protest: the colonials are making merry while Alsace and Lorraine are in pain. There were even petitions and demonstrations with banners. Enough of waste! Alsace, yes; Tonkin, no! But were they not duty-bound to give the Marchand mission a fitting sendoff, to celebrate the establishment of the protectorate of Madagascar?

Back at home, cheeks pink, features festive, Marguerite did not speak to us but went straight to her room and locked the door. Late into the night we heard her talking, regaling Gabriel the First, my unknown grandfather, with the latest news of Levallois and of the French Empire, which would very soon be strong enough, in alliance with Mexico, to push back the Americans—a band of moneyed, ill-bred upstarts. But the volume quickly rose. She railed against her Hidalgo for leaving her so soon. Seven days! As if in seven days you could take the measure of a woman, a woman of Lyon! Inexperienced in bed, perhaps, but unchallengeable in the kitchen. And to bring him back, she called out the names of dishes renowned between the Saône and the Rhône: braised carp, chicken Célestine, *tablier de sapeur, bugnes, radisses.*

On the other side of the door Louis whispered to me, "She's right, believe me, your grandmother is right; a woman is worth more than seven days." The hypocrite; he never formed a lasting attachment.

## IV

Marguerite measured things. Empire zealots are like that. Without warning she would stand me against the eastern wall of the kitchen, where my preceding measurements, with dates, were inscribed *(3 ft. 7 in. June 1, 1890; 3 ft. 8 in. March 13, 1891).*

"Isn't this child ever going to grow?"

And for the umpteenth time she would change doctors, forcing us to travel around Levallois in ever-widening circles and obliging me to consume ever-stranger diets. By the time we celebrated my fourth foot I was on celery sticks in the morning ("For the fiber, Gabriel, the scaffolding of the body"), on lentils at noon ("Packed with iron, more scaffolding, just think of the Eiffel Tower, Gabriel"), on tea in the afternoon ("It rids us of excess plumpness, Gabriel, but mind, it must be drunk weak"), on cod-liver oil at eight in the evening ("I shall be frank, Gabriel, this potion, which I agree is loathsome, will do you no good at all, but the action of retching as you swallow it will relax your muscles and contribute to your growth").

At one point Marguerite attributed my stagnation to her measuring devices. She possessed all kinds: yardsticks, dressmaker's tapes, surveyor's measures. Behind Louis's back, she often took them to Sèvres. I helped as best I could. Yardsticks are heavy.

"Our house is overheated, you see. I believe our yardsticks may have stretched. That's why you aren't growing."

The officials at the Bureau of Weights and Measures welcomed us with open arms.

"What a pleasure to meet people like yourselves, lovers of truth. And what a splendid lesson in precision for the lad."

They would take away our measuring devices to compare them with the standard, returning a few moments later.

"All is well, apart perhaps from this one made of cloth. It is indeed just a shade too long. Perhaps the lad plays with it when you are not there? You should advise him not to."

"What temperature do you suggest?" Marguerite asked.

"Sixty-eight degrees."

"Humidity?"

"Sixty percent."

"You see?" said Marguerite on the way home. "We were right to make sure."

But let's be quite clear. Gabriel was not Marguerite's only cause for disappointment on this matter of size. Any excuse would do for her to deplore France's dimensions: the width of the Seine ("Do you realize, Gabriel, that you can't even see the opposite bank of the

Amazon?"), the rate of local precipitation ("Unless more than four inches fall in an hour, don't even call it rain!"), the size of eggs ("Decidedly, Gabriel, temperate-zone chickens no longer lay properly").

But she reserved her keenest distress for the world map. No matter how high-spirited she might be on her return from the receptions, a single glance at the globe would plunge her into despair.

"Look, Gabriel, our little pink spot is nothing compared to America or Russia. Besides, our Empire has been stagnating for years. No denying it, my poor boy, you take after France."

This heredity weighed heavily on my shoulders.

There were many other reasons for my small size. No matter what Louis and Marguerite said and did, I sensed an absence just above my head, a void, a chill, just above me, just at the place on my genealogical tree that should have been occupied by the newborn's young mother, the very one who had fled the hospital, leaving us alone with the squalling parturients and the nuns in their winged coifs. A kind of blank that might one day swallow me up. Now, now, the blank would say, that's quite enough of pretending to be alive. Gabriel, who has no mother, has never really emerged from the void. . . .

This being the case, it seemed better not to grow but to remain somewhere down low.

Later on, much later on, only a few years ago, on a sunlit terrace on the boulevard Saint-Germain, where we were celebrating the liberation of Paris for the hundredth time, Louis would say to me, "You know, I did everything I could to replace your mother." He spoke slowly. Bourgeuil wine loosens the tongue but does not improve the diction. He gripped my arm. "Gabriel, I did everything, everything. You noticed, I hope?"

Gabriel had noticed.

Not simply noticed, but encouraged and even lent spice to his father's unbelievable amorous career. Because of my allergy to nannies (every one of them inhuman), Marguerite and Louis took turns looking after me. But what can a man do when he is burdened all day long with an infant of tender years? Fathers do not like going for walks; fathers do not like playing with blocks. It was because of me, it was thanks to me, that he began to receive guests.

At first they shut me in my room. But I had not prevailed over inhuman nannies to end thus in exile. So I howled. At once Louis appeared, his loins curiously girded with a bath towel. There there, there there, Gabriel, he said, and settled me down next to him, next to them.

But I would not have you assume that Gabriel was tossed carelessly into the fiery and acid universe of sex. His apprenticeship was gradual. It began with his hearing. Since his small legs could not yet support him, he lay in his soft cradle protected by a screen of tawny wicker, punctuating with his approving chirrups the yeses, the yes-yeses, the no-not-thats, the please-oh-yes-pleases, the oh-yes-yes-yes-pleases! Later, once Gabriel could hoist himself upright, came vision. But spring bloomed slowly that year, so the athletes remained for the most part beneath the eiderdown, emerging only rarely and briefly to perform against a wall or on a rug. Not until summer could he witness complete scenes, and even then they were obscured: women wore their hair long then and chignons never held up; the first brisk engagement and they would come undone despite forests of hairpins. Furthermore, if my father's partner happened to be a high-strung type, this gripping spectacle was quite often interrupted. "Who on earth is that?" the guest would suddenly shriek, having finally noticed my presence.

"Only my son, darling."

"Well, I can't go on. That child's eyes turn me to ice."

"Come, come, darling, at his age?" replied Louis.

"You're an odd family and no mistake," the lady would mutter as she got dressed. "And when I say odd . . ."

How did Louis meet all these women?

To this first question the highly envious Gabriel has the answer: through the bookstore. Sent there by city hall officials, by travel agencies, by the ministries where Marguerite had pinned their leaflets, ladies on their way overseas came in for information. They would enter the bookstore shyly.

"Is it dangerous in the colonies?"

But ladies not going abroad also came in, and much more boldly: Would you happen to have a book that would take me out of myself?

Gradually the conversation would slide into the suggestive mode. Without seeking to detract unfairly from Louis, this slide—a necessary but far from conclusive condition of the operation—was abetted by his fair visitors' curiosity, always of the same kind:

"Tell me, is it *really* hot over there?"

"Are the natives *really* savage?"

It is beyond this point that the mystery begins.

How did Louis manage, almost every time, to convert this equivocal climate into one of crude interrogation: Would you care to call on me at home? It is a question to which Gabriel, that son highly envious of his father, still finds no answer after years and years of speculation. He gives up.

And to this let us add a truth as hard to swallow as a ball of cotton wool: unlike me, my father was tall and handsome. Hazel eyes, and cheeks the opposite of mine—hollow, as if sucked in, giving him an untamed look. And that isn't all. As I was saying, he had an untamed look, but tender, too, for toward the bottom of these hollows, as if extending his lips, were two small dimples. In short, my father's face offered women everything they could desire, violence and gentleness, the promise of caresses but the possibility of cruelty. As for the rest of his anatomy, you'll never know. Filial respect imposes limits. Don't be disappointed. Consider what this confession of envy has cost me, and be satisfied.

Coming back to the house, Marguerite sometimes encountered one of these guests powdering her nose in the hall mirror before leaving or, worse, asking Louis to pull her corset tight.

"Oh, excuse me, madame!" my father's lady friend would stammer. "Oh, excuse me!"

She would snatch up her things ("It's quite all right, young lady," said Marguerite) and bolt.

"You see, Mama," explained Louis, "out there in the colonies this choice will no longer be available to me. In the tropics all women are alike. It's like the weather. There are no seasons out there."

"But I didn't say a word, dear boy."

Marguerite was unperturbed. She considered every object she owned and every event that took place at no. 12 on the brand-new rue

Cormeille with the equanimity of the Creator: the proud certainty that all was as it should be.

Today I understand my mother's flight: in such a creation a normal woman would inevitably have felt suffocated.

I also remember Sundays, and for good reason; everything flowed swiftly on Sundays: hours, money, the Seine. Louis would appear in my room early in the morning.

"Get ready for the races!"

For a long time I wondered what kind of getting ready Louis had in mind: knocking on wood, lighting a candle? In any case I dressed and we sallied forth into the morning, father and son, one whistling, the other skipping. To soothe our consciences we went by the docks. But the passenger boats, packed to the gills with horseracing enthusiasts, made no move in our direction. We were obliged to reach Longchamp on foot.

"Faster," said Louis, "or we'll miss the first race."

He was talking for himself. This was the time when he planned our future.

"If for any reason we don't leave for the colonies, I wouldn't mind moving to Saint-Cloud hill. On the eastern balconies you'd only need binoculars; you'd see every finish."

For Louis, the horseracing fraternity was a kind of model: it was the best you could expect of this world, human nature and the planet being what they are. As soon as we were through the entrance gates he embraced crowd, trees, track, weighing enclosure, ladies' hats, stands, in a broad sweeping gesture.

"This is what life should be like, Gabriel!"

He was probably right. In that case we would all have much sprightlier names, like Vale of Love or Golden Vine. We would sport our owners' colors, and the rules would be so much simpler. Every hour, we would line up for a new race and begin all over again. Whenever we discussed horses Louis studied me gravely; perhaps he expected me to help him replace our world with a racetrack. Later on, we never again mentioned the subject. He was doubtless disappointed. I had not supported him wholeheartedly enough. During races he gnawed at his lips, abruptly very pale as if about to weep. As the pack neared the finish line he squeezed my hand harder and harder. Gabriel yelled with the crowd. The Orsenna family would have time to lose two or three races before lunch. Besides, the real eating came later, after the last race, while we "let the crowds thin out." The crowds slowly deserted the track, some disappearing into the woods toward Auteuil or Neuilly, some returning to Paris by river. We were regular customers at a portable café erected only on Sundays, just behind the mill.

"Celebrating a big win?" our racetrack acquaintances would call out.

"I see the gentleman has the good sense to take his time," said the café owner.

"Yes, time . . . it's like my hot tip today; sometimes it doesn't exactly fly."

Suburbanites who had flopped down at nearby tables joined us in thanking providence that they did not live in the capital; at least we could afford to "let the crowds thin out."

Soon it would be time for the last ferryboat. Louis helped the café owner dismantle his parasols and load chairs onto his cart. The Seine's water was black, and the water bus, stopping first on one bank and then on the other to pick up passengers, made slow headway.

"A strong current tonight!" said my father.

"And it would help if they didn't open the Suresnes lock every Saturday night," said the ticket collector.

By the time we reached Levallois it was dark. We came ashore next door to the Cavé boatyards. Ships on dry land take on strange shapes in the dark. The water bus went on toward Clichy, Gennevilliers, the north. We were left alone amid the smells. Louis put a hand on my shoulder. He removed it at once.

"What an idiot I am to put extra weight on you! What if you had chosen just that second to start growing, eh, Gabriel?"

He was not twenty-eight yet. I had long since reached the age of reason.

Gabriel has many other horses in his memory and yet another racetrack, at this very same spot by the Seine. Next to the Clément Bayard bicycle factory. The municipality had built it to lend glitter to our city. Go out and thank the horses, said the posters; they are increasing the value of your property. Louis turned his back on it all;

you did not promote real estate values on the backs of thoroughbreds. Once again, he was right. Levallois's horseracing aspirations fell flat. The racecourse enterprise was fleeting. Its mile-and-a-half-long track did not last ten years. They tore it up in 1900. . . .

It was there that the Levallois Trotting Club staged a contest so tawdry it made Louis ill: Colonel Cody, alias Buffalo Bill, versus the well-known bike champion Meyer, the former on horseback, the latter on a bicycle (made by Clément). The purse: 10,000 francs.

The contest inflamed the press: "Will tradition prevail over the future at Levallois tomorrow? This newspaper boldly predicts that human ingenuity will humble the animal."

There was no question of Louis associating himself with this charade. That day he remained glued to rue Cormeille. With whom? Probably another noisy guest, Mademoiselle Isabelle or Claudine the bookbinder, women it was impossible to love without alerting all your neighbors, unless you happened to live by a sports stadium at match time at the very second a goal was scored; they screamed so loud, you see. . . .

So far Gabriel had known few historic days in his life. Since some newspapers had declared this to be such a day, he strove to appreciate it and to call to his aid all the (meager) scientific rigor of which he was capable.

The people of Levallois supported modern industry. The people of Neuilly, solid show-jumping fans, cheered on the animal. The rest were split right down the middle.

And Gabriel, turned against Buffalo Bill by Marguerite's stories (this Colonel Cody was a damn Yankee, a murderer of Indians and Mexicans, etc.), focused all his attention on the bicycle, astounded at the sight of the champion Meyer eating up the bumps on the track, noiseless, feather-light, ethereal, neither flying nor rattling, appearing to brush the earth, to stroke it, sovereign—and leaving no trail of droppings.

He tugged at his grandmother's sleeve.

"But how does Meyer bounce that way?"

"Rubber, Gabriel. His wheels have rubber rims."

When he returned home, Gabriel gazed with new eyes at a soft red rubber ball he had until then neglected. He stopped doing what he was told, he consented to sit down to table only if he had the ball, and as his right hand sought the shortest passage from his plate to his mouth, his left tapped his new friend up and down, bouncing it again and again off the kitchen tiles in a movement later to be called dribbling by basketball players the world over.

Thanks to that meeting of the Trotting Club, Gabriel can thus set a precise date for the birth of his rubber vocation: 1893, his tenth year; you can easily check it in the newspapers of the day. And I believe it was Louis, kissing me good night, who first said, "My bouncing boy, sleep well and bounce from dream to dream, my bouncing Gabriel."

But let us leave the ever-present Gabriel for a second and return to the facts. Despite the best efforts of the champion Meyer, the cycle was defeated; Buffalo Bill and his mount won the day. Great that evening were the rejoicings of the horses, the legions of Levallois horses. Yes, that night they celebrated their victory. Neighed, blew through their nostrils, bucked, escaped, galloped down the streets, pissed waterfalls more sonorous, more odorous, and more generous than usual. Although accustomed to this four-legged presence, to which they owed most of their income (and the enjoyment of several ancillary perquisites including the discreet arrival in Levallois of battalions of ladies ready for anything, exhilarated as they were by the wild atmosphere we generated), the people of Levallois were unable to get a wink of sleep through the whole of this night of saraband, and next morning twenty-seven of them presented a written complaint to city hall, concluding with the hope that Levallois would soon cease to be the biggest stable in the Republic.

A not-too-distant future would take it upon itself to grant their request.

When horses disappeared, to be replaced by automobiles, they left human beings alone on the earth, with no other source of emotion than speed. In the exchange, travelers lost a part of their soul and traveling lost its warmth, the warmth of a steaming rump and the rolling trot of a live animal.

## V

There were days when we stayed at home. Alone. Louis and Gabriel. Without lady visitors. Louis studied for his exams. Distant exams. Entrance exams for a school yet to be created. In fact he read books, every conceivable book about the colonies. And then, when he had finished them, all the others, all the books every bookseller receives from every publisher.

"This isn't how you study for an exam," said Marguerite.

He fully agreed. "Well then, give me the examination schedule. But you're sure I won't be too old by the time the school has been created?"

"I'll get you a dispensation."

And Marguerite went off again to badger the Ministry.

I believe years went by. Without properly realizing it, Gabriel had entered time. His toys changed. Lead soldiers replaced his little wooden horses, an irrefutable sign of adulthood's approach. But Louis, anxious no doubt to provide fixed landmarks for his aging son, always told him the same stories at the same time of day, just after tea:

"Story of the man who seeks a land where nobody dies.

"This story is about a man whose mother was very old, and who wanted to find her a land where nobody ever died (Marguerite is not yet old, Gabriel. But one day you and I will also have to find such a land for her). Anyway. The son set out to find this land. Whenever he reached a place and saw graves he went on. He wandered through every land without ever finding one where there were no graves. Then a man said to him, 'Why are you always going off like this? You never stop traveling; you wander the world leaving your old mother all alone!' (It was a good question, Gabriel; never will we leave Marguerite all alone. Never.) Anyway. 'I seek a land where there are no graves,' the son replied. 'If you agree to pay me a wage,' said the man, 'I will undertake to show you a land where there are no graves.' 'Show me a land where nobody dies,' replied the good son, 'and I will give you everything I possess.'

"They set off together and reached a land that indeed wanted for nothing except graves. They ordered their camels to kneel and spent the night with natives of the land. Next day the guide said to his companion, 'Now give me my wage, since I have shown you a land where there are no graves.' The first man gave him everything he possessed. The guide took his due and disappeared. The good son sent for his mother. And together they lived peaceful days in this land without graves. But one day he left to wander in the country round about, leaving his mother asleep at their hosts' house. When these people saw her asleep, they cut her throat, divided up her flesh, and set a portion aside for the son. When the son returned they said to him, 'Your mother was near death; we cut her throat and we have divided up her flesh. Here is your portion; we set it aside for you.' "

Since then, I have come across this story again. It is from a *Tamachek Grammar* by Louis-Joseph Hanoteau, general and scholar, who was born and died (1814–1897) at Decize but who spent his whole life in Algeria, for he had only one interest on earth, the Tuareg Blue Men. He spoke their language, knew their customs, even understood their extremely rare and abstruse rock inscriptions. Perhaps he felt bluer and more nomadic than he did French and a general?

## VI

"How does the moon stay up?" asked Gabriel.

"This question proves you are becoming a man," Louis replied.

Looking deeply moved, he cleared his desk of all the books and maps piled upon it, pulled up a stool for his son, smoothed out a large sheet of paper, seized a pencil, drew spheres, ellipses, and crescents, and launched into a confused explanation that successively considered the representation of the world by the ancients, the trials of Galileo, the fall of apples, the movement of the tides, and so on. At about eight, Marguerite put her head in to summon them to dinner.

"Can't you see I'm discussing serious matters?" said Louis.

And on he went with his diagrams and his calculations, none of them appearing to bear the remotest relation to the moon. Clearly Louis was out of his depth.

"You understand?" he kept asking. "You understand, you're sure you understand?"

Gabriel nodded. To please him. For the immense explanatory flow did not satisfy him at all; to be candid, it even bored him stiff. Gabriel already had his answer, a much simpler one, and this one was irrefutable. One night, someone had hurled a rubber ball to the ground, like his own but white and gigantic, and had hurled it with such force it had bounced all the way up into the sky. All he needed now was the name of this champion bouncer. So there's no need to get so complicated, Louis. "I'm hungry, Papa, can't we put the rest of your story off until tomorrow?"

Later, as he was undressing, Gabriel heard Louis's voice through the half-open door.

"I am afraid our child may not have a very scientific mind."

"And so?" replied Marguerite. "Did Savorgnan de Brazza have what you call a scientific mind? That didn't stop him pushing on through the jungle!"

## VII

That evening father and son were seated side by side on the Mexican sofa in the Mexican living room on rue Cormeille, Levallois. What is a Mexican sofa? Leather smelling of wax; Marguerite waxed it every week. What is a Mexican living room? A room the Hidalgo Gabriel the First would like when he finally returned from Puebla: on the walls small pictures of ocher sierras and white churches, on the mantelpiece a silver riding crop, a bright red and green rug with cubic bird head (or panther head, or snake head, or turtle head, hard to say), on a small table a bottle of tequila, unopened and replaced every quarter, and so forth. Marguerite had a simple strategy for attracting those who had disappeared: win their trust, make them feel at home.

Everything was ready to welcome Gabriel the First. But alas, Gabriel the First refused to come back. The tenderest, the most faithful, the most Mexican of ghost traps ever laid in the Old World failed to work.

That evening, then, father and son were seated side by side. The two porcelain candlesticks (a specialty of Vera Cruz) were lit, the mark of a grand occasion.

"Don't come in, don't come in!" Marguerite shouted every five minutes from the kitchen.

On all grand occasions we were banished in this fashion to the Mexican living room, barred from the kitchen, as if grand occasions were cooked up in there among the pots and stove tops.

And then: "Close your eyes," said Marguerite. We heard the door of the chest creak, glasses ring, the rustle of fabric ("That's the lace tablecloth," murmured Louis). "Keep your eyes shut." The sound of footsteps receded. From afar came another rustling and then yet another ("Heavens, Mama is changing"; as we know, nothing about women's clothes was foreign to Louis). "There, you may open your eyes." The sound of footsteps returned, accompanied by a whiff of scent that blended uneasily with the smells of chocolate escaping the kitchen.

Vision confirmed hearing and smell; this was without a doubt the grandest occasion ever experienced by the Orsenna family. Even Christmas was surpassed. Even the opening of the bookstore. Even the visit, one Sunday in June, of friends from the Ministry. Double place settings. Flowers on the table (anemones). Water glass, wine glass no. 1, wine glass no. 2, champagne glass. Abundance. Eggs Meurette. Pike Nantua. Creamed veal Orloff. Six cheeses, one for each side of the French map: Pont-l'Évêque, Muenster, Tomme des Alues, Picodon from Dieulefit, goat cheese from the Abbaye de Belloc (Basque country), Caillebotte from the Vendée. To cap it all: cake—chocolate planisphere.

The last mouthfuls. Marguerite rose, tapped her champagne glass with the tip of her knife.

"Give your father a big hug, Gabriel; he has *passed*. A friend from the Ministry informed me of the examination results. They will be made public tomorrow. You see, Louis, I was right to persist. The Colonial School has finally opened. And you are in."

Enormous pride, eyes full of tears, evening of glory in the Orsenna home.

Once upon a time, at the end of the last century, there was a happy family.

Happy Louis. Snugly curled up inside his school (a Moresque palace on avenue de l'Observatoire), he wanted to stay there forever. Here, he said, I shall wait for my son. Soon he will join me. Life will be easier when there are two of us. Happy Louis: from one class to another his teachers led him over the whole world. To Laos on Mondays: "Kinship systems among the Meos." To Africa on Tuesdays: "Irrigation problems in the Sahel." Back to Paris on Wednesdays: "Native code, law of 1887." "Don't forget that once you are in the bush," the teacher would stress when attention waned, "it will be your task to lay down the law. And to make sure it is respected. So listen carefully. 'The law of 1887 limits punishments applicable to natives to two weeks' imprisonment and one hundred francs in fines, and limits punishable offenses to sixteen: (1) nonpayment of taxes and refusal to perform compulsory labor; (2) refusal to respond to administrative summons; (3) firing off a gun during festivities within five hundred yards of the district commissioner's residence; (4) disrespect in word or deed toward a representative of French authority; (5) hiding or concealing oneself during a census; (6) sheltering a criminal; (7) destroying or moving road signs or markers; (8) abandoning dead animals; (9) burial outside official cemeteries and sites; (10) public expression of sentiments of a nature to diminish the respect due French authority; (11) refusing to give statistical information or deliberately withholding information; (12) failure to appear before a district commissioner during a judicial inquiry; (13) failure to render aid in case of danger; (14) failure to carry out, in cases of epidemic, sanitary measures decreed by the district commissioner; (15) usurping the functions of village chieftain or district chief; (16) allowing herds to stray and refusing to gather them in.' " And Thursdays were reserved for Indochina: "Rubber cultivation in the Saigon region."

He had found his refuge and would gladly have lingered there under the allegorical frescoes until I arrived. He would guide me in my studies. We would leave together, two colonial administrators assigned to the same district despite the regulations (and thanks to a new dispensation wrung from the Ministry by Marguerite). I am convinced he spent hours picturing us seated side by side under a silkwood tree, surrounded by lady friends and dispensing justice. An indulgent justice. Our own kind. Nothing to do with Napoleon. An Orsennaic code.

Happy, earnest Gabriel, he was acquiring age. In fact he was hungrily devouring all the age available in his immediate vicinity. He wanted to accumulate years not simply to join his father in the Moresque palace but also to embark in his turn upon amorous adventure. And in this respect his ambitions, fanned by Madame de Lafayette, Lamartine, and Alexandre Dumas, knew no bounds. He would: (a) prove to Louis that a single Love is infinitely better than countless conquests; (b) prove to Marguerite that Love has no need to die in Puebla (Mexico) to endure; and (c) prove to the whole world that short chubby men also have a chance with the ladies.

And so, as soon as a gap yawned between two classes, he would squeeze through it, race across the Luxembourg Gardens, and plunge into adolescence although, a few scant moments earlier at the Lycée Montaigne, he had still been a child. At that time the Latin Quarter offered everything that adds years to a boy fresh from his home suburb. The café tables you could lean your elbows on, provided you made yourself bigger: easy, all you had to do was raise your buttocks discreetly from your seat and slip into the space thus created either your folded leg or a thick coat. Café conversations, in the course of which the world was daily remade, in the course of which you learned the names of the architects at work on this vast construction site: Bonnal, Thiers, Tocqueville, Guesde, Marx, some in favor of a fresh coat of paint, others advocating that everything be destroyed in order to begin again from scratch. Wine to warm your stomach. The girls, often red-haired, who came into the cafés and who, when they were low in spirits or low on funds, occasionally allowed a rolypoly lad to escort them home and take advantage of the steepness and narrowness of the stairs to put his hand where it was a mortal sin but where the moves essential to every Great Love were learned.

Following such temerities Gabriel went back across the Luxembourg Gardens yelling at the top of his lungs, "I'm only thirteen, I'm only thirteen!" bringing frowns to nannies' faces, making the babies howl, and scattering the pigeons from their habitual perches on the marble skulls of France's queens. Breathless, he reached school and returned to his seat just in time for a mathematics test.

With this unpleasant interlude out of the way, Gabriel gave his father the latest news. The geography teacher who succeeded the science torturer was of liberal temperament. Nothing surprised him. Neither rowdiness nor paper (and prophetic) airplanes nor my rhythmic knocking on the back wall of the classroom. As everyone knows, the Colonial School was next door to the Lycée Montaigne. And according to the scientific calculations of my father and myself, on condition we chose the right seats, we sat, each of us in his respective establishment, back to back. Communicating in our very own Morse code was the birth of art. After all these years, and now that Louis has disappeared, I am going to be frank; our dialogues were generally strange, surreal. Skipping from subject to subject was the rule, as were non sequiturs and outright misinterpretations. But to jump from this to the conclusion that I was not communicating with my father—that someone else, the bursar of the Lycée Montaigne or even one of those Indochinese nabobs who would one day run our Empire, might have been intercepting our secrets and exploiting our complicity . . . I do not know, I do not wish to know, I do not want to come to conclusions. That's not my job. That is what death is for.

But happiest of us all was Marguerite. The prospect of the great departure for the tropics flooded her with joy. Blossoming amid her preparations, she was on the move from dawn till dusk.

We began our farewell rounds very early.

"You think we should already be doing this?" asked Louis (it was October, a full year before final exams and postings).

"Yes, we must forget nothing and nobody. And leave-takings are like apartments, you have to settle into them."

She had reconstructed our family tree. We visited all its branches one by one.

The Orsenna family set forth every Sunday at dawn. As we walked to the bus, Marguerite outlined the plan of campaign for the day: this Sunday her female cousins on "Uncle Joe's" side. They all lived in the ninth *arrondissement,* the home of theaters, of boulevards, of authors. Marguerite told us on Uncle Joe's side of the family they were like that; they lived for art. She rang. Inside you heard feverish activity and now-who-could-that-be-at-this-hour, followed by the maid's trotting footsteps. Close behind her came our cousin. In a filmy peignoir.

"Forgive me, I had company last night. How nice of you to come. So you're off? I think you are wise to go. France is shrinking. Why, last night the theater was almost empty. On a Saturday! Don't tell anyone."

They offered us port wine. They gave Gabriel pomegranate syrup whatever the hour, a theater habit no doubt, drinks the color of a theater curtain. They chucked him under the chin.

"You won't be scared of the lions?"

He looked at their breasts.

After a discussion of the colonies, which always aroused a degree of interest, the conversation quickly flagged. We had risen early. Gabriel would have fallen asleep on his seat had it not been for the clucking of the cousins and the incessant movement of their legs (extended by slippers with fur pompoms), crossing, uncrossing, recrossing, the peignoirs falling open.

In the next room you heard coughing, the desperate hack of a smoker waking up. The cousins came out to the staircase with us. They leaned over to wish us good luck and who knows, once you've made your fortunes perhaps you'll come back to our old ninth *arrondissement;* the Gymnase is up for sale. What would you say to a Grand Théâtre Orsenna? They bent over the stair rail. Their breasts bulged out of their mauve or fuchsia peignoirs. None of the cousins resembled each other and yet, each time, the two white half suns glowed with the same glow in the gloom of the stairwell; I could not tear my eyes away. Several times I almost fell.

"Watch out for that kid, Louis," a cousin called out. "He doesn't look where he's going!"

In less than three months we had exhausted our immediate family circle. The collateral branches offered other attractions: craftsmen and inventors scattered through the eleventh and twelfth *arrondissements*. On this side of the family we were born with manual dexterity. They showed me the tricks of their trades. This might be useful to you out there in the colonies. They asked us to stay for dinner.

"Don't go yet, the kid's interested."

We had to stay for testing of their new inventions, share the long-awaited moment to see if their gadget would start. We hugged one another amid the din. They bade us farewell with shouts of: "Well, take care then, and let us know if you decide to start up a factory, I wouldn't mind going at all; what about you, Madeleine?"

I no longer remember their different specialties. All I can say is that they were not in transportation or in freight or in hauling; otherwise they would have been our neighbors in Levallois. But which of them was a toymaker and which one installed plumbing?

All I can now recall is one big machine, explored Sunday after Sunday. . . . All told, our family tree was more prolific in gear wheels than in leaves and branches.

We left no one out, not even the most distant, the most nonplussed to see us appear, the most suspicious ("This isn't about money, is it?"), and the embittered ("Well, your grandfather certainly struck it lucky, getting his hands on the weekend house after the death of . . ."). The volume shot up. I was asked to wait outside in the street.

We spent the whole year on these excursions, our minds awash in addresses and in the problems of getting from Ivry to Lilas, from Gennevilliers to Montrouge, trailing from bus stop to bus stop.

"What about my work at the school?" Louis would storm.

Ashamed for him, we dragged him along: How can you learn without knowing your roots? You would forget everything.

My grandmother would give me a joyful wink: What a baby your father is!

Gabriel agreed. Role reversal usually comes later; a son does not take over his father's care until he has reached maturity. Louis became my firstborn before I was fifteen. I had grown a wing just to protect him. Perhaps the reason for this precocious reversal is to be found in the schedule of the Colonial School. The Lycée let its pupils out earlier. I went to pick up Louis every day, waiting for him under the chestnut trees among lady friends and a handful of relatives. He came running out and I asked him if he had had a good day in school.

* * *

In April, Marguerite declared herself satisfied. There, now we can go with a clear conscience. We had finished our goodbyes. Now came the most important part: France. How could we take our leave of her? One Saturday soon after Easter Marguerite dragged us off to Angers. Why Angers? You'll see, replied Marguerite. Louis and I imagined some ultimate forebear, a tutelary ancestor, paramount chief of the clan, kept till the last, to bless us before the great adventure. We were far off the mark. . . . In the train we played guessing games.

"Got it! We're going to tour the Loire châteaus! Not a bad idea, it's the heart of France. We're going to miss them out there, especially Chambord. I'm right, aren't I, Mama?"

"You will see."

"Or are we going to look at Balzac's house in Tours?"

"Why not Rabelais's house at La Devinière near Chinon?" Since his forays into the Latin Quarter, Gabriel liked to put on rakish airs.

"You will see."

In any case, we did not see Angers. As soon as we arrived, Marguerite stuffed us into a small horse-drawn carriage headed south. A pity; it seemed such a nice quiet town, a town of just two colors, the walls white and the roofs dark, the faintly creamy yellow of tuff stone beneath the black of slate. As for the local château, Louis described it to me; he alone could see it through the little porthole window: Round, Gabriel, you would like it. Meager information. I am no wiser today.

After two or three hours the carriage stopped outside a low-roofed house, the door open, fishing poles on the right, fishing poles on the left, a muffled hubbub within. All around as far as the eye could see: vegetable gardens, vegetable gardens that would make a vegetarian of you until the end of your days, so delectable-looking was the tiniest leaf, gardens more tenderly nurtured than any flower bed, more profuse than any greenhouse, free-growing vegetable gardens without stooping human forms, as if nature in these parts always knew what to do and when. A little way off, gray, flush with the fields, in fullest spate, flowed the Loire.

"In we go," said Marguerite.

Next moment there began the tenderest dance of gratitude Gabriel is ever likely to behold. A woman behind a counter cried out, "Here they are!"

And the innkeeper came running up, bald, somewhat ruddy-complexioned, but with astonishingly pale hands now raised heavenward, now folded across his stomach. "It's you! A Lyon woman back among us! I didn't believe it when I received your letter. Welcome, welcome to you and to your two friends."

And as he sat us down at his best table overlooking the river and called for a clean tablecloth—the whitest, please, the very whitest, and let's have some flowers—Marguerite was telling us that her first visit here went back forty years, with her father, when the latter was president of a dining club of the Saône region. "Mind you," Marguerite whispered, "don't go thinking that the cooking here is better than in Lyon, but the Loire is France; anyway, he'll tell you all about it. . . ."

Which the innkeeper proceeded to do, not leaving us until it was time for us to go. He hovered over us, served us himself, served us again, examined each dish in the sunlight, made us sniff it before setting it down, asked our opinion before each mouthful . . . an attentiveness that in the long run would have been annoying if it had not been accompanied, in the calmest tones, by an exhaustive description of springtime in the Saumur region, those glorious April weeks when everything comes in at once: salmon, sorrel, dew, new turnips and vine shallots, the real secret of beurre blanc—what, you don't know beurre blanc?—a half glass of wine vinegar, the same of dry white wine, two generous spoonfuls of butter, salt and pepper, you'll say you don't need the Loire for that, you'll say there are low flames and wrists supple enough to whip butter at the proper speed all over the world. . . . So? So you'll be forgetting the main thing, the heart of beurre blanc: why, the gray vine shallot, of course, glazed in jars beforehand. Marguerite and the innkeeper exchanged superior smiles; oh, these young people!

For three days we tarried in these gardens: Gennes, Les Rosiers, Chênehutte, Saumur. The sun was back and the Loire was receding; little by little, sand replaced water. In the evenings they knocked at our door.

"If the asparagus come up tomorrow, shall I save you some?"

They were the white ones, picked the very morning they came up, before the harsh light of noon, and even more melting in the stems than at the tips.

"Everything in its season," said Marguerite. "In France, vegetables. Over there, rice. One should never confuse things in life."

She was a most methodical person. She would have been a peerless organizer aboard Noah's Ark. By the time we left, Gabriel could tell a pike perch—which has nothing, nothing whatsoever in common with pike—at the very first mouthful.

On the return train ride:

"I wonder if this trip was a good idea," said Marguerite.

None of us said another word before Paris. The Orsenna family was no longer very sure of its colonial calling.

## VIII

Much later, at the Liberation, Louis and I talked a great deal about the women of that period.

"The world is beginning again," he said. "We must tell one another everything; the world can be rebuilt only on transparent pasts. . . ."

I was not convinced he was right. But I listened to him, I listened to him. There were some superb years for Bordeaux around that time: '45, '47, '49. You could spend hours in restaurants listening to your father, to your best friend of a father, drinking Bordeaux, gazing through the window at the blue sky, not saying a word. You would have plenty of time later to talk, all alone, when the wine would not be so good, when fathers had disappeared.

"There was one," said Louis, "whose name was Odile and who always asked after you. And you know when?" No, I didn't know. "Well, during; can you believe that? Right in the middle. I would hear her squeak, 'And how is Gabriel?' She thought I answered badly, without details. Breathlessness was no excuse, she said. She ordered me to love you more."

With a smile I thanked him: Thanks, Papa, it's a fine story.

But I never, never told him about the visits of the Irish girl, Miss O'Mahogany. Throughout my schooldays she came to get me—do you hear, Louis; wherever you are, you have a right to know—every first Tuesday of the month she was there. She had given me my choice of day: Monday or Tuesday, which day is sadder for you, which day do you need me more? We agreed on Tuesday rather than the eve of a vacation day like Wednesday or Friday, and on Mondays children's sadness lacks bite, a little Sunday warmth still lingers. No, sadness did not really get into its stride until next day, Tuesday. Every first Tuesday of the month she was there, tall, redheaded Mahogany.

I journeyed through my schooldays as if under her protection. When there was a licking in store for me, when a big (a normal-sized) kid trapped me in the playground, he suddenly froze, fist an inch from my nose, remembering the redheaded apparition of the first Tuesday of the month. And remembering the only time she lost her temper. When she saw me that day I was crying; I had blood under my nostrils where my mustache would one day be.

"Who?" she asked.

I pointed out the puncher, a new boy ignorant of the first-Tuesday rule. She walked up to the puncher, busy holding forth in the center of the playground, a spot absolutely off limits to relatives.

Petrified, the playground supervisors looked on and the pupils drew aside. She measured the puncher with a contemptuous stare, head to foot, foot to head, before letting her gaze come to rest on his fly; for years and years, scores of witnesses were quite clear on this point.

"So you like hittin' small kids," she said in rich Irish tones. "That means you must have a little one, a reelly little one, d'you hear me, a *reelly* little one, and it won't ever get any bigger. Ever."

And she grabbed my hand and hauled me off to lunch. Without written permission, without any kind of excuse, which nobody requested of her and which she naturally did not possess. From this I deduced a truth rarely useful in everyday life, even on Tuesdays, but which I cherish: the academic world is scared stiff of redheads.

We always ordered the same dish.

"Would you like something from my country?" she would ask.

"Yes, yes."

"All right, haddock and poached egg then."

She wanted to know what I was studying. As soon as we were seated she asked for paper. I recall lunches piled high with drawings and figures.

"So are you interested in trigonometry at all then, Gabriel?"

"In what?"

"Useful, reelly useful, Gabriel, for working out something's height without moving. What about Magdeburg hemispheres?"

I did not listen, I stared at her hands resting one on top of the other, two Magdeburg hands; where was Magdeburg?

"They create vacuums, understand, Gabriel; not even galloping horses can pull them apart."

Miss Mahogany had a marked preference for scientific subjects. She foresaw a future in science for me, like our Fleming or your Arago. She did not encourage me too wholeheartedly in the study of the English language: Take your time, Gabriel, that's where I keep my secrets hidden. Naturally it was only in this field that Gabriel was ready to move mountains. She was also concerned about my health, much more than you were, Louis. She cautioned me about germs that have the peculiarity of striking when love is lacking: If you get my drift, Gabriel, when you do it without any feeling. She was an expert on contraceptives, or at least on their terminology; she knew all the names, she blushed as she said them: French letter, French tickler, French johnny, French cap, French cloak, all those French things to make life better, why French, it doesn't matter to me, I'm Irish, but still and all—she kept on—rubber, condom, deb's delight, preservative, safety nipple, safety sheath, love glove. She made me swear: Promise me, Gabriel, when you do it . . . you know all about rubber . . . they're made of rubber now, no more skin jobs, please, promise me. . . .

"Are you screwing her?"

Your son is not properly speaking a seducer, Louis. You even looked down on him, gently but undeniably, for this very reason for years and years, on walks, vacations, at dinners. And if today we can speak as equals, it is because of a circumstance independent of our two wills but which has the merit of bringing you back down to my level, a cruel circumstance if you like but, admit it, a human one: your death and my continuing life. So. Well, then, I have two things to tell you.

1. Your son who is not properly speaking a professional seducer (although in the long run I spent my life trying to advance, step by step, into the dreams of the two sisters of whom we shall hear more, rest assured), your nonseducer of a son was nevertheless the recipient every afternoon of the first Tuesday of each month and sometimes the next morning, a Wednesday, and even the day after that, a Thursday, throughout his final school year, of this flattering question, whispered in classrooms, at study, in the corridors, in every tone of voice, wheedling or threatening, in the recreation yard: I'll give you five minutes by my new watch to answer; come on, don't be a shit, come on, tell us, are you screwing her?

2. Never—do you hear me up there, down there?—never did she mention you to me. Yet you were not far away, in the adjacent school, in the next room, on the other side of the wall when she came to take me home; it would have needed but a gesture from her, pushing the door open, leaning on the bell, calling your name, anything at all. On reflection I even believe she arranged it so that you would be there, nearby, so that you would hear, just to show you that she loved me and not you.

There was nothing between you, a Magdeburg vacuum, Louis, even though it was through you that I met her, even though she inhabits a page in your catalogue of forgotten loves. Nothing. There was nothing between you. You have to accept this irrefutable truth. From where you are, you see differences better, Louis, you can distinguish between breeds invisible to living eyes. Among men who think only of women, there are two kinds—are there not, Louis?—the seducers, like yourself, those who can begin, and then the imprinters, like me, those who can never finish. We've each had our share of women, Louis, each in his own way; answer me, you think it was a fair share, don't you? Certainly fair, that's not the problem. But faithful, faithful to the way we have lived? What does your silence mean? Could it be that the frontier does not run where I have just drawn it? Could there be seducer-imprinters on one side and on the other side the imprinted-seduced? You and I reject this possibility, don't we, Louis, it would be too sad, wouldn't it, too antidemocratic.

## IX

The three steamer trunks were delivered one evening at the end of May. One each, said Marguerite. But Gabriel hasn't yet lived much, he has less to pack, he'll lend us a little of his, won't you, Gabriel?

They were big black wooden boxes with pale wooden hoops, and they sat in the Mexican living room in the space vacated by the erstwhile Mexican sofa, now stored beneath the ersatz veranda to await a purchaser. (Despite the advertisements handwritten one Sunday morning by the whole family and stuck up at the butcher's, the baker's, the dairy, and at the Auvergnat purveyor of coffee, firewood, and coal, no buyer ever came forward. Perhaps Mexican sofas interested no one. After a few weeks out of doors the sofa faded, and its colors no longer deserved the name of Mexican. Unknown to Marguerite, Louis and Gabriel were in favor of scratching out the word "Mexican" on the ads. But they had disappeared, replaced by others: two tortoiseshell cats, one Breton box bed. . . .)

The arrival of these three steamer trunks brought our leave-taking to an end. Or rather it ushered in another season, much more painful: a season for selecting. Selecting from a multitude of possibilities the handful of things that would make life (colonial life, anyway) bearable.

Each of us chose in secret. But Gabriel spied, Gabriel rose in the night, stealing into the erstwhile Mexican living room and raising trunk lids inch by inch: What do my father and my grandmother love better than anything else in the world?

Initially Louis considered taking his glass plates, the photographs representing his loves. With infinite care he padded the bottom of the trunk and then alternated layers of photographic plates with layers of crumpled paper. Impossible not to make a hideous racket at night, a horrible rustling of old copies of *Figaro,* as you sought to rediscover the smiles of those young ladies. Gabriel persisted. After all, they had belonged to his life as well. One evening he felt Louis standing behind him.

"Beautiful, weren't they? There will be others, I promise."

Together, with great reluctance, the seducer and his son decided not to take them along. Gabriel had offered the hospitality of his own trunk. But no, they would never have survived the shocks of the voyage.

"You see, Gabriel, women are at once very fragile and very heavy."

One by one they were withdrawn amid the complaints of the crumpled *Figaros* and piled up on the ledge around the fireplace. So should we consider Louis's final selection the expression of his true preference? Or of resignation? Let me itemize: sunglasses, marine print representing Dieppe in winter, guide to the cheeses of France, Longchamp racing forms, names of horses (Val d'Ajonc, Schéhérazade, Margot 2, Fleur de Seine: all, he insisted, were syllables potentially useful in the colonies). And then in one corner, nicely tucked away, almost hidden, the photo of a dignitary whose identity Gabriel pursued for weeks. A young candidate for a history professorship finally told him that it was beyond the shadow of a doubt a Rothschild, English branch, the wealthiest.

Thus was revealed to me one of my father's dreams: wealth. Alas, a dream never to be fulfilled, nor even to approach fulfillment despite repeated efforts, some of them quite harrowing, as this candid history will reveal.

As for Gabriel, he did not hesitate a second. For want of partners he had thrust his amorous ambitions into the background since Easter and had launched himself on the gigantic task of modernizing the world. In any case these two ambitions, love and modernization, struck him as complementary, since the light shed by the latter would encourage the former to quicken and bloom.

"We must strip our feelings of the trappings of religion. Thought must follow in the wake of Science and Industry. . . . The great challenge today is to put order into our mental chaos."

Such were his obsessions and their inescapable consequences: an accelerated rate of serious reading, a paler complexion, and the decision to study—even if it meant doing so by correspondence—for the entrance exam to the august École Normale Supérieure, wellspring, mother, and seedbed of all intelligence. We may look upon this period as Gabriel's awkward age. Hitherto so gentle, so calm and reflective, Gabriel became curt, arrogant. At the smallest domestic oversight—two sugars in his coffee instead of one, a window left open to admit a draft—he heaped his grandmother and father with strange imprecations.

"You're both still bogged down in the theological age!" (And Gabriel raised his eyes heavenward to confirm the vacuum reigning above.)

"To be alive in 1900 and to have remained so metaphysical!" (And Gabriel shrugged, a modern and industrial gesture if ever there was one.)

And before the appalled gaze of his parents (what's happening to him? what can he mean? is this some sort of code?), he began to pin edifying texts extracted from the Great Explanation on every wall of the house, even in the erstwhile Mexican living room, even in the lavatories.

In Marguerite's bedroom, just below the bronze crucifix overlooking her single bed:

> In the theological state the human mind, essentially directing its inquiries toward the intimate nature of things, the primary and ultimate causes of all the effects that strike it, in short toward absolute knowledge, conceives of phenomena as the products of direct and continuous action by more or less numerous supernatural agents, whose arbitrary intervention explains all the apparent anomalies of the universe.

On the sideboard, prominently tacked up behind the family photos:

> In the metaphysical state, which is basically but a simple modification of the former, supernatural agents are replaced by abstract forces, veritable entities (personified abstractions), inherent in the world's various entities, and conceived of as being capable on their own of generating all observed phenomena, which could thus be explained by assigning to each its corresponding entity.

On the wall of the WC behind the chain at handle height, a text several times rewritten, for the paper first blistered and then tore as a result of a slight leak in the flush mechanism:

> Finally, in the positive state, the human mind, recognizing the impossibility of obtaining absolute notions, ceases to seek the origin and

> destination of the universe and to know the intimate causes of phenomena, in order to devote itself exclusively to discovering, through a judicious blend of reason and observation, their effective laws, that is to say their invariable relations of succession and of similarity.

"What are we going to do with him?" asked Louis. "Do you think this kind of madness lasts long?"

"A little tropical air will do him a world of good," said Marguerite. "In any case, I like him better this way. How would it be if he spent all his time in cafés and fell in love with a girl who'd sleep with anyone for a glass of absinthe?"

And she was utterly reassured when, on inspecting Gabriel's bedroom, she discovered the unhinged one's credo glued to his night table at a spot normally remote from prying eyes.

> At every phase and at whatever mode of our existence, individual or collective, we must always apply the sacred formula of the positivists: Love as a principle, Order as a foundation, and Progress as a goal.
>
> For love seeks order and inspires to progress; order consolidates love and guides progress; finally, progress develops order and returns us to love. Thus conducted, affection, speculation, and action all tend equally to the unceasing service of the Great Being, of whom each individuality can become an eternal organ.

"Come, Louis," she said. "Come. I have something to show you."

It was not easy to read the credo in that position. They had to lie on the bed and lean back, necks twisted. It was in this posture that Gabriel discovered his father and grandmother, a posture the Positivists would not have been alone in judging equivocal. He could have uttered an oh! and discreetly closed the door. But he preferred to listen.

"Well, do you have anything to say to this?" Marguerite was asking.

"It's perhaps a little—how shall I put it?—impenetrable," answered my father.

"Well, I agree with its general tone."

Deafened as they were by the edge of the mattress and the roar of blood in their ears (their heads hung backward over the edge of the bed), they spoke in stifled gasps. Gabriel took this syncopated diction for neophyte enthusiasm.

"Victory. I've convinced them," he said to himself.

It will thus be readily understood that Gabriel (without a second's hesitation) packed into the bottom of his trunk:

1. The six bound volumes of *A Course of Positive Philosophy* (Bachelier, Paris 1880).

2. *System of Positive Politics, or Treatise on Sociology Instituting the Religion of Humanity,* four volumes (Mathias, Paris 1851–1854).

"I hope that is all," said Marguerite.

No doubt she was thinking of the pitiful line of native porters groaning through the jungle beneath the weight of Auguste Comte.

"One more," said Gabriel.

And Marguerite yielded, highly intrigued by the title, or rather by the subtitle: *Catechism of Positivist Religion, or Summary Exposition of the Universal Religion, Eleven Systematic Discussions Between a Woman and a Priest of Humanity,* one volume (author's edition, Paris).

"Lend me that one when we get there," she said.

Gabriel glowed.

Marguerite took longest of all to pack. She would close the bookstore early and make the rounds of the dressmakers of Levallois and its environs. The hills—Puteaux, Suresnes, Saint-Cloud, Sèvres, Meudon—teemed with seamstresses. They headed for Paris every morning, dark rings under their eyes, cases containing their night's work in their hands. Squeezing into the omnibuses as best they could, they went right on sewing. Passengers would comment on the style and color of the dresses. But Marguerite had only one requirement: lightweight fabric.

"It will be so hot out there, you see."

They showed her samples and she waved them aside.

"Have you nothing lighter?"

She would grow impatient.

"I'm not going off in wool or velvet, come now! Are you trying to kill me?"

But the dressmakers had no experience of tropical wear. My grandmother had to forage herself for the right fabric, immersing herself in travel books and accounts of dog days in the tropics. Gabriel would hear her railing against authors who went into endless detail about tiger hunting, pug marks, and rifle calibers but remained mute on the question of clothing, as if the nature of a person's second skin were a trifling matter! She found what she was looking for in English publications devoted to Queen Victoria's travels.

"Now there's a woman who knows about clothes!"

Indian weavers, it seemed, had invented a miracle of lightness and sheerness, a shimmering wild silk called cloth of Tussore.

"I want a dress of Tussore silk," my grandmother ordered.

Our dressmakers had never heard of it. Diffidently, they suggested a hybrid material, half linen, half cotton: nothing better for sunlight, madame, and we can satin-stitch the collar for you.

"I want a dress of Tussore silk," my grandmother insisted.

She came home at night, frustrated and empty-handed, and collapsed on the erstwhile Mexican sofa.

"The fact is, Louis, I wonder whether France truly has a colonial vocation. Look at the English; they found the proper cloth. That kind of attention to detail is the hallmark of a people who deserve their empire."

"We have our own way of doing things," my father said loyally.

"Do you think it will get any hotter than today?"

"Mainly more humid."

"Even if we are far from a river?"

"Even."

Muted, filtered, their voices reached Gabriel: disembodied voices, not altogether alive. The window was wide open, but the double curtains were drawn. Outside it was still light, the undying daylight of early June. Yellow and then blue and then gray, and finally black. Outside, Levallois stank as usual. The stench would reach its height in summer, not far off now. From time to time, Marguerite broke off and whispered, "Are you asleep, Gabriel?" The said Gabriel held his breath and made no reply. Out on the veranda the conversation resumed.

"Do you think people can train for the heat?" asked Marguerite.

"The best way to train for it is to eat salt," said my father.

At length night fell.

* * *

It was now (with the Colonial School about to publish the latest exam results and the tropical postings that would follow in their wake) that a towering wave of medical books broke over Levallois: Dr. A. Le Dantec, *Essentials of Exotic Pathology* (O. Doin, publisher); Dr. A. Legrand, *The Health of European Troops in the Tropics* (O. Doin, publisher); Dr. Just. Navarre, *Handbook of Colonial Hygiene* (O. Doin, publisher); Dr. Ad. Nicolas, *Work Gangs in Malarial Zones* (G. Masson, publisher); etc. Marguerite (this isn't a hospital!) wanted to send them back. But Louis did not agree; he held that a bookseller should welcome every conceivable aspect of reality, no matter how unattractive. And with the most innocent of expressions he would open these charming works, seemingly at random, at their most instructive passages.

" 'Guinea worm: this is a filiary, reaching upwards of twenty inches in length, encountered in the skin of the lower limbs and in the intestines' "—"Louis, I beseech you!" said Marguerite—" 'and in the region of the shoulders in water carriers. The natives extract the worm with great skill by twirling it little by little around a twig. As soon as they meet the slightest resistance they stop twirling so as not to break the worm, then resume the maneuver next day until extrusion is complete.' "

"How revolting!" said Marguerite. "Do stop, please."

"No, no, you merely have to twirl the stick gently. We will hire a very patient boy." And he went on. "Let me see now, what have we here? Verruga peruana? We have no possessions in the Andes? Then it does not concern us. The Oriental pustule? Of no interest, a small benign lesion. Ah! here's one called ainhum. Listen to this: 'Spontaneous development of a constricting band of fibrous connective tissue at the base of the toe, progressively choking off circulation until the toe falls off.' "

"I suppose you think you're amusing? Go on if you like," said Marguerite. "I am going to bed."

"One more, the last tonight, I promise. Yaws, or frambesia tropica: 'A contagious disease, thought to be transmitted by flies and characterized by the appearance on the skin of papules generally leading to an extensive rash that rapidly scabs over. At a certain point in their development these fleshy nodules have the appearance of raspberries' "—"and I do believe we happen to be in the middle of raspberry season this very minute!" commented Louis in his inimitable manner—" 'hence the name frambesia.' And listen to this, this is too good to be true: 'Scientists long believed yaws to be a manifestation of syphilis, but such is not the case. The same patient can be a carrier of both diseases.' Wonderful, wonderful! O admirably prolific Nature!"

Marguerite had already slammed the door.

## X

This little scenario, begun as a joke, quickly turned into a nightmare. From all these manuals of tropical medicine swarmed demons that tormented Louis. The closer we came to the fatal day of departure, the less he slept. Scarcely was he abed than he was up again, settling for the night into our up-to-date bathroom (Marguerite's pride and joy) as if the bathroom, the part of a house most closely resembling a hospital, were a sanctuary that microbes might think twice about entering. There he spent his nights in the wavering light of a big kerosene lantern, curled up tight on the blue bath mat, right forefinger locked onto left wrist to check his pulse, gaze now lowered upon a work rich in terrifying descriptions, in limbs detaching themselves from bodies, in worm-devoured entrails, now fixed on a round mirror he had set up against the copper tub the better to scrutinize his fear and his sickly appearance, his body trembling with cold despite the very reasonable June weather and for this reason covered with an army blanket (why army? it was khaki, I recall) from whose folds he periodically withdrew a thermometer, muttering, "Ninety-eight point six; that's it: apart from fever I have all the signs, fever is just around the corner. . . ." And when Gabriel came tiptoeing in, wrestling with the kerosene lantern to stop it from smoking too much, reaching out a hand to the shivering colonial administrator, asking him if he needed anything, Marguerite's presence or a doctor, Louis would answer in a dying voice, "No," very slowly, "no, Gabriel, no, all is well; as you can see I am dying, and whatever you do don't tell Marguerite. . . ."

After two weeks of stoicism, two weeks of pitiless struggle against his armies of imaginary diseases, Louis surrendered. Gabriel, as was his habit, had come in at around three in the morning to ask how Louis was feeling. Eaten up by mosquitoes (he had doubtless forgotten to close the transom window), Louis was shining the kerosene lamp up and down his arm and babbling. "My God, my God. Ah! is that you, Gabriel?" Yes, Papa. "Gabriel?" Yes, Papa. "Gabriel, I know we are going to cause Marguerite enormous sorrow"—he spoke like a man on his deathbed, stumbling from one gasp to the next—"but do you think it would be wise to leave in my condition?"

"You are right, Louis. It would be madness. Your health is already so delicate. . . . You would never stand up to the microbes out there. Let's stay, Louis, let's stay here!"

In answering thus Gabriel twice sacrificed himself: as a Positivist (it is a Positivist's duty to modernize the planet, particularly its remotest and least developed corners) and also as a future lover. Exoticism. He had noticed from his reading that virtually all heroes loved by women had black hair: D'Artagnan, El Cid, Casanova, Figaro, Fabrice del Dongo, and so on; every one of them was dark. Why this dearth of fair-haired men in literature while blond women teemed and triumphed? For a fair-haired young man like Gabriel, the colonies had held out a promise, the promise of lending him that touch of exoticism that might have made the lady of his life forget that he, unlike all other seducers, was not dark.

But Gabriel was an exceptional son, his father's friend, you see, his father's dear friend.

"No, Louis," this exceptional son went on, "resign, abandon this career; don't worry about Marguerite, you're just not strong enough for the tropics."

"I had noticed that you too wanted to stay on here. It is a relief to me. I would not have wanted to deprive you of a memorable journey. Besides, France herself is in urgent need of modernization."

And at once Louis was cured: he threw off his khaki blanket, stood up, embraced his son without a thought for contagion, and the two of them went to the erstwhile Mexican living room to pour themselves a glass of schnapps, that fiery spirit of France's lost provinces.

"You see, Gabriel, our true illness, the Orsenna family's truly serious illness, is our dreams. What do we possess that is real, Gabriel? You have your rubber, I my lady guests, Marguerite her Mexican living room. It is not sufficient foundation for a real life. Gabriel, we are afloat in dreams."

"Speak for yourself. I am very real. I am studying the most real philosophy in the world. I will meet a real and living woman and I will love her and she will love me. A woman who is unique, unlike all your acquaintances—"

"Poor Gabriel, you still speak like an unreal person. A unique woman is the least real of creatures. As soon as you live with a woman you'll ring her round with dreams—you're my son, you're just like me, you can't help it—you'll besiege her with your dreams of other women. Gabriel's poor unique woman, and poor Gabriel. No, no, believe me, Gabriel, this is serious; dreams prey on our family. Good dreams and bad dreams. Imaginary illnesses and real feelings. These are our true enemies. And it is hard to fight dreams. We must help one another, join forces. Promise me you will be more real, Gabriel, swear you will try. And I too will do everything I can. Gabriel? Yes. Let's sleep now. We have to be in top form tomorrow to begin fighting dreams."

Gabriel hunted high and low for the device that makes our dreams; he finally believed he had found it. Behind the mirror, behind faces, behind true and false faces, the faces that are truly ours, the faces that scan you wide-eyed and somewhat pityingly—yes indeed, my friend, that is beyond a doubt you—and then the false faces, the false and beautiful faces, the faces that take the place of real faces the moment you close your eyes.

Perhaps all childhoods are the same: you cannot grow accustomed to your face, and it is this disgust that starts the dream machine working out there on the other side of the looking glass, amid bathroom smells, the smells of damp washcloths and toothpaste.

## XI

A man sat in our Mexican living room's last surviving armchair, his gloves resting on his knees, butter-colored gloves at variance with an otherwise ruddy and vigorous appearance. Marguerite sat facing him bolt upright, studying her nails. "Leave us, Gabriel."

There was a silence, time for Gabriel to disappear and to glue his ear in exactly the right place for listening, against the keyhole, an indiscretion perhaps, but memory does not sustain itself without a little help.

"Well, Orsenna, this resignation. Can you explain it to your lady mother here and to me?"

The man with butter-colored gloves addressed Louis with a spurious-sounding severity, a severity that failed to convince; somewhere behind it you sensed a very specific directive to display indulgence. My father breathed in again, very loudly. I still recall that hissing inhalation. I keep it in my head like a relic, a moment of courage from my father, and we know that courage was not his outstanding quality.

"I am not leaving."

"And could you tell us why? Yes, why?"

For the whole of the life my father and I shared, this man with butter-colored gloves was to remain the prototype of a race we scorned: flunkeys-sent-to-demand-an-explanation.

"I am not leaving," my father said again.

Nothing escaped my ear, not Marguerite's silence, not the rubbing of her hands, not the creaking of the Mexican armchair as the man with butter-colored gloves rose.

"In that case I must leave. Like your colleagues, incidentally; they are at this very moment shipping out. But you know there are always ships. Really, then, no regrets? Very well, then, madame, my respects."

Thanks to my faithful ear, my memory fed itself both on the kiss the man with butter-colored gloves bestowed on my grandmother's hand and on the various groanings of doors and of wheels, on the clip-clop of the horse's hooves on the (recently laid) paving stones of the rue Cormeille. I barely had time to straighten up and jump backward. My father came through the door and took my shoulder. We watched together through the open window (it was high summer) as the carriage disappeared from view.

"You see, Gabriel, that's the Colonial School's delivery wagon. They use it for every kind of job. And he is the human equivalent of that wagon. They use him for every kind of job too. He takes care of everything that goes wrong, from the boiler that breaks down at midnight to the model Vietnamese pupil who suddenly, during Midnight Mass, bursts into tears. Why would a Buddhist burst into tears on Christmas Eve? Find out at once, there's a good fellow. That's his job, finding the answers to countless similar questions put to him daily by the school director. So we must forgive him, Gabriel—avoid him and his kind like the plague, but forgive him, Gabriel, forgive him."

## XII

After Louis's resignation, we remained indoors throughout the month of August 1900, shutters barred, as if in the grip of an all-consuming love affair. You heard letters being slipped under the door and passersby wondering if the empty house were for sale. Marguerite had forbidden us to go out; since they believe we have left, no one must know. . . . Only Gabriel was permitted to slip outside as evening fell. He walked like a ghost, the way he thought ghosts walked, so close to the walls that you bumped into them. He avoided Levallois, heading out to Neuilly and the Monceau flatlands to buy bread, oil, and essential provisions. He discovered odorless neighborhoods where everything cost more but the Orsennas were unknown. On his return the air smelled more strongly than ever of horse. And Marguerite said nothing.

She had taken her Mexican memories into her bedroom—the saber, the tequila, the photo of Gabriel the First, the photo of Eduardo G., the man devoted to the wholesale fish business—and spent her days seated on her bed. She studied her hands. And said nothing.

At first Louis was not too concerned. But when Gabriel drew his attention to the miracle he uttered a cry, flung open the door: Take good care of her; I'm going to get the doctor. This miracle Gabriel had stumbled upon by accident on a day like so many other days as he studied his grandmother through the keyhole. Her movements were quite simple, such as rising from her bed to go over and open the window a crack. Yet these normal, everyday movements seemed suddenly strange, as if emerging from a dream and doomed to return to it. For a few seconds, Gabriel sought the reason for this sense of dream. A second later he understood. He understood that Marguerite and Marguerite's life no longer made any sound. Neither her bedsprings nor the window latch squeaked, nor did the floor creak: bed, latch, and floor that had formerly been three separate and distinct generators of sound.

Gabriel immediately called Louis, who first refused to believe it and then was forced to admit the evidence of his senses: it was true, Marguerite's life no longer made any sound. It was then he let out his shout and started out to call a doctor. Gabriel pulled him back just in time. What could a doctor do in such a case? What description could they give him of the malady? Our grandmother and mother is suffering from silence? Our grandmother and mother's life has become soundless?

Together they agreed to postpone the consultation, conferring at length over the unpredictable nature of a sorrow that could begin one fine day to devour all the sounds of a life, a life in which sound would henceforth be pointless, since there was no longer anyone on earth to cock an ear in her direction, to pay her attention. No, an affliction of this nature was not within the purview of medicine, not even tropical medicine. And they decided to keep secret a family eccentricity that might harm your career, said Louis, if people knew. . . . Remember what I told you, Gabriel. Our family is sick, very sick.

## XIII

Beware of temperate regions. France too has her jungles, invisible to the outsider. All you see is schools, noble façades, flags, lofty sentiments carved in stone (French Republic, Liberty, etc.), great men carved in stone surveying posterity from their lofty niches, timorous pigeons in residence on the heads of the great men of stone and flapping fearfully every time children yell, the streaks of their droppings down below. . . . People walk up and down the rue Saint-Jacques and boulevard Saint-Germain, sniffing the ozone-rich air of the Latin Quarter, suspecting nothing.

Even today Gabriel remembers the door with painful clarity. Every morning he went into grotesque squirming spasms of hesitation in front of that door; all right, this time I'm really going in, right, just getting my breath, I'm counting, one, two, three, ready or not in I go. . . . Yet the door was commonplace enough, its lower half of dark pine, its upper half glass-paned, with a slightly drooping brass handle, a door like countless other doors. Nothing frightening about it at all, rather a friendly door in fact, a door most assuredly distressed by the commiserations showered upon Gabriel as soon as he went in. "Why, here's our roly-poly friend. Doesn't he look pale!"

"That's from not getting enough sleep."

"Naturally he's anxious, he can't keep up the pace!"

"Take some advice from a friend, Gabriel, for your health's sake give it up!"

This flow of sweetness had always subsided somewhat by the time I reached my place. But you still couldn't afford to relax for a second. It was market time, in a very special market. Only false information was for sale. Hey, I've unearthed a fabulous article on Kant; the trouble is it's only in the Orléans library and I couldn't take it out; would you like the train schedule, Gabriel? Let me give you some advice for the Livy translation, consult the Trévoux dictionary, volume eight (it has only seven volumes). . . . They were all false leads, nothing but a wallet with sewn-up compartments. For this was the law of the academic jungle: if you can't actually eliminate a rival, at least you can try to slow him down.

And this was only a prelude. Now the teacher came in. And the worst began, the tapestry session. The master gathered his star pupils around him. Are you ready? Good, perfect. The others scraped and pecked about in hopes of the occasional crumb. Gabriel, who, beyond certain fantasies about women, really understood nothing except Auguste Comte, listened in terror as his class wove perspectives, embroidered systems, stitched families together. Rousseau was more the son of Aristotle than of Seneca. . . . Had it not been for Spinoza, Kant would have been a Thomist. . . . Homer was to Scudéry what Horace was to Madame de La Fayette. . . . Drawing strength from the dense dank atmosphere, family trees blossomed and flourished. To get on, you had to fight. They would have fought over a water faucet. Under such pressures the atmosphere swiftly became stifling. Later, through his work, Gabriel would know many tropical forests, and not the minor ones but Annam and Amazonia. . . . Well, he is quite categorical about it: muddled concepts are more impenetrable than mangrove swamps. . . . This painful impression was not universally shared. Hooting contentedly, the star students swung from liana to liana. But the needy ones, the plodders, had more and more trouble breathing and shyly asked for the windows to be opened.

"So that the Henri Quatre crammer can steal our ideas? Thank you very much! You would be better advised to listen to this reading of Dante by Mother Arnauld of the Port-Royal convent. According to Sainte-Beuve . . ."

And in the omnibus bearing me home to Levallois I would take stock of my knowledge: three more or less clear ideas about Kant; six, but mediocre ones, on Plato; and poverty (two ideas) regarding Pascal. As for Grotius, sheer destitution (scarcely one idea). I make an exception of course for Auguste Comte, about whom I knew pretty well everything but who had already been long out of favor. Yet to hear the specialists talk, there was no point turning up on examination day unless you had at your fingertips an average of twenty *original* perspectives for each author on the syllabus.

It was thus a somewhat undone adolescent who returned to the bosom of his family, Louis-laden-with-women and Marguerite-the-soundless, before vanishing into his room to practice his scales—the fussy little Latin assignment: translate as many lines of Cicero as possible without a dictionary—until, having reached the limits of his endurance, he foundered in sleep. If you start dreaming in Latin you can consider yourself on the right track.

Often, since then, I have told foreign friends the story of that last school semester of 1900, the story of my aborted intellectual calling. They stare at me in amazement.

"But what outlandish exam could possibly call for such mental gymnastics?"

"An exam on general education."

"Only in France could they dream up such an idea! Relax, Gabriel, relax," say his foreign friends. "And let's drink to your country, France, so endearing. How on earth could you pour such passion into—what's the French term again? oh, yes! you just told us—'general education'?"

Fifty years on, Gabriel strains his ears: it is raining. A lowering December. Pens squeak across white paper. The star pupils pant. Today it is a fragment of Virgil: translate into French Alexandrines (rich rhymes) the distress of a majesty named Dido, queen of Carthage and madly in love with a Turkish wayfarer: *uritur infelix Dido totaque vagatur. . . .*

The teacher's pets cursed, floundering amid these Mediterranean outbursts. Step by slow step they advanced into those heaped-up sorrows. They sighed, they opened their dictionaries and scanned them and slammed them shut, as if every variant for sadness could be contained in a dictionary!

Suddenly the click of footsteps reached us. First from afar, then closer and closer. The teacher's pets raised their heads. Who could be coming to violate the sanctity of our Latin unseen translation at this hour? Since the top half of the wall separating the classroom from the corridor was of glass, we soon recognized the principal's hairless dome.

The door opened and the class sprang to attention.

"Sit down, I shall be brief. What are you translating, Virgil? Excellent, Virgil. Just the right degree of difficulty. Your rivals at Henri-Quatre are on Seneca today. I have my spies. Easier, Seneca. Carry on with Virgil. Well, I shall be brief. I have an urgent message from the vice-chancellor to deliver to you. As if the vice-chancellor were unaware that you are studying for an examination. *The* examination! But orders are orders, here we go. . . ."

The headmaster always addressed his senior class in clipped, military language. Was the examination not a war?

"Here we go. The new Republic of Brazil has chosen Auguste Comte to be its leading intellectual light. But nobody in Brazilian ruling circles knows Auguste Comte. So Brazil has requested our educational support. Republics must help one another. There are not all that many of them, after all. In short, are you willing to go and teach Auguste Comte to Brazil's ambassadors in Europe? Our government has decided to start with them. To cut down on travel costs, no doubt. So, then, ten days of intensive positivism during the Christmas vacation! Not interested? You're sure? Nobody? I quite understand. You are studying for *the* exam. You are right. I shall send the vice-chancellor a full explanation. Henri-Quatre is still ahead of you in Greek. Keep it in mind. Well, goodbye, and good luck with your Virgil."

The principal was already leaving the room when a hubbub recalled him, a hubbub scarcely flattering for Gabriel, a hubbub imploring him to put his hand down. What use was Auguste Comte? What would you do with an ambassador? Where was Brazil? A hubbub that proved beyond a doubt I was not a dangerous rival, that I belonged more to the breed of popular mascot than that of future student at the École Normale. In any case, there sat the volunteer, hand upraised, sheepish smile on his lips, eyebrows stubbornly knit. The principal turned to the teacher. High-speed palaver in telegraphese. And no need to be a student at the École Normale to guess its content. Who's that? Orsenna. Does he stand a chance in the exam? None. Fine; does he know anything about Auguste Comte, then? It's his hobby.

Whereupon the principal, all honey and smiles, hastened with quick little steps to the volunteer's seat.

"Bravo, Orsenna. I shall inform the vice-chancellor at once."

Fifty years on, I strain my ears, I strain my ears, I hear the classroom door close behind him, the principal's receding footsteps, the sarcastic congratulations: You must punish your ambassador severely, Gabriel, if he doesn't study properly. I hear the teacher's piping voice: "Come on, gentlemen, back to Virgil." I hear the silence gradually return amid the squeaking of pens on white paper and the renewed sighing, I hear myself murmuring Brazil, Brazil, syllables like a gusting wind, like a ship outward bound, like the kindling of flames. You may travel all you like, said the teacher, but pray do not disturb your classmates.

The walls of the Foreign Ministry were lined with red velvet. In the room where the modest reception took place beneath gilt moldings, a sepia tapestry recalled the jungle of yesteryear, peopled by nymphs and fauns. The floors shone like glass. Outside the high narrow windows were a gravel driveway and a crescent-shaped lawn with two gardeners raking at invisible leaves. Around me twenty fellow positivists stood mute and rigid, very young people brought together as if for the ogre's banquet. We are a gift from France, thought Gabriel. A France eager to reestablish diplomatic ties with the ogre?

A door opened. A minor official wearing a chain of office cried out, "His Excellency the Minister!" And—preceded by two more chain-wearing flunkeys—Foreign Minister Théophile Delcassé came in.

"Thank you, lads," he said.

He moved among us, shaking hands.

"Good luck, lads," he said.

And he returned to his foreign affairs.

An attaché handed out envelopes with our names. You may open them. Everything had been taken care of: tickets, passports, instructions, destination, even labels to stick on the trunks. Gabriel was to go to London, 14 Pelham Crescent SW7. Excellent, said the attaché. The gift from France was escorted to the door. The positivists took careful little steps because of the floor, slippery as glass. "Good luck," said the attaché. He spoke just like the minister, same tone, same diction. He even added "lads," but in a low voice as he turned away, like someone afraid to borrow someone else's uniform. Passersby watched us descend the ceremonial stairway. It was cold and dry.

A question from Gabriel, in the train:

"Tell me, Louis, do you think people dream in big countries as well, with all the reality they have around them?"

On December 20, 1900, there was once a father who braved the journey to Le Havre, braved the farewell embraces—England must be a good place for our disease, Gabriel; hurry up and get settled, I shall be there soon with Marguerite—braved the last scenes, Gabriel's luggage being checked and taken through customs, his son climbing the gangway and vanishing into the belly of the ship that gradually pulled clear of the dock. There was once upon a time a father who grew smaller and smaller under the sea gulls. And I glimpsed in the small crowd at the far end of the dock one arm waving goodbye and the other also waving, more abruptly, with the back of the hand, the way you shoo away unwelcome people. Poor Louis, already wrestling with our ghosts, the newborn's mother and Buffalo Bill, Levallois and the Luxembourg Gardens, silent Marguerite and the Mexican living room. . . .

I had left him to cope all alone with my childhood.

Then Gabriel, knight of the round face, left the stern with its hawsers coiled like gleaming snail shells and its passengers already green with seasickness, walked past the lifeboats and their peeling paint, and made his way to the bow. Ahead, beyond the mists, lay London, the world's largest city, capital of the Real.

## POLITICAL

*To keep your files up to date as I prepare to leave France, I am anxious to overlook nothing and nobody. Let us therefore invite an eleventh-hour guest aboard ship, the young Archduke Maximilian, the one Napoleon III placed on the Mexican throne.*

*Louis often mentioned him to me.*

*"He asked nothing of anyone, you see, unless it was to ask the Adriatic, which he could see through his window, to inspire him to write a few acceptable lines:*

> "Oh that my feet might tread that tranquil path!
> The path that 'neath shy myrtle wends its way,
> There would I sing of Science and the Muse—
> Sweeter to me than Gold or burnished Crown. . . .

*"His wife Carlotta, née Coburg-Gotha, was of course ambitious, but was this not a peccadillo shared by all archdukes' wives?"*

*Marguerite was less indulgent. She would put her hand on my shoulder, look gravely into my eyes, and say, "Now you, if an emperor made you a gift of a throne, you would show yourself worthy of it."*

*Alas, Maximilian lacked the virtues of Gabriel Orsenna. He was unable to govern ungovernable Mexico. Our armies abandoned him.*

*"Well, don't you think it's natural, Gabriel," Marguerite would ask, "for the French to come back to France?"*

*And the Mexicans shot Maximilian.*

*"Of course it is sad," said Marguerite, "but you have to agree it was no fault of our emperor's. He gave him his chance."*

*Later I learned the rest of his sad story.*

*Once he was dead, Maximilian hoped to be able to resume the life he loved. Basically, the status of ghost suited him rather well. A ghost can dream of poetry without having to write lines people will sneer at. He can spend his summers on the Adriatic and leave for other climes as soon as damp mists begin to gather. He can even love his wife, gently, with his fingertips, without being swept away by the inborn ambition of all women named Carlotta, née Coburg-Gotha.*

*But please, said the ghost Maximilian, now leave me in peace.*

*They did not leave him in peace.*

*After his death, friends flocked to him. Friends scandalized by the attitude of Bonaparte III, friends ashamed to be French. All warm and well-meaning. But so noisy! Alone among them, the painter Manet was a pleasant and helpful companion. Instead of shouting, he transferred his anger to his art. Thus was born in the year 1868 a powerful, brooding canvas of the firing squad, the guns, the officer commanding the squad, a few observers, and the short-lived emperor of Mexico, white shirt thrown open, chest bare. Throughout the gestation period, Maximilian abstained from calling on the painter. Then the work was done, and Maximilian invited himself in. And there before his eyes was his death all over again, the freezing black dawn, his death pinned to the canvas like a beetle on a cork display board, his death killed all over again; all that was missing were the Mexican stage props of that dawn, the two or three vultures, the guardian volcano. The artist had been quite right to limit himself to essentials. Then Maximilian waltzed and swooped around the artist's studio. Thank you, Manet, thanks to you my death is dead and you have magnificently enthroned me in the memory of men; I must kiss you—and he bestowed on the creator's forehead a kiss in which he put all the warmth and all the love ghosts are capable of.*

*Alas, a few months later Manet's conscience nagged at him. His Maximilian was a failure. He removed him from the composition. The executed man's despair can be imagined. Of course there was a hope that he might one day be reborn as a handsomer, more splendid Maximilian. But the former emperor of Mexico was something of an artist himself; he knew how these people think, one whim begets another. Alas, alas, he told himself with an enormous sigh, my hour has passed. But perhaps the blank space on the canvas will intrigue people as much as (more than) my face would have done?*

*But alas, a few years later Manet died. His heirs squabbled over his pictures. And cut into four pieces (yes, cut into four pieces) the death of Maximilian, whose pieces were scattered.*

*Later still, enter Edgar Degas. Was it in honor of Maximilian's memory? No, probably in honor (alas) of Manet's. Whatever his motive, he set to work and one by one retrieved the pieces. Manet's death of Maximilian, minus Maximilian, was together again.*

*Alas, Degas died. Once again, Maximilian trembled. But the National Gallery was on the alert. At the great sale of 1919 it purchased the four pieces of the death of Maximilian, which have ever since (and forever?) been reunited on a London wall (Trafalgar Square).*

*How could I possibly be a Bonapartist?*

*There it is: if we add the short-lived emperor Maximilian to the passenger list, my ship is full. It is up to you to draw your conclusions and pen the portrait of Gabriel, politically speaking, as the year 1900 draws to a close. I wish you luck. As for me, I shall continue my journey.*

# 2

# *Matters Botanic*

## I

A STORM. AN ANGRY SOU'WESTER. Gale force registering over 10 on the meticulous Beaufort scale. The gulls high above the shuddering vessel no longer squabbled or struggled but were swept swiftly overhead, drifting from Spain to Lapland. White breakers marbled the dark-green sea. The French coast appeared and disappeared astern. An unpleasant sense of eclipse when you love your country. Up ahead we butted into unending gray: sometimes the foaming gray of the sea, sometimes the watery gray of the sky.

The second we were outside the harbor's protective arms, the second the pounding began, every sensible passenger wanted to turn back.

"Captain, we insist you put about!"

"Captain, you will drown us all!"

"Captain, be warned, I have friends in high places!"

But alas for the fearful, our sole master under God had the broad torso and brick-red complexion of the Armorican race, that granite-hard western branch of the Aryan trunk, one of whose foremost mental qualities is its refusal ever to change its mind. That is why Bretons are cherished by shipowners. They do not turn back, whatever the weather. Luckily the earth is round, or once gone we would never again set eyes on them. . . . One by one the protesters gave up hammering on the glassed-in bridge, became steadily paler, and, after a last attempt at dignity, clapped hands to mouths and dashed for the nearest railing. It was at this moment that the dining room bell rang for the first lunch sitting. As best he could, sometimes crawling upward on all fours, sometimes racing wildly downhill, Gabriel made his way to the ship's restaurant.

The dining room was empty and the chairs were chained to the floor. Bottles clinked rhythmically behind the bar. From one end of it to the other, from port to starboard, slid a big ashtray flaunting the name of that admirable aperitif, Suze. Clinging to the doors for support, the ship's stewards hailed the intrepid arrival with the restrained enthusiasm of a porter at an English club: Do come in, sir, would you like a drink? I should be most surprised if we had many customers in weather like this.

I remember most fondly those fraternal smiles, that pride in belonging to the aristocracy of the sea, to those unaffected by seasickness, for they mark the very end of my childhood. Afterward, immediately afterward, the adventure of adulthood began.

A family appeared, four units emerging unsteadily from the aft gangway, father, mother, and two little girls, holding one another by the hand as if roped together. Gabriel had chosen a table to starboard. As evidence of their perfect manners, tact, and consideration for others, the four unsteady units headed cautiously to the opposite side.

"Oh, Papa!" cried the youngest of the ladies. "What if we invited this young man who isn't vomiting to have lunch with us?"

"Ann, I beg you!" cried the father. "Please forgive her, sir, she must be tired; she rose very early this morning."

At any other time of his life, Gabriel would have blushed and stammered, Pray think nothing of it, sir, lowering his gaze and spooning down his solitary vegetable soup. But the roaring of the gale, the first swallows of the Médoc he had ordered, perhaps too his (recent) admission to the aristocracy of the sea, had sent boldness coursing through his veins. He rose and bowed.

"On the contrary, sir, this young lady voiced my very thoughts, for I myself wished to invite you to a collective celebration of this crossing. May I introduce myself: Gabriel Orsenna, trainee diplomat."

Following a brief exchange of civilities, broken by rather tense silences as the downward rush of our restaurant into the trough of a wave brought stomachs brutally to throats, it was decided that Gabriel would join their table.

Until then he had known only his own family. And one's family is not an acquaintance, merely an extension upstream and downstream of oneself, a kind of annex, warm and always in the way.

And now, across a table thrown into disorder by the buffeting of the sea, a strange gentleman, truly foreign to him, a foreigner with merry eyes behind round glasses, was handing him his card:

Markus V. Knight
Music Director
London Office: d'Arblay Street

So it was that in the midst of this storm a door opened for Gabriel onto a whole succession of sumptuous existences, onto what would in the hotel business be called a suite.

"I hope you have taken note, Gabriel—please allow me to call you Gabriel—music director, not impresario. God deliver us from impresarios; they are a blot on our Art. No, music director, which is to say permanent traveler, talent hunter: as soon as I hear of a right note somewhere I'm hot on the trail!"

"You should also explain to our friend Gabriel," said the mother in the gentlest of voices, "that the obscurer the talent you unearth the more lucrative our contracts are."

The two little girls spluttered with laughter. The music director half rose, arms widespread. "I shall say no more, Gabriel, you now know my entire fate: in my case, hunger for money, in theirs hunger for food. For just try feeding these three feminine creatures less and you'll hear them raise the roof. But what about you, Gabriel, do you play the violin, the piano?"

Too late, too late to reply.

Gabriel had fallen.

Caught up in his emotions, wholly preoccupied by his determination not to blush, a task universally known to be all-absorbing, he had forgotten to hold on to the arms of his chair. A sudden lurch of the ship flung him to the deck.

"We shall all perish!" cried the mother.

"Oh, my gosh!" said Ann, the daughter who had invited me to join them.

"Have you broken anything?" asked the other little girl, the older one.

Her lower lip was trembling, the way it does when you're about to cry.

Poor Gabriel's knee was hurting quite cruelly. Indeed, the scar of this historic wound is still visible today.*

He climbed back on his chair as best he could.

Throughout these happenings, the music director had not stirred. He resumed the conversation as if nothing had happened.

"So, Gabriel, neither the violin nor the piano?"

"Alas, sir . . ."

The music director had leaned close to Gabriel and was whispering a curious blend of confidences and highly indiscreet questions. "It's obvious, isn't it, that they don't have much respect for me. True, for a whole year now I have found no one suitable. But you'll soon find out, they think everything is easy, they think virtuosos grow on every tree. But you, Gabriel, if I may be so bold, how do you plan to earn lots of money discreetly? Believe me, you must have both at once; lots of money is essential but far from enough. The important thing is discretion. Women cannot abide too-obvious striving. Yes, lots of money, discreetly come by. That is the secret to cordial relations with the female of the species. I have paid dearly for this knowledge. One day I'll tell you all about it."

The three ladies across the table were deep in communication. From time to time one of them would stop speaking and raise her head, shamelessly studying our hero before returning to her murmurs and her splutters of mirth. Clearly they were not listening to this male talk; they had other subjects of interest. Relieved, Gabriel gave his companion a little information about himself, the bare minimum.

"My field is positivist philosophy."

"I shall be frank, young man: philosophy worries me, positivism reassures me."

Ignorant of the facts of this life though he was, Gabriel was expecting this reaction. All fathers, and first and foremost those involved in art, want their daughters to choose companions with steady professions. How could you blame them?

"Please don't take it the wrong way," said the music director. "I like you immensely, and the main thing is to have a calling."

*Romantic Gabriel! I've looked everywhere, even in summer while you're asleep, and never found a scar *(note from Ann)*.

Gabriel nodded. Without a calling you were adrift. He had just discovered his own: to follow this family forever and everywhere.

They brought in the leg of lamb with mint sauce.

"It's the worst crossing for nine years," the steward told them proudly. "The assistant dishwasher has broken his arm."

The three women, absorbed in handling a lunch that circumstances had rendered perilous, had for the moment cut short their investigations. They kept their eyes on their plates, on the mouthfuls they attempted to build before bearing them to their mouths, and they chatted of Christmas, of the gifts they hoped to receive—isn't that so, Markus; do you hear, Papa?—if, of course, this ship ever reaches port.

Gabriel took advantage of this respite to acquaint himself with his love. Until then he had not looked at them. He had merely kept telling himself that he was sitting across the table from a miracle. And he had kept that miracle at arm's length, just where it was, across the table, even at the risk of appearing boorish. He stared at places near the miracle: above it, below it. But never eye to eye. No confrontation with the miracle. But now the time had come. Let me see, said Gabriel. He took his courage in both hands. Let me see. And he cast his first glance at them, and then another, and yet another. . . .

And it was thus, by bits and pieces—a cheek, a forehead, a soft-skinned temple, a pouting lip, golden down on the nape of a neck, a timid way of closing the fingers, a mocking way of narrowing the eyelids—it was thus, fragment by fragment, that they entered Gabriel's life and were assembled fragment by fragment within him. His first impression had not lied. There was indeed a miracle across the table, a dangerous miracle. It was worse than he had foreseen. More beautiful, more mocking, more lost, more to be seized tumultuously in his arms, more everything, more forever. More forever elusive.

Today, the old Gabriel telling you this story must forget the intimate knowledge he has of all three of them; he must seal three distinct wells of memory one by one in order to return to what was clear on that afternoon of December 20, 1900: they were extensions of one another. In age, for example, it was as if they were but one person at three stages of her life: at six or seven her name was Ann, at ten or eleven she had a name Gabriel did not yet know, at thirty (at most thirty-one) she had become Mrs. Markus Knight. Or in hair color and facial structure: two golden braids, round face (the youngest one); auburn ringlets, somewhat severe, framing an oval out of a Sienese painting (the elder sister); a thicket of black curls (May I remove my hat, with all this rolling and pitching? Mama, you'll be so ugly. Ann, I implore you!). And Gabriel blushed, once again, as the very young mother withdrew one by one the giant pins holding the feather-and-velvet creation in place.

Other details of the three women were harder to place; they seemed to live their own lives. Without renouncing membership in the Knight family, of course, they nevertheless demanded a measure of freedom. I mean Ann's dimple, a minute hollow on which side now? Yes, I see it again, to the right of her chin, every time she became serious again for a second (such dimples are a rarity, dimple experts would later tell me; "normal" dimples appear either at the moment of laughter or else are permanent). Well, neither the elder of the two sisters (why shouldn't I jump ahead, I can quite well call her Clara) nor their mother possessed anything of the kind. Likewise, since I have just mentioned Clara, her neck: a prodigy of length (she was only ten, at most twelve), of whiteness, of fragility. Gabriel stared at it as if at something never seen before on earth, a part of her body she might have invented specially for him, a distance between the head and the rest: sometimes, when she was upright, a firebreak or no-man's-land; sometimes, when she leaned forward to swallow a mouthful made particularly recalcitrant by the rolling of the ship, the arch of a bridge.

And Gabriel was beginning—oh! step by small step (let us bear in mind that apart from certain episodes in the Latin Quarter he knew nothing, absolutely nothing, about women), oh! circumspectly, so as not to blush—Gabriel was beginning to imagine other features, other even more intimate characteristics, when something nudged his right boot, a pressure he briefly believed must be that of the giant Suze ashtray. But no, the ashtray was navigating down at the other end of the dining room. So then?

So then existence almost stopped. The lights went out and every article in Creation vacated the place allotted it since civilization began, giving birth to the most barbarous of dins: glasses and bottles exploded against bulkheads, furniture not bolted down skittered noisily across the deck; as for human beings, seamen, stewards, or passengers, they lost all dignity. Unable to walk, two seamen under orders to put out the beginnings of a fire crawled forward on all fours toward the stove used for broiling lobster, which had overturned. The Le Havre–Newhaven packet was beam on to the swell, lying far over on her port side and in no hurry to right herself. Gabriel and his miraculous family hung on to their chairs as best they could. Lunch had vanished; the leg of lamb, the mint, the boiled potatoes, the glasses, plates, cutlery, salt, and pepper had all gone to join a mountain of debris down in the nethermost corner of the dining room. All that remained was the white tablecloth, now stained by a long, winding streak of dark-brown gravy. And during those endless critical seconds Gabriel contemplated that long spreading streak, that endearing, brotherly vestige of everyday life. I want to live, he silently screamed. I want to live; this is no time to die, with this miracle across the table from me. At long last the ship came back, slowly and reluctantly, to a posture more nearly vertical. In short, she righted herself.

"Well, well," said the music director.

"I'm hungry," said Ann.

Love is mightier than death. Gabriel, a survivor of the gale of December 20, 1900, still remembered in meteorological annals, can vouch for it.

In an attempt to mask the several symptoms of his confusion, Gabriel went into action, busying himself with first-aid assistance beneath the approving gaze of the music director, who told himself that in the makeup of this likable Gabriel the reassuring positivist side was decidedly stronger than the disturbing philosophical side. Half an hour later a second portion of reasonably hot lamb, smothered in a mint sauce comparable to the first and seemingly even runnier, with potatoes more boiled and shrunken than their predecessors, sat waiting for Elisabeth to give them her attention, for the miraculous mother, at that moment busy removing a stain from Ann's red wool pullover with the end of a napkin, was called Elisabeth. And quite out of the question to start eating before Mrs. Markus Knight, Gabriel properly told himself.

After a few minutes the stain finally realized it was a nuisance and disappeared. Elisabeth wished the company a hearty appetite. The conversation resumed. Gabriel's miraculous companions would be in London for only a few days. (Alas, a thousand times alas, Gabriel had hoped that all the maritime buffeting would impair some organ inside the music director—oh, nothing serious, just enough for a convalescence of, let's see, a few months, long enough to gain a foothold in this miraculous family.) Then they would be off again to explore northern Hungary ("Do you know Budapest, Gabriel?"), eastern Czechoslovakia, and southern Poland; they had been told of some promising fiddlers scattered in the backwoods as well as an "infant magician on the keyboard" (as the music director expressed it) between Chelm and Brest-Litovsk.

"How, Gabriel, my dear erudite friend, would you explain the geographical fact that Central Europe is the great mine of music? Sometimes my ladies and I would appreciate a change from eternal cold, eternal sleds, eternal boiled potatoes. We have tried the Mediterranean, we have ranged its perimeters, ears alert. Commercial and musical yield: nil. Nothing to offer refined audiences, only wailing muezzins, irritating arpeggios, syrupy mandolins."

"But still . . . Italy," ventured the positivist philosopher.

A mistake. A hideous mistake.

"You are thinking no doubt of opera," said the music director in abruptly glacial tones.

"No, no," replied Gabriel. "Lully, Vivaldi."

Too late. The harm was done. All four of them stared at Gabriel, dumbfounded, horrified, as if he had just killed Beethoven with his bare hands. The Knight family unanimously loathed opera. As you may readily imagine, Gabriel never mentioned this subject again.

So he still does not know what lay behind this phobia. Was it an involvement of the music director with some coloratura, one of those long-pardoned crimes buried beneath years of silence and now hauled back from the dead by this little ass Gabriel? Or had Mme. Elisabeth succumbed to a tenor? There might also have been some kind of professional dereliction, a breach of contract for example. Singers love to cancel at the last second, with the theater already packed, the curtain about to rise, and the understudy nowhere to be found. And then who is to blame, who has to announce the ugly news to the public amid catcalls, who has to refund the tickets? The impresario, whether or not he has changed his title to music director. But I am speculating. I know nothing for sure. The Knight family will disappear and its secret with it. I am not going to reopen the inquiry fifty years after the event!*

The sea was calmer. The immense white cliffs of England now sheltered them from the wind. And opera had ruined everything. Gabriel attempted to change the subject, asked increasingly original questions. How do you recognize talent? Is the violin more difficult than the piano? But there was no reply. The Knight family pretended not to hear, pretended to be watching the gulls or details of the coastline through the portholes—"Oh! the old keep, I had quite forgotten it; there are the houses that all look alike again"—nobody paid him any more attention. The miracle was fading rapidly into the distance, left behind in the storm no doubt, beyond the horizon, in some place where opera did not exist.

"I think it's high time we looked for our luggage," said the music director as he rose (and offered Gabriel his hand). "Goodbye, young man. Delighted to have made your acquaintance, and good luck with your philosophy."

And he left the dining room. Then it was the turn of the mother and of the elder sister with the as yet unknown name; she smiled on him most kindly but granted him nothing, not the promise of a rendezvous, not the merest hint of an address. The miracle was collapsing. Had it not been for Ann, blessed and cursed be your name, as utterly blessed as eternally cursed, for had it not been for her, for the few words she uttered, innocently, as she took her leave—Come and see us, 21 Sloane Street; my father is never in his office—Gabriel's life would not have been this battlefield, this void, this paradise.

And they disappeared. By the time Gabriel had found his two suitcases, they had disappeared. The hem of a navy blue dress, two snowy ankle socks flashing suddenly on the other side of a porthole—a very young girl must be climbing a gangway to the pier—and then nothing. In vain he raced all over the ship, asking, calling for Mr.

*I should hope not! *(note from Clara)*.

Knight, Mr. Knight, quizzing the customs officers, would you have seen the Knight family? Nothing. Marguerite's grandson, like his grandmother, had let his miracle escape.

He almost had to be carried aboard the boat train by a sympathetic policeman, and he did not recover his spirits until much later, past Croydon. Then he took his favorite rubber ball from his suitcase and began bouncing. In any train compartment in any other country they would doubtless have cried lunatic and put this demented youth in a straitjacket. But the English are a tolerant people. Gabriel's traveling companions observed this spectacle with indifference. A bearded, pipe-smoking young man, the kind who uses props in an attempt to appear older, stopped smoking for a second and said, "I say!" At this intrusion into someone else's private life, the other passengers turned shocked countenances on their garrulous companion.

And it was thus that Gabriel entered London (Victoria Station), bouncing his ball and ready for the second set.

## II

The assemblage of arms, legs, and lap draped in black (or at best in gray) and leading a life of its own (desolate and all too proper) below Marguerite's blue gaze cannot really be considered a woman's body. Of course Gabriel had sought shelter thousands and thousands of times within those arms and on that lap. But a grandmother has no body. Nor did Louis have a body. Fathers do not have bodies. We are astonished that our parents die when all the while the death of parents is simply punishment for the unimaginative children that we are. Perhaps if we paid more attention to their bodies, our parents would not die. Or would die less.

The first body Gabriel took an interest in, the first not to laugh at him, not to flee; the first to welcome him, to accept his stares, his visits, his questions; the first body that let him do everything he wanted was London. He immersed himself in it the way a lovesick medical student immerses himself in anatomy: with an ogre's frenzy. Since the Brazilian embassy was deserted, since with the exception of the albino doorman everyone there appeared to be away on Christmas vacation, Gabriel tirelessly roamed the city's streets. Night and day he strode, examined, measured. No matter what the hour. In all directions. In all weathers. He checked stock-market quotations and pushed through doorways, stuck his ear to the ground and listened to the walls. He rapped on the city's joints as well, to test its reflexes. Which led to a few brawls in the East End and an arrest in Hyde Park. But the albino's intervention soon set him free. He merely said, Ah, you too? English and Brazilians are very fluid when it comes to morals.

And in the evenings, refining his map of London, he discovered the cartographer's very special intoxication. I advise you to give it a try: a distinctly voluptuous experience. As you transpose your day's discoveries to a map your heart beats slower but stronger and pride overflows you. Suddenly you are absolute master of the streets you have traced, the squares and embankments you have walked. You become their guardian spirit.

He very soon distinguished the three juxtaposed cities that are London. To the east the docks. In the center the banks. In the west the residential areas. To the east, from all over the planet, came the infinite diversity of things. In the center, the banks transformed those things into wealth. In the west lived the wealthy. In the east teemed things as well as people so poor that the things had accepted them into their domain. In the center, paper was king, for the bankers, concerned first and foremost with hygiene, considered it their highest priority to transmute the malodorous sloshing about of things into odorless notes. In the west, gardens bloomed and the wealthy strolled.

And Gabriel slipped from one London to another, constantly modifying his appearance in order to remain anonymous, to melt into the crowd. Sometimes the smallest detail is enough to transform you. A neckerchief and cloth cap, and he was an East End docker. A crush hat casually substituted as he strolled around the Tower, and he entered the City like a true apprentice stockbroker. A white dickey slipped on in a dark corner at the end of Fleet Street, and he was at once a gentleman's gentleman from an impeccably West End address—Belgravia, Kensington, Chelsea. This constant shifting of disguises filled him with pride. It seemed to him that he reflected every facet of London, that he *was* every facet of London, the only one qualified to fix it on a map. Here you are, he would one day tell the Geographic Society, presenting them with what was more a portrait than a map, here is London's only true likeness. . . .

This passion for cartography has never left me. The older I get the more clearly I perceive in it the working of that consistent capacity for empathy that sets apart certain human beings, a most exalted science, a true physiology of places. One day I will describe Cannes for you; you'll be amazed, you won't believe your ears. . . .

## III

On the morning of December 31, Gabriel was awakened by a kind of singing: long-drawn rhythms abruptly cut short, incredible vowel modulations, a few quickly swallowed shushing sounds, like the crunching of a beach beneath bare feet, a blend of the sun and of yearning for the sun.

"That's the Brazilian language," he said.

And he leaped out of bed. The embassy rang with voices. *Como vai?* Merry Christmas. How was your trip? And your love life? What news from Rio?

He was dressing as fast as he could when there was a knock at his door. It was the albino.

"Sir, Reinaldo Aristides Lima is expecting you."

Gabriel finished knotting his tie and examined himself closely in the tiny mirror: Do I have the face for the job? But he had no standard of comparison. What was a positivist supposed to look like? I should have worried about it earlier. Never mind. And he ran downstairs.

The room was hung with somber velvet almost hidden by pictures. Numberless tropical vistas. Gabriel studied the giant trees, the churches piled high with colonnades and cherubs, the markets teeming with Negroes, the much paler beauties surprised on their evening promenade, two distant yellow sails approaching harbor. . . .

"Welcome to Brazil," came a very gentle voice from the gloom. (Chargé d'affaires Reinaldo Aristides Lima did not like the light.)

Gabriel went forward, stammering what he considered to be appropriate civilities. "My respects, Your Excellency, may I—I mean may France—my respects, Your Excellency." Little by little the features of a large weary fish swam into view, illuminated by the most benevolent of smiles. Curiously enough it was his hair, his excessively black hair, that highlighted his baldness. His plump fingers toyed with a small shiny letter opener. He spoke flawless French, the kind you reserve for marriage proposals and for receptions at the Institut de France.

"Monsieur Orsenna, your philosophical beliefs must be strong indeed for you to brave the rigors of this climate in order to spread the word among us. Such courage on your part compels me to honesty: I am of the other camp. I will confess that after the fall of Dom Pedro II I awaited—I hoped for—the Emperor's return. I believed republics to be by their nature ephemeral. But since the new order has endured, the responsibilities of this post oblige me to learn newer (and doubtless excellent) ways of seeing the world. Please accept my gratitude."

He rose, stretched out his hand.

"We could hold our first class in an hour. Would that suit you?"

Walking Gabriel to the door, he stopped before a glass-fronted cabinet.

"This is my collection. Are you interested in paper knives, Monsieur Orsenna?"

Gabriel, doubtless influenced by his diplomatic surroundings, replied that a reader as avid as he was could scarcely have remained indifferent to them.

Whereupon the chargé d'affaires took me in his arms. Not until much later did Gabriel learn the meaning of this embrace in Latin America, a simple expression of politeness. But on December 31, 1900, he believed it denoted affection.

We must try to understand him. Stripped of the Knight family, he felt utterly alone in London, bereft of all warmth. He therefore offered Reinaldo Aristides Lima what amounted to a declaration of love for Brazil, for exiled diplomats, for red velvet. The ambassador said to himself that this young, this very young French republican was decidedly most likable.

On that morning and with that exchange their friendship was born. A friendship of which Gabriel received proof a few days later when he was summoned just after dawn to a most secret ceremony, the visit every Monday by an assistant barber to dye the black hair, the never-black-enough hair, of the sixty-year-old—and much more than that—Reinaldo ("I have invited you backstage, Gabriel!"). A friendship that was to last exactly three months and nine days until the tragic death I must alas, and perforce, describe.

An embassy is like a family boardinghouse. And as in all such boardinghouses, a sense of exile dwells amid the colors of furniture bought or rented from predecessors and the smells of cooking and gravy permeating its walls. A mania for gossip, a passionate interest in people's pasts, an indiscreet curiosity about the day's mail, a few dreams of promotion lost amid the general resignation, the sense of living among caricatures of human types (the spinster obsessed with exercise, the confirmed bachelor, the counselor's wife in love with her body, the cipher clerk amassing notes for a future novel), and above all else a double question: Is this really a family? Is this really life?

In this Curzon Street boardinghouse, located in London but in every other respect in Brazil, the head of the family was absent. Was Rio attempting to express its displeasure with Queen Victoria over this or that issue in world affairs? Or was it simply that tropical wisdom had dealt with the delicate problem of nomination by postponing it? Whatever the reason, no ambassador of the Republic of Brazil to Great Britain was there. A mere chargé d'affaires presided over the affairs of the family boardinghouse. The very shy and very polyglot Reinaldo Aristides Lima, declining to use the massive mahogany desk—reserved, he said, for the plenipotentiary alone—worked beside the desk, squeezed in between the window and the glass-fronted cupboard, on a tiny credenza piled high with files.

"And what if the ambassador eventually turns out to be you?" Gabriel asked him later, when they knew one another better.

"Then I shall change places. But it is infinitely improbable. Two quite different destinies. Believe me, Gabriel, I have no reason to complain. To each his own level. And I am so very close to the top."

It was true. His credenza touched the big empty desk.

"This is where decorations are awarded," the albino whispered to him as he led him to the embassy reception room.

The staff awaited him in hierarchical order, from Reinaldo Aristides Lima to Maria the cook, through first counselor Gabeira, coughing into a silk handkerchief; the very intense second counselor Victor Neves; the contract attaché Xavier Guimaraes; and the gardener-handyman Edward, who had nothing to do with Brazil, all quietly seated on gilt ceremonial chairs.

"Monsieur Orsenna, we are all ears," said almost-ambassador Lima with an orchestra conductor's wave.

Gabriel cleared his throat, had time to notice that not one of his listeners had come prepared to take notes, and was off. "Isidore-Auguste-Marie-François-Xavier Comte was born on January 13, 1798, at Montpellier into a family of Catholics and monarchists" (the chargé d'affaires nodded vigorous approval). "In 1814, tutored by Daniel Encontre, professor of higher mathematics at the faculty of Protestant theology at Montauban, he entered the Polytechnic School, which was closed in April 1816 for being Republican and Bonapartist" ("Splendid," said the chargé d'affaires). "Auguste Comte then hit upon the idea of creating a new polytechnic school in the United States of America, for in his opinion democracies needed mathematics" ("But do we need democracy?" murmured the chargé d'affaires). "It was a failure, happily for the history of philosophy. For Auguste Comte now began to construct his system. Rejecting all notion of the absolute, a synthesis of Montesquieu, of d'Alembert, and of Rousseau—positivism . . ."

Out of scientific principle, Gabriel was determined to move rapidly from biographical anecdote to focus on pure ideas. After a quarter hour of this diet, the first counselor, racked with coughs, left the drawing room. Maria, the rotund Bahian, escaped shortly afterward—not for lack of an excuse; on the morning of December 31 a cook is her own mistress. The rest of the audience had fallen asleep, discreetly and with dignity, as only diplomats can. Only the second counselor and the chargé d'affaires continued to stare at our speaker.

"The preceding distinction suffices to explain why it has hitherto been almost universally believed that we should proceed from the particular to the general, and why today on the contrary we must proceed—"

At eleven sharp the chargé d'affaires raised his hand.

Gabriel stopped short in the middle of his sentence:

"My thanks," said the chargé d'affaires. "Our thanks. We shall resume tomorrow. Same place, same time. But I fail to understand what all this has to do with my country, Brazil."

We must picture Gabriel's sad white room after this educational fiasco: Auguste Comte's sad indigestible books sitting on the brass bed, his sad preparatory notes scattered on the small table that wobbled despite many attempts to brace its legs, the sad sash window, sad sad Saint Sylvester's Day, 1900.

There was a knock at the door.

Without waiting for Gabriel to open it, second counselor Victor came in: a huge smile, round glasses, very pale complexion, coal-black hair parted in the middle. He pounced on our orator and seized his hands.

"Thank you, thank you. Those are exactly the ideas Brazil needs today."

He clenched his right fist, he pounded the air; those were concepts on whose foundation republics could be built.

Gabriel sighed. "I am deeply moved. But you saw what happened: utter fiasco."

"What else did you expect? My country's diplomatic arm is gangrenous from years of empire."

Gabriel sat back down on the bed and shook his head. "It's not that, I bored them. They were yawning, all of them, or nearly all of them were yawning; the others were asleep. What a triumph!"

"That's why I'm here, I wanted to . . . a piece of advice. . . . Do you mind? Empire engenders bad habits: the craving for stories, fables, anecdotes. Emperors' mistresses, empresses' fevers, crown princes' sorrows. . . . You see what I mean? For quite some time yet Brazil will continue to crave romance. So be more anecdotal."

"You think so?"

"I am sure of it. But I will not lose hope. Little by little Brazil will realize that only ideas have beauty. We shall shake off the straitjacket of romance. A republic is a regime without a past. Nothing but free human beings and battles of ideas. Don't you agree?"

To be candid, Gabriel had not given much thought to republics. To be even more candid, he would probably have preferred a reasonably obscure republic containing quite a few empires. But the secretary's enthusiasm was a tonic.

Listening to him, you would have thought Brazil was a new country fresh from its mother's womb, like the United States the century before, and that you could make anything you wished of it.

"So Auguste Comte planned to found a polytechnic school in America?"

And Gabriel had to go back in detail over the great dream of 1816. At every sentence, Victor nodded. Yes, Brazil must have a polytechnic school. Yes, mathematics was indeed a splendid seedbed for democracy. . . .

Then the two new friends shook hands and Victor returned to his diplomatic duties.

Toward three in the afternoon Gabriel had the idiotic idea, the arrogant and ridiculous idea, of challenging the stars that so clearly frowned on him that day. In other words, he directed his steps toward Sloane Street, no. 21, the address Ann had breathed into his ear before vanishing into the crowd.

Sloane Street is a handsome thoroughfare that leads up from the river Thames to Hyde Park, and number 21 was cream-colored, with two fat columns flanking the front door. According to the small plate above the bell buttons, the miraculous family lived on the fourth floor. The young mother, Elisabeth, opened the door.

She spoke very rapidly.

"Oh, it's you, Gabriel? What a pity! They've left. We have to be in Antwerp tomorrow morning. Because of a Mozart mass of which my husband expects great things. I am off to join them at the station. I was just closing the house down. Goodbye, Gabriel. You must come back again. Perhaps you could take this bag down. Leave it at the bottom of the stairs. Now you promise you'll come back, Gabriel?"

"When?"

"I don't know. Mercy, such questions! With Markus there's no telling. In a month, perhaps. Keep an eye on our windows. You can see them from the street. If there's any movement, come upstairs. You promise, now? Farewell then, Gabriel."

Elisabeth closed the door and Gabriel walked down, down, endlessly down. He was still walking down when he heard a voice behind him.

"You're still here?" Elisabeth was staring at him. And our Positivist must have looked truly despairing, for she cried out, "Very well, Gabriel, you may come with me to the station. Poor Gabriel, do you think that will do you any good?"

In the cab she said poor Gabriel again and took his hand.

"Since you are in love with my two daughters, let me explain things to you: the first one is always afraid and the second one never. It won't be easy, poor dear Gabriel. I don't want to give you advice, but believe me, this absence will be good for you; you must seize this chance to season yourself a little. Oh, no! It won't be easy, my poor Gabriel. Fortunately they are still very young. Yes, you must use this time before you see them again to season yourself. Is it a promise?"

They had just turned left into a street called Pimlico. Elisabeth moved closer to him. He felt the closeness of her leg, her hip, her arm. She turned toward him. She took both his hands. She gazed straight into his eyes, eyes of which he felt ashamed, the eyes of a sorrowing schoolboy, eyes he wished he could then and there exchange for the eyes of a seducer, metallic, laughing, but nobody was trading eyes on Pimlico Street that day.

"Gabriel, before everything that is going to happen begins to happen, I wanted to ask you. What is a woman to you?"

Very loud, Gabriel heard the noise of wooden wheels on the road, then Elisabeth's voice.

"Gabriel, I asked you a question, what is a woman?" The cab had stopped. Around them porters were shouting: Which train? What platform? They had arrived. She said, "Kiss me, Gabriel."

But it was she whose lips brushed his.

And he was alone in Buckingham Palace Road with Elisabeth's scent, a scent that was new to him and that clearly was not part of the Oriza repertory, even though Oriza was perfume purveyor to the Russian royal family (as its posters proclaimed on every wall in Levallois), yes, to the Russian royal family and to several other royal families, perhaps even the English one.

* * *

Next day Gabriel radically altered his teaching methods. His audience had shrunk: the only ones present were the chargé d'affaires, the republican second counselor, and the contract attaché. But those absent had an excuse. It was January 1.

"According to Auguste Comte," Gabriel began, "the elaboration of thought is inseparable from the blossoming of the emotions."

His three listeners, ready as yesterday to slump into diplomatic ennui, sat up straight on their gilt chairs, all ears.

"Auguste Comte met Caroline under the arches of the Palais-Royal. . . ."

And with a wealth of detail Gabriel outlined the world's oldest profession as it was exercised under the said arches and in the adjacent furnished rooms. Shocked, the chargé d'affaires raised his eyebrows. The speaker anticipated his objection by recalling Christ's example—He too had shown kindness to Mary Magdalen—and the eyebrows fell. As for the contract attaché, his nights in London had proved to him that whatever else one might say about paid loves their diversity was infinite. He itched to raise a forefinger and ask for specific information about the Palais-Royal, its exact address, hours of business, prices. . . . In short, Gabriel had his audience's attention.

He told how Mme. Massin, an actress, had sold her daughter Caroline's virginity to a lawyer, M. Cerclet. How the girl, quickly abandoned by her purchaser, had become a prostitute. How she implored one of her customers, Auguste Comte, to teach her algebra. How a mutual affection was born.

Alas, Caroline's past weighed on their relations. . . .

Little by little the reception room filled with people. Mysteriously alerted, a packed audience stirred impatiently. There were a few English there, but the vast majority were Latin American. Every gilt chair was taken. The last arrivals had to stand. As if by chance, Maria the cook had deserted her range. She stood rocking from one foot to the other, avid for the rest of the story.

Then Gabriel looked Victor, the republican second counselor, straight in the eyes; the time had come to blend a few positivist precepts into his narrative. So Auguste Comte thought about marriage. He wrote asking his parents for their permission. They refused.

For the obvious reason, his betrothed's misconduct? Not at all. They had learned that Auguste and Caroline had been living under the same roof before receiving the sacrament ("Oho!" said the audience; "Sshh!" said Maria).

The philosopher set forth on a positivist crusade. The opposing forces were clearly defined: on one side closed minds and unyielding tradition, on the other modernity and love. Ladies and gentlemen, transition periods are the most difficult of all times to live through: the new thinking is not yet strong enough to overcome selfishness, and religious beliefs are no longer quite strong enough.

A woman rose to protest. Gabriel had time only to glimpse her mantilla; neighbors had already forced her to sit down again. In the front row of gilt chairs, Victor was nodding approval. Well done, well done, he was mouthing, moving soundless lips, the way you speak to a deaf person. Well done, Gabriel, well done. . . .

Terrified at the prospect of appearing one day in a book by their son Auguste as examples of enemies of human progress, the Comte parents finally gave their consent.

The philosopher's witnesses at the ceremony were his old mathematician friends. But who had Caroline chosen?

And on this question, the lecturer left the hall.

I do not know whether Gabriel advanced positivist ideas one iota. But for several weeks his serial drama attracted a faithful audience. The Brazilian embassy turned people away at every episode. And what a shame, the lecturer would say to himself, his gaze sweeping the rapt faces of the men and women before him, what a shame the Knight family had left London! They would have realized that music was not the only thing in life. Alas! on Sloane Street the curtains never stirred.

Our young Orsenna had left truth behind him. Intoxicated by his success, overwhelmed by storytelling zeal, he launched into stories that no longer had any connection with Auguste Comte. He attempted to justify himself in an introductory address. He proclaimed, for example, that *The Three Musketeers* was in fact a philosophical tale. Did not Aramis represent the age of theology, Your Excellency, ladies and gentlemen, Athos the metaphysical age, Portos the positivist age, and d'Artagnan the philosopher running from one to the other?

His audience nodded—splendid, splendid—but let us not waste time; what happens to these musketeers?

And with great relish our hero told them the story of Mme. Bonacieux and of the queen's shoelaces, all adventures of undeniably bouncy heroes.

"Already?" The audience sighed when he stopped. "What was tattooed on Madame de Winter's shoulder? Please tell us or we won't get any sleep tonight. Anyway, long live positivism! Even though Aramis is the one I really like. . . ."

Some evenings these days, in his house at Cannes-la-Bocca, most often after a good Médoc, our hero wonders whether he has not lived another life than his own. It was his passion for bounciness, he suspects, that may have led to his mistake. Which profession, indeed, stands more in need of bounciness, the manufacture of rubber or the creation of a narrative serial? A real soap opera, the kind that brings a whole nation to a standstill at the same hour each day so that people can follow it, a serial that feeds conversations and breeds impatience, a true soap opera with numberless twists and turns, whose plot never comes back down to earth but spawns wars and cities, endless intrigues, love children, dozens and hundreds of characters, a vast multitude of characters by turns affectionate and cruel but always capable of peopling the worst of solitudes, even those that fall on Cannes-la-Bocca at night when the watchdogs bark to each other from empty villa to empty villa.

## IV

No point in sitting at coffee tables leafing through Janeiro newspapers, reciting Portuguese irregular verbs, or taking your first steps in tropical lepidoptery through the pages of fat red books: the days refused to speed by. Time hung heavy between positivist story sessions. Watches stagnated. Although inured to the spectacle of boredom, the diplomats felt a tug at their hearts when they looked at Gabriel. They invited him into their offices, sought to distract him with news from the other side, offered him coffee from São Paolo, and plied him with stories.

"You know, Gabriel, when I was stationed in Copenhagen, and God knows Danish time is hard to kill, I began to carve ivory privately, in my office—small narwhal teeth—and that was how I discovered a hidden law which I shall gladly share with you. My dear Gabriel, you seem so unhappy, here it is: the tinier the scale you work on, the faster external time will elapse . . . the faster the durable will evaporate."

But the sickness grew worse and the embassy lived in dread of losing its tutor, such a charming tutor, and one who made the rigors of theoretical philosophy so painless to swallow. And without a positivist, how did you learn positivism? And without positivism, how did you make headway in modern, republican, and positivist Brazil? The chargé d'affaires summoned his senior colleagues.

"We must give this young Frenchman something to do or he will leave us."

The first counselor sighed. "You know what that means, Your Excellency."

Every diplomat nodded. They knew. So rare were tasks at the embassy that dropping even one of them raised the general boredom quotient several notches. After much discussion, however, they were obliged to resign themselves to the sacrifice.

At crack of dawn next morning, contract attaché Xavier Guimaraes came to get Gabriel. His expression was black: So you have taken my job away from me? In vain Gabriel protested. Guimaraes refused to believe him. For him, laundering was the calling of callings, a secular religion. He sulked all the way to the docks.

"This is Saint Catherine dock."

It was the ark, the catalogue, the whole planet, commerce run amok, a frenzy of trading bales for crates, hogsheads for sacks, a piece of Ceylon for a bit of Trinidad, Murano glassware, elephant tusks as yellow as if they had been smoking, Boer prisoners surrounded by soldiers, Lloyds insurance men, a timekeeper from Greenwich with the real time in his hand, a Salvation Army patrol. . . . To reach the wharf you butted across the four corners of the earth, you were jostled by a consignment of tea, crushed beneath a cargo of cloves, and hounded by wine and by the aromas of coffee and cinnamon, by whiffs of ilang-ilang, by the sournesses of vinegar and herring.

Through this sea the attaché briskly swam, alternating the breast stroke with energetic punches, shouting, "This way Mr. Orsenna, this way!" Suddenly the ship appeared, immense and white beneath haughty rigging, sails furled and decks bustling: unloading had begun.

They had to fight again to gain possession of the huge wicker baskets. A zoo director claimed they were Malayan monkeys; a Fleet Street trader swore it was his Bolivian silverware, by Jove; they came within an inch of blows. Policemen ran up, the baskets were opened. "You see," said the contract attaché, "nothing but dirty laundry from America." Then where are my monkeys? cried the zoo director. A customs officer appeared: "Your laundry is not contaminated, is it?" We showed him our papers. Then waited another two hours for the arrival of the wagons that would have to cleave these crowds. By now it was daylight, sometimes blue, sometimes black; clouds sailed swiftly overhead from the west.

Enthroned on a mountain of ropes, ledger open on his knee, inkwell held steady in his left hand, steel pen poised in his right, the contract attaché kept tally. One by one the fifty-eight brown wicker crates were hoisted onto the wagons: São João Branco family of Belém, present; Medeiro family of Vaz d'Obidos, present; Nelson, Constancio Alves, and João Goanha families of Manaus, present; present the very cream of Amazonian society, said the contract attaché as he called the roll, the aristocracy of rubber. He was glowing with pride. "If I might offer you some advice, Mr. Orsenna, you must be most meticulous in taking inventory. A single bundle gone astray and the chargé d'affaires explodes. That is what makes the day go by so swiftly, Mr. Orsenna, the obligation to perform well, responsibility. Moreira family of Porto Velho, present; Baron Canudos de Litivia, a lone wolf, that one, present; are you sure that was the last one? Very well, then, sign here." And step by step the convoy heaved into motion, three rumbling, rocking wagons wrenched from Saint

Catherine dock. A sepia Sikh giant from the port police cleared a path for them: Make way, make way for the cargoes from Brazil.

"Where are we going?" Gabriel asked most positivistically.

"To Cornwall. That's where the waters are purest."

"And do many Brazilian families have their laundry done in England?"

"The cream, Mr. Orsenna, the Brazilian elite. You see, our best people are staunch believers in purity. If you could see the Amazon you would understand. It is not a river, it is floating mud. Would you like to do your laundry in mud, Mr. Orsenna?"

Gabriel said no, of course he wouldn't.

England slipped slowly by, a land of green gardens and white houses with black shutters. At nightfall—which came swiftly, as swiftly as in Brazil, the attaché remarked (they were his first words since London)—the convoy halted outside an inn. Stains and all, the fifty-eight crates were brought in out of the rain and stored in a barn.

Before he fell asleep, Gabriel lay wondering if the laundry business was a good way of training for difficult loves. How did you go about seasoning yourself? He dreamed of redheaded laundresses with rough knuckles and soft palms; ample, peppery, colorfully spoken women free with their caresses; he dreamed of beauty spots, of dazzling bosoms, of aprons to be unfastened, of rotundities to be nibbled, and of hollows to be filled. And one last detail, this dream was permeated by a smell utterly out of place in Great Britain: the ubiquitous cool scent of French household soap.

Next day the crates were counted and loaded again and the convoy moved on. The weather had deteriorated and the horses' heads drooped as though they sought gold coins on the highway. The coachmen had raised their collars and pulled their caps low, so that all you saw at the head of each wagon was a black bundle with a whip stuck in it. Downpour followed downpour, sometimes normal ones (Gabriel means vertical ones), sometimes horizontal. Usually the rain dropped straight down, in the manner so well described by Newton, but a sudden squall would lash you head on with icy water that forced its way between buttons and multiple layers of wool to reach the skin; then it trickled down, either in the back, down the spinal column to the seat, or else in front, via chest and navel on the way to a member already—it must be confessed—far from frisky. Once this phase of the drenching process was complete the downpour abated. Rain gave way to winds, to gales. After a few minutes of this blowing, your clothes, even the most sodden, had lost all trace of dampness. For a short while the sun broke through, doubtless to add a finishing touch to phase two, the drying period. But a fresh procession of clouds quickly swallowed it whole. Already the next downpour was upon us, its first drops striking the grass in the very next field.

After hours and hours of this treatment, Gabriel was forced to admit that the Brazilian elite was right. Doubtless there were absolutely irreproachable laundries in Latin America, but laundering was part and parcel of the very spirit of Cornwall; it was written into its climate.

By midafternoon Gabriel was overwhelmed by cold and hunger. He missed Levallois so badly that a kind of warmth was born close to his heart. And he sat huddled over this warmth as if over a stove fed log by log and regret by regret.

Suddenly, right in the middle of a particularly violent squall, the attaché emerged from his silence and yelled in his ear, "We're there!"

Gabriel raised the hood of his cloak a fraction of an inch. They had reached the top of a hill overlooking the sea. For acres all around them, white shapes hung from lines.

"You see," said the attaché with growing elation, "all we have to do is hang out the clothes, and the Atlantic launders them."

Far below, sheltered by a gray stone jetty, was a tiny harbor filled with shrimp boats. Smoke rose from a solitary house and was almost immediately dispersed by the rain; small bright dots came and went on the beach or settled on upturned hulls: sea gulls.

Gabriel sat as if turned to stone. His arms and legs refused to respond. He was hoisted from his seat by one of the coachmen and almost carried to a peat fire. He waited until he felt between his fingers the edges of a cup and, rising to his nostrils, the soothing aroma of tea, before he could wipe his eyes and look about him.

A terrible disappointment. And your positivist, more perhaps than others, is sensitive to disappointment.

The laundresses had no breasts (unless they were stuffed away beneath their navy blue uniforms), did not have red hair (unless it was imprisoned in starched coifs), did not smile (unless they smiled inwardly and most selfishly), did not even possess hands (hidden by gloves). You could have sworn they were a squad of nurses, a brigade of hospital sisters, and matronly ones at that. They wasted no time. The contents of the fifty-eight crates were dumped onto great checkered tables, and the sorting began.

On the right, saliva, bodily fluids, leaks. In the middle, blood. On the left, natural products, crushed mango, maracuja pulp, cocoa stains. The contract attaché made sure family names were clearly handwritten in India ink on each garment, in a spot that would not show, the inside of a cuff or collar. Catholic laundresses would have crossed themselves, *Ave Maria confiteor,* at the sight of some of these Amazonian stains. But these Anglicans maintained their self-control, their utter detachment, perfect qualities in a laundrywoman. Not a laugh, not a comment. Yet occasions abounded. What could the Goanhas have been doing in their nightshirts to soil them in this way? And the Riobaldo women? Did you ever see civilized people get a blouse so filthy? And those sweat stains, those semicircular halos around the armpits, was that simply the climate, the terrible equatorial climate, or was it other kinds of heat, more intimate, more urgent? And blood, why all this blood, on shirts, pants, sometimes mere roseate spots, as if from a bite, sometimes scarlet stains as wide as dinner plates? What on earth went on in Brazil?

Finding himself thus drawn into the more intimate fringes of the savage life, Gabriel felt his cheeks burn like fire. Desperately he sought an accomplice among the laundresses. A hint of a gleam in an eye, a beginning of voluptuousness in a bodice. But no. They went on calmly sorting.

The attaché appeared on the threshold.

The instant he saw Gabriel he ran up to him.

"Quickly, quickly, Mr. Orsenna, the manageress is expecting you."

Gabriel followed him.

People today have lost all memory of the real Great Britain, the one that ruled the world. We have lost all feeling for empires. With a backhand swipe at his ball, Gabriel would like to help take you back in time to experience that world anew. The meanest St. James bootmaker and Piccadilly jam manufacturer felt they were vice-emperors.

The tradesmen of England believed they were what made the world tick. Every morning they rose to assume their illusory daily burden, making the world go round. And indeed the sun never set on their endeavors; they felt they were members of the planet's ruling circles, part of its private entourage. Whence English pride.

Gabriel would like you to expunge from your imagination any hint of your common or garden-variety shopkeeper, your insignificant tradesman, your petty black-market operator. Think instead of a queen, a First Elizabeth, a Great Catherine, snowy hair tightly imprisoned in a headband, long face, prominent cheekbones, the look of a Mother Superior.

"So you are French," she said. "I might have guessed. The French are so dirty."

Then she turned to the attaché. "I have never understood why. France has rain, just as we do, and streams."

Gabriel went underground. He remained there for the rest of the day before returning to London in a Spanish diplomat's carriage (a few wealthy Madrileños also had their shirts laundered in Cornwall).

Gabriel Orsenna, businessman, almost-Companion of the Liberation, in love his whole life long with the same two women, should have been more careful of his appearance. Those closest to him are unanimous on this point: Gabriel has often been somewhat slovenly. Gabriel pleads guilty. This journey to Cornwall is not an attempt at exoneration. It simply helps explain his distinct (and unforgivable) taste for dirt.

## V

Gabriel would gladly have held on a little while longer to his job as a diplomat-storyteller. There was no denying the public success of his lectures, and certain of his regular female listeners, in particular Amaranta, daughter of the Dominican ambassador, a sixteen-year-old she-devil who managed to swing her hips even while seated, and

Mrs. Shandy, a Scottish novelist in the full golden bloom of her thirties, let him know by dint of winks and pouts that the cult of Auguste Comte could just as conveniently be celebrated in a tête-à-tête behind locked bedroom doors.

It must be admitted that the positivist content of his little talks had been considerably cut back. Despite the admonitions of the republican second counselor Victor ("You have a decided streak of the Cariocan housewife in you, Gabriel, with the same proclivities for mush"), he no longer spoke of anything much but love, limiting himself to just one weighty maxim per session ("The real superiority of the Great Being stems from the fact that his expressions are themselves individual and collective beings"; "This common sense so rightly advocated by Descartes and Bacon must today exist in purer and more vital form among the lower orders, thanks to a fortunate lack of book learning that leaves them less at the mercy of habits of vagueness . . ."), a weighty maxim he would coat with sugar, the endless account of a marriage, or with brimstone, the beginning, oh! just the beginning, of a disrobing.

And it was in his white bedroom with the sash window, reclining on his excessively soft bed, that he spent his days preparing for his nightly lectures, reading *Dangerous Liaisons; The Life of Marianne; Moll Flanders; Clarissa, or the History of a Young Lady*. From time to time he looked up, took a few steps, went to look out through the window, and lay back down again with a sigh. These women are truly terrifying! Do I really have the calling for a great love? But he very quickly recovered and returned to his reading, wishing he could cable Mrs. Knight wherever she might be: BECOMING SEASONED STOP GABRIEL BECOMING TOO SEASONED STOP YOU WILL FIND HIM RADICALLY CHANGED ON YOUR RETURN STOP READY TO TAKE ON ALL SISTERS IN WORLD STOP.

Alas, Queen Victoria died on Tuesday, January 22, in Osborne House at Cowes on the Isle of Wight. And this earthshaking event upset everything. Including Gabriel's apprenticeship.

The chargé d'affaires called in the whole staff.

"Ladies and gentlemen; dear friends. The late queen could scarcely have been called a friend of our beloved Brazil, but now is a time for forgiveness and I would like to remind you of what is required of us on an occasion of profound mourning."

His eyes misted over as he uttered these words. This display of emotion goaded republican second counselor Victor to fury. Leaning toward Gabriel, he gripped his arm hard enough to break it.

"Are you aware that the rubber tree is the source of the Amazon's wealth?"

"Yes," Gabriel replied.

"Did you know that our rubber trees will grow only in the wild, that all efforts to domesticate them have failed; did you know that? No? It is because of Brazil's soul, Gabriel, Brazil's untamable soul. Well, Queen Victoria gave orders for the seeds of the rubber tree to be stolen from us—do you hear me, Gabriel?—stolen! Queen Victoria was the greatest thief in all the annals of theft, and the criminal entrusted with the foul deed was named Wickham. Remember that criminal name. He stole seventy thousand seeds from Brazil. And these seeds came through London. And they were exhibited at Kew Botanic Gardens. And our chargé d'affaires thanked the queen for inviting him to this exhibition. You hear me, Gabriel? He *thanked* her! And then the seeds were sent to Singapore and Ceylon, which are tropical zones but domesticated, unlike Brazil, Gabriel, and our rubber trees are growing there like corn, Gabriel, like corn, like tomatoes, like peas, more shame to them. But if I may say so, Gabriel, our republic is in the shit. What will we do with Amazonia if Asiatic trees are in competition with it? What can a young republic do with a huge forest of trees that serve no purpose?"

Shocked, Gabriel was discovering at one and the same time the petty side of queens and the scope of geopolitics. Kidnapping forests, transporting flora from one end of the planet to the other the way you change a dahlia's place in a garden. . . . No doubt about it, empires were not without their gall.

Bathed, soaped, shaved, powdered, heartily fed (mangoes, bacon, red beans), the last sartorial touches applied as night's blackness gave place to the gray of day, and ready to leave, gloves on, cape lightly fastened across his chest, at about eight-fifteen, eight-sixteen, although the audience was not until eleven: "Come on," said the chargé d'affaires.

"So soon, do you think?" asked Victor.

"One day you will learn that a true meeting of minds requires you to immerse yourself beforehand in the ambient air. Besides, anything at all might happen en route, and no one, not even a republican, has the right to keep a king waiting."

So we made our meandering way across London as if in the middle of an Atlantic Ocean, first to port, in the direction of Aldwych and Waterloo, then on a starboard tack to Hampstead and Regent's Park, but never, never in the wind's eye, never straight ahead, never to our port of call—to Buckingham Palace, where Edward VII was expecting us. Forgetting all about us, the chargé d'affaires sailed under his country's new colors, blue and yellow, sea and sun, plumes and gold and sweetness and wealth; he pitched and rolled in his landau drawn by four white horses, the picture of half-breed ostentation, order, and progress. Every now and then, at a crossroads, the coachman turned around. "And now which way?"

"What time is it?"

"Half past nine."

"Then let us continue. The king must feel that I love London almost as much as he does. It is delicate touches of this kind that mark your true diplomat. In this way, and in no other, can one forge ties of friendship, yes, of friendship, with Great Britain. You know, it would not surprise me if the king asked for my confidential advice. He saw me at the funeral, he appreciated my tact in not troubling his old mother with this rubber business, he is aware of my admiration for England. I have no ambitions here, I am of neither party, hence my advice might well be of use in determining his domestic policies. The king will say to me, 'Just between us, my dear Ambassador'—he will call me Ambassador; in his lofty position you do not distinguish one diplomatic rank from another—'so, my dear Ambassador, pray tell me about my kingdom, I get about so little.' 'Your Majesty,' I shall reply, 'your people prosper, but they dress so drearily. Why not straw hats instead of bowlers?' "

So ran the chargé d'affaire's dreams that morning, dreams of friendship with the king of England and of the world. He sailed along under the light English drizzle, his right hand on the black corner of his cocked hat, often raising the hat in response to the huzzahs of passersby (English huzzahs, polite ones: "I say, a general, so early in the morning?"). And the other hand inside his waistcoat, stroking the vellum of the very brief memorandum he himself had drawn up during the night and whose opening words were—let me see now, oh, yes!—"The milk of the rubber tree, as Your Majesty knows full well, is Brazil's lifeblood."

"I am aware of the problem," the king would reply. "I have already taken steps. The world is certainly big enough for us not to step on one another's toes, is it not?"

Reinaldo Aristides Lima thought of his mother, the old dowager Dona Betanha, native of Ilhéus: what a pity she was not here. She would not be able to see him leave Buckingham Palace in all his glory, the savior of the Amazonian forest, the great defender of rubber. It had stopped raining; he could have invited her up into his landau, and a fig for protocol! What a shame she lived so far away. He wrote her every Sunday, letters more beautiful than Stendhal's (a minor run-of-the-mill diplomat) and Chateaubriand's (execrable diplomat and warmonger). . . . He was still loitering at the foot of Tower Bridge, drunk on dreams, as it struck half-past ten. He had to gallop to the palace.

Two fellow diplomats were waiting in the antechamber, the Italian and the Swiss, their appointments set respectively for twelve-fifteen and twelve-thirty. Sadness flooded Reinaldo Aristides Lima's soul. He had believed that King Edward, sensing a friendship was about to be born, had made himself available for preluncheon sherry, for luncheon, perhaps for the whole afternoon. At first you have to give friendship time, enough temporal mulch for friendship to *take*. These two Italo-Helvetic appointments were quite simply an error the king's advisers would swiftly repair. Please accept our apologies, Mr. Ambassador, Mr. Ambassador, come back next week, His Majesty is busy with his Brazilian friend. Besides, simply on the basis of objective, incontestable fact, since Brazil was twenty times bigger than Italy its representative should remain twenty times longer with the king, I shall therefore take my leave at five P.M., the ambassador said to himself. Well, four at the very earliest. I hope my coachman waits. . . .

And as he mumbled thus to himself, a footman summoned him and opened two doors. Edward VII was there. And greeted him (most warmly, thought the diplomat). My turn, to the attack!

"Your Majesty, the milk of the rubber tree is Brazil's lifeblood—"

"How is our cousin Pedro?" the king interrupted him.

A quarter past eleven struck. The footman entered. The interview was at an end. "A useful preliminary contact," Reinaldo Aristides said several times as he described the interview to us, "His Majesty and I got to know one another better. Yes, I am most sanguine as to future prospects. . . ." He asked to be dropped at the nearby park, St. James's ("Go on without me, I shall walk back, there are conclusions I must mull in the wake of this meeting, decisions I must weigh"). As they did every day, the ducks had invaded the lawns. The chargé d'affaires was soon mobbed. The boldest of them, black-and-white Icelandic ducks and a russet-headed pochard, nibbled at his trouser cuffs. A fair-haired little girl with square spectacles asked him if he was the pope. He was obliged to beat a retreat by way of Haymarket and Regent Street.

Until the very end, until his tragic death, the chargé d'affaires bore the countenance of men who are certain, men lit from within by Hope. Even a month later, after his call on the Foreign Secretary who arrived 121 minutes late ("Oh! the House! In your country you have no parliament, I believe?") and was therefore able to grant him only a few moments.

"What may I do for you, my dear Ambassador?"

"Mr. Secretary, the milk of the rubber tree is Brazil's lifeblood. Yet smugglers—and scientific accuracy compels me to identify them as British—are even now stealing rubber seeds from us—"

"Thank you for your candor, my dear Ambassador, I shall mention the matter to my honorable colleague in Customs and Excise, and once again I thank you for your unvarnished language. It is exactly this kind of mutual confidence that I want to see blossoming between our great nations. . . . Again, thank you, and a good day to you."

Outside, the air was pale. A sickly sun shot timid rays. This time the chargé d'affaires returned along a westerly route. What does a ruined forest look like? he wondered. And with his thoughts on the Amazon, he reflected that whatever Edward VII might do or say, Hyde Park had precious few trees.

* * *

Did the chargé d'affaires despair? Absolutely not. Diplomats are like storytellers, they cling tooth and nail to their dreams. To cut short Brazil's rubber hemorrhage the chargé d'affaires hummed to himself, the chargé d'affaires briskly rubbed his hands, the chargé d'affaires had a solution. He was on his feet again. His eyes sparkled. The liver spots on his hands and the red blotches on his cheeks disappeared, abruptly swallowed up by this return of youthfulness.

"Gabriel, my dear young French friend, we are going to open negotiations! I am happy for you. You are about to have a living lesson in what diplomacy is all about. Everything depends on the wording. Did you know that the right noun in the right place can prevent wars? Did you know that the proper deployment of commas brings continents together? Believe me, I have nothing against writers, but what *we* write is so much more useful.

" 'Given that recent progress in transportation threatens our national botanic heritage; given that, for the human species, the vegetable kingdom is a last haven of calm in a sea of wars; given that, without the majestic spectacle of the seasons, our very survival would be at stake—' " The embassy had started writing again.

"All very fine, these 'givens,' but what are we proposing?"

"Calm down, calm down, let the idea ripen: you can't hurry the Foreign Office."

It was now, in the middle of the night—for with diplomats only great fatigue gives birth to great ideas (Maria Clementina was brewing those root teas resorted to at the full moon by the widows of the *sertão* to rekindle the ardors of departed spouses)—it was now, as we writers paced up and down, that the chargé d'affaires solemnly announced his plan for an International Conference on Universal Botanic Harmony. The embassy rang with bravos. Even the albino applauded. Maria served champagne and *caipirinhas*.

When I think of my unhappy companions at the crammer, Gabriel said to himself, probably buried at this very instant in frantic revisions, while I—without false modesty—while I busy myself with world affairs . . .

Spring returned, and with it the social season. The chargé d'affaires sallied forth to suppers, cocktail parties, openings.

"I am plowing the soil, Gabriel, I am tilling it, I am aerating it.

Once the Rio agreements are signed, presto! what a harvest we shall reap!"

As his contacts multiplied, he gave out enticing hints, tidbits of information.

"I would be extremely surprised if Rio let spring slip by without an announcement of major importance. . . .

"Speaking quite unofficially, I am delighted to inform you that a certain excitement currently reigns in our Cariocan ruling circles."

His diplomatic counterpart from the West or the young civil servant from the Foreign Office would nod: "Old Europe expects great things of your Brazilian vitality."

And we would return in high spirits to Curzon Street.

"The ground is ready! Let us pray the harvest will not be long in coming!"

Every morning the protocol attaché and the private secretary sorted boxes of invitations and calling cards, drew up schedules, calculated the length of each visit. And the marathon began, from drawing rooms to stately homes, from Kensington to Belgravia, from smiles to kissed hands. Occasionally, just to catch up, I tried to cut corners.

"What can you be thinking, Gabriel?" the chargé d'affaires would cry. "How do you imagine ideas grow? We must plow the whole field!"

And so it was that one fine afternoon the official embassy landau, Order and Progress, drawn by its four white horses, trotted merrily toward Richmond. At the gates of Kew Gardens the coachman showed our invitation to the guard:

Joseph Dalton Hooker<br>
Director of the Royal Botanic Gardens<br>
and<br>
James Collins<br>
Curator of the Pharmaceutical Society's Museum<br>
have the pleasure and the honour to invite<br>
His Excellency the Ambassador of Brazil<br>
to an exhibition of new products from Ceylon

Inside the conservatory the speechmaking was already under way. On a platform draped with bunting an austere-looking gent held forth, notes in hand, a gent sporting side-whiskers, black morning coat, striped trousers. "Ladies and Gentlemen . . ." From the entrance all you could hear was a rumbling interspersed with phrases more forcibly uttered than the others: "Ladies and Gentlemen . . . the Empire takes pride . . . with all due respect to Holy Scripture . . . Noah confined his concern to the animal kingdom alone. . . ."

There was a sudden burst of applause and every eye turned in our direction. We were pushed toward the platform, where the speaker—hear, hear! cried the crowd—where the speaker cordially greeted us. "In the name of His Majesty the King I salute in your persons the priceless vegetable abundance of the tropics. . . . Long live Brazil!"

Whereupon the speaker clapped his hands. Four assistants climbed onto the platform bearing a silver platter laden with an enormous brownish ball.

"That is rubber, Gabriel," whispered the chargé d'affaires, kneading my shoulder, "that is *our* rubber!"

The speaker called for silence.

"Your Excellency, ladies and gentlemen, this is the very first Asiatic rubber; it is my great pleasure to announce that our plantations in Ceylon and Singapore are a complete success. It is now a certainty: the rubber tree flourishes in the East. Long live our botanic gardens, and long live Brazil, which so generously made the seeds available and has behaved throughout with most consummate fair play. Long live the Empire, long live Great Britain, long live the King!"

And before anyone could applaud, the strains of "God Save the King" rang out under the glass roof, reverberated, and were lost amid the luxuriant foliage. The chargé d'affaires had disappeared. Gabriel rushed outside. Guards answered his questions. The honorable gentleman had gone in that direction. The honorable gentleman had been heading west. The honorable gentleman had taken Hawthorn Alley. I believe the honorable gentleman is up in the pagoda. Gabriel ran, raised his eyes. At the top of the Chinese tower a small figure straddled the railing.

* * *

The chargé d'affaires's fall was of great purity, a perfect arc, with the wind carrying him clear of the pagoda. He did not crash down onto the lower levels but glided out toward the great trees. For ages I reproached myself; we could have spread sheets, rushed straw to the base of the pagoda, broken his fall, softened it; he did not so much fall through the air as dawdle in it, he took his time. He lived all his lives again. At the very top: Glory, sun-bathed, emerald and gold, sanctified by History, prime mover of the International Conference on Universal Botanic Harmony; and then, lower down, lower and lower as gravity pulled on him, came bleaker pictures: the useless life of a diplomat, the rare interludes, the tiny pleasures, *tableaux vivants* of Reinaldo Aristides Lima as a lovesick fifty-year-old, as a punter at the greyhound races, as a far-off and too-affectionate son. You felt him smile or scowl as he passed from stratum to stratum of his memories, moving ever faster now, like an express train racing through stations of himself. By the time death took him he was quite young; yes, death came in his youth, a brutal sense of coolness, an instant odor of damp loam on the crashing face (fortunately they had just watered it, the day had been so warm). He lay on a bed of the rarest kinds of heather. The English onlookers at once thought: I say, an unhappy love affair.

## VI

It was night, ice-cold night, probably the year's last ice-cold night, winter's last fling. Fog had descended on London, as if a vaporous light were pouring in through a rent in the immense black curtain of night. The shadows alongside Gabriel trembled with cold and fear. Diplomats do not make good front-line troops. Who had dreamed up this crusade? Hard to say. A general feeling of revolt circulated when they brought in the broken body of the poor, gentle chargé d'affaires, the one who had so loved Queen Victoria. A feeling of rage. Oh, diplomatic rage, of course, restrained, polite, heedful of good manners and of the proprieties. Oh, beyond a doubt History has remembered more violent instances of rebellion against British domination: the Boers, for example, India's sepoy mutineers, even the French before Fashoda. But the discreet, the very discreet and mostly forgotten Brazilian crusade also deserves mention. For almost the entire staff of an embassy to decide one fine evening around eleven to go and avenge a superior—that is unheard of in the long annals of diplomacy, in the endless banquet which is diplomacy, where all you ever do is swallow insult after insult after insult.

The only ones left behind in Curzon Street were the tubercular first secretary, excused, and the albino, who was waiting for his beloved ("Be frank, Gabriel, do you think albinos disgust her? But what will she think if she returns in the middle of the night and doesn't find me here?"), also excused.

Everything had gone smoothly. The gates were open. Who would dream of guarding a botanic garden? The only difficulty was the fog. Visibility was down to fifteen feet. But my fellow crusaders knew the area by heart. When their spirits were low they often went to Kew to admire the orchid collection that so reminded them of the tropics. . . . The grieving little band trooped slowly down the side of the main walk, one foot on the grass border, the other on the gravel. Regular visitors to the gardens told Gabriel about things he could not see: on the left giant araucarias from Chile, on the right a clump of aloes from the French Riviera. . . .

And then we went into the hothouses, leaving the fog outside. The Brazilian crusaders halted to inhale the smells of moss, of moist bark, and a very powerful odor that dominated all others, ilang-ilang. Victor closed his eyes and asked me to listen.

"Don't you notice the difference?"

I heard nothing. Dripping water, feather-light rustling in the foliage, the rattling of the broadest palm fronds. An almost perfect silence held prisoner in the damp.

"What's missing is the animals. The real Brazil has noise."

And we set to work. All night long we sabotaged, politely, diplomatically, without smashing anything. Sometimes Gabriel had trouble with rusty faucets. He would call the cipher clerk, a man with wrists of iron. Once we had turned off all the heating, once we had thrown open every window, door, shutter, skylight, and bay, we watched the icy fog roll into the hothouses.

"On a night like this every plant will be dead by morning," whispered the cipher clerk.

Thus we took our leave of the poor and very gentle chargé d'affaires, the way you scatter ashes on the sea. And we went home to bed.

As soon as news was out of this "dastardly attack that augurs most unfavorably for what will be the twentieth century" (as the opening words of the *Times* report put it), the whole country was up in arms. Soon regiments of donors were on their way to Kew Gardens.

They came on foot and in carriages, one bearing a Malayan fig, another his epiphyte orchid, in earthenware pots, in glass globes, in hollowed-out elephant feet. Everyone had dug deep into his personal hothouse, reached far into his colonial past, and on the sidewalks idle bystanders applauded, shouting "Up the museum, down with the plant killers!" The Jews of course were often blamed (rootless people with no sense of the soil). Outside the gates the throng of donors could make no headway; there were queues and obstructions. Street vendors took advantage of the windfall, selling tea and chestnuts; fires were lit to re-create warm climates for the plants; people swapped memories of the Indian Army, of the good old days in Jamaica; people resigned themselves to stopping overnight; householders along the way offered to take in the more fragile plant species, they were passed from hand to hand with an exaggerated wealth of precautions, with real tenderness, umbrellas were opened, cotton was packed around them to protect them from the cold. By comparison, mere flirtation would have been a small thing; for the plants, people would have disrobed. They would have given away coats and shirts for the greater comfort of a few wild pistils. The evening papers, the police, the clergy, and the King himself had to appeal to donors to stop coming forward. "Please bring no more; the museum is once again fully stocked."

"The British deserve their Empire," said Victor as evening approached. He had written his letter of resignation; he was leaving his country's foreign service. "Diplomacy is dead. Republics must find new ways to fight."

The next day Gabriel took the train back to France. Kent's thousands of greenhouses glittered in the newly returned sun.

* * *

I forgot somebody. Perhaps. I am not sure. I would not like to start lying to you.

Did Marguerite come to London for the burial of the queen? There are times when I see her in the gloom of the embassy corridor, trying to knock on the door of my white room with the sash window. But how could I have heard her if her life no longer made any sound? I can also feel her arm on mine, both of us lost in the crowd, in the immeasurable crowd of the funeral procession. Please, Gabriel, find out for me, it's raining so hard, my black coat, will the colors run? The old lady with the blue gaze, huddled on a bench at the station—don't wait, Gabriel; what time is the train? Promise me I haven't done your career any harm. That old, old lady, was it Marguerite?

# 3

# *On Efficiency,*

## *or*

## *Nine of the Joys of Clermont-Ferrand*

### On Efficiency

Why Clermont-Ferrand? Why rubber? Why this marriage of Clermont and rubber?

Our Gabriel, erstwhile Londoner and just off the train from Paris, wandered through the city wide-eyed and uncomprehending.

1. The people of Clermont did not seem to be jumpity, bouncy folk. They clearly belonged to the class of humans who live with their feet on the ground.

2. The stones of Clermont were hard, black, unyielding. Nothing in common, for example, with the friable stone of the Loire country or the shimmering granite of Brittany (probably ready at the drop of a hat to bound onstage and exhibit itself in the glare of the footlights). No such likelihood with the building blocks of Clermont-Ferrand. Gabriel verified this by carefully stroking two church façades, Notre-Dame-du-Port and the cathedral. Under the bewildered gaze of passersby he placed his hands on both buildings and pushed hard, but managed only to bruise his palm. It was proof enough: this building material was quite without elastic properties.

3. The surrounding volcanoes were extinct, utterly extinct; everyone from the station employee to the streetcar driver assured him of this. No bouncing to be expected from that quarter.

4. The local hero, Blaise Pascal, had been interested in many things, arithmetic, literature, wagers, but never in rubber, which in any case

had not yet reached Europe in his day. Furthermore, this Blaise Pascal had supported Jansenius against Loyola. Now, which of the two, Jansenists or Jesuits, are the subtler, the more rubbery? Clearly the second group.

5. The sea was far away and Brazil farther still. Those who know both the Amazon and the Auvergnat stream named Tiretaine will vouch that there is no possible connection—absolutely none!—between these two watercourses.

So?

When you understand nothing about a city, the thing to do is pick a medium-size restaurant (small ones are too crowded, and in big ones people are circumspect in their speech) and order the specialties of the house, its most expensive dishes, without stinting on wine or extras. This approach makes the customer welcome and the restaurateur talkative.

Which is what Gabriel did. Although still young, he had a flair for getting information. He entered the Café Bancharel.

"Tell me, sir, why is the city of Clermont so fond of rubber?"

"It is very simple."

A long and involved family history ensued, whence it emerged between solicitous queries ("Do you like this tart? What do you think of my jugged hare?") that Elizabeth Pugh Baker, wife of the first co-founder of the Clermond-Ferrand Farm Machinery Works, was the niece of the Scottish scientist Macintosh, who had discovered that latex was soluble in benzine and had subsequently invented the modern waterproof raincoat.

An Italian would have concluded, The answer to your question, the thing that has made Clermont the world capital of rubber, why, it is love, young man!

The restaurant owner was more chaste. He merely muttered a few words about chance before presenting the bill (which was extremely reasonable). A little unsteadily, Gabriel went out onto avenue Charras. The local wine had warmed his heart: in every Clermont woman, big or small, young or old, he saw Ann or Clara. Luckily for his career, he had sense enough not to call on his employer in this condition. He made his way to the Hôtel du Puy on boulevard Desaix, where he slept twelve unbroken hours of most fruitful sleep.

In his dreams he saw the people of Clermont bouncing as if

mounted on springs. In his dreams he saw rekindled volcanoes in slow, ruddy eruption. In his dreams he saw elastic cathedrals whose narrow Gothic portals stretched themselves into wide Romanesque doors to admit big Sunday-morning crowds. He saw Blaise Pascal in a tantrum of frustration: every time he threw a solid out of the window in an attempt to gauge some air pressure or other, the solid barely touched the ground before bouncing back tauntingly in the scientist's face. He saw the Tiretaine turned mud-colored and thronged with canoes.

When he awoke he understood: rubber was the secret garden, the hidden yearning of Clermont-Ferrand. Rubber and Clermont were complementary, made for each other. You had to be blind not to see it. And after lathering his cheeks with soap, shaving off his down, pomading his hair, brushing his teeth, and fortifying himself with two enormous rolls, he made his way to the Works. He whistled. Victory was in his soul. He gazed mockingly at the city: I've guessed your secret, I know your hidden dreams, I know what you are concealing behind your forbidding appearance.

At place des Carmes a M. Drouard greeted him.

"So then, young man, do you have the calling?"

"Since childhood, monsieur. I can truthfully say I was fonder of rubber than of candy."

And to screw up his courage (for stage fright had struck him as he entered the somber office), he kneaded the rubber ball hidden in the depths of his pocket.

"But remember, young man, rubber is but a means to an end. Here you will acquaint yourself with the peerless possibilities of the inflatable tire. Just listen!"

M. Drouard threw open the window. A streetcar went past in a hideous clatter of groanings, squealings, and scrapings. Iron pitted against iron, wheels against rails.

"Have you any idea what the world would be without rubber? Uproar, permanent war between things. So many young men of your age choose the colonies or banking. Useful activities, no doubt of it, no doubt of it! But with pneumatic tires you will be entering the very core of life. There is no time to lose. When would you like to begin? We have heard good things about you. You are not much of a Catholic, admittedly, a bit of a Mason in fact, am I right? Now don't deny it, you're not the first: Auguste Comte's influence. . . . But I wager that within a month we'll have you back in the fold. You'll see, we don't force anybody, but we have our methods; recalcitrant cases are rare. . . . The influence of latex, that's all. Are you ready? Splendid. I'm going to start you at the bottom of the ladder, unloading gum. You'll feel quite at home. Welcome to the world of the inflatable tire."

Of the ten years that followed you will learn nothing. Or next to nothing. I have no wish to bore you.

Apprenticeship stories have stock themes: love, puppy love, cupboard love. Mother, sister, cousin, girl next door, Mme. de Rênal, the woman of thirty, the professional. . . . As a good father, I could assume a pompous air and point out that there is more to life than love, that Stendhal was small-minded indeed to concern himself more with La Sanseverina than with the progress of the steam engine. But I shall take care not to. There are limits to my hypocrisy; had Ann and Clara been nearby I should have lived for them alone, straining my ears for their approach, making up excuses for meetings. That is why I have abbreviated those ten years so ruthlessly. That is why I have shrunk those ten years up so very, very small. You cannot fight human nature. Just as children are born loving chocolate, so readers prefer amorous sentiments to industrial passions. We are made that way. God has willed it so. For those who are exceptions to this rule, and only for them, I have drawn up the following brief catalogue of my pneumatic joys. Just write to me at 13 avenue Wester Wemys, Cannes-la-Bocca, and let me know which particular joy you are after. I shall be delighted to describe it to you in greater detail. I won't even request a stamped return envelope.

## NINE OF THE JOYS OF CLERMONT-FERRAND

### *Botanical*

First-quarter schedule: familiarizing yourself with every plant, tree, vine, cactus, root, and fungus capable of producing latex. Meticulous joy for the one who can reproduce a *Manihot glaziovii* on a scale of one to a hundred in India ink. Taxonomic joy for the one who knows that

*Euphorbia intisy* does not belong to the asclepiadaceous family. Divine (or poetic) joy in naming—and by the same token creating—*Hevea brasiliensis, Hevea guianensis, Sapium thompsonii, Castilloa ulei, Ficus elastica, Funtumia, Landolphia, Cryptostegia grandiflora, Parthenium argentatum, Scorzonera tau-saghyz, Taraxacum kok-saghyz, Isonandra, Palaquium, Payena, Mimusops, Ecclinusa.* Linguistic joy: it is sweeter to learn Latin from flora than from Caesar's *Gallic Wars.* Democratic joy: numberless are the chosen plants, bearers of the precious sap.

## *Geographic*

Every afternoon, on the old, creaky terrestrial globe in the municipal museum, identify the production zones: Amazonia, Mexico, Tobago, Guatemala, Madagascar, the Ivory Coast, Turkestan, Southeast Asia.

"Take it easy, young fellow," the museum guard would say. "You're turning it too fast. Why not walk around it yourself and let it stand still? You'll see, it will come to the same thing."

## *Olfactory*

Oh the aroma of smoked gum, the whiff of vast forests, you had only to close your eyes and open your nostrils and you were there, far from the fogs of Auvergne, O Brazil of all the fragrances!

## *Chemical*

Piercing the mysteries of blending. Moral joy: my employers have faith in me. Culinary joy: for a long time chubby Gabriel, a hearty eater as we know, could cook only one dish: rubber tire à la Clermont-Ferrand. Take pure latex (free of sugar, vegetable fats, and other parasitical substances or organisms). Add plastifying agents, oils, suets, paraffin, then protective agents, white of zinc, kaolin. Stir briskly, adding sulfur and vulcanizing agent. Pour into cylindrical compartments (see fresh pasta). Transfer to mold. Blend in accelerators and coolants to ensure that cooking is uniform throughout. Then simply pop into oven and the tire is ready. And don't expect Gabriel to give you the recipe. Secret, secret, secret (the delectable joy of possessing secrets).

## *Tactile*

The science of pneumatic tires (or pneumatology) resembles the act of physical love. Only crueler. More complex. As in the act of love it is all a question of skins, the road's skin and the tire's skin. How best to proceed so that the two please one another, attract one another, mesh with one another (to avoid fatal skidding), but without being too closely welded (to avoid wasting engine power)? How to ensure that the road's skin does not bear too abrasively on the tire's skin (be on the lookout for wear, which quickly leads to a blowout) but still tightly enough (without holding, no tenderness)? It is to answer such questions that all tire experts run their hands over every conceivable kind of road surface: gravel, dirt, asphalt, different kinds of paving block, concrete, grass, even, or sand. Thus they gradually learn the texture of things. That is the essential condition for daring to marry a car to a road, the compromise of all compromises, the most Pascalian of wagers.

## *Handyman's Joy*

Let's say a flat tire. How to repair it in the shortest possible time?

Of all the joys of Clermont-Ferrand, possibly the most esoteric, not to say the unlikeliest.

Some of Gabriel's colleagues derived undeniable pleasure from all this dismantling, patching, and reassembling.

Not Gabriel.

Even today he claims the right to be a tactile human being but not a handy one.

## *Official Validation*

On the first Monday of every month we took the morning train, a grim-visaged three-man team: M. Drouard, to whose wrist the precious briefcase was attached by a steel wire; M. Guillaume, his assistant, who never let the briefcase out of his sight; and Gabriel, assigned to keep his eyes open for spies. As soon as they reached Paris the trio hopped into a taxi. The doorman at the ministry greeted us like old friends. "A very good morning to the gentlemen from Clermont! And a pleasant journey, I trust? I shall tell Monsieur Glavani you are here. I won't show you to his office; you know the way by now!"

The waiting room at the Patent Office looked like a junkyard: prototypes of all shapes and sizes lay about, clumsily wrapped so that you saw only mysterious shapes. The doorman flung weary arms aloft. "It's no good telling them 'Just draw a picture, that will do the trick; in any case leave your wonders out in the courtyard,' they never listen."

Indeed, the atmosphere there was tense in the extreme. Each inventor sat with his treasure in his lap and his arms clasped tightly around it, unless (for greater security) he was sitting on it. Everything depended on the aforementioned's size. And whenever a tyro, a newcomer, ventured a question, even a harmless one, with a friendly expression, such as "Mine's electricity, what's yours?," there was no reply. Or at most a grunt. M. Drouard warned me to be very careful. Patent applicants were the worst kind of thief, and cunning too; they could reconstruct anything, real Cuviers; give them a tiny bone and they'd draw the whole dinosaur for you. They'd worm your secret out of you while you weren't looking; you wouldn't suspect a thing. Far better to keep your mouth shut.

The department head, M. Glavani, was a friend of France, of the automobile, of the inflatable tire. He received us like royalty.

"Well, what news this time? A hundred and twenty an hour on snow without mishaps?"

M. Drouard unfastened the three locks one by one and laid on the vast chestnut table our reports on the new tread (a steel-studded leather device), or the detachable rim, or the spare wheel. . . . M. Glavani clapped his hands. He was by nature an enthusiast (which had done his career no good, or so the doorman informed us). He pulled out his large black imitation-leather ledger. "Here we go, I'm issuing you Patent Number 72387. I would love to spend more time with you, but your colleagues expect you back and will tolerate no delay. Until next month, then. Bring me a nice surprise."

We left his office with martial step, hearts overflowing with peace, bodies filled with the gentle warmth legitimacy confers; this was the joy of official validation. Back through the waiting room we went, riddled with glares from every inventor. Some protested aloud: "It is disgraceful, disgraceful, a representative of the Republic should keep his feelings to himself"; this was favoritism. They probably complained to the minister. Whence our supporter Glavani's limping career.

Sometimes, before the return train ride, I just had time to return to Levallois. Marguerite no longer railed at my profession. She had finally realized that if Alexander the Great had known about tires he would at the very least have conquered Japan. As for Louis, he made no pretense of reconciling himself to my absence.

"It's to your benefit, Gabriel, I know. But the days go by slowly without you. I have a plan which will bring us together. For now my lips are sealed. I will surprise you later. . . ."

Gabriel returned to Clermont both moved and anxious. He had learned to be wary of Louis's plans, particularly the affectionate ones. And this anxiety somewhat diminished the joy he felt at official validation.

## *Competitive*

History's first Grand Prix race took place in the year of grace 1906.

All Clermont-Ferrand, with the exception of women, the ill, lovers, and pious folk with a marked distaste for all things modern, wanted to be at the Sarthe racetrack. A selection had to be made. Gabriel ended up among the elect, proof of the excellence of his performance at the Works.

On learning the good news, Louis flew into the most terrible rage. The paternal telegrams came thick and fast:

ABSOLUTELY FORBID IT STOP RISKS TOO GREAT

SKIDS STOP EXPLOSIONS STOP SUICIDE GUARANTEED

Gabriel ignored them.

Was it the smell of human fear (the fear dogs smell so keenly before they bite)?

Was it the indescribable thunder of the engines (which gave back to silence its nobility and its feather-lightness)?

Was it the memory of colors (the reds of the cars, the greens, the blues flashing by, coupled together like a many-colored train and enduring for long minutes within your eye, vibrating, refusing to be extinguished even though the track was empty again)?

Was it the fluid curves of the cars for one who had never known a mother?

Was it the anger of women hating this man's game?

Was it the end of the straight where you had to choose whether or not to brake?

Was it all this theater, these repeated false starts, these cars ranging far out into the surrounding countryside before returning to cross the finish line?

Was it the stopwatch itching in your palm?

Gabriel gives up. He has no answer. He knows only that he had a whole day's respite from his loves, not one thought of them, not the slightest vision of Clara, not the smallest recollection of Ann. He rushed up to the officials.

"Do you plan to organize more Grands Prix?"

"Of course, young man, all over the world."

Gabriel jumped for joy. He had realized that a double love as difficult and eternal as his own needed a holiday in order to regain its strength, a very short and very intense holiday. For Gabriel it would be Grand Prix races. They would be his sleep, his very own deep sleep. Since even in his dreams he saw only them, Ann the golden-haired, Clara the elder.

### *Advertising*

Michelin Man was created in Gabriel's image. Was this too a joy? Guess.

"A woman is waiting for Gabriel at the Grand Hôtel de la Poste!"

This cry of horror, uttered on one of those dull afternoons so typical of the year 1902—(1) already more than three hundred and sixty-five days without Ann or Clara; (2) the tedium of twentieth-century afternoons was even more marked than its nineteenth-century predecessors—almost ruined Gabriel's career forever. His colleagues let fall the tire they were dissecting and stared at the rake, full of the spurious concern of which only colleagues are capable. And M. Drouard went up to him and laid a hand on his shoulder.

"What's the matter, Gabriel my friend? What's up? Aren't you happy here with us? Be careful, Gabriel, don't destroy yourself."

Should this be taken to imply that tiremakers are puritans? This reaction might lead one to believe so. Wrongly, however. Tiremaking is a science of blending, of contacts, of touch, a science infinitely removed from false modesty. But for the people of Clermont-Ferrand and perhaps for other human beings, women—and let us be specific: that nomad species that is neither man nor mother nor wife nor sister—women then represented at once distraction and drift, two qualities unacceptable to a tiremaker, as every driver will attest. And so it was that his co-workers and M. Drouard suddenly looked on

Gabriel as the devil and muttered cryptic words: a woman, de la Poste, she's from Paris of course. And Gabriel too was stammering: family, just for a few minutes, I'll be back. . . . Removing his gray work smock, he ran—Is it Clara? No, probably Ann?—ran to the place de Jaude.

He dashed breathlessly up to the reception desk. A bored clerk pointed: Behind you, monsieur. Gabriel rushed in the direction indicated, bursting in a great crash of parting foliage through a screen of potted plants—

"Calm down. Hello and calm down," said their mother, yes, Ann's mother, Clara's mother. "Here, dry your forehead with this handkerchief. Your cheeks are bright red."

With unforgivable tactlessness (unspoken tactlessness, fortunately), Gabriel was thinking, What luck, it's only their mother! I feel dirty, I feel ugly. What a disaster if Ann or Clara were here. From now on I shall approach them only at a stately walk, and even then only in winter. In summer I shall keep quite still so as not to sweat; women hate men who sweat; there's no love where there's sweat; thank you, God. . . .

"Good. Are you feeling better now? Would you like something to drink? No? Very well, we must talk seriously. I am here because I find you most likable. I believe my daughters also find you likable."

Gabriel's rapid heartbeat, which had begun to slow down, set off again at a faster gallop than ever.

"Oh, let me be frank; you are not the only one they find likable. My daughters are like that. But when they speak of you their eyes shine in a special way. A mother recognizes that gleam. And you, Gabriel, forgive my forthright questions but we have so little time—I must return on the next train—do you love my daughters?"

"Er, well . . . yes."

"So much the worse for you. Another question, Gabriel. Are you Jewish?"

"No."

"Don't pull that face, it isn't the end of the world. It's just that not being Jewish you can't have the slightest idea about Jewish mothers."

Gabriel acknowledged his ignorance.

"Jewish mothers are the best in the world. And not just where food is concerned, as certain prejudiced persons would have you believe.

In love too. A Jewish mother is capable of taking an ice-cold train to an ice-cold city to tell a young man who is sweating—forgive me for laughing at you, Gabriel, Jews are like that—to tell him: so, you love my daughters and it is possible they will one day love you; all the conditions for the catastrophe are already in place. Would you agree to give up my daughters, Gabriel?"

"No."

"I thought not. Very well, then, I shall do my duty as the best mother in the world and try to deflect as much unhappiness as possible from you. I will come here from time to time, Gabriel, if you are willing. I will tell you about them. You shall tell me about you. You shall get to know them better. I will advise you. Agreed, Gabriel? I understand your hesitation, Gabriel. Not to have a mother of one's own and then to run into a Jewish mother-in-law, what a shock."

Gabriel nodded his head like a very small child: Yes, madame, yes, I agree.

"Splendid. I don't have much time, I must return tomorrow. Let's take the older one first. Now this is what you should know about Clara. . . ."

Thus began the first of the lessons given by Elisabeth Knight to Gabriel Orsenna in the lobby of the Grand Hôtel de la Poste, place de Jaude, Clermont-Ferrand, behind the screen of potted plants. Later they would change their routine and take the steam-driven streetcar all the way up to the Puy de Dôme, leaving from the place Lamartine, going up the whole length of the avenue de l'Observatoire and climbing amid grunts and showers of sparks to the summit.

Up there, looking out over Royat, Riom, Chamalières, Puy-Guillaume, the Charade track, and the Mont-Dore thermal baths, she worked me into shape, as they say of trainers.

"You must first season yourself, Gabriel. I don't want to dishearten you, or else why would I be here? But it will be hard; there will be ups and downs, scenes, long dreadful silences. Nothing like my own love, Gabriel. Markus and I share the same life, you see."

"What exactly do you mean by 'season'?" asked Gabriel, not going too close to the rail for he suffered from vertigo, even in Auvergne.

"It means developing a little indifference, yes, a little indifference. Learning to think of something other than my daughters."

Gabriel thanked her. "I shall try, madame, I shall try."

Mrs. Knight drew closer. It was often cold up on the top of the Puy de Dôme. She put one hand on Gabriel's shoulder and rubbed her nose with the other.

Emboldened by this sudden sense of closeness, Gabriel took breath and courage in both hands and asked, "Do you think a woman, I mean two women, could love a man with plump cheeks?"

Then Mrs. Knight laughed, laughing the way you laugh in winter, little gasping laughs, mouth only half open.

"But of course, Gabriel, what a question! Heaps of women like plump cheeks. Shall we go down?"

And doubting Gabriel (did she say that just to please me?) took a last look at the plump, roly-poly mountains of Auvergne, my roly-poly brothers.

Picture Gabriel arm in arm with Elisabeth, sheltered beneath her hat, those vast works of art that were the hats of those days, authentic patches of jungle, foliage, ostrich plumes, perched birds; picture Gabriel for once delighted to be short (had I been taller my head would have bumped into the jungle); picture the beautiful, the very beautiful lady and Gabriel crossing the place de Jaude, one pressed against the other under Clermont's astonished stare.

"If you wouldn't mind some advice," M. Drouard muttered with a blush next morning, "don't be so conspicuous."

On this matter, so long after the event, now that the statute of limitations has expired even for ridiculous behavior, Gabriel owes it to himself to acknowledge a ridiculous instance of personal vanity. Elisabeth was always strikingly elegant, sometimes in the height of fashion, sometimes in ready-made clothes, depending on the ups and downs of her recruiter-impresario's fortunes. Around 1910 and 1911 fashions changed: suppler, simpler dresses with raised waistlines, often with an Oriental air. But it was the colors in particular that changed. Reds, greens, and royal blues replaced lilacs, mauves, aquamarines, and soft hydrangea tones.

Wonderful! Gabriel told himself. Elisabeth has noticed my progress. She knows I no longer fear women. She dresses as she pleases.

And at night, in bed, he rubbed his hands: intimacy with women is mine, the freedom of women is mine, to us, to them, to me, to all three of us, Ann and Clara!

Ridiculous Gabriel. Grotesque lapdog Gabriel, thinking his yapping caused the sun to rise.

Elisabeth was simply following fashion. The sun had set on the designer Worth. Paul Poiret's word was now law.

As I write this I see your youthful eye light up. You dare not say it, but I know the question burning on your lips: Did you sleep with her? It is clear you know nothing about Clermont. Discretion does not exist there, as the town's few adulterous couples will agree. Everyone knows everything. The slightest guilty caress is reported within the hour to the management of the Works. Summons. Dismissal.

The hotelkeepers of Riom will confirm it. They had seen it as their mission to extend an incognito welcome to the errant men and women of Clermont. Not a chance. Riom was too close (9 miles) to Clermont. You had to go as far as Vichy (36 miles) or, better still, Moulins (57 miles) to escape the all-seeing eye of the Works.

Since Gabriel never left Clermont except for Grand Prix races, such suspicions are grounded solely in gratuitous malevolence. Either that, or every one of Mrs. Knight's visits would have had to be marked by a most improbable series of coincidences along the following lines: that, in consequence of some mischance during the descent from the Puy de Dôme, the mother of Clara and Ann had been thrown violently against our hero and, still dazed from the impact, remained snuggled there; that back in the lobby of the Hôtel de la Poste the receptionist had turned his back to them, admittedly such people adore fussing over the room keys; that the elevator operator had been absent from his post because of a bereavement or his mother's illness (and Mrs. Knight—you see, I am being frank—knew how to work the long brass elevator handle); that the corridor was deserted, with the chambermaid busy on the floor above; that the door to Room 314 did not creak; that Gabriel did not emit those ludicrous babblings typical of virgin (or near-virgin) males when you undo their Sunday cravats; that laces did not squeak and corsets did not rustle; that Gabriel, aflame with impatience, did not send his boots flying against the far wall of Room 314, as absolutely all young people so fortunately placed are prone to do; that Mrs. Knight neither cooed nor sighed nor clamored at any point. And the fact is—although perhaps you do not yet realize it—when you come from Paris just for this you do coo, you do sigh, you do clamor.

Coincidences, admit it, coincidence heaped on coincidence. Gabriel has already told you but he will say it again: there are no coincidences, simply regrets. No, we would do better to stick to the facts. Gabriel was not dismissed from the Works. So his conscience is clear. And many statistics (which for political reasons we are unable to publish here) confirm it: a Jewish mother is more faithful than other women.

In fact it was a quite different relationship, in appearance utterly legitimate, that nearly shattered my tiremaking career for good. Gabriel loved streetcars. Rubber specialists might poke fun at them (poor, railbound vehicles), but he loved to watch these great insects scurry about town, their antennae waving skyward, their legs hidden in turbulent sparks. He often treated himself to a ride with no precise destination just for the pleasure of the clattering and lurching and the heady sense of modernity it gave him. Without boasting the same soothing virtues as Grand Prix races, streetcars eliminated sadness. Ann and Clara seemed closer and a future with them a little more certain. For streetcars, by definition, never switched routes. And the sight of such constancy was comforting. We have never fully realized it, but their replacement by buses, particularly of the fickle variety, the kind that constantly switch lanes, must have secretly but profoundly disoriented city souls, imbuing them with thoughts of adultery.

But to return to our subject, that morning Gabriel was going up the avenue Charras, comfortably ensconced in his streetcar.

And who was sitting on the terrace of the Café Bancharel opposite the Hôtel du Midi? Louis.

The son stood up in his seat, jostling two peasant women just in from the mountains to sell—judging by the smell—Saint-Nectaire cheeses, and leapt down to the street. Louis was already rising. They embraced hard and long. How-are-you-well-and-rubber-well-and-Marguerite-still-sad-and-your-love-life-too-lively-and-yours-not-a-thing-we'll-soon-fix-that. It took repeated admonitions from the next streetcar for father and son to release one another and let it go by.

"Love is a beautiful thing," said a voice behind them.

They turned.

"May I introduce Dr. Ligier," said Louis. "My partner."

Poor Dr. Ligier, was all Gabriel had time to think before he was shaking hands with a colossus and returning the colossus's smile as best he could. Overall result: five crushed fingers but a warmed heart. For the colossus, massive shoulders, Praetorian neck, cannonball skull, had the friendliest smile in all France.

"Of course you'll have lunch with us," Louis decreed.

*Cousinat* (soup: onions, chestnuts, leeks, celery, heavy cream, Salers butter)
*Falette* (stuffed breast of mutton, white beans)
*Sweet aligot* (fresh tomme from Planèze, garlic, mashed potatoes flambéed in rum)
*Local wine,* Chanturgue

As course followed course, Louis unveiled his new scheme. And the deeper he delved into the details of the operation, the more glasses of Chanturgue Gabriel poured himself in order to drown the deep-seated pessimism he felt about all his father's plans.

"Let me explain, Gabriel. As you know, people who settle in the colonies are often afflicted with poor health. And for my part I do my utmost to promote the progress of tropical medicine, without which there would be no Empire. You'd have thought all Frenchmen would rally behind such a cause. Well—have some more cousinat, doctor—a few months ago a Parisian publisher (I'll give you his name, Gabriel, you might come across him one day; avoid him like the plague), anyway, the Spa Press, 3 rue Humboldt, published a scurrilous piece of claptrap entitled *Châtelguyon and the Colonials,* and with an even more revealing subtitle: *Many colonials diagnosed with liver disease in truth have intestinal disorders and could be treated at Châtelguyon.* See their game? An underhanded commercial ploy to drain Vichy of its colonial clientele! And by the same token, force Vichy into bankruptcy. All men of goodwill are resolved to fight back."

"Had it not been for your father, Vichy would have gone under," confirmed Dr. Ligier, the colossus.

"And here is the result—I wanted it to be a surprise—*Vichy for*

*Colonials and Tropical Residents* by Dr. Gandelin, Orsenna Press's very first book."

Gabriel wiped mouth and hands and began to leaf through it:

PREFACE

Colonials and residents of the Tropics are insufficiently informed of the effectiveness of Vichy waters and their preventative and curative action on tropical ailments. They know that the Vichy thermal establishment is useful in the treatment of liver and gastrointestinal complaints. But the profound and absolute certainty of a cure or of a definite improvement in cases of tropical disease has not yet entered the collective conscience, with the result that people often fail to visit Vichy in search of a cure.

"Well, what do you think?" asked Louis.

The Vichy cure is the sovereign remedy for all these ills. Under treatment the skin becomes firm and supple, the complexion clears. Thin faces fill out. Good health returns. At the same time facial puffiness disappears, the cheeks lose their flaccidity, skin tone reverts to normal, and bloated features once again assume the appearance of good health.

As I read I heard my father speak.

"You'll see, doctor, Gabriel too has a scientific mind. It was not chance alone that led him to settle in Pascal's birthplace. He may be of great service to us."

"I am sure of it," said the doctor.

Vichy is for persons afflicted with weakness, listlessness, anemia. Colonials fit this category. There need be no outward symptom of disease.

Vichy is the ideal sanatorium. Colonials and patients from tropical climates should go there to seek health, to rebuild strength, and to heal themselves of distempers contracted in the Tropics. No need to fear tuberculosis, for no consumptive is ever admitted there.

Vichy is the fountain of eternal youth for Colonials.

Those who drink at it recover their health, their strength, even their youth.

"That's it, you're done, I deliberately kept it short so that the truth could shine forth. Well, what do you think?"

"Remarkable," said Gabriel. "Devastating, too, from the point of view of other spas" (to which, fifty years later, Gabriel offers his apologies, but Chanturgue blurs the judgment where spas are concerned).

"You're not saying that just to please me?"

"No, it's true."

"What did I tell you?" said Louis to the doctor. "Yet another ally!"

"Welcome to the ranks of the Vichyssois," said the doctor.

And we endlessly toasted Vichy, Science, the Empire. Streetcars shuttled back and forth. By the time they had finished drinking, Gabriel was utterly bemused by this endless streetcar endlessly circling Clermont, just like city ramparts on wheels.

The months that followed (up until the arrest) are represented in our Father-Son saga under the chapter "Confessions," also entitled "Nudities."

Gabriel and Louis met every Sunday at the Café Bancharel.

"The surest proof of my dedication to the truth," said Louis, "is my choice of Vichy (thirty-five miles from here). Had I chosen to champion Châtelguyon (thirteen miles), these trips would have been shorter."

"Indeed," replied Gabriel.

"The doctor has invited us for next week."

"Thank him for me, but I can't."

"What's the matter, Gabriel? Ann again, Clara again? Come now, you're not being reasonable. We must talk. Let's order first. What about a Mousteyrol, followed by a picoussel?"

And as the beef, ham, chicken, and vegetables reached the table, followed (after the cheese interlude) by the plum and herb soufflé, Louis spoke to his son of love.

"Women leave, Gabriel.

"Perhaps men can begin, Gabriel, but women finish.

"If the women who leave only had a grave, Gabriel, at least there would be an end to the journey."

He grew gloomier and gloomier. His surroundings must have had something to do with it, all those extinct volcanoes. And of course the

Mousteyrol. When the doctor was not there it was as if Louis drank dark thoughts.

After these gloomy encounters Gabriel would hurry to the Works. The gatekeeper would be astonished.

"Coming to work? On a Sunday evening?"

Only there, little by little, buried in his work, could Gabriel recover peace of mind, that trust in things, that sense of solid ground beneath one's feet induced—in the absence of love—by sheer efficiency.

Despite the doctor's loud protests, Louis was shortly thereafter arrested: practice of (tropical) medicine without a license. Charitable souls—or, more accurately, mistreated intestines—had denounced him. Châtelguyon was avenged.

# 4

# *The Adoptive Life*

## I

THERE THEY WERE: a big table by the windows, a mass of blue flowers amid the glasses. There they were: Elisabeth in red, the two sisters in off-white, Markus wearing an ancient boater at a rakish tilt; there they were, the four Knights, in Paris, surrounded by skinny youths (in all likelihood the revolting virtuosos). There they were at long last. And unaware of Gabriel's arrival with his two suitcases, deaf to the beating of Gabriel's heart. They went on talking as if nothing had happened, explaining the menu of the Washington and Albany hotel to the little prodigies, ordering white wine to start off with. Just as Gabriel (all courage drained) made ready to give up and leave, just as the dream seemed doomed to remain a dream, a memory of a storm-lashed Channel crossing, forever a dream, nothing more, just as life was about to become a life again, ordinary, happy perhaps, a Clermont-Ferrand wedding to some Marie-Bénédicte, a successful career in engineering—just then Elisabeth exclaimed, "There's Gabriel!" followed by the other three, "Gabriel, it's Gabriel!"

They rose, they milled around him, they embraced him; Gabriel was introduced to the revolting virtuosos, "This is Gabriel, my son-in-law," added Markus Knight, seating him on his right as the whole dining room, the other tables, waiters, and headwaiters, looked on. They looked on as this dream became reality. Suddenly a kind of uncertainty hovered in the lukewarm air. Should they applaud? Without applause an emotion is hard to sustain, but no, the diners smiled, dinner resumed, the clatter of cutlery on plates, the glasses ringing anew. This seventeenth day of July, 1913, Gabriel Orsenna took up residence in his love.

On the ship: "How old was I?" asked Ann. "Are you well?" asked Clara. "Don't exhaust him, he's only just got here," Elisabeth broke in. Question, answer, bedlam, nobody listening, everybody talking instead of embracing; so wide was the table, we lobbed words across it, words like aerial pontoons: "You haven't changed a bit," murmured Clara, eyes reaching for Gabriel. "Ah! you think so?" said Elisabeth with a wink at Gabriel. "I find him—how shall I put it?—seasoned." "We'll see, we'll see," chanted Ann, and every word was a promise or a recollection opening a door forward or astern, to the future or the past, and a warmth was rising, a warmth Gabriel would never again feel and would never forget, the strange market that is love, a giant trading post: you enter a world and that world enters you. So much exchange warms the air, thus the sensation of summer heat.

Such intense sweetness becomes painful; a diversion is needed. You feigned interest in the revolting virtuosos. And what are you working on just now? Ah, Chopin's Nocturne No. 6. That's the one with the tricky sixteenth bar, isn't it? How will you tackle the fingering?

And Gabriel, who knew nothing about music theory, who therefore understood nothing of all these discussions, was comforted to discover the *technical* character of music. He told himself that in love too there must be levels of skill, beginning with mandatory apprenticeships; he felt equal to any task, for the future rubber king feared nothing so much as charm, charm and its tyrannies, its total injustice, the laborer who had only to present himself at the eleventh hour to receive his due.

The youthful virtuosos were not misled for a second by all this exaggerated attention. They knew they were merely an intermission. If there had been less noise you could have heard the rumble of their anger, particularly when the recruiter-impresario forbade them to cut their own meat.

"Let us help you, you have an audition tomorrow, you mustn't clench your fingers around your knives."

And it was then, as the whole Knight family (including the son-in-law to be) sliced beef up into little cubes, it was then that Mr. Knight suddenly announced the wedding date.

"It will have to be the thirtieth of August! We leave for London the very next day!"

"I shall take care of everything," said Elisabeth. She contemplated

Gabriel with the slightly condescending smile of Creator contemplating creature: So, are you satisfied? You see, it was worth waiting for.

"What are you talking about?" Ann asked.

"Nothing, a secret between Gabriel and me. I'm not going to let you gobble him down raw, my darling daughters."

And the sisters blushed. Because of their auditions on the morrow, the youthful virtuosos were denied champagne.

"Splendid! Now, where are you going to sleep?" asked the impresario.

Clara turned pale; Ann echoed her father in a child's small voice. "Oh. Yes. That's true. Where on earth will you sleep?"

The hotel manager was summoned to the table.

"Alas, sir, the hotel is full for the night. Now, tomorrow, I can assure you . . ."

It was therefore decided that the betrothed would spend the night with the virtuosos—all men together, right, Gabriel? You won't mind, will you? Naturally, Gabriel would have preferred a little privacy, for he was not without plans for the night. First to luxuriate at leisure in this summer heat, and also to acquaint himself with an utterly new presence at the core of his being, a reality so solemn and joyful he wondered if it might not be his soul. To answer such a question requires solitude. But could Gabriel begin his relationship with his future father-in-law with a wounding refusal? He therefore replied that of course he would be extremely flattered to share a room with these good gentlemen whose rest he would in no way disturb, given that he had no intention of reading in bed after this memorable evening.

"Wonderful, Gabriel!" said the impresario.

Should I kiss Ann? Should I kiss Clara? our hero wondered. He decided that such a demonstration would perhaps be judged premature. He therefore rose, took up his two suitcases, and walked to the elevator, tormented by the stares he felt on his back. What if I have disappointed them? What if it's all over by tomorrow?

When the door to communal room 217 was closed and locked, when the lights were not immediately switched on, when there gushed into the gloom insults and still more insults in an unknown language rich in consonants, when menacing shapes drew near, one brandishing an oblong ashtray, one a briefcase, one a shoe tree, Gabriel thought he had seen his last day as a son-in-law. Circling around a small table, he attempted (now, now, gentlemen; now, now, my friends) to negotiate.

"Remember tomorrow's audition, gentlemen, you might damage a knuckle. . . ."

His mollifying tones, his precise diction, his recourse to English and a few snatches of German were in vain: words accomplished nothing and blows began to fall.

So, bounding onto an armchair, he leapt, via the bed, to lock himself in the bathroom. And it was here, reclining on a pile of soft bathrobes emblazoned with the heraldic crest of the Washington and Albany hotel (starred flag and ducal coronet) that Gabriel spent his first night as a man-who-has-left-the-dream-and-entered-love. His head was jammed against the bathtub and he had to curl up his legs like a sleeping dog to avoid bumping them against the commode. Through the white door he heard the squeal of violins and the tinkling of mute pianos. How can they even hope to keep a woman with the din they make at night? wondered the son-in-law. Perhaps they are condemned to sleep forever alone, to love only in brightest daylight and on the run. . . . And Gabriel was overcome by sympathy for the victims on the other side of the white door, a sympathy progressively gentler and more benevolent, a sympathy that little by little, and despite the uproar next door, turned into the deepest of sleeps.

When he awoke, Room 217 was silent, free at last of the slightest note. He peeped through the keyhole. It seemed deserted. The odious virtuosos had probably left for their audition.

Such was the first skirmish in the endless war that pitted Gabriel his whole life long (and even today, in hoary old age) against the myriad and ever renascent hordes of his rivals, those in love with Clara, those inflamed by Ann, those in love with and inflamed by them both. Yet there they are, ladies and gentlemen, in the very next room. The voices you may be hearing are theirs. They live where I live, at 13 avenue Wester-Wemys, Cannes-la-Bocca. In the long run, Gabriel won the war.*

They are here, at least for now.

*Absurd male pride *(note from Ann).* Come, come, Gabriel has the right to a little pride now and then . . . after all the things we did to him! *(Clara's reply to her sister).*

* * *

Gabriel arrived very late at the rue Bergère, just missing the audition. A crowd pressed around the recruiter-impresario. Where do you find these prodigies? How do you do it? And so handsome, too! Champagne glass in hand, the recruiter-impresario feigned modesty: Very simple, really, all you have to do is listen at keyholes. And somebody slapped him on the back: Get along with you, you old charlatan, just when everyone thinks music has fled Europe, presto! you pull another Slav out of your hat. . . . The offers began. "I'm organizing a charity ball at Biarritz in a fortnight. I'd love to have one of your pupils." Which one would you like? It makes no difference: they all command the same fee, for now. And Markus leaned over to whisper the figure in the music lover's ear.

"You're insane! A fee like that for an unknown!"

"Take it or leave it. Don't forget the ability to play quickly *and* slowly. How many musicians do you know who can play quickly *and* slowly? Ah, Gabriel, I've been waiting for you."

The crowd turned, whispering. Who is this? Another discovery?

The recruiter-impresario seized my arm and drew me aside. "I wanted to talk to you about the wedding. Don't think I am obsessed with marriage vows. But life is only possible when you are married. Believe me, Gabriel, it is our only safeguard against madness." He held out his glass to me. "So, it's settled, you'll join the family?"

Ann was answering reporters who were lost amid the alien consonants.

"The tall sad one there, who played Liszt—"

"Terzansky?"

"That's it, can you spell it for me?"

And so it went, Lorincz Miksath, Jan Szczucka, Emil Fucik. . . . Even today, when he closes his eyes, Gabriel clearly hears every sound that accompanied his decision: the background of worldly chatter, the clink of glasses at a toast, Ann's voice spelling out the consonants, a few queries about me (the one speaking to Markus, who is he?), the constant swishing of the revolving door, and finally the phrase *safeguard against madness*. "I assure you, Gabriel, the only *safeguard against madness*—"

"Very well, I put my trust in you," Gabriel replied.

Then the recruiter-impresario embraced me and raised his champagne aloft. As Gabriel recalls it, there was a burst of applause.

(Although, thinking back, this was highly unlikely. The heroes of the hour were the revolting virtuosos. Not Gabriel Orsenna at all, even in his brand-new guise of official future son-in-law.)

Immediately afterward began the period when the two sisters kept disappearing. Already gone in the morning when Gabriel came down to drink his breakfast coffee from cups as round and heavy as those in dining cars. Already in bed by dinnertime. You must forgive them, Gabriel, Elisabeth would say, their days are so exhausting. (What was so exhausting? the future son-in-law would have loved to know, but he stifled his questions; above all, oh, above all, never give the impression that he might be an indiscreet young man, for artistic families value their freedom above all else, do they not?)

They went past like a breeze, Ann and Clara, arm in arm, crossing the hotel lobby with long strides, Ah, there's Gabriel, excuse us, Gabriel, we are extremely pressed for time; sudden fits of uncontrollable laughter, the young elevator operator, the one who trembled if Ann merely said good morning, monsieur, the young man in love with Ann closed the doors, and the glass-and-mahogany cage slowly rose: See you tomorrow, Gabriel, we must meet more often, and they laughed, laughed enough to sear his soul, then the car stopped between floors. The operator was obedient to their every whim, it had become a routine, this intermediate stop: Tell us you aren't angry, Gabriel? Forgive us, all these preparations. . . . He heard them without being able to see them properly, they were already too high, just the hems of their dresses, one patch of white, another of royal blue, through the bottom of the elevator cage.

Our table dwindled day by day; one by one the virtuosos left on musical engagements. First Jan, then Emil and Gregory. Only Lorincz remained; he needed comforting and spoke constantly of returning to Budapest, since nobody here wanted him. Elisabeth held his hand. He had very long fingers with gigantic half-moons in the nails that made those who looked at them for extended periods want to vomit (Gabriel is merely reporting, with complete objectivity, the facts of that period).

"This career of yours, Gabriel," asked the recruiter-impresario. "Still rubber?"

"Still."

"Wonderful. I would never have given my daughter to a man without a vocation. I remain somewhat doubtful as to whether rubber is a true vocation, but you will convince me, won't you, Gabriel?"

"Yes, sir."

"Come now, call me Markus."

"Yes, Markus."

"In any case, Gabriel, I trust you about rubber just as you trust me about marriage, isn't that right, Gabriel?"

"Of course, Markus."

Then Markus rose, kissed Elisabeth's hair, told us sleep well, and left to make his nightly prospecting rounds.

"I must," he told his wife. "The French have taken all my virtuosos from me. What is left to take to London?"

She smiled at him a little sadly, wished him good hunting; be sure not to wake me when you come in.

And Gabriel was left alone with his (still undetermined) love's mother. Around them, the dining room filled. Mainly with day-trippers, full of stories about their adventures in Paris, and a few businessmen seated alone and picking over their newspapers the way one pares one's toenails in order to shed once and for all the cares of the day just completed. Elisabeth looked at me, her elbows on the tablecloth, her head on her hands. She had removed her hat, one of those works of art that had so intrigued Clermont-Ferrand; the work of art sat on the table among the glasses. Its feathers and foliage stirred softly in the breeze. Beside us the virtuoso nobody wanted smiled, his head in the clouds.

"Well, Gabriel?"

"How can you expect me to decide if I never see them?"

"Come now, Gabriel. Surely our talks at Clermont-Ferrand were not in vain? It's not a question of deciding but of ascertaining. You follow me? Of ascertaining within yourself which slope is the steeper. And then marry her."

"But you, you know me—"

"You mean which of my daughters would I, Elisabeth, choose for my wife if I were you? No, Gabriel, I am very fond of you, very very fond of you, but that I cannot do for you. A marriage is a personal matter."

Soon the diners went their ways, one by one, the headwaiter addressing them all by name—good night, Monsieur Seyrig, good night, Mademoiselle Hertling, good night, Monsieur Enard—bowing slowly as he handed them their room keys as if they were not allowed to leave the hotel again that night. The dining room was empty and, for a moment, very white; they had laid the tables for next day, set out the napkins and tablecloths, and nobody sat on the chairs. Then they turned down the lamps, all save ours. Elisabeth called for an herbal tea, a complex concoction that was different every evening, a marvel of botanical alchemy that would send her off to sleep on the right note. She dictated the recipe to the bartender, becoming indignant at his deficiencies. What, you have no sage? no savory? Later, she drank with eyes closed.

"First things first, Gabriel. What is a woman to you?"

Sometimes we would still be discussing my marriage when the recruiter-impresario returned. He came and sat down with us. He ordered a brandy. They lit another lamp. At the reception desk, behind the teak counter, the night watchman received his last instructions from the porter.

"The Republic is decidedly unfavorable to music. What a misery these French instrumentalists are! To reason is not to play, you see, Gabriel. We shall be forced to return to Europe."

To him, Europe was those areas rich in musicians: Germany, Poland, the banks of the great rivers, the Danube, the Vistula. . . .

He took my arm. "Let's walk up to the second floor together. I'm going to tell you what I really think, Gabriel; it's Elisabeth you need. In the end every likable man I meet (for I do like you very much, you know, Gabriel) needs Elisabeth. Perhaps that's why I place such great stock in marriage. Perhaps it's just luck, Gabriel, simply luck. Good night, Gabriel."

"Good night, sir—I mean Markus."

"Your wedding, your wedding, as though a wedding were sufficient reason to drop good old Louis, as if an adoptive family, with adoptive relations considerably more intelligent and richer and more amusing than the real ones, living in an adoptive climate considerably brighter, lighter, and more stimulating, as if the adoptive life were an excuse, Gabriel, for forgetting the banks of the Seine and Oriza perfumes and the number of the omnibus that in less than an hour could whisk you to Levallois; time for us to give you a hug, Gabriel, and to make sure (without importuning you in any way) that this wedding will be beneficial to your health, time for us to give you a little news of our life, considerably less glittering than your adoptive life but a life just the same, beginning with our address, which has changed: Île de la Jatte, Gabriel, dangling our feet in the water; we are already thinking about the spring floods, but your old Louis can now fish from his window, which certainly is not the case with you, Gabriel; in an adoptive family one travels widely, one has always to be where others want one to be, always perfectly presentable, am I mistaken, Gabriel? Is the adoptive life not exhausting? Yours is not the only wedding, Gabriel; it must not deafen you to the sounds of other preparations, of other festivities perhaps as joyful as your adoptive ones, Gabriel, for example the polishing of our silverware, the first laundering since 1866 of our biggest white tablecloth, the rattling of armies of glasses that have been in the dark since Maximilian's execution; in a word (if the adoptive din is not too loud, if it allows you small moments of silence from time to time, if the wind is right and you still remember the way to Levallois), you cannot fail to realize that another ceremony draws near, a ceremony that concerns you, Gabriel: your old Louis is also embarking on the adoptive life, like you he is starting again with a clean slate—her name is Iris, pretty little English name, don't you think?—in short, your father is getting married, and if you feel the need to plant your roots back in the shameful-but-real before facing your adoptive jungle, the glorious-but-perhaps-false . . . in short, Louis awaits you. I embrace and await you."

That was the purport, concentrated, summarized, of the innumerable letters received by the obliging receptionist of the Washington and Albany and at once delivered to the future son-in-law.

And here is my chance to complete the portrait of the sprightly future son-in-law (all smiles, all tenderness, and all attentiveness in his adoptive universe) with a darker touch, much darker. For like Saint Peter in the Garden of Olives, he denied his father right up to the last cockcrow of the great day: Another love letter for you, the man with the golden keys loudly announced so that everyone, including and especially the Knights, would hear. Oh, her again! answered

Gabriel in the same loud tones; there's nothing I can do about it, please, take it away, please, and do the same with any others that arrive.

## II

> Divide each of the difficulties to be considered into as many discrete units as possible and as would be required to best resolve them.
>
> RENÉ DESCARTES

We must remember that Gabriel is an engineer. And that engineers, whether famed or obscure, whether experts in civil engineering or in rubber, are crusaders for the truth. Everything that is untrue is painful to them, and what is unclear is even more painful than what is untrue, for the untrue is still a part of the true, the same thing only opposite, and can be made true simply by taking the necessary corrective steps. But the unclear, what can be made of that?

We must therefore picture Gabriel the engineer particularly at a loss before these two sisters.

The face of the one you are going to love—where does it come from? Love is already there, but the woman before your eyes does not seem to have completed her journey and may never altogether arrive. To be sure, she has already dispatched a small regiment of feelings ahead of her, sweet wild feelings, what the magazines call a bolt from the blue. But the woman herself, her body, her looks, her fragrance, she lingers, she unpacks her bags, she stares at us, motionless, as if through a mist that prevents us from seeing her clearly. And Gabriel the engineer, anxious in the extreme, scanned the horizon (the hotel lobby, the fickle elevator) where Clara and Ann came and went without being able to distinguish clearly between them. Logically, he told himself, this single love for two separate beings was not possible. But who was one and who the other? Where did one end; where did the other begin? Oh, if this love is going to be like Marguerite's, if it is no more than a dialogue with ghosts, I should cut my losses right away.

Does this deliberation, fitting in an engineer, constitute an excuse for Gabriel's subsequent behavior? History will judge. In any case our future son-in-law, transformed into a crusader for the truth, opened his investigation with Ann. Shadowing her was easy; the young woman's gait was free, rapid, determined, unfaltering, as if in a conquered city. Every morning at eight-twenty-five she entered a building, number 2 on small secretive rue Auber, not far from the Opéra and just across from the publisher Calmann-Lévy. For lunch every day except Thursdays she made do with a hard-boiled egg and a glass of fizzy liquid that looked from afar much like lemonade. In the big café on the boulevard des Italiens where she seemed to be a regular customer, nothing happened, not a conversation, not a tryst, not even a response to the many compliments which her beauty, her solitude, and her general appearance (androgynous air, mocking smile) naturally elicited. Having refreshed herself, she returned to rue Auber, where the crusader for truth had no trouble ascertaining the object of her unvarying (except on Thursdays) routine: a black marble plate imprinted with gold letters was fixed just under the doorbell: ADVANCED STUDIES IN ACCOUNTING AND INTERNATIONAL MANAGEMENT (4th floor), an institution whose modernity was demonstrated by a phenomenon then extremely rare: it was coeducational. But Mlle. Knight appeared to be the only member of the fair sex to take advantage of this opportunity, for apart from her only men, youthful, mature, or aged, entered and left number 2. The future son-in-law could not have been more pleased by the results of his investigation: (1) she works, (2) in a field that has nothing whatever to do with art, and (3), in conclusion, I have the strong feeling that this Ann is my ideal. Thursdays aside, those mysterious Thursdays between noon and almost four, which would keep their secret for two and even three weeks. For during the first week the crusader for truth dared not ride the same omnibus as his potential betrothed. As no cab was to be found in the neighborhood, he lost the trail. The following Thursday, seven days later, well before noon, he sat hidden in the depths of a carriage and devoured by curiosity some twenty yards from the bus stop. Love, oh, love! commented his driver, a ruddy-hued man with an astonishingly deep voice, all the way from the Opéra to the place des Ternes. There she got off the bus, quickly followed by Gabriel, went down the rue Cardinet, and disappeared into a hotel named Paris-Plage, not emerging for another two and a half hours, ten minutes after a family, blatantly American and ignorant of the Thursday cult, four minutes after a sad-looking gentleman, very elegant, flannel suit and subdued tie—a lawyer? a banker?—but preceding by almost a quarter of an hour a robust gentleman with a yachtsman's cut to his jib, in his fifties, brown hair gray at the temples, blazer with gilt badge, his lips hesitating between smiling openly and whistling a catchy tune. In the face of such uncertainty, our crusader was obliged to return a third time (but cabless, straight to the rue Cardinet, hoping they did not change meeting places every Thursday). And at around three-thirty, exactly fifteen minutes after Ann's departure, there appeared on the threshold of the Paris-Plage, in the plain light of truth, the yachtsman, apparently just as contented as he had been the week before.

You are about to conclude that the file on Gabriel's marriage was now closed: exit the impure Ann, enter her sister Clara, my wife. Wrong! Deeply wrong. A crusader for the truth is not necessarily a puritan, far from it.

Hardly had the yachtsman rounded the corner of boulevard de Courcelles than Gabriel was seated at a sidewalk café on place des Ternes, at the precise spot where the Brasserie Lorraine would one day stand. He ordered a German beer, one of the very last of its kind to be served in Paris, given the deterioration of the international situation. And he closed his eyes. And Ann entered him. That is, she finally emerged from the mist. Her features acquired sharper definition. He knew her reality: smooth-skinned blonde, golden tan in all seasons (good investment for winter), a broken upper incisor slightly overlapping its neighbor, a wide domed forehead accentuated by prominent cheekbones, lips neither thin nor sensual, the discreet projectors of appetite, hands with long fingers made to seize anything, anything, Gabriel, even you (he opened his eyes long enough to order another beer), small breasts, or so it seemed, and legs most assuredly long but athletic (at that time you saw nothing of the legs without seeing all the rest as well), the sort of legs that never run away, they simply go elsewhere; and then her look, a laughing look, a candid accountant's look (Gabriel was to verify it at dinner that very evening at the Washington and Albany), the look of an honor student, of the pride of the rue Auber, of a future international manager: are you tempted? So am I. Then let's go. A look that left your own only to examine and assess lower down. Alone in his café on place des Ternes, in the month of August 1913, Gabriel blushed, blushed and told himself, This time there is no doubt, I'm in love with Ann, she's the one I love; oh, Louis, wish me good health, this Ann will take me far, already I'm thirsty from the journey: "Waiter, another beer."

"Will French do? We're out of German."

It was thus as a quite subsidiary undertaking—and because a crusader for truth is duty-bound to explore all facets of a situation—that Gabriel took on Clara's case.

Dreams, bags, and baggage, the crusader had settled into the Knight universe. And had shed fifteen years in the process, for adoption is a kind of miracle, obliging you almost to begin your life anew. It was therefore an adolescent Orsenna who sat upright on his chair at the head of the table at the Washington and Albany, eyes riveted on the hothouse rhododendrons. The Knights had forgotten him. They were exchanging those intimate details that are the staple of family conversation.

"Are you still constipated, Ann?"

"And how are your hemorrhoids, Markus?"

"You know very well I hate veal, Mama."

All of which delighted our crusader (I'm in, they have accepted me, I am one of them; truly, this clinches it forever).

Then one of them turned to Clara. "And how goes the violin, my dear?"

"It's coming along, coming along."

Gabriel thus learned that for years Clara had been preparing for a concert, a concert that would be the best-present-any-father-had-ever-had, a concert that would make the world press say, Why, oh, why did the recruiter Knight search so far afield for what was so near? Obviously, such a concert demanded arduous practice. So Clara had been meeting her teacher several times a week for years, and more and more frequently in recent days as the date for handing the present (the concert) to Markus drew near. I must follow her, the crusader for truth told himself in the glow of the results of his previous investigation.

While Ann progressed through the city as if in conquered territory, the way an American woman goes shopping—I want this, I want that, this whole shop, this corner of blue sky, this contented yachtsman (to whoever was there to pay the bill)—Clara retreated. She was like a spy abandoned in hostile country, a blown agent whose nerve has failed, her head pulled in between her shoulders, her movements quick and birdlike, flashes of panic in her eyes: I know that stroller is staring at me, that building is about to collapse on top of me; look over there, the sidewalk is splitting open. . . .

And Gabriel had to force himself to repeat, It's Ann I love, it's Ann I love, it's Ann I love, to keep from rushing to take Clara in his arms, to brush the dew of fear from her temples, to swear by all he held dear, by his Louis of old, for example, that all was well: it is August, Clara, the skies are clear, soon it will be warmer still, your father loves you, the elevator at the Washington and Albany is the quietest and happiest place in the world. Paris will always be Paris. . . .

Soon she left the rue de Rivoli, turned up the rue d'Alger, and pushed open the door to number 17.

On the mailboxes above the garbage pails in the narrow entranceway, no hint of music. Nothing but high fashion. KATY MILLINERY (second floor), EVENING WEAR (mezzanine), MARGOT AND MARIE, GLOVES MADE TO MEASURE (fourth floor, end of corridor). Just one name was out of place, on the third floor, MORBIHAN CERAMICS, stranded on rue d'Alger after who knew how many bankruptcies. Figures came and went in the gloom, bearing hatboxes or dresses held at arm's length, wrapped in tissue paper to prevent wrinkling, and each time the crusader for truth obligingly made way, flattening himself against mailboxes, hearing the smart young milliners rail against grand occasions: Why do the customers all want to be dressed at once?

And in the rare moments of silence between these comings and goings, Gabriel strained his ears: nothing, not the faintest scraping of a violin, not the slightest hint of a concert being rehearsed at number

17 rue d'Alger. Perhaps Clara had lied, perhaps she was preparing the most beautiful dress in Paris, for her father alone, the kind of dress that must be tried on over and over again. . . .

And then Clara appeared, in tears, followed by a wobbling tower of round packages; behind her a piercing voice repeated, "Hey, young woman, if you're not going anywhere let me by."

Then the crusader for truth at once forgot his previous betrothed, the yachtsman's friend. Then the crusader for truth seized the girl's two hands and shook them, shook them without the slightest restraint, since those hands were no longer fragile, no longer hands preparing for a concert. And he cried out, but in a low voice, a strained murmur, "So you're not a violinist, eh, and this has nothing to do with the violin?"

And the girl stared at the crusader for truth, considerable surprise in her eyes.

"Is it any of your business?"

Then:

"Do you plan to stand here all night?"

She freed herself.

They went out into the rue d'Alger, into the sounds of the city, the heat of the stones, the August light.

"Do you know what fear is, Gabriel?"

She gazed at me, looking lost, but haloed by a faint flickering light, as if by a lantern swinging inside her head just behind her gray eyes.

"You did not follow me just by chance, correct? I am Clara. You agree? Clara, and not another? Then you deserve to know everything. I have never liked music, I hate music, music is too frivolous, it puts things to shame, musicians' daughters have no right to things. Let's walk a little, Gabriel, you don't mind? You see, Markus has told us so often that music alone . . ."

It is hard to listen to a walking woman, especially in the din of the city; you must always stay one half step ahead of her, body leaning toward her, and give her your ear by turning your head at least forty-five degrees, so that the words go straight from her lips to your ears, and all this without losing your balance, without stepping on her foot, seeming neither obtrusive nor awkward but attentive and unself-conscious, a charming companion—in short, I have never been able to do it.

And you pass so many hotels, the temptations are unceasing, exacerbated by the light touches, the smells, the contacts with her thigh, a breast that grazes your back in a dense crowd (blessed be crowded avenues), the vertiginous dampness when you take her arm to cross, and that cruel yearning to kiss the back of her neck, the most fragile spot, those first hairs, the sweetness of little girls, to inhale the nape's particular musk, while she, the walker, realizes nothing, or pretends to realize nothing, and says, What splendid weather for walking. . . . And crueler still is the torture if her dress is of silk or of linen. You could swear they were accomplices, the woman and her accursed dress, that they whispered salacious secrets to each other, like a countess of old and her chambermaid as her lover waits outside at the foot of the tower, shivering in the snow. . . . And don't forget my size; I had to walk on tiptoe, casually hopping along to seem a decent height. . . . I was on the rack, my heart was beating too fast.

I suggested that we stop: It's so hot, Clara, why don't we have a lemonade in this café or catch our breath on this bench? Alas, she would not reply, or if she did it was to say, Why, Gabriel, are you tired?

I used to have such foolish pride. I did not want to say yes to such questions.

So we continued, day after day, to walk along side by side. She explained everything to me; I have forgotten most of it, wretch that I am. My memory isn't much even when I'm sitting down, worse when I'm up and walking. . . .

Three times a week I went with her to the rue d'Alger. During her classes I stayed in the garden, always in the same spot, on the Terrasse des Feuillantines at the corner of place de la Concorde. It did not rain once that summer. The regularity of my schedule intrigued the nannies and mothers. At exactly five o'clock Clara came into view, exhausted, trembling (Oh, Gabriel, if only you knew how hard it is), her body broken, bent double as if to give the enemy the smallest possible target. . . . I stood before her on the sidewalk, shifting from one foot to the other, dancing my futile jig and saying, All will be well. She seemed at the end of her tether, overcome by her distress, racked and racked again. And every time it was pride that gave her the courage to keep going.

"A fear like mine . . ."

Suddenly she was breathing better, pulling herself upright, managing to smile.

". . . a fear like mine, don't you agree, Gabriel, it deserves to be published? Let's get out of this street, I need air."

On the way she told me of strange cases, Mlle. Dora who was losing her voice, little Hans who lived in dread of horses, an intelligent man obsessed by rats. . . .

"Be honest, Gabriel, do you not find my music phobia more interesting?"

Through the days of August 1913 we walked and walked. I finally (and inevitably) understood the deeper reason behind these walks. Clara needed to check, neighborhood by neighborhood, to see whether (despite music) the city still existed, to see whether the Creator, overwhelmed by music, had not wearied of things, to see whether He had indeed completed His *real* work. But Clara had no faith; she trembled at one day discovering some instance of divine laziness, an emptiness, a hole, a hole just in front of her, threatening to swallow her up. She explained to me that people were very wrong to make so much music, especially so much religious music, the fools. One day God would realize that notes meant more than things. He would leave us in the lurch on our ugly planet and go somewhere else to play the piano in peace. Do you understand, Gabriel? God will abandon us, we won't exist any more. We must stop the music, Gabriel, stop it now; tell Markus, I don't dare to, oh, Gabriel. . . .

I took her hand at painful junctures, when we left the street, for instance rue Boissy d'Anglas, and emerged onto place de la Concorde: Is the obelisk still there? Yes, Clara, I swear it. Or on the Montmartre funicular, where we turned around and scrutinized the city slowly, slowly, the way you look for your name on a list of examination results. I did my best to reassure her. I told her God had not yet chosen music; yes, Paris still lay at our feet, like a good dog panting after the hunt. . . .

And as Clara checked on the state of Creation in this way, as this adventure both exemplary and amazing went on at Gabriel's side, what was our hero's one thought, what was the one obsession tormenting Gabriel, the wretched little knight of the round face? Alas, it must be admitted: to make love to his tall gray-eyed companion—a shabby, rabid desire, a butterfly collector's mania—to pin that indefatigable walker once and for all to a flat surface.

## III

To sleep.

No doubt about it, Gabriel was scarcely at his best that teeming summer of 1913. Extraordinary events occurred in his immediate vicinity and he failed even to notice them, obsessed as he was by two bodies, two biological mechanisms: Clara's, as we have seen, and his own, broken by walking and lack of sleep. For you sleep all too seldom in the adoptive life, what with concerts, with after-concert suppers, with after-supper rehashing, with after-rehashing gossip, and with the clatter of an awakening hotel when you have barely begun to sink into the bosom of the healing ocean.

Worse still from this standpoint was the Sect. What strange disdain for sleep from people whose raw materials were dreams! As long as they could drink and discuss the soul, its adepts would willingly stay awake for a day and a night and quite a few more days stretching into quite a few more nights. In vain did Gabriel, for love of Clara (I'm so glad you're here), choose the most uncomfortable armchair (thank you, Louis XIII) with the stiffest back and prop his eyelids open; he knew full well he would not stay awake for long.

And his resistance always failed at the worst possible moment.

Yet at first all went well. One of the decisive jousts in the history of mankind's study of man was taking place in London. A joust (experts now claim with the wisdom of hindsight) no less important than the Council of Trent. Clara had chosen this occasion to introduce Gabriel to her circle. The concierge admitted them without challenge to the extremely elegant building at 54 rue de l'Université (you'll see, Gabriel, soon we will defeat our enemies and all live in the seventh *arrondissement,* doctors and patients alike; she took him by the hand). The hostess greeted them with a brief smile: Hurry and find a seat; you're just in time, Witold is calling England, we're about to get the latest news.

"This is my brother," Clara said, motioning to Gabriel.

And for a second the future son-in-law hesitated; could this new brotherly status be considered a step forward in his suit? Yes, without a doubt, a brother is closer than a walking companion and any increase in proximity implies progress in love. It was therefore a lighthearted Gabriel who was introduced to the bearded gathering of soul doctors, a Gabriel exuding charm and garbed in the subtlest humility: I am full of good intentions, but unqualified, alas. That need not distress you, Gabriel—you don't mind being called Gabriel?—we will assign you a mentor who will explain what is at stake—and it is considerable, Gabriel, considerable—in tonight's debates. And Gabriel was overcome with gratitude. In short, he charmed everyone there—apart from one surly fellow (why this need to win us over, my dear Monsieur Gabriel?) but let us ignore this killjoy—which so delighted him (Clara will see that I am likable and cannot fail to draw her own conclusions) that he almost failed to hear the ambiguous words uttered several times behind his back: Clara seems to have found the perfect brother this time. "This time." What did "this time" mean?

Having made his round of the guests, Gabriel was steered toward the only empty chair, the ubiquitous Louis XIII.

And his mentor appeared, dark-haired with flashing black eyes and low-cut Spanish dress.

"What do you wish to know?" asked the mentor.

"Everything. And first, what is happening in London?"

"An international medical congress. They are debating the psychoanalysis issue."

"Splendid, splendid, and who will be there?"

"The Frenchman Janet, to whom neurosis is a kind of syphilis of the soul—"

"How very stupid!" said Gabriel. (Note the carelessness of this remark: in his desire to please at all costs he might have destroyed his chances forever by some irremediable faux pas.)

"Yes, how very stupid," agreed his mentor. "And Jung will also be there, preaching theories of a psyche without sexuality, can you imagine, without sex-su-ality—"

"Grotesque," ventured an emboldened Gabriel.

This conversation (your narrator can still hear it as if it had taken place this very afternoon; oh, the illusion of sound standing still!) was doubly stimulating, both to the mind and to Gabriel's vision: where to focus his gaze on this mentor? On her eyes, dark, or on her dress at the neckline? It was an impossible choice. Hence a perpetual shifting of focus that gave their conversation an almost athletic charm, like a body shaking itself awake, like an early morning run. In short, Gabriel felt a strong attraction for his mentor, and Clara, realizing it, came over to interrupt them.

"Is everything going well, Gabriel?"

"Everything."

"So I see."

And she rejoined her specialists. Just then the telephone rang. It was London. Bad news about the joust, it seemed. The hostess replaced the receiver, and everyone began talking. The low-cut mentor joined the fray. Gabriel was left all alone. Alone with the meager theoretical baggage he had just been given. Alone confronting a war of which he understood nothing: libido, psychasthenia, stylographic method, uterine presumption. Lost in the great varnished room. Far off, foreign words resounded; far off, Clara had forgotten him and, cheeks suddenly flushed, was crossing swords with a Bosnian on the theme of the vital impulse.

What, under such circumstances, could a crusader for the truth do but try to muse in scientific terms on the state of his loves?

So he attempted to apply his skimpy and recently acquired knowledge to Clara's case. Once again he recalled things Clara had said as they walked together.

"Gabriel, don't you find it strange, the way that little girl is nibbling the rim of her glass in front of a gentleman in all likelihood her father?"

"Oh, Gabriel, see how that horse prances before entering the tunnel!"

"Why do you think that woman dropped her umbrella (which you so obligingly picked up for her)? Did you notice the shape of the handle?"

"This bicycle-riding fad, now, that saddle, you're not going to say it's innocent?"

If Gabriel had understood the words of his low-cut mentor, Clara was *pansexual,* like all members of the Sect. The difference between the two sisters leapt out at once. Clara saw sex everywhere, whereas Ann saw sex nowhere but in sex. This made Gabriel's problem simple, at least in its formulation: what should a future son-in-law do to ward off the ever-present temptation of Ann and channel toward a locked room (complete with bed) the countless manifestations of sexuality encountered by Clara in the course of a day?

It was then, all of a sudden, that he fell asleep.

Later, much later, the big lustrous room rang with veritable howls, victory howls. The soul doctors hugged one another, broke into dance. In the end, and against all expectation, the Welshman Jones had successfully defended the cause. Jung had been heaped with ridicule. The purity fanatics were defeated. At long long last, sexuality would be elevated to its proper place. Long live Freud! The rest of the century would be splendid. Long live the year 1913!

Now that psychoanalysis has triumphed, burrowing down beneath humanity to new subterranean strata (id, preconscious, subconscious, paraconscious, superego, pit, orchestra, mezzanine), burrowing so deep that in order to get in touch with ourselves it is no longer enough to be silent and listen, we must take the elevator; much later on (now that cities have adopted the mania for depth and riddled themselves with underground parking lots), it sometimes vexes me that I fell asleep at the very heart of that decisive debate.

I could have crisscrossed the globe—and I love to travel—giving lectures in Rio, Tokyo, Los Angeles. The heroic beginnings, the triumph of the pansexual: I would have adapted the topics to fit the circumstances, I would have overflowed with anecdotes about rivalries, the neuroses of the Welshman Jones, the denunciatory telegrams sent to François, René, Eugène, Ursule, Denise, yes, mademoiselle, Freud, 19 Berggasse, Vienna, Austria, everything that inflames the heirs, the adepts of the second, the third, and quite soon the fourth generation. . . .

And I picture another life, yet another: Clara lives by my side. Sounds reach me from the next room, the sounds of the art whose birth I witnessed, someone murmuring something, the scratching of a pen.

## IV

Revolving doors. This roundabout way of moving from one place to another suited Gabriel's temperament: regretful when called upon to leave, bashful when required to enter. And revolving doors possess so many other endearing traits: their knack of swinging the overimpatient user through a complete turn and bringing him back to his starting point, their propensity for cruelty, their penchant for pinching, for hurting you. Moving from one place to another is already a journey. Our heartfelt thanks to the revolving door for reminding us of it.

But precisely because of his fondness for these small circular odysseys, our hero hated it when his hand was forced, when someone behind him imposed on the rotation a rhythm he would not have chosen for himself. To put it differently, going through a revolving door was for him a solitary pleasure. You can imagine the time he wasted waiting for a propitious moment during rush hour, when the Washington and Albany seemed to be filling and emptying all at once. . . .

That night, a particularly empty night, a night without Clara, without the low-cut mentor, he suddenly felt that someone had entered the compartment behind his own. He turned, stumbled, smashed his forehead against the glass. When he came to his senses, half prone on the sidewalk, Ann was kissing him. Well, well, Gabriel, aren't you the secretive one; here we are both getting home at the same late hour; it's an omen. And she took his hand firmly, her lover's fingers gripping Gabriel's indecisive ones. And she told him to get up.

"Come on, Gabriel, you're not going to lie there forever because of a simple little bump on the head, come on."

And the night watchman, a Portuguese student of Thomism (with whom Clara spent far too much time in discussion), stuck his head out from behind the row of green plants where he kept his camp bed and his row of cream-colored books (Vrin publications) and with a strange grin wished them good luck.

And Ann, still leading Gabriel, went in search of the elevator, which was neither on the first nor the second floor, and Gabriel climbed the stairs four at a time behind her—but why the elevator, what need have we of the elevator, we're already on our floor?—which was where they found it, stopped, blatantly slumbering, protected by a small sign hanging on its door: SERVICE SUSPENDED UNTIL 7 A.M.

And Ann brushed the sign aside and gave the order, "Let's go, you'll see, the two Knight sisters are not untouchable; don't worry, I've watched how this is done," and she pulled the lever, and the elevator began to rise. Ann did not look at Gabriel, and as it rose the elevator groaned, with terrible grinding and creaking from the mahogany cabin, a racket that could not fail to rouse the hotel, the guests would soon be pouring out of their rooms and we would be unable to hide since the elevator cabin had glass windows, and the scandal would spread like wildfire and your parents would no longer trust me . . .

With a last crash and rattle (can anyone in Paris still be asleep?), the elevator stopped. "Here we are," said Ann. The elevator had climbed beyond the top floor.

Gabriel raised his eyes. The great greasy pulley hung just above them, and above that were only roof and sky.

"So," said Ann.

Gabriel strained his ears, leaned over to scan the stairway. It would not be long before the roused sleepers rushed to the assault.

"So," said Ann.

Silence had returned, the silence of the middle of the night when you hear nothing but the frenzied beating of your heart, and Ann was right: the beating of a heart has never wakened a hotel.

Now Gabriel stared at the elevator floor, a particularly bristly-looking kind of mat.

"I always do it standing up," said Ann.

He turned very softly, so as to avoid creaking. She was leaning against the far wall, arms raised. Her head rested on the instruction board. She looked at him without a trace of a smile.

"Start with your tongue," said Ann.

Then the year 1913 burst from its bounds and bore fruit. Summer begat summer, a summer for Gabriel's loins as he knelt before her at the waistline of the white dress, a summer for her belly turning and burning like a Catherine wheel, a summer for her throat, no doubt touched by the sun, a nomad sun of the night, a summer for Gabriel's hands although he could no longer tell whether it was he or she who was burning, a summer for his head although he had always been of the belief that men with round cheeks were not entitled to torrid seasons, a summer of low tides, swollen with humid odors, kelpy, vegetable, half-opened clams, and still more and many more summers, and the elevator resumed its climb, leaving beneath it the great greasy pulley, soaring up from the roof to reach that place where summers are made and which resembles the swell of the open sea. Naturally it feels so hot, we're under the eaves, thought Gabriel, still seeking an explanation for things. Everything is under control. Everything is under control. She wore a dress of white lace, buttoned to the neck, a dress that unbuttoned into two vertical halves from top to bottom. Her right leg beat a little too quickly, like a spasm of the eyelid.

Later, when the elevator had resumed its station beneath the greasy pulley, when the summers one by one had flickered out, when the creaking had subsided and the elevator had returned to their floor, Ann replaced the sign: SERVICE SUSPENDED UNTIL 7 A.M.

She kept her white dress separated in two.

"Who would see us at this hour? Good night, Gabriel."

Obviously Ann is the one, he told himself while digging through his pockets and not finding the key—ah, here it is—while managing to open the door to his room, while deciding not to turn on lights (I'll be going to sleep immediately), while undressing in the dark, while bumping into an armchair—what a day! what a day!—while making sure the curtains were drawn and the bolster replaced with a pillow; it's so obvious now, how could I not have known? Ann is my one and only love.

It was not until the last moment, when his own weight was pulling him down onto the bed and he had already told himself good night, Gabriel, in his loud clear engineer's voice, that he felt a presence.

"I realize you are tired," Clara said, "but the important thing is our future."

She had taken his hand.

"You know as I do that everything is sexual, Gabriel, including the absence of sex, so there is no hurry, and good night, Gabriel."

And she rolled onto her side.

And I truly believe she was instantly asleep.

It was in the dining room that Gabriel made his choice known. The family's happiness was a joy to behold.

"Bestowed, a hand most happily bestowed, my dear Gabriel!" said Markus as he leaned toward his son-in-law. "I'll say it again, it was the only decision to make; outside marriage a man risks madness."

Clara did not look at him; she was staring at the plants in the conservatory with the smile of a royal consort. At the other end of the table, Ann and her mother were as usual engaged in an endless low litany. From time to time they turned laughing toward Gabriel, and it seemed that, I can't swear to it, but it seemed that this morning he read on their lips that saying Elisabeth loved so well and had taught so well to her daughter: Life is long, Gabriel, I am happy, we are happy for you, but life is long, Gabriel. . . .

The businessmen sitting at a nearby table asked the reason for all these high spirits. "I am giving away my daughter," answered the recruiter-impresario.

So they ordered champagne, the best. This is how businessmen give expression to their joy. Some were from Chicago, some from Lyon, and they had just signed an important agreement. In textiles. Luxury textiles, the pair from Lyon specified. Our contract needs a godmother. "Which one is the bride?" Elisabeth pointed to Clara. "Wonderful, just write down your address here, Chic International Inc. will send you dresses."

"Yes, where will you live?" asked Ann.

Clara wrote *Hotel Washington and Albany, Room 212.* We raised our glasses to love, to marriage, to Chic International, to Room 212, to the cities of Chicago, Toulouse, Paris, Washington, Albany. Is Albany really a city? Gabriel wondered. One of the Lyon businessmen kept murmuring into the bride's ear. "You'll see, our dresses will be most becoming to you. Perfect for you, absolutely perfect." Then he went around the breakfast room taking the two yellow roses from the center of each table and offering the resultant bouquet to the younger sister, Ann, "so that no one will be left out."

The waiters smiled. The Knight family and their future son-in-law were very popular at the Washington and Albany.

My very dear son,

Should you chance to meet the forgetful Gabriel in the lobby of your grand palace-hotel, be so good as to tell him the date of a certain ceremony involving his father, and at the same time remind him of that father's name (Louis): the first of September, 12 o'clock, D'Alésia church, fourteenth *arrondissement,* Left Bank, and of the reception, Île de la Jatte. And this time, this time, the old reprobate really has put all his eggs in one basket, all of them, do you hear? including the sacrament of marriage, the glue without which life falls apart. But, as absence makes a poor adviser, particularly for the above-mentioned Louis, it would perhaps be best if you could be there to hold my hand. I am sorry, I had wanted you to have the place of honor, but Marguerite insists upon taking over the Île—sorry, taking me down the aisle.

Signed: Louis.

P.S.: Since I have placed all my eggs in one basket, my life has begun to list sideways just like the tower of Pisa, so come back, Gabriel, I'll give you half my eggs and regain my balance.

Any normally constituted son receiving such an appeal would immediately have rushed to the new address on the Île de la Jatte to help straighten the tower of Pisa. But not Gabriel. He stared at the bellhop.

"Must be congratulations, sir," remarked that lover of tips, fanning the air with the silver salver on which the heartrending letter had sat just a few moments earlier.

"Yes, Roger, congratulations, and in addition the news that all is ready. We shall therefore be getting married on the first of September, at exactly noon, anywhere, so long as it is on the Right Bank."

He smiled at Clara. Beside him in bed in Room 212, she pulled the sheets up to her nose and rolled her eyes like a blushing little girl. And, demonstrating an unself-consciousness about his roly-poly form that had hitherto eluded him, he leapt out of bed, foraged through the pockets of the trousers discarded by the window the night before, found the coin he sought—"And this is for you, have a good day, Roger"; "Congratulations again, sir"—and rejoined Clara. "You understand, it's my wedding, I can't let him come; I want happiness for me and me alone, just once, especially happiness with a woman. Later, the next day, or even that very evening, I'll introduce you to Louis, but not before."

"Who is this Louis?" Clara asked.

But Gabriel could not allow remorse to tarnish the luster of those delectable days. And the thought of a lonely father once again putting all his eggs in one basket, scaling and rescaling the slopes of happiness with no help from any quarter, is enough to spoil the most selfish happiness. . . .

And so, on the evening of August 31, when it was really no longer possible to cancel the next day's ceremony, Louis received the longest telegram ever sent from Paris to the Île de la Jatte.

Gabriel, heedless of the stops chopping his message to pieces, announced that he too was putting all his eggs in one basket and would be

GETTING MARRIED SEPTEMBER 1 AT NOON IN SAINT-AUGUSTIN CHURCH STOP INCREDIBLE COINCIDENCE DON'T YOU THINK LOUIS STOP PLEASE DON'T COME STOP ORSENNA RECORD REGARDING LONGEVITY OF ROMANCE NOT IMPRESSIVE STOP PERHAPS FATE WILL STRIKE THE TWO OF US IF TOGETHER SO LET US TAKE OUR CHANCES SEPARATELY STOP WHATEVER THE COST STOP I EMBRACE YOU.

Late that night, with Clara and Ann still not back from the Parisian hideaway where they buried their lives as sisters, and with Gabriel lying sleepless, torn between calling the vice squad and fleeing to the Île de la Jatte (it is true, I know it now, my sister in life is my father), an extremely agitated man, half in tails (he was missing the waistcoat), appeared at the reception desk of the Washington and Albany. "The groom, which floor?" he asked. Do you mean Monsieur Gabriel in Room 212? "Thank you, thank you." And he flung himself into the stairway, despite the shouts of the Thomist Portuguese student: But monsieur, he is asleep! Flinging open the door, Louis said breathlessly, "Consider me not to have come, consider me to be but a telegram: proud have such mature son stop alas comply with tragic provisional separation stratagem stop."

And he kissed his son, cast a brief glance at what Room 212 of a palace looked like—"I am going, I am going, Gabriel, consider me not to have come"—and his eyes were so full of tears as he crossed the lobby toward the revolving door that the Portuguese Thomist night watchman, instead of insulting him, wished him a good night and a good day to follow it.

Since that August 31, every time anyone has mentioned a father to Gabriel, or introduced one to him, he compares and is unable to repress a doubtful look.

"Really, that's a father? You're sure you have a father? Do you know what a real father is?"

Occasionally during this period, after one of our meals or coming upon me in the lobby, Markus would take my arm.

"I know we have spoken of this before, Gabriel, but if you could just tell me a little about what your profession entails. Something to do with rubber, isn't it?"

I would explain patiently all over again.

Despite his best efforts a girl's father is unable, deep down, to believe in the reality of his future son-in-law. At best he is nothing but an amiable ghost. The good thing about ghosts is that they do not inhabit beds, no matter how often they drape themselves with sheets. The said future son-in-law's career looked like an ill-defined commotion somewhere out in the mist.

"Ah, wonderful, yes, I see. But have you never thought of entering the diplomatic service?"

For Markus Knight, ambassadors were kings, untutored, disdainful kings, ever-present at concerts, dozing off in the best seats, always ready to lionize established stars, never disposed to lend aid to a newly discovered virtuoso or to an impresario temporarily down on his luck.

"But you, Gabriel, you love music, you would not be like them, your door would be open to artists, true artists, I would help you distinguish the true from the false and France's prestige would be thereby enhanced. Don't you think we sorely need diplomats who aren't fools?"

Gabriel would continue to describe his career in rubber.

Markus would give in.

"True, true, no doubt you are right. The invention of the telephone has done diplomacy no good; it has made ambassadors so much less useful. So go with rubber. In any case you know I trust you, Gabriel, you do know that, don't you?"

So the two ceremonies took place on the same first of September at the same hour. And every precaution had been taken to protect the eggs in their separate baskets and thus finally thwart the evil star that had until now shone so banefully on all Orsenna couples.

1. A more than reasonable distance, plus the Seine, separated the two churches.

2. The projected paths of the processions ensured that no unexpected encounters would occur.

3. The guest lists were so ordered as to exclude the slightest possibility of the same person being invited to both ceremonies. "Is there anyone you would like to invite, Gabriel?" Elisabeth had asked him. Like Saint Peter the betrayer (and future pope) he had replied, "You are my only family!"

4. After the reception, Louis would remain on the Île de la Jatte whereas Gabriel would leave for Brazil.

So where did Louis and I slip up? How to explain what followed?

Today, after much reflection, I suggest that it was the telegraph office. Perhaps the evil eye can be transmitted by wire. For as soon as the sun rose on the great day a veritable frenzy of telegram-sending seized father and son.

FINAL DECISION WHITE MORNING-COAT

RED CARNATION AND YOU? KISSES.

LOUIS (8:12 A.M.)

TAILS FOR ME RIGHT SHOELACE BROKEN AFFECTIONATELY.
GABRIEL (9:15 A.M.)

LEAVING ILE DE LA JATTE CAN REMEMBER YOUR FIRST STEPS
COURAGE. LOUIS (11:01 A.M.)

BIDDING TEARFUL FAREWELL WASHINGTON AND ALBANY
STOP RIDICULOUS. GABRIEL (11:28 A.M.)

The grooms approached their destinations. This great telegraphic flurry and the constant coming and going of uniformed messengers shrouded them in mystery. Guests in the respective wedding parties whispered their theories: It must be a former mistress who won't give up. Or long-distance speculation on the New York or Amsterdam stock exchanges. . . . As for the two Orsennas (until now everyone had been wondering what was so special about them as to inspire marriage), their market value inexorably climbed. As I entered the church Elisabeth slipped her arm kindly under mine (since you have no family), the harmonium hummed, the verger moved forward, a small fair-haired messenger broke through the lines (another dispatch for you, monsieur), and throughout the solemn wedding march Gabriel attempted to open the envelope with his left hand. As he took his seat he slipped the form between the pages of two Holy Days and under a mask of piety made out:

IF EMOTION INDUCES RAPID HEARTBEAT ORDER YOU INTERRUPT
CEREMONY LIE DOWN ANYWHERE AND CALL DOCTOR ORDER YOU.
LOUIS (12.07 P.M.)

Clara missed none of this. Her lips were so tightly shut that guests wondered how her murmur emerged: "I hope this time it's goodbye."

*Et introibo ad altare Dei,* the nuptials began.

The wedding went as all weddings go: the smell of incense, swelling organ music, strained atmosphere, sense of disenchantment, who can halt the drift of the continents? Facing us (Clara and me, Gabriel, seated on our big red chairs), a priest (old) went through the steps of the mass, opening the book, reading from the book, carrying the book, folding the vestments. . . . Several times he turned to us, to Clara and me, smiled at us, murmured, "My young friends," and continued his work. Time went by.

Then came the sermon, a long deterministic saga. Since the dawn of time Clara Knight, crossing Germany, Poland, Hungary, Czechoslovakia, the Baltic provinces, music, had been marching toward Gabriel. While he, infinitely more of a homebody, had merely left Levallois for London one fine day. And aboard ship. . . . Who could still believe in coincidence? You know, dearest brothers and sisters, the frequency of connections between France and England. How infinitesimal were their chances of meeting! No, for generations upon generations, God's plan had been ripening. . . . Down to this very day a road had been abuilding. . . . Blessed be the Lord. . . . (We were no longer anything but figures in a tapestry, Clara and I, destinies intertwined by divine fingers, woven together for eternity.) Oh, two parts of the whole at long last joined . . . ! My young friends, I wish you, I wish you. . . . He stopped talking. Amen.

The mass resumed, ever slower; you felt the priest was near breaking point, suddenly exhausted by his calling, by his daily chore of breathing the divine spirit into earthly weakness, of propping up a people hazy in their views with a semblance of scaffolding. He smiled at us, Clara and Gabriel, "My young friends," he wore an apologetic air; you wondered whether he would be able to go on.

After the *Ite missa est,* he approached me.

"I beg your forgiveness. There were so many deaths again this week. . . . I am not so resilient as I used to be, I can no longer move so quickly from one service to another. Given the circumstances I ought really to cancel, to rest, pick things up later on. But I cannot; what would the families say? So forgive me and try to make do with this, this poor ceremony."

I reassured him. No, no, you are mistaken, it was a beautiful wedding.

He looked at me with a smile, "You are too kind"; he didn't believe me. And he returned to the sacristy, slowly, with an old man's walk, one step, then another.

Outside the church the guests were waiting. For the rice throwing, the hurrahs.

"So, Gabriel, what were you doing?" I felt Clara's hip against me and her lips brushing my ear. "Still had some packing to do?"

And we descended the stairway under a triumphal arch of bows, flutes, and metronomes. The impresario had done well; all his new discoveries, his apprentice virtuosos, and even some established ones had come. And the Portuguese student too, the night watchman from the Washington and Albany. All of them, every one, kissed Clara.

In the carriage a heap of telegrams awaited me:

WHAT IS HAPPENING? MINE OVER AND DONE WITH
ANSWER (12:26 P.M.)

OBVIOUSLY RAPID HEARTBEAT WAIT TILL PULSE DOWN TO 80 BEFORE
RESUMING CEREMONY (12:35 P.M.)

WHICH HOSPITAL EVEN IF BAD LUCK AM COMING (12:49 P.M.)

That first of September, like every first of September, must have gone on until nightfall. But Gabriel remembers nothing. There must have been a wedding feast, theatricals, singing perhaps, more telegrams. But Gabriel has in his ear no hubbub, no reminiscent echo of a nuptial party at that hour; and when he closes his lids he fails to see the tiny figures that usually crown the wedding cake, the groom holding his bride's hand while she holds a candle.

But one scene does come back to him, a railroad-station scene. In the gray light filtering through the dirty window, the Knight family, or what is left of it, just three persons now, the reduced Knight family stands on the platform, the train is about to leave, the young newlyweds have lowered the window and are leaning out to talk to those staying behind.

"So it's decided, this time it's rubber?" says Markus.

"Yes, I believe it is decided," replies Gabriel.

"You hadn't told me that rubber requires you to stray so far afield!"

"Yes, yes, I assure you, you were forewarned. The company sends us all abroad before investing us with higher responsibilities."

"Then I misheard; no matter, Gabriel, I have faith in you, you know I have faith in you."

The women swear to write to one another. A loudspeaker asks

those traveling to Rouen and Le Havre to board their train.

"And Gabriel," Elisabeth cries, "we very nearly forgot to tell him goodbye!"

They kiss me on the corner of my lips. For once I am taller than they are. As the wagon lurches into motion, Ann looks me straight in the eye. "Take very good care of yourself, Gabriel, and life will be long."

Elisabeth once again warns Clara never to drink unfiltered water. Now Markus seems not to know us. He compares the time on his watch with that on the great clock hanging like a chandelier above us. People run the length of the train, wave handkerchiefs. Not the three Knights. They stand motionless. The impresario holds his two remaining women, a hand on the nape of each neck. And then they vanish. An adoptive life comes to an end.

*That is how your father (Gabriel) and your grandfather (Louis) were married on the same day. I am telling you all this in so much detail because it is very difficult to make a selection from the various components of your own life. When you are older you will see that once you open the door to memory the past years surge forth, whole or in fragments, but always garrulous, with neither organization nor shame. You and the attorney will each select from them the elements most useful to you, the extenuating circumstances as well as the incriminating ones. To each his allotted task; attorneys defend, sons judge. Naturally. Very well, I'll return to the story. I shall delay the trial no longer, I want the dossier to be complete. You left me on the station platform; here I am on the ship. Will you look like me? Will you love travel as much as I do?*

# 5
# A Crossing

THE TIME HAS COME, now that Gabriel like his illustrious predecessor Christopher Columbus is aboard and cleaving the high seas, the time has come to compare their two experiences.

## *1. Points of Similarity*

Gabriel, like Christopher, had to allay his shipmates' fears.

> Sunday, September 9, 1492.
>
> On this day they lost all sight of land. Fearing they would not see it again for many a day, several among them lamented and wept. The captain comforted them with grand promises of plentiful land and wealth so that they regained hope and lost the apprehension they felt at so long a journey. . . .
>
> This day he sailed nineteen leagues and decided to record somewhat less so that his men should be neither frightened nor discouraged in the event that the voyage went on much longer.

Let us be quite clear: Gabriel's daily labor of appeasement, for better or for worse, did not concern the Booth Line crew (phlegmatic seafaring men) or its regular passengers (planters or practical businessmen) but only Clara, a lost Clara, terrified of the ocean, a Clara whom Gabriel had to take in his arms to protect her from the Atlantic swell with his own rocking, like a voyage within a voyage, like those children who sail their little paper boats in the excessively blue swimming pool of a liner herself plowing through the real (emerald-green) sea.

But if you will admit that marriage for love is a hypothesis as risk-fraught as was that of the earth's roundness in the fifteenth century, the similarities between the crossing of 1492 and that of 1913 become striking.

The first night, just after France disappeared, I took my very young bride to the prow, thinking that her soul would open at the heart-rending spectacle of the setting sun and that I would be able to slip inside it for the night and even longer, so boundless was my optimism in those days. Alas, Clara took but one distracted look at the fiery orange sphere marbled with darker veins (and appearing as if sharks were swimming inside it). She took no interest in the struggle, usually so moving, between the old resisting sun and the leaden clouds pressing upon his brow, the old sun gathering all his remaining strength, becoming scarlet with the effort, the false-hearted clouds impassively increasing the pressure until drowning ensues. Clara was as unimpressed by this killing as by the greenish radiance said to accompany it. She let go of my arm, turned around slowly, and stared out at the liquid wasteland.

She muttered under her breath, "Everything is empty. Look, there are no more things. . . . This is what the whole world will be like once music has prevailed."

Realizing that our love could expect no help from romantic twilights, I led my very young bride to the dining room and seated her in the place that seemed to me the most *real*, the most likely to reassure her, under a lamp between two Argentinian dealers (they sold livestock on the hoof). And throughout dinner I wore myself out steering and sustaining the conversation around the wealth of the pampas, deadly boring, but I hoped it would set Clara's fears to rest and prove to her once and for all that South America, the object of our voyage, did indeed exist, was tangible, dusty in summer, muddy in winter, full of lowing cattle smelling of dung, a continent whose existence was nowhere near dissolution at the hands of music. Alas, she did not listen, nor did she eat; she peered fearfully through the portholes. So I cut short our tour of the pampas. When, at a nod from the chief steward, platters of cheese began arriving on the tables, we rose and returned to our cabin, not to leave it again: a mark of discourtesy everyone gladly forgave, given our newlywed status. ("Your table companions from the first night out have been asking after you," the steward with the Swiss accent told us every day as he brought in our meals with the customary white rose or dwarf hydrangea blossom or carnation sent by the second mate who looked after passenger morale. "What should I tell them, sir, madam?" That all is well, isn't that right, Clara? that all is well. And off he shambled, his footfalls as halting as his accent, to spread the good news—all is well in cabin 18—the crew probably winked knowingly; nothing like a cruise to anchor a love. A paradox, right, lieutenant? A paradox!)

## *2. Points of Difference*

Fundamental.

Catholic Isabella, claiming official duties, remained ashore. Whereas Clara came with me. Christopher Columbus would therefore not have experienced the extremes of communal living, twenty-one days in a red mahogany box pierced to no purpose by a boarded-up porthole and provided with a bed too small for two (one of them endowed with respectable breasts) and yet so large it took up every inch of space between an oval dressing mirror and a nuisance of a hanging wardrobe whose brass handles glittered at night and whose compartments creaked with the swell. As for our cabin doors, one opened just three times a day to admit the Swiss steward and his silver platters, whereas the opening and shutting of the other (which gave access to the delightful comfort station in which everything was in miniature, from the handle of the chain to the width of the mauve paper) were less predictable, as you might expect when you change your eating habits and your time zone all at once.

Come now, you will say, at some point Gabriel must have escaped to smoke a manly cigar on the bridge, to walk in the wind and regain that fine manly solitude alone, face to face with the wild fraternal ocean.

No.

I did not miss one single second of mahogany. I stuck it out right up until the second mate's announcement that the voyage was over, that the salt water was turning fresh. I gorged myself on communal living. I must have sensed that after twenty-one days such a life ends. I hoarded within myself all those womanly gestures, and I now lay them out before you, one by one, souvenirs of a cramped marriage.

Daybreak, a trickle of pale light through the sealed porthole, manifested itself in Clara by the quivering of her nostrils, wingbeats so tiny that only a loving, that is to say, only a watcher with cat's eyes could detect them. Then began the stretching, first the legs, slow undulation of bedclothes and Gabriel's flight to the far edge of the mattress so as not to disturb her, then rotation of the body until finally she lay on her back, her hands emerging from the sheets on each side of her head, two pale butterflies perched at the summit of two white lily stems (her arms), a moan—"Good morning, Gabriel, the sea seems calm today; don't look at me, I look frightful"—a leap from the bed, Clara's back running into the comfort station.

Intermission: Gabriel would close his eyes and calm himself as best he could, with words—she is big, I am small, we are complementary—listening; water flowed, hair crackled under the brush—what electricity! have you ever listened to a storm? "I wonder if Markus has found anything in Poland"—she was talkative only during these moments, to camouflage the sounds of her intimate operations—"you can turn around now, Gabriel, here I am."

Then two possibilities: either the Swiss steward was late, and without wasting a second the newlyweds . . . (I shall return to that), or else the Swiss steward knocked, in which case Clara would cry out, wrap herself up in order to preserve decency (without which the majority of the Swiss drop breakfast trays), and Gabriel, before going to the door, would tuck in the folds of a sheet most decidedly familiar with his wife's derrière (the Knights' chaste term) and breasts.

The time of torture was upon them: a communal meal in a mahogany cabin in which the slightest noise echoed and crashed like thunder.

Clara chewed discreetly, lips closed in the approved manner, whereas Gabriel, terrified at the noises brought on by the smallest mouthful, ate nothing, swallowing only his coffee, thimbleful by thimbleful, stretching his head as far away as possible.

Then followed the hunt for crumbs, seemingly essential before any woman, however ready to endure the worst outrages, can relax, thrashing about and uttering cries of horror the second her thigh or buttock encountered the tiniest speck of croissant or stray particle of toast in the farthest reaches of the bedding. An erotic variant on the childhood tale "The Princess and the Pea," about the girl who detected the presence of the tiny green pellet in her bed despite the intervening layer of five mattresses and thus proved herself truly a princess. Thwacking, then, in every direction, pillows severely chastised, irritable commands: Get up, help me. By the end of the voyage she had commandeered the silver scoop and the soft-bristled waiter's brush that made the rounds of the tables at the end of each meal, after the cheese and before the dessert, purging the tablecloths before the banquet's climactic delight. Such was her assault on our conjugal bed. And at last she said, There, and replaced her tools on the dresser. And . . .

And the caresses we exchanged will remain secret. Secret because they are the best known, the most often repeated, the most dreamed of by animal species for as long as the earth has turned. To unveil them would be to risk losing the heady intoxication of invention. Be very careful if you decide to tell my story. They will write to you (readers are merciless), or someone will raise a finger during your lecture to a culture-hungry Lion's Club: There is nothing very new in what you have so blushingly outlined for us, my dear sir, my wife and I (we live in Chamonix), Roseline and I started doing the things you are talking about every week, at least thirty years ago, well before the spread of the railways. . . .

Be as quick as you can to learn modesty in the matter of erotic propriety, it will protect you from countless disappointments. Don't emulate Gabriel, who spent those twenty-one days at sea puffed up with pride and confident in the belief that he had invented a new position, fondly and frequently recalling that glorious spectacle, Clara in front of him on all fours, and he, the inventor, behind her, drawing unending bliss from this memory until the melancholy night in Tournus, much later, at the start of the thirties, when he landed in the Hôtel Le Rempart (for what reason, an automobile race?) and found on the night table a specialized manual in which he read, with supporting iconographic references, that the famous discovery had been in practice since the Hittites and was referred to as "the doggy position" in the oldest of all systems of hieroglyphics.

The doggy position, then, in the course of which (and this is the only one of those caresses Gabriel will reveal) Clara turned her head toward her invader and gave him a half-wearied, half-comic look: are all these acrobatics truly Catholic?

When it was all over the newlyweds implored one another, "Swear you won't look at me while I'm asleep"; so they swore, they slept, and, of course, the first to awake broke the promise. Often Gabriel emerged from a dream and felt the sun's warmth of Clara's two eyes traveling over his face and body. Terrified, he would pretend to be still asleep, then, still blindly, would draw his very young wife into loving, less from love than from fear: to end that scrutiny as quickly as possible, that scrutiny that might truly (as they say) "open her eyes" and drive Clara (what am I doing naked next to this naked man?) to flee him forever.

Other actions of Clara's were harder to catch and are therefore remembered with the peculiar relish familiar to all collectors. They were part of her daily grooming ritual, the secret backstage activities of a woman, and were captured only with the stealth of a Sioux, with the patience of a crocodile, long feigned sleeps ("What luck that you are a heavy sleeper, Gabriel!"), eyelids raised millimeter by millimeter ("I'm sure you're not sleeping; if you watch me plucking my eyebrows, Gabriel, I'll leave you").

At the very heart of his collection in that treasure chest of intimate activities, Gabriel (to avoid boring those less fascinated by women than he—all tastes, and even alas indifference, are to be found in nature), Gabriel will acquaint you with just two, his favorites: your very young bride sitting spread-eagled on the floor and leaning forward, her left hand grasping curly black hairs and pulling gently while the right, armed with mustache scissors (Gabriel's), prepares to clip a tuft deemed (how mistakenly!) too abundant by its owner. The second intimate image is more childlike, almost a masquerade, as if she had pulled on a clown's loose white fancy dress trousers, Clara bent double in the miniature tub of the comfort station, nothing but a calf visible, sheathed in white, a woman's secret recipe (milk of sweet almonds? sap of rare herbs?), fingers, her fingers, clenched around the little gray block of pumice, polishing the leg, progressing, stroke by stroke, toward the ultimate sweetness, seat of the most painful regrets, maker of exiles. . . . And as evening fell (not quite dark, the sea's phosphorescence through the sealed porthole and a yellow gleam from the wardrobe handles, Clara folded herself in two, cuddled up within herself, like a foundling in a floating wicker basket—"Good night, Gabriel"; "Sleep well, Clara"—and off she went alone, I have no idea where, to roam the night.

I have not unveiled everything. There are still tricks up the magician's sleeve, four realities, the inner aspect of the left upper thigh, inner aspect of the right upper thigh, oh, miracle of places spared abrasive contact, the outskirts of the black forest like two frozen gestures, you have only to gaze at them to feel caressed, at peace with the world. And then those two so sorely underrated popliteal hollows of which most women know nothing, not even their address (behind the knees) and of whose value they are unaware, a grain of sand in an hourglass, the lukewarm brine of a slack tide, two plus two and there are the four capitals of sweetness.

There, the visit is over. These twenty-one red mahogany days, ladies and gentlemen, are *proof* (a) that Clara exists, (b) that I too have led a communal life.

You require evidence? Nothing easier. Go to London, capital of the Real, headquarters of the Lloyd's insurance company that knows where every ship in the world ever has been, is, and ever shall be, day by day. Open the register to the year 1913, autumn, check under Booth Line, steamship *Wellington,* passenger list, letter O, the very young M. and Mme. Orsenna, no extra baggage, guests on September 23 at the captain's table,* uneventful crossing.

Those twenty-one days also furnish proof that the Orsennas make progress from generation to generation: remember, Marguerite's love lasted just one week.

*Forgive this small inaccuracy on Lloyd's part: in fact, we declined the invitation. I have kept it as a souvenir, ornate card embossed with dolphins, unintelligible Latin motto.

# 6

# *Gabriel in Love*

## I

WE FINALLY ventured out.

So long had we roamed within the confines of our cabin, sometimes swept away by our bodies, sometimes basking in the sunlight of our feelings, that a kind of vertigo had taken hold of us. We longed for something solid, something safe, a land, if possible a continent. I had assured Clara so often of Latin America's existence that she now wanted to find out for herself. After twenty-one days she was close to believing that everything was a dream, a dream and a lie. She stared at me with the strangest of expressions, as if I had spun Latin America from cobwebs, as if I had told so many untrue stories that I myself was fictitious.

So one fine morning we pushed open the red mahogany door and like all liberated prisoners blinked in the light.

"They're out, the French couple has come out!" The news ran through the ship. "Bravo, France!" "Twenty-one days!" The captain wanted to meet us.

"Because I do enjoy young people!"

It was his expression. He never tired of saying it to us.

"Come up on the bridge with me, the view there is so much better, and I do enjoy young people. . . .

"If you're bored, feel free to go to my cabin and find yourselves books to read, because I do enjoy young people. . . ."

And the steward who knocked on our door around 10 A.M. without coming in used exactly the same words:

"The captain would like you to join him at his table, because he does enjoy young people."

He sometimes puts his hand on my knee, Clara would tell me in the evening. But no more than that. Just a captain's hand doing nothing on my knee. Don't go making a ridiculous scene, now. . . . This passion for young people was a secret between us. He never confided it to anyone else. But he would regale Clara and me, a hand on each of our shoulders, with his view of the world. He believed that time was a landlubberly notion. At sea, you understand, time doesn't exist. In port, that's where the trouble starts. Believe me, if we didn't have to put into port we would never age at all! Look at me: I'm fifty-five. How old would you have guessed, Clara, forty? Forty-five? In his opinion sailors withstood age better than other human beings. Look at seaports: most ships don't come in and tie up, they drop anchor out in the harbor approaches. They don't want to be contaminated by time.

Once their curiosity was satisfied (what will these French newlyweds look like after twenty-one days?) the passengers took a dislike to us because of Clara's regal habit of rising abruptly during a meal: "Are you coming, Gabriel? It's too, too boring here."

It was not the politest of formulations. But at bottom she was right. Conversation had begun to languish the moment the ship left London, and now our table companions had only the scrapings of the conversational barrel to offer one another, like dinner guests infinitely protracting their small talk because it will not stop raining outside.

"What's happening to the Atlantic?"

The whole dining room rushed to the portholes or out on deck.

All but the seasoned travelers, old hands at the crossing, who merely exchanged grins and winks.

"No need to worry," the captain told us, "it's like this every time."

We rose in our turn and followed the others.

A wide dark stain, the blue of the past few weeks, was falling away behind the stern ensign. Everywhere else the sea was ocher.

"This is fresh water we're in. The River Amazon is so powerful it washes everything out to sea. Soon there'll be no Latin America left."

Leaning over Clara, the captain continued his lesson.

"I too sometimes feel I'm gradually slipping out to sea."

"Come now, captain," said Clara.

I was not looking at them. But I could swear she had laid her hand on his uniform or at least on his captain's gold braid. I was getting to know her. I knew that such and such a tone of voice corresponded to such and such a movement of her body.

This freshwater harbinger of land somewhat dampened the excitement of our arrival. When Latin America finally appeared, there were no oohs or ahs. The passengers gazed in silence at the low line on the horizon. There were no cliffs.

"That's forest," someone said.

"But they told me there would be gigantic trees," replied a woman's voice, close to tears.

The old hands stayed inside playing whist and drinking mint juleps and whiskey sours, the last few quaffs of the crossing. They joked with John and Pedrinho, the two bartenders, making them promise: You'll remind us now, won't you, if we should happen to forget your tip in the confusion of landing. . . ? Clara would not leave her seat by the piano because of the fan turning just overhead. I delayed a long time before going back out on deck. There was something cloying about the aura of farewells hanging over the ship. And in the advice people offered me: You'd best get out there sharpish, young man, or you'll miss the estuary. . . .

The ship was steaming slowly up a wide shoreless arm of the sea. The forest marched into the river, the river flowed into the forest. An Italian couple rolled terrified eyes.

"Do you think there will be any dry land at all?"

They had planned to open an automobile business and were already talking of going back, "But we sold everything we owned in Milan; it was you who insisted on coming." Gradually their consternation gave way to an angry scene.

A seaman was bombarded with questions.

"Is all of Brazil like this?"

"Is it always as hot as this?"

"Is the sky always so overcast?"

He mumbled a yes here and a no there and confided that steerage passengers were sometimes so disappointed that it was necessary to turn a fire hose on them to soothe their feelings.

The ship was moving slower than ever. A small fleet now possessed the channel: canoes flush with the water, boats with blood-red lateen sails and hulls of every hue, orange, white, pale blue. The passengers wanted to know if these were Indians. The captain, where is the captain? He should be telling us! I turned my head in every direction. This was Brazil. Brazil, at long last! The forest full of wild rubber. The world's storehouse of elasticity and bounce. Long live Brazil, our hero chanted with undeniable bombast. He pulled his red rubber ball from his pocket. In the shelter of the lifeboats where no one could see him, he abandoned himself to his favorite pastime. Greetings, Brazil, long live Brazil. Brazil, here I come! Then quite suddenly Brazil disappeared: Bye-bye, Monsieur Gabriel, see you tomorrow. Night had fallen. (At the equator the sun does not set, the sky is already too low for that; it suddenly flees, the horizon swallows it, and it is night.) The air turned black, the heat of the air turned black, and was instantly striated with sounds as if the day, in departing, had opened the door to the pack, to the infinite multitude of sounds held muzzled by the light: shrieks, birdcalls, croakings, an animal screaming in the distance; the whole world crackled. And from the water all around the liner, from the total darkness of the water, conversations, laughter, and whisperings rose from the canoes.

Huddled against one another, the passengers fell silent.

"Have these savages been pacified?" a man asked in a shrill voice. "Could they climb on board in spite of our height?"

I returned to the bar. The old hands were grouped around the pianist. They must have roused him from a brief nap. The poor Englishman had not even had time to put his shirt on properly; you could see his chest, small nipples sagging amid russet hairs. Please, please, I haven't stopped playing since London; let me be. But the regulars wanted music. They forced him to drink. Mr. Süshind, a sturdy businessman from Hamburg for whom I felt a real liking because he did not stare at Clara, grabbed the unhappy musician by the nape of his neck and forced his head toward the keyboard.

"All right, all right, I'll play."

He began with "God Save the King." The officers sprang to attention. The old hands raised their glasses. And at once the night replied: at first a little sporadic hand clapping from the canoes down on the water, then whistles, rhythmic chuckles, crashes, the whole river, forest calling to forest, wished long life to the king of England; then in like manner it accompanied the "Marseillaise," *abreuve nos sil-*

*lons, sillons, sillão,* the Brazilians on board crowding around Clara, Victor Hugo, Mademoiselle, Auguste Comte. . . .

And so it was that on October 3, 1913, the steamship *Wellington* arrived off Belém do Pará.

John, the head bartender, had advised us to wait. ("Since Madame Clara dislikes crowds, and it's bedlam here when a ship comes in from Europe, believe me, you'd do better to wait until the crowd thins out. You can keep me company while I take stock.")

He had lined up all the bottles on the bar and was taking inventory, a notebook in his hand.

"It's strange, you know. On some crossings, people drink. On others, not."

Around us and in the passageways the hullaballoo was gradually dying away. Clara swept the bottles with her gaze, smiling a stray, fleeting, pallid smile. The existence of Latin America, henceforth confirmed, was of no comfort. She knew that soon we would have to get up and leave the ship. I think she would gladly have stayed aboard for the return voyage, even if it simply meant coming back again. After all, the crossing was a kind of adoptive life. I had my vocation to help me, but she . . . I stroked her wrist, where the veins are. She did not notice. The bartender continued to expound on the state of his supplies.

"Well, well, only two years ago I would have been out of curaçao by now. These days nobody asks for it."

For long minutes now not a single form had passed by the portholes. Except for the distant rumble of her engines, the *Wellington* had fallen silent again.

So I took my very young wife's hand. The bartender wished us good luck without raising his head.

We walked down the gangplank behind our trunk, hefted by two seamen. They made heavy work of it and complained: Thank God this is the last one; what do they have in here? (Beginner's mistake: I had given them their tip in advance.) They dumped it at the feet of waggish Customs men who were already pointing at the Washington and Albany label.

"Paris?"

"Hotel in Paris."

They rummaged at leisure through Clara's underwear.

And there we were in the Brazilian night, the two of us, my new young wife and I, seated on our trunk that here and there sported the Washington and Albany label, place des Pyramides and rue de Rivoli, hot and cold running water, elevator, telephone (Paris).

After a while a white suit approached us.

"You wouldn't be . . . ?"

He spoke French with no accent but oddly enriched with superlatives.

"I had begun absolutely to lose hope. I told myself that you had not come because of recent most sinister events."

"Forgive us, my wife was briefly taken ill."

"Oh, what dreadfully sad news, and how is she now?"

Fully recovered. Restored to health.

"Most excellent. Then let us lose no time. Allow me to introduce myself: Loïc Huet, Monsieur Revol's secretary. And Madame Revol will be anxious. They are giving a dinner in your honor."

We loaded the trunk into a brand-new Voisin that moved very slowly because of the potholes, if you can call such quagmires potholes. The secretary wanted my opinion. Did I think relations between France and Germany would continue to deteriorate, as people were saying? Were we headed ineluctably toward tragedy? I did not answer. I was too busy trying to remain seated amid all this jolting. And between bumps Clara bade me never again—do you hear me?—never use her health as an excuse.

The dinner was the same as all such dinners: a meal to welcome anyone just in from the other side of the world. An immutable scenario, familiar to all travelers. Good evening, I hope you're not too tired? You'll find the time change easy to get used to, whereas the heat . . . speaking of which, how's the weather in France these days? The hungry homesickness of the exile: How is the Marne, how is Nogent, how is the post office, how is Fallières, how are the banks of the Seine, how is *Le Figaro,* how is Montmartre, and Lucas-Carton, and the separation of church and state?

"Let him eat," said Mme. Revol, our hostess. "Speaking of which, have fashions changed? What's become of Worth?"

Clara was watching me with bemused eyes as I struggled to keep up my end of the conversation. Let me see now, I met this young man at the Washington and Albany, Room 212, and here I am this evening eating chicken *basquaise* at the edge of the jungle; what is happening to me?

At all these welcoming dinners they introduce you to local Francophiles, generally as the cheese course draws near.

"You know," said Mme. Revol, "our friends the Velosos are great lovers of France."

"Delighted."

"Oh, yes, João here did some of his architectural studies in Paris."

"Let me think back now, what was that street called, Rasmaille?"

"Boulevard Raspail."

"That's it. Boulevard Raspail, wonderful, wonderful memories!"

"Not another word, João, or else your wife, Branca—on your right, Gabriel, I hope you don't mind, it's our custom here to go by first names, because of the heat—or else Branca will start to get ideas." Our hostess (heavy waves of musk) leaned toward me. "Branca is one of the driving forces behind the Alliance Française."

"I do hope you won't be too bored. Time here just stands still."

"My dear, you exaggerate. What about yesterday's concert? You missed a magnificent evening of Schubert, with performers brought all the way from New York."

Terrified, I looked at Clara. Luckily she had heard nothing. Almost asleep, she was swaying slightly in her seat.

M. Revol was explaining. "My wife is from Brittany, a Breton from Dinard. So, of course . . ."

I went along with him. "Yes, of course."

The dinner ended amicably. Later, over coffee, I tried to ask a few questions of a professional nature. "Well, what about the rubber industry?"

"Tomorrow, tomorrow, when you've had some rest; rubber can wait!"

"Just what I was telling you," said the Breton lady from Dinard. "Everything waits here. You are exhausted, my dear Clara. I know just how you feel. Guy will take you home right away."

But the Francophiles protested. They drove us home. You will dine with us tomorrow night. What luck to have you here. I've heard that you're a great expert on Auguste Comte. What a stroke of luck; enjoy your stay in Belém. You should have seen it during the boom. Oh, no, you'll see, the boulevard, what was the name again? Raspail. Ah, yes, Raspail and Montparnasse.

Clara had dozed off on my shoulder.

Then the Francophiles' car stopped. They pointed out at the night.

"It's at the very end, the house is most charming. Enjoy your stay in Brazil."

We walked trustingly into the darkness, unable to see a thing, except for a white form emerging little by little, a form that spoke. "Ah, madame, ah, monsieur"—I translated for Clara, my linguistic abilities, acquired in London, coming back to me without too much trouble—"impossible to turn the lights on because of the mosquitoes, Jesus be praised, this is your house, all right, put your trust in Jesus, watch how you go; I am Rosa Marcelina; France is the eldest daughter of the church; the bed is made, sleep well, daylight will bring you the house, thanks be to Jesus and Mary."

My new young wife collapsed under the double mosquito netting. I ran my fingertips down the length of her body: it was as moist as it had been at the Washington and Albany. And I was afraid, my eyes wide open in the darkness, I trembled at the thought that I might not be the equal of a climate that could impart to my new young wife, only just landed and not yet knowing anyone, the same moist warmth as at the Washington and Albany. Several times I thought it was daybreak. Equatorial cocks crow all night long.

Clara smiled. Smiled and slept. Lost no doubt in some deliciously cooling dream of Central Europe, perhaps a sleigh ride, or else an after-concert supper in Warsaw. Gabriel went out onto the balcony alone. Before him, Belém sprawled along the banks of the ocher river as far as the eye could see. Daybreak. Gabriel recalled the advice given him by his positivist friends in London: Beware, beware of the equator's spell. Don't let the tropics bewitch you. For such magic is the opposite of progress. Once you're over there, Gabriel, all you have to do is dissect the charm and note its ingredients. That's the best way to protect yourself from it.

Daybreak. Elbows on his balcony, Gabriel applied himself to his task. What are the precise phases of the breaking of day in Belém (Brazil)?

First the light. It was like a punctiliously observed agreement between two powers. After centuries of negotiation, shadow and sunlight had divided the city between them. Every morning they retreated unprotestingly to demarcation lines calculated down to the last millimeter. For shadow: the alleyways, the mango-lined walks, church porches, warehouse eaves. For sunlight: all the rest, the squares, the ocher river, the too-broad avenues, the open carriages, the hackneys, incautious bald-headed men.

Then the heat. Pressed on the town like printing on a blank page, heavier and heavier, hour by hour, crushing. And coming from straight overhead; flight was useless. But heat's tyranny was not passively accepted. Barely awake, still groggy, the heat was vulnerable to attack. Gabriel watched from his balcony as battle stations were manned. Traps were set: armies of ventilators resuming their daily chore as night faded, a little naked girl's bedroom door set ajar to create a draft, a big black man and his lighter-skinned helper delivering ice blocks. The black man drove the cart, his helper running alongside, pausing at all the imposing-looking residences to deposit a hoary block that was quickly pulled inside by the hand within. The wagon kept moving. The strategy was obvious: harass the enemy. Isolate pieces of heat and quietly destroy them. . . . Urban guerrilla warfare.

Finally, the colors. They came from the ocher river in launches converging on the marketplace: the greens and yellows of fruit, the reds and blues of caged parrots, the glossy blue-greens of *surucucu* fish, the paler tints of sea cow, the spotted splash of jaguar hides, the black of twists of tobacco, the knobbled sepia of alligator skin—all these glowing hues miraculously torn from the dull emerald monochrome of the forest. While from the city, from the city's houses, other less colorful denizens came out, with the more subdued shades of everyday life: heaps of hammocks woven from raw hemp, cartloads of brown water filters, boots, machetes, black medicine boxes, bottles full of roots, flesh-and-blood crucifixions, blue Madonnas, varnished sandals. . . .

Now the women came out to shop in orange, violet, purple, and snow-white dresses—Negresses, mulattoes, Portuguese women, German women—and men seated themselves on the ground, backs against the walls, heads lolling between their knees, only their straw hats and their floppy blue pants visible. Photographers set up their fat boxes on long giraffe legs, and dogs began to prowl and children to run; suddenly heat, light, shadow and sunlight, colors and sounds, all were mingled; the city teemed. Day had broken.

To avoid succumbing to the spell (enemy of civilization) on his very first morning, our hero left his balcony and set forth.

"The *travessa* Campos Salles, please?"

The replies were an early barometer of local conditions.

"Ten years ago you would just have followed the crowd."

"Clearly the gentleman enjoys being depressed!"

Guy Revol, the company's agent, was waiting on the veranda.

"You should try to be on time, Gabriel."

"I'm sorry, monsieur, but I got lost and—"

"Oh, I mention it purely for your own sake. You'll find that punctuality is a pillar of strength in these places because, frankly, local work habits . . . And call me Guy. We're both in the same boat, if I may say so to someone who has just landed."

Revol's body was a curious piling up of component parts: a very round head set on very narrow shoulders, swelling just below into a respectable stoutness perched on a pair of bony legs lost farther down in flapping beige trousers.

He looked at Gabriel with kindly eyes.

"They've recalled all my assistants one by one since the slump began, all transferred to Asia, the Saigon region. Some of them still write. They don't advise me to come. They're dying of boredom on those plantations. Of course we're bored here as well (you'll find that out soon enough, Gabriel), but it's nothing compared to boredom on the plantations."

He seemed delighted to have found someone to talk to. Someone with whom to discuss the different forms of boredom in this world.

"We'll take care of your new young wife, don't you worry; all will be well."

Gabriel too, since the end of the twenty-first day, had tried to make himself very young. Everyone wants to protect very young people. A humanitarian reflex. Like helping a blind man to cross. And Gabriel, whose new young wife was busy sleeping, sleeping and smiling, wanted to be protected.

Along the alleyway men in white shirts sat waiting by telephones. At some invisible sign a child rose, went to fetch drinks from the tavern, came back with a tray. Then nothing moved, except for the drinkers' hands and the speakers' lips in continuous low-voiced conversation. From time to time, someone would address the official in charge of transatlantic cables, a young black in a blue cap. Yes, Galileo? Nothing, senhor.

Guy Revol led him on a tour of the premises, a kind of gigantic log cabin, pale green with shuttered blinds.

"We used to call this our headquarters, the company's central headquarters in Brazil. Who would dream of calling it a headquarters now? Would you, Gabriel?"

Walking through the empty rooms, Guy recited the names of all the employees who had once sat in those chairs, had once kept those books.

"Many have gone back to France. The rest were Brazilian."

"What about you, Guy?"

"They wanted me to stay, just in case. . . . Apparently the fever could flare up again any time. If so, they want to have someone reliable on the spot. But in fact I'm closing up shop, as gradually as possible."

"And what will my job be in all this?"

"Oh, you! You'll probably be the only one doing anything at all useful for the home office. Come along, I'll explain."

We went back along a different set of corridors. Guy introduced me to two clucking secretaries and to Alberto, a gaunt mulatto with white temples and a wide smile: he had been there since before the boom.

"I've put him in charge of records. If you need to know anything about the past, he's the man to ask."

We were back on the veranda, seated at a mahogany table. From the ocher river rose a faint, almost cooling whisper of breeze.

"As you see, this is the best part of the building to be in until around eleven o'clock. After that, until siesta time, I move on to my second office, at the western end of the building. My third office, in the evenings, is in the east. You'll soon have your own little itinerary worked out! That's the good thing about empty buildings. You're free to choose any spot you please."

"And my job, Guy, what will my job be in all this?"

"Well, now. The company has lent money, lots of money, to the *seringueiros,* the people who used to tap the rubber out there under the trees all over Amazonia. Money for essential supplies, Gabriel, tobacco, alcohol, guns. . . . Their debts are nowhere near repaid, and they must be collected quickly because, with the slump, they will be less and less able to pay us back. Your job is to recover this money, Gabriel, do you understand? Apparently the company considers these debts very important, but surely they told you all this over there? I have calculated the total amounts, region by region. We will plan your trip together. I wonder whether your very young bride—"

"So my job is really to put us out of business?"

"Well, yes. . . . Like me, Gabriel, like me! They don't say so officially, but I have the feeling the company wants to pull out of this territory. You and I are the last two left in Latin America. After that we'll have to make up our minds to leave for Asia, for that's where the future lies, or else give up rubber altogether. Do you want to go to Asia, Gabriel?"

"I don't know, possibly."

"That's right, you're young. But I'm no longer flexible enough. First Europe, then Africa, for I've served my term in Africa too. We couldn't have children, my wife and I, so of course . . . always ready to travel. But you reach an age when you balk at changing continents. You'll get that way too, Gabriel."

Just then a telephone rang across the alleyway.

"See what it is, Alberto," said Guy Revol. "One last piece of advice, Gabriel: in these countries it's best to wait until noon before you start drinking."

The records keeper was across the alley in a few strides. He was back at once with his wide smile.

"Yes?" asked Guy Revol.

"Nothing, senhor, the same price as yesterday."

"In other words, rock bottom. Nothing but war will make it pick up again. Wars are extremely good for raw materials; you must learn that, Gabriel. You should have seen the commotion during the boom, right, Alberto?"

"Oh, yes, senhor."

"The whole city was here, the telephones never stopped ringing, the yelling burst your eardrums—How many dollars to the pound? Who wants a thousand tons of grade A?—there was never enough beer in the tavern, do you remember, Alberto?"

The records keeper nodded his head: oh, yes, senhor.

"Ah, noon already," said Guy Revol.

Alberto rose; the records keeper was also the bartender.

"Nowadays of course we have all the beer we need. . . ."

Baba Rosa Marcelina was waiting for Gabriel, standing with three letters in her hand. "Monsieur, monsieur, what has happened, oh, monsieur"—and she brandished the envelopes above her head—"oh, monsieur, oh, Lord-Mary-Jesus, it's not my fault; you will curse me and it's not my fault. . . ."

"Of course it's not your fault," said Gabriel. "But what is not your fault?"

And he gently took the letters from her, two of them from France—"They must have come in on the same boat as us, do you realize, Clara?" he shouted—and a third in unfamiliar handwriting, with no return address, a message from Belém. Later, Gabriel said to himself. First the news from Levallois.

Gabriel,

1. I have measured the Atlantic from Brest to your Belém: well over 6,000 miles unless I am mistaken. Is the distance between you and your father now sufficient? The next step would have to be the Antipodes. Is this what you are contemplating? Do please keep me informed.

2. I have studied Belém's location on the map. Agreed, you are not strictly speaking in the forest. But admit to your old father that this Belém of yours is completely surrounded by trees. This being the case, Gabriel, here is an abridged list of the illnesses to which you will most assuredly succumb, unless you return with all haste. It is Science addressing you, not I; do you think you are above Science? Here it is, then: First amoebic dysentery—diarrhea is no kind of life, Gabriel—and of course malaria, including its most hideous form, *Plasmodium*

*falciparum,* or else leishmaniasis; do you want ulcers all over your face, Gabriel, do you think Clara will like that? And what about onchocercosis; I know you don't miss your father, but is that any reason to go blind? I shall make no mention of meningitis, of cholera, or even of the plague, those you might catch just strolling through one of our own charming cities in the south of France. Oh, and smallpox; have you been vaccinated? And leprosy, Gabriel, are you aware that leprosy and scrotal elephantiasis are endemic to Brazil? Forgive all this detail but a father must tell his son everything, can you picture yourself advancing on your new bride with balls as big as watermelons, yes, almost trailing on the ground, do you truly imagine that even an immense love, that even the love she feels for you could survive such a hideous sight? Think about it, Gabriel, you're a man now; you must lead your own life. But please, never, never venture into the forest. I have not mentioned the complications that will inevitably—do you hear me? *inevitably*—erupt the second you set foot in that green rotting mass. Weigh it carefully: on one side, the above-mentioned horrors (abridged, Gabriel, don't forget, highly abridged). And on the other, the curse with which your father might be afflicted in matters of love, and I do mean "might." For this curse is still a mere hypothesis, and my happiness these past few days would tend to prove that the curse is losing its potency. But let us wait for confirmation. If I were truly happy for a long time with a woman, you would come back, wouldn't you, Gabriel? You would no longer have any reason to risk your life in those festering climes. Your answer, which I expect will be affirmative, oh, certainly affirmative, gives me courage to continue in this insane enterprise called marriage.

3. For I have started out well in married life, Gabriel. This time it's happening, do you hear, all my eggs are in one basket, including the rotten ones. Without rotten eggs a marriage cannot succeed, Gabriel, you must learn to live with them, and swallow them from time to time—indeed, every day—since that's what seems to be required.

A big kiss and a hug from your Louis of old; you would have trouble recognizing him, he's improved so much.

P.S.: If you think I'm lying or have invented all these diseases—I know you believe me capable of such chicanery, yes, I know it—then ask around you; there must be an honest doctor there, not a Brazilian of course, he would claim that his country is as clean as Greenland, but a Swiss, the Swiss are the most sensitive in matters of hygiene, or write directly to France, not through me, to the Pasteur Institute in Paris; they'll tell you.

My Gabriel,

Answer me honestly: is life different in a *very big country* (sixteen times the size of France if I am to believe Louis)? What is the predominant feeling, one of finally having *space* or one of affiliation at long last with *power?* Answer quickly, I need to know.

There is another question I would like to ask you, but with all your ideas about modernity your answer cannot fail to be biased: Can a republic manage so vast a territory? Don't you think it would have been better to remain an empire?

Be careful when you reply. I imagine all correspondence is censored out there in the tropics, and I wouldn't want to hurt your career, even if I don't always understand it. But everyone chooses his own life, everyone except Marguerite, for had it not been for her state of mourning, you see, she would not now be living on the Île de la Jatte (where your room, facing the Neuilly bridge, is waiting for you), but in Fashoda or Lang Son.

Lovingly,
Marguerite.

I am not leaving you. I am going away, Gabriel. If the fear keeps on, what is the point in being two?

Clara.

It was thus that Gabriel made the acquaintance of his new young wife's handwriting: decisive, somewhat angular, the words all connected. He raised his head. Rosa Marcelina had not moved, white eyeballs still rolling, hands still clasped.

"Madame didn't leave anything else?"

"Oh, no, monsieur!"

"Madame didn't say anything else?"

"Oh, no, monsieur!"

But can you say you truly know a person's writing from a single line? Handwriting experts tell us no.

So Gabriel asked no further question, did not raise his voice, did not call out to his new young wife, *Where are you?* Did not rush down to the docks, did not tearfully search the house from top to bottom, opened no cupboard, no drawer, did not look at the bed, did not bury his face in the right-hand pillow where a trace of her scent must still linger, uncorked no bottle, neither whiskey nor gin nor *cachaça,* did not let fly with a kick at the little yellow dog, last night's parting gift from the Francophiles (to keep you company, madame, until you have a baby) and christened by her George Sand, shredded no photograph, did not crumple into a ball the twenty-two-word letter, *I am not leaving you. I am going away, Gabriel. If the fear keeps on, what is the point in being two?,* did not put it to the flames with his flint lighter, sent no telegram to the Île de la Jatte nor to the almost-palatial Washington and Albany in Paris, did not run feverish hands through his hair, did not vomit into the swiveling bowl that served as a washbasin, did not violently rip the mosquito netting to shreds, did not take out his rage on the door, no more on that royal-blue Brazilian door than on all the other doors in the world that never keep anyone in, and especially not wives, did not snivel, did not shout *There she is!* at the first crunch of footsteps outside in the street on the other side of the bougainvilleas. Gabriel Orsenna sat down, he took a wicker chair, quite similar to the one called Mexican in his youth, he dragged it from the living room onto the veranda (and the noise that it made was utterly normal, the noise of a chair dragged over a wooden floor in anybody's house), from the living room to the veranda to take advantage of the cool of the evening, he made certain he could see a stretch of the ocher river through the mango trees, and he sat down. And remained seated in that same spot for exactly ninety-three days.

## II

Don't expect a blow-by-blow account of this disaster from Gabriel.

Engineers have their pride.

Understand simply that it was a disease, a disease that attacked hours, minutes, and seconds the way poliomyelitis attacks the muscles: time was paralyzed; time no longer went forward.

Many poets, many women of a certain age, many weekend philosophers (like the captain of the steamship *Wellington*) have begged heaven to visit them with that very disease: O time arrest your flight!

Politely but firmly, Gabriel would have them put an immediate end to such arrant nonsense and officially rescind their prayers, for time standing still is the sharpest of all pains.

Time was dead, and what could you do when time was dead? Open your eyes? Room 212 at once appeared, just beyond the Brazilian garden between the aviary full of sleeping macaws, yellow, red, and blue, and the white gateway. Close your eyes? To see the bed in Room 212? And Clara's head above the sheets? Open your eyes again? To see Clara's interminable thighs you had only to follow down, down to the state of absolute bliss, the very heart of the adoptive life. Close them again? Clara was still there. As was Room 212. An engineer can weigh the evidence: time was indeed dead, no need to hold a mirror to its nostrils or check its pulse. And Gabriel felt that death within him, felt like a woman for feeling such a presence inside him, a doomed woman bearing a corpse *in utero,* the still, cold body of a very young bride who was no longer there. At one point he sat bolt upright in his chair, startling George Sand, who barked. But he very soon slumped back again. What good is flight? There is no escape when time is dead. How can you kill time, how can you assault something already dead?

So Gabriel remained sitting in a wicker chair on the veranda for ninety-three days. To keep him company, Rosa Marcelina surrounded him with everyday household objects: the portable washbasin, the revolving bookcase reserved for treatises on rubber, the box containing all Louis's telegrams since the dawn of time, a small table of rough-cut bamboo, a lectern with the day's periodicals, and the grandfather clock whose pendulum swung unavailingly to and fro, fooling no one. At night, Rosa Marcelina hung above him a double thickness of mosquito netting, turned out all the lights, and, leaving him under the protection of São João, São Sesfredo, São Alavico, Santa Rosa, São Zé, São Raymundo, São Ribaldo, São Marcio, São Felisberto, and Santa Otacilia, she wished him good night and disappeared.

Just now Gabriel hinted to you of privacy. Don't accept this unquestioningly. His misfortune became the favorite spectacle of the people of Belém, a goal for family walks, the subject of every conversation. People came to watch this seriously lovesick Frenchman sitting motionless on a veranda. People observed that France was clearly equal to her reputation. Women turned on their men: You would never love me like that. Parents scolded children whose first impulse was to throw fruit, eggs, and even pebbles at the sufferer. People wondered whether the disease might be contagious. They decided not. So they edged stealthily closer, as close as possible to the veranda, to learn the details and discuss possible cures. What could be done in cases of acute lovesickness? Everyone had his own approach. For Rosa Marcelina the strategy was obvious: first, ceaselessly remind all the saints that they had work to do on earth and would be better occupied helping humans than snoozing in heaven; second, increase the dose of pepper in the food. And when she saw Gabriel wince as he swallowed a chicken *moqueça* or a piece of grilled *surucucu,* then guzzle down pint after pint of water, cheeks aflame, forehead slick with sweat, she would raise her hands heavenward; Oh, Mary, mother of God and ever virgin no matter what went on up there, *seu* Gabriel is warming up, recovery must be near. Such a diet wreaks havoc on the intestines. Rosa Marcelina didn't care. Very gently, with little tugs, she removed the sufferer's trousers, to the great joy of the onlookers, who cried out, Oh, what beautiful buttocks, they're so white; are Frenchmen's buttocks always so white? Rosa Marcelina paid no attention. She washed the sufferer's trousers, scrubbing vigorously and fondly in the stone tank behind the house. And then she hung them up and waited for them to dry without taking her eyes off them (a great many of the local women would willingly have stolen them as relics). The crowd's greatest disappointment was Dr. Lezama, his studies at the University of Lisbon notwithstanding, who paced around the patient, muttering, "Oh my, I've seen this before, I've seen it before, no doubt an acute allergy, but to what, Lord God in heaven? I must have inoculated him against every single tropical antigen by now, one by one," and back he went, more crestfallen than a schoolboy in a dunce cap, to attend to his regular patients. M. and Mme. Revol didn't know the secret for setting time in motion again, either. They would arrive one after the other toward the end of the morning, after the announcement of rubber futures (unchanged, still at rock bottom).

"You can get me something to drink, Rosa, a beer, but put some water in it. Whew! This heat; it makes it hard to talk but talk we must. Gabriel, I know what love is; Gabriel, we too, Mme. Revol and I, we also went through our period of doubt. And believe me, to doubt is to suffer! So there you are, Gabriel, love is no excuse. You must pull yourself together. Lean on your vocation, Gabriel. Few men are lucky enough to have something so solid as a true vocation to lean on, a vocation such as yours. And you know that I am ready to help you, that the company is ready to help you, but please, you have to do your part."

Mme. Revol would arrive a little later. Showing exemplary tact she always chose a seat some distance from her husband, so as not to let on that they were a couple. And she smiled most sweetly at Gabriel throughout the visit, and as they left together she would turn and wave goodbye just as she passed through the little gateway and disappeared behind the leaves.

The Revols were not very successful. They failed to draw crowds. Whereas General Manager Abel, director of the Hôtel de Paris, basked in public popularity. He never appeared alone. He was always followed by a multitude eager for his stories. For General Manager Abel was regarded as Belém's unchallengeable expert on matters of love. As he told anyone who cared to listen, he had chosen the hotel business for but one reason: the pageant of love. Honeymoons, four days and four nights without coming out; and by contrast the haste of adultery, a half hour, at times less; angry scenes, lovers' reunions, hand-holding in the dining room, titillation, sidelong glances, touches, love letters. . . . It was meat and drink to him. People even said the mirrors in rooms 7 and 11 were two-way. As for the wall between Room 6 and the private suites, it had more holes than a Swiss cheese. . . . He had his own theory about a course of treatment for Gabriel: prime the patient's pump. And in furtherance of this goal he told tales about his guests by no means lacking in imagination, tales, believe me, my dear Rosa, considerably hotter than all the pepper on earth. General Manager Abel called three times a day, just before each of his three big rush hours: at dawn, when guests were asleep and not yet asking for their breakfasts; a little later on, when the taste of their breakfast coffee still lingered in their mouths, preventing them for at least an hour from thinking about lunch; and finally toward the middle of the afternoon. I know, Gabriel, I could have come earlier, but if I were not there for the siesta, what would I be able to tell you? As for staying on here after six P.M., who would take care of dinner? An establishment like the Hôtel de Paris has certain standards. Can you believe that yesterday, Gabriel (and if I call you Gabriel without first asking your permission it is because deep down we are brothers twice over, brothers because my country, Lebanon, is so like France, isn't it, Gabriel, and brothers also in our passion for love), so can you believe that yesterday evening as I made ready for bed I heard a noise? Not the usual creaking of springs and human panting (the staple of every self-respecting hotel) but a kind of sizzling I was unable to identify, and as God is my witness I have a memory for sounds and I've heard them all. I made an immediate sortie. Rapid reconnaissance of all strategic locations. Situation normal in Room Six. Room Seven was empty; alas, if you could have seen Seven during the boom! But in Eleven . . . I must explain that Eleven is my very quietest room, Gabriel; its window overlooks a giant bougainvillea. This marvel of a room is occasionally occupied by a silver-tongued young lawyer from the local courts. Naturally I cannot reveal his name. Otherwise how would I deserve the trust of my guests? On the eve of a difficult case, this silver-tongued barrister often comes to rehearse his speech in his room above my bougainvillea. Well, last night he was sitting on a chair; but instead of the usual heap of files on the table there was a small portable stove in which he was twiddling a fork. I was on the point of intervening—cooking is strictly forbidden in the rooms, our houses are made of wood, Gabriel; we don't have firefighters like your Parisian *pompiers*—I was about to fling the door open when he removed a small round fish fritter from the stove and blew on it several times. Then he moved toward the bed where, I had not noticed till then—as you can see my thoughts were strictly scientific, Gabriel—there lay a mulatto girl, extremely young I have to admit; we have no regulations like yours, adolescents are as entitled as anyone else to frequent hotel rooms. The red skirt worn by this particular adolescent was raised to her navel. And she was pretending to read, this child, seemingly absorbed in a magazine whose pages she turned after wetting her index finger. Well, Gabriel, our silver-tongued lawyer asked her, gently and politely, 'Is it too hot?'; she didn't answer, and he slipped the little golden sphere, done to a turn, all the way into her vagina. He waited a few moments, then retrieved the fritter and swallowed it, eyes closed. And repeated the operation three times. At which point the youthful reader asked "Finished?," lowered her skirt, picked up the money waiting on the table, threw a leg over the windowsill, and disappeared into my bougainvillea. Twice during the course of the night I returned. The stove had disappeared. The files sat on the table and the lawyer was working furiously away as though nothing had happened. A very odd story, wouldn't you say, Gabriel? And yet another perspective on the inexhaustible diversity of love. Well, I must be off. If I'm not there for breakfast there'll be hell to pay. But I hope to have new stories for you soon. With the weather we're expecting, I wouldn't be at all surprised."

"What filth!" Rosa Marcelina muttered throughout this tale. "Nothing comes out of your mouth but filth, oh, *seu* General Manager, no doubt about it"—she pressed both palms tightly against her eyes, but her ears were visibly twitching—"yes, what filth!"

The citizens of Belém, those who flocked to the house at every one of General Manager Abel's visits, seemed to savor it. Endless comments were heard. Sometimes during siesta after Gabriel's ordeal by pepper, as Rosa Marcelina snored supine in her white hammock, a little girl, never the same one, would come and sit on the wall of the veranda and watch Gabriel dozing in his wicker chair (futile slumber, for even in sleep time had ceased to flow) and swing her legs back and forth, one after the other, the light steady brushing of flesh on lightly bruised flesh, a small, endearing, and futile human clock. . . .

"Well, well, I see the pump is already being primed."

General Manager Abel's visit at that hour, four-thirty or five o'clock in the afternoon, was always the longest, the most leisurely.

"I can't wait to tell you, my dear colleague in love, Gabriel, they are back! Every three months or so they come to my hotel for just one night. Neither of them lives in Belém, they lived here two years ago; then they separated. I think it was she who left, if you will forgive the reference, Gabriel. She left him for one of the engineers on the Madeira–Mamoré line, you know, that insane plan to build a railroad through the heart of the jungle. Well, public works are none of my business. The important thing, Gabriel, is that they come back. They always take two rooms, Seven for them and Six for the children,

children they pick up anywhere, down on the docks or in the marketplace, before checking into the hotel. The first time they came I wanted to throw them out. Adolescents in the rooms, fine, but children no. But they begged me, standing side by side at the reception desk. Which is rare, Gabriel, usually one of them registers and discusses terms with the desk clerk while the other hangs back, staring at the floor, toes turned inward. Not this pair, no, both together: please, please, Mister General Manager. And I gave in. They went to their room, number Seven, and the children to number Six. The rest is quite simple. Like everyone else they make love, Gabriel. But just before they finish the man strikes the dividing wall a heavy blow: Go on now, off you go and play. And the children in Room Six begin to shout, to argue, to make typical kid noises. Then the woman begins to moan and the man puts his hand over her mouth: Shh, the children will hear, shh-shhh. The woman continues to moan under the man's hands. You can't hear anything but you can guess from her eyes and the convulsive jerking of her neck. When it's all over they get dressed and hug. They depart one after the other. I am forced to make them leave through the kitchen, for they are both still crying, and red eyes don't make a good impression on the other guests.

"What do you think of that, Gabriel, tell me honestly?"

Later on, after dinner (pepper, always pepper), when the mango trees were a round and indistinct mass in the gathering dusk, when nothing stood out against the sky but the giant eucalyptus, couples would amble up arm in arm to view the spectacle of lovesickness. Without much care for the flower beds, without much regard for the night, they came and pointed out the mosquito netting, the man curled up in his wicker chair next to a yellow dog, and the cloud of insects all around them, for Rosa Marcelina now left a kerosene lantern alight over the front door, to ward off the wilder animals, she said. The female half of the loving couple would murmur, "It's true, he doesn't look very happy." The man would reply, "The French are so intense."

"Yes, our own sorrows are much less painful, aren't they, Raymundo" (or João, or Zé).

And they would stroll home to bed, but not before trampling a few more flowers. Rosa Marcelina would find them dead next morning and bury them in a veritable concert of imprecations: Brazilian sons of whores, Saint Mary ever virginal, Brazilians not even worth the shit dangling from their backsides, O Lord of all mercies. . . .

You would think that after all these visits, all this pageantry, time would finally throw in the sponge and condescend to revive somewhat. Alas, not one little bit. Every time anything interesting happened in the garden, or General Manager Abel began a story, it was as if duration headed off on a different tack, one that had nothing to do with real time, the kind of time that moves clocks forward. And Gabriel proved it to himself each time: when the happening was over, when, for example, the hotelkeeper returned to his hotel, Gabriel, who had been enthralled by the misadventures in Room 7, would at last glance at the dial. A wasted effort. The hands had not budged. And to confirm that time was dead despite the efforts of his Brazilian friends, that other room, 212, returned to take up residence in Gabriel's head, with yesteryear's long thighs leading to the center of the earth, toward sweetness, and Room 212 would yield its place only to the steamship *Wellington* on her way back to France, a steamship that had no reason to hurry, since the concert Clara was attending wasn't yet over. And since the virtuosos were now playing slower than ever.

## III

Gabriel must now give literature its due. The agent of his miraculous cure was not Rosa Marcelina's peppers, or Guy Revol's increasingly rarefied lectures on vocation, or his North Breton wife's increasingly compassionate gaze, or the ever saltier stories from the Hôtel de Paris, but a book. Just published in France, according to General Manager Abel. "Apparently it's all about love, your turn to make yourself useful, read it and tell me all about it. I don't have time, with the hotel, but it might be of service."

So Gabriel embarked on a reading at first somewhat boring for an engineer. Bedrooms of yesteryear, Sunday lunches, lilacs and budding groves, family strolls, sometimes one way through the village, sometimes the other. But suddenly the adventure gripped him. A man loved a woman and grappled with that love with such intelligence, such invention, such prolific pain that an honest engineer could only raise his hat in salute. His own unhappiness suddenly seemed a trivial matter indeed, so trivial that he was ashamed. How could he hope for Clara's return if he continued to wallow in such trivial unhappiness? He resolved to rise to the challenge, to suffer in the manner of the gentleman in the book. And it was thus that he emerged from stupor to enter jealousy. A jealousy in no way related to the trifling doubts and sudden anxieties he had felt in the past: this was a consuming jealousy, the kind that monopolizes life in conquered countries, by night and day, nights worse than days.

Entirely recasting the operation, he launched into a series of mathematical calculations at which one might legitimately be tempted to scoff. But engineers are not engineers just because they build bridges (which we are incidentally quite happy to cross) or design new kinds of mechanical devices (which multiply our muscle power tenfold). Engineers call upon Science in all circumstances, not least for the management of personal difficulties. With the help of many additions, subtractions, and recollections, Gabriel now drew up a kind of almanac, an ephemeris, to establish the phases of her Parisian day when Clara in all likelihood would be behaving herself as should a new young wife temporarily separated from her husband. And then the other phases.

Statistically speaking, when do people make love?

"Midnight to two-thirty.

"Eight to ten (when you wake up).

"Two-thirty P.M. to seven, except for lovers inconvenienced by husbands or by regular working hours. For such unfortunates the lunch hour, one P.M. to two-thirty, may be substituted. But such was not Clara's situation. This being the case, and given her appetites, why should she deny herself a meal?

"Ten to midnight."

Taking the time lag into account, Gabriel could therefore consider himself a more or less carefree husband four times a day (Belém time):

"Midnight to two A.M.

"Four to eight-thirty A.M.

"One to four P.M.

"Eight-thirty to midnight."

All told, thirteen carefree hours out of twenty-four. More than one hour out of every two. Hard to count that as true unhappiness.

Gabriel exhaled softly and stretched. He felt the presence of the air on his skin: the light breath of movement, the movement of time once more flowing.

Next morning, when Rosa and General Manager Abel met at the garden gate, they glanced at the spot where their employer, friend, and associate had been sitting for three months. But the wicker chair was empty, and the mosquito netting lay heaped on the floor as though tossed down without a care for the tangles that would take hours and hours to unravel. As for Gabriel and his yellow dog, they were nowhere to be seen.

From the kitchen came a sizzling as of bubbles popping, and at the same time a smell of fried eggs.

"But—but he . . . oh, lord of all the saints!" cried Rosa.

"He is cured. I was sure he would be, he is cured," said the general manager.

A little unsteady on his feet, a little puffy from mosquito bites, but with a genuine smile, Gabriel greeted them: Thank you, thank you for everything, I will never forget.

Then they all embraced. General Manager Abel kissed Rosa and Gabriel; their young employer and French associate was on the mend.

And as Rosa Marcelina hurried off to spread the good news, the manager of the Hôtel de Paris headed for the kitchen to find a bottle of that excellent drink from the Highlands, Scotch. He took our hero's arm and the two of them returned to the veranda where they proposed toasts, unusual at this early hour—to love, no matter what the cost, and to recovery!

"I have not yet recovered," said Gabriel.

"Come come, I knew this would happen," the general manager interrupted between two swallows religiously savored, eyes turned heavenward. "I knew it; our own troubles pale by comparison with the sufferings of this new French writer. Once again, the Jews lead the way. Of course we men with round cheeks can suffer equally as well, much better even than gaunt men. But the Jews are better still. I'm not offending you, am I, dear friend and colleague Gabriel?"

The last-named was doing sums in his head.

At this hour across the Atlantic, 9 A.M. in Belém, and therefore 3 P.M. in Paris, Clara had four roles to choose from:

The normal young wife: shopping in department stores with her sister or her mother. Possible. Optimistic, but possible.

The loving young wife: she has gone to her room for a nap and sleeps alone, the fingers of her right hand clutching the return ticket stamped Le Havre–Belém and dreaming of passionate reunions. "Forgive me, Gabriel, terror seized me, but the evil has now been uprooted; if you still want me we can begin again, swear you forgive me." The most morally satisfying scenario, but oh, how improbable!

Third role, the waverer: lingering over lunch. Clara has not yet finished her dessert (hot fudge sundae: vanilla ice cream, chocolate sauce, roasted almonds) and is at this very moment musing over how she will spend the afternoon: alone (cf. preceding scenarios) or escorted (should she decide to go along with this violinist who for want of anything better is nudging her ankles under the table).

Although more than 6,000 miles stood between him and this wavering, Gabriel's whole body hurt, as if the pans of a giant scale were thudding into his ribs, first on one side, then the other.

Fourth role, the unfaithful wife: already recumbent, Clara, now, yes, at this very second, is favoring one of the countless virtuosos or soul-healers living in Paris (or merely passing through) with a tour of the center of the universe, the capital of bliss, the easiest place in the world to reach: simply follow the slope of two extraordinarily long thighs.

Gabriel killed time as best he could as he waited for the bed on the other side of the Atlantic to stop squeaking. He paced back and forth on the veranda, ran around the garden several times, threw George Sand into the flower beds, and pissed through the aviary wire onto the blue and red macaws: all actions to be expected from men crazed with jealousy.

Appalled, General Manager Abel trotted after him, saying, "Come now, Monsieur Gabriel, you shouldn't allow yourself to suffer like this; come, Monsieur Gabriel, stop torturing yourself." At long last the clock struck one. Gabriel glanced across the Atlantic. Whatever might have happened earlier, Clara was now behaving herself, getting ready for dinner.

He let out his breath, smiled at his friend the hotel manager, begged him to take a seat—"Thank you for spending this entire morning with me despite your hotel"—and talked to him with the demeanor of an utterly normal, even civilized, man.

A woman in love will of course change her habits readily; like everyone else, engineers are acquainted with this truth. But Clara less than most: her soul doctor, René A., had strongly advised her to accept herself as she was, that is to say as a regular eater and a sleeper at set times.

His faithful friends were there. Each shook the convalescent's hand or clasped him to his breast, convinced that his own prescription had remedied the disorder.

"You see, all it took was priming the pump," said General Manager Abel.

"When you have a vocation nothing can hurt you too deeply," said Guy Revol. "Well, now we will have to prepare for your journey in double-quick time. With war on the way there'll hardly be enough time to call in our debts. As far as the company is concerned, you realize, you're already on your way. . . . Ah, yes, I took that risk. You won't make a liar of me, will you, Gabriel?"

"Stop talking to him about work; let him be at least until tomorrow," said Mme. Revol. "I was sure you would get better. That's how Bretons are, especially those from the north: they dive down to the seabed, give a kick, and pop back up to the surface. You are of northern blood, aren't you, Gabriel?"

Leaning over him, Rosa painted his mosquito bites with a greasy ointment that gave off the double odor of camphor and marjoram.

"Just you wait, *seu* Gabriel, this secret medication for your outsides and pepper for your insides: in a few days the real *seu* Gabriel will rise up and rule over Belém!"

Out in the garden, General Manager Abel's legs performed a curious jig, undoubtedly in celebration of the wonderful news but also to avoid George Sand's teeth, for the dog had concluded that cream-colored trousers had no need of cuffs, an opinion widely subscribed to among yellow dogs.

As for the book, the only true agent of his cure, it disappeared. Gabriel did not discover its fate until his return from Amazonia months later. Rosa (may she be forgiven) had carried it off to the assistant parish priest of Rosario-dos-Homens-Pretos church, who had at first received it somewhat dubiously.

"Alas, the Holy Spirit of Pentecost has not granted me the gift of the French language. Are you quite sure this material is morally sound, my dear Rosa?"

"It saved *seu* Gabriel."

"In that case . . ."

And he welcomed it into his vestry and spoke of it from the pulpit, displaying it with much pomp and ceremony even though its little gray cover, almost green by now with mildew, looked sadly shabby alongside his plump gold and leather missals.

"Here," he said, "here is a French bible that restored sanity to a French visitor who had gone very far astray. Brothers and sisters, never dip more than a toe into worldly passion, for it is a stream infested with piranhas. Divine love alone is without fangs. Should you yield to human folly, beloved brothers and sisters, come and restore your strength here, before this miracle-working French bible."

*Swann's Way* thus remained on display in the chancel for two months, resting on a eucalyptus-wood lectern not far from the small flame marking the presence of Our Lord. Never had the faithful been so many, for the tale of the Frenchman sick with love had spread throughout Belém and its hinterland.

But in March 1914, after terrible and most unseasonable rains, the roof of the old Rosario-dos-Homens-Pretos church, dating from the middle of the eighteenth century, collapsed. How could you conduct mass under the pitiless equatorial sun and the sardonic stare of the vultures? It had to be repaired at once. And in order to repair it, the church had to find the kind of money no family, no matter how pious, no matter how devout, was prepared to offer in the wake of the brutal collapse (resembling that of the holy roof and perhaps predictive of it) of rubber prices.

So the church authorities decided to part with the auxiliary bible *Swann's Way* for cash: the profane was destined after all to be restored to the profane. The book was picked apart and its pages cut into tiny squares as small as relics in response to the demands of a considerable clientele.

And the few fragments of the Grasset publication that failed to find immediate takers were displayed alongside lamb fetuses, garishly painted devils, Spanish fly, and aphrodisiac roots in the specialized stalls of Belém's market, notorious for its thieves and in consequence nicknamed Ver-O-Peso, meaning "check the weight."

On his return from the forest Gabriel was thus able to acquire two pieces of the auxiliary bible. One was apparently from the title page; it read:

> ard Grasset
> Publisher
> e des Saints-Pères

and the other, torn from the text:

> ever have made them understand the emotion that I used to feel on winter mornings, when I met Mme. Swann on foot, in an otter-skin coat, with a woolen cap from which stuck out two blade-like partridge feathers, but

Gabriel has held on to two proud memories of that rather painful period. One reflects the worldwide influence of our nation's peerless literature. Fragments of Mme. Verdurin's salon, cattleya petals, Forcheville's fatuity, had proved as potent as tropical and equatorial magic. The other proud memory concerns me. Even today, according to sources I have no reason to question, my sad tale is part and parcel of the local language. In Belém, they say, "as unhappy (or as much in love) as Gabriel."

Who can say more?

Whose heartbreaks are remembered by a city fifty years on?

*"To have loved me so," said Clara (at exactly the moment she knew our infallibly punctual cleaning woman would arrive to*

*cut short any gushing), her gaze remote as she returned this portion of the manuscript, purloined the night before.*

*"I hope you intend to talk about me as well," said Ann, looking threatening but distracted, as if she had thus far read nothing of my notes, one morning as we went shopping (fresh sardines, thyme, tomatoes), along rue d'Antibes, in Cannes.*

## 7

# Notes from the Rain Forest

WHY A PRIVATE JOURNAL? Because the death of time is a curse, and I had resolved at all costs to avoid a relapse. Do you understand? And a private journal is incontrovertible proof that the days are indeed passing.

So here are my "notes from the rain forest." Just excerpts, have no fear.

### *July 13, 1914*

Mud.

Nothing but ocher as far as the eye can see.

The riverbanks have disappeared. Not a tree. Not a sound. Save that of machinery, muffled explosions, like a too-heavy heart. And everything is atremble, the bridge underfoot, the chair beneath your buttocks, the glasses of whiskey or of assahy, the English prints on the walls (familiar Kentish foxhunting scenes). Even voices tremble, even the mist-shrouded reveries that have taken the place of sleep, even memories of Paris, Room 212. And our ship conveys no sense of forward motion, rather the certainty of standing still. No bow wave, merely a wake that immediately fades. Even the most optimistic passengers believe it is the world behind us that is retreating, carried astern by the current. From time to time a dark shape comes into view, and an Indian paddles slowly by in a dugout canoe, flush with the water.

In any case, it is best not to look too much. The heat gets into you through your eyes.

*July 15*

Reading all day long. Two examples of marriage.

1. Louis Orsenna, last letter received in Belém before departure.

My dear if silent son,

You may travel far, as far into the forest as it is possible to go, I cannot forbid it. The Atlantic will not do; put as much distance as you can between yourself and your poor father, a man clearly unable to make a success of even the merest little marriage. You will remember that I put all my eggs in one basket. But all the eggs in the world are of no avail against a single stroke of misfortune, an impossible coincidence when you consider how vast Paris is: to find oneself face to face with one's spouse, she walking down the rue d'Antin and myself leaving a hotel where I had just placed yet another egg in my basket by breaking off, yes, Gabriel, I swear, breaking cleanly and forever the last of my illicit attachments.

Yes, flee, Gabriel, and do not return until the risk of contagion has died down.

Permit me one last piece of advice, Gabriel, before I cut myself off from you for so long. Beware of the tiny candiru fish. It insinuates itself into any orifice, front or back, Gabriel, taking up residence in the body and fomenting fatal infections. A father owes you this further note of scientific caution, scientific, do you hear me, Gabriel: the candiru fish can even climb the urinary stream and make its way thence to the bladder. All conscientious doctors advocate chamber pots for survival in Amazonia.

Your good old Louis, refusing to lay down his arms, once again tackles life anew and, prior to vanquishing misfortune and presenting you with the image of a sire serene in wedded bliss (an image I acknowledge all sons are entitled to), embraces you.

2. Mme. Godin des Odonais.

The celebrated *Abridged Account of a Voyage into the Heart of South America,* by M. de la Condamine, a man dear to my heart, for it was he who first brought rubber to Europe. At first sight it is but a geographer's narrative, richer in natural phenomena and in friendly natives than in beings truly human. But you have only to open the book at the epilogue, if you are fortunate enough, as I am, to possess the rare Maestricht edition (1778). There you will find the story, sad beyond tears, of Mme. Godin des Odonais, "The Dreadful Adventure of a Gently Nurtured Lady Who through a Succession of Events Beyond the Scope of Human Precaution, Found Herself Lost in Impenetrable Woods Inhabited by Fearsome Beasts and Dangerous Reptiles, Exposed to All the Horrors of Hunger, Thirst, and Exhaustion, Who Wandered for Several Days in this Wilderness after Witnessing the Deaths of Seven Persons, and Who Alone Escaped all these Dangers in a Manner Bordering on the Miraculous." This Mme. Godin des Odonais was a married woman, like Clara. Two essential differences: the period, since her terrible adventure took place in 1769, and the sentiment: the lady in question crossed the whole Amazonian forest from Riobamba (Quito province, Ecuador) to the Atlantic to rejoin her husband, posted at Cayenne. Reading a biography is among the most useful of tonics. In bad moments, you have to cling to earlier lives. Little by little they take you out of your rut, although not without straining, the way a yoke of oxen, for example, will haul a cart out of a ditch. But once this chord has been struck (long live biography!), cold reality reasserts itself: to be sure, the boldness of Mme. Godin des Odonais inspires optimism, there are women who actually love their husbands, but I must bow to the evidence: Clara is not one of their number.

*July 19*

Portrait of a passenger: Signor Pizarro, presenting himself as a descendant of the great Francisco Pizarro. He is here to claim his rights in Peru. Shows everyone his papers, certificates from an Italian notary proving that Pizarro was Italian. His antecedents are impeccable: a direct line of descent. According to the steward, there are still dozens every year who go up the Amazon in this way to reclaim their share of the inheritance of Señores Pizarro, Cortés, Almagro. . . .

*July 20*

Today the boat is moving up two rivers at once, one to port, of familiar ocher color, and another, coal black, to starboard. My fellow passengers forget the heat and clap their hands in delight. "Look! Oh, look, the waters aren't mixing." The purser shrugs, no need to get excited; the black stream is from Colombia (Rio Negro), the ocher from Peru (Rio Solimões). "How wonderful!" cries a fair-haired woman in a little straw hat. She almost swoons for love of Brazil when the day's second attraction appears, freshwater dolphins. They leap and swim at the exact meeting point of the two colors, as if trying to stitch the two rivers together.

### *July 21*

Manaus at last. The city has no piers. Because of the tidal ebb and flow of the Amazon River, there is a fourteen-foot difference between winter and summer water levels. The docks are floating pontoons that pitch and roll underfoot, as unstable as rubber futures. The jungle has reconquered its lost territory. Tall grasses choke courtyards, the roots of silk-cotton trees crack terraces, eucalyptuses thrust their branches through shutters, vines coil tight around street lamps. The only part of town where this vegetable army dare not encroach too far is the area between the cathedral and the warehouses, a few alleyways occupied by a lethargic, seemingly defeated marketplace. People shuffle along at a snail's pace, a dense throng lacking all animation. Natives of the Nordeste with long mystical faces, dazed-looking Indians with dark salmon skins walking in their own world and jostled by everyone, a few bearded Slavs of beer-yellow complexion, the occasional Chinese, the only ones moving at a brisk trot, and the instantly recognizable breed of defeated men no longer possessing race or color, fugitives from the forest with the lost eyes of beings returned from the depths.

The customers, the pathetic customers, mill to and fro in front of the stalls without ever stopping, before the half-angry, half-resigned eyes of traders from the Near East who came here at the start of the boom, Lebanese, Syrians, Egyptians, whose lot in life is to be killed, killed by heat and sluggish trade, a handkerchief permanently held to their faces, permanently mopping, permanently grumbling, flapping their hands in the air to get business going again, to urge those buying nothing to make way for others. Move along, ladies and gentlemen, move along; look at my watches, prices slashed, guaranteed three hands, who wants my watches, don't let time go by on its own; take a look at my mirrors, ladies, come now, ladies, take a look at what the men are seeing. . . . At regular intervals they shake their fists at their lesser rivals—at squatting peddlers crouched over a single carpet strewn with shoddy trifles, laces, buttons, pins; or at ambulant merchants, market porters, shoeshine boys, water bearers, tortilla vendors, sellers of sacred pictures, many-bladed Swiss penknives, bird cages, apologetically hawking their wares, their voices rising timidly. A colored Saint Sebastian to ward off mosquitoes: small size, 1 milreis; large, 2 milreis. A Saint Otacilia for constipation: small photograph, 1 milreis. God bless you. . . .

To wander for any time in this strange moneyless market, in the midst of this aimless throng, is to understand that trade, even simple barter without the exchange of money, is the only way to hold off the forest. To show it that we human beings too can live intertwined lives. That we have our own tangles, our own exchanges, our own metamorphoses. Let there be no doubt: Manaus is a city under siege. The market is the last square still standing against the invasion of the green.

## *July 22*

To all but the blind or deaf (or simply uninformed) of Manaus, Senhor Guilherme Moreira is a well-known attorney, a most conscientious attorney, wise in the drafting of deeds and implacable in the recovery of debts, a married attorney, father of two grown children—the first, Joaquim, a student of philology at Cambridge (Magdalene College), and the second, Enrique, a budding executive on Wall Street (Drexel, Morgan and Co.)—a moderate attorney, neither stout nor scrawny. And the last time he was seen entering the Place Blanche brothel, that reputable establishment on Libania Street, was on that night two years ago when the humidity was unbearable and the rain refused to come, when all the demons of every citizen of Manaus, even the best concealed and most somnolent of them, awoke and ruled the city until three in the morning, when the storm broke. But since no one that night was blameless, since every human being, young or old, woman or man, was caught, whether down by the river surrounded by naked children or packed into a carriage drawn up in front of the theater, since every one of them had indulged in the reproachable, the city entered into a sort of unspoken pact, an agreement to forget, thanks to which attorney G. Moreira maintained his stainless reputation.

For others, for the curious, for those who can fit little disconnected pieces together, such as a man's disarray on Sundays or his inordinate use of graph paper, for those who like details, for all these, Senhor G. Moreira is a positivist before he is a father or a husband or an attorney. And a member of a good dozen secret societies, all dedicated toward one goal: progress. And my three knocks on the door of his chambers on the twenty-second day of July, 1914, validated this opinion in accordance with the following equation: nervous gestures = Frenchman = Auguste Comte = positivist = attorney Moreira.

I waited on the threshold. Modest, eyes lowered in the manner I adopt for important occasions, a little girl in white ankle socks.

"Come right in," cried Senhor Moreira, "come right in; anyone from the land of Descartes and Lavoisier is welcome!" A drawing room occupied by four other men, four men of somber mien whose arms were nevertheless opened wide to greet me. There ensued an embarrassing scene, a heaping of tributes at the feet of our old country, France, mother of letters and of laws; France, birthplace of inductive and deductive reason; France, midwife of democracy: Montesquieu, Robespierre, Victor Hugo, and on and on.

Nonplussed, I stared alternately at my toecaps and at the procession outside the window. They were loading a small pyramid of Cheops and the Sphinx (in three sections) onto a cart, props for *Aïda*, all looking somewhat the worse for wear. At long last the litany died away. So many sugared words had made the air as sticky as syrup.

"So, dear friend from France, you see Brazil with virgin eyes. Tell us honestly, do you think we will ever put any order into these tropics of ours?"

"Well, you know, I've only just arrived . . ."

"Please."

"Well, then, I would say (and of course this is just an opinion), I would say it will be difficult for you; there is no doubt you will succeed but you will need to muster all your resolve, for, let me see now, life here is—perhaps it's not the right word: yes, life here, this comes closest to my meaning—life in Brazil is totalitarian."

"Totalitarian? Totalitarian as in a dictatorship?"

"Totalitarian. I am not a chemist, but it seems to me that I can sense Europe's *composition,* the ingredients of the cocktail: three approximately equal parts, one third life, one third (or perhaps a little more) death, and one third an intermediate stage, neither life nor death nor forward progress nor immobility, but waiting. Europe is at least one third waiting. Flowers wait to grow, corpses wait to rot, loves wait before bursting into flame—"

"Most stimulating, most stimulating to the mind, pray continue. Is your drink to your liking?"

"Here, nothing waits. You are ninety-nine percent life, one percent death, and zero percent waiting. Look at your corpses; they start to rot the moment they die, as though life resented yielding an inch of its territory to death. Forgive me this morbid example, but we are all scientists here, are we not?"

His positivist audience concurred, dreamy smiles on their faces, *"Enrichissantissime!"* they murmured. "Invaluable perspectives."

I was ashamed to have spoken at such great length. Since Clara's departure the merest swallow of whiskey opened floodgates of words within me. I overflowed with theories, introductory lessons, exhaustive analyses of the world. I talked, I talked, more and more gaily, confidently, certain that Clara had no choice but to rush back as quickly as possible to share life with such an incisive conversationalist.

After hours of penetrating ratiocination I returned to earth. The positivists were obviously waiting for something. I racked my brain, but I had utterly forgotten my starting point. So how could I reach a suitable conclusion? At last, after a silence that threatened to become embarrassing, I found the thread again: ". . . And from all this it follows, dear friends, that you will succeed in your quest for order. France the mother of laws was not so very long ago as hirsute as your own Amazonia. Remember that; covered with forests."

In these climes friendship blossoms as swiftly as plants. In the space of two hours we had progressed from everyday casual interest to life-or-death mutual involvement. And such was the warmth between us that the outside air seemed cool. They fought for the honor of putting me up. I'm already asleep. Clara.

*July 24*

I went there and I can vouch for it: Manaus Opera House reeks as strongly as Levallois, Levallois on the worst summer days, when every horse from every carriage in Paris has pissed and defecated at once. Chickens hopped from seat to seat. Trees grew from the orchestra pit. Onstage the curtain had been hiked on high like a woman's dress, the flies exposed to view, three canvas backdrops as full of ruffles as a petticoat: the Barber's piazza, Violetta's bedroom, Norma's forest; three dogs squabbled over a sheep's head in front of the prompter's box. Whole families had taken up residence in the stalls. Snoring, chattering women, a crying baby, turtledoves roosting in the monumental chandelier.

To avoid twisting the knife in my friends' hearts I decided to keep this visit a secret.

*July 25*

We finish off our day at the Café Byron, a floating restaurant moored directly opposite the main warehouses. My friends arrive one after the other, reeling across on the pontoons. Dr. Lauro Cavalcante, a giant pediatrician and a bachelor, most opaque concerning his private life; President Somebody-or-Other (I do not even know his first name), who presides over the Lodge, the Football Club, the Tropical Zoo, the Library, the Sculling Club, the Angler's Association, the planning committee for the new golf course—clubs and associations whose gatherings and financial difficulties he tirelessly relates to us, invariably ending on the same note: I did not assume the presidency of such and such a club, such and such a zoo, such and such a fellowship, such and such an association, in order to preside over its demise!

And Pedrinho Martins, manager of the Brazil–Peru Steam Navigation Company, who often speaks of a gigantic wave born every ten years far out at sea, the pororoca ("great roaring" in the Indian language), which rushes upriver as far as Santarém, washing away everything in its path. Monsignor Macedo, bishop and positivist, who had dreamed in his youth of a floating cathedral, the Christophorus, most useful in these waterlogged places, wouldn't you say,

Gabriel? And Walid the Syrian dealer, who has profited from the slump to climb to the "top of the heap," which is how my friends refer to their circle. The others are a little contemptuous of him, but they support his idea for the formation of yet another association, whose purpose would be to coerce the authorities into establishing an official land registry system for the Amazonian region. The proposal is assuredly not disinterested, since Walid has a monopoly on fencing supplies and barbed-wire imports. But without land registry—in other words, without clearly defined property lines—how can you achieve progress?

It is touching to see them meet openly in this way, in broad daylight, all these members of secret societies once camouflaged by the din of the boom and now laid bare by the slump, like big fish left high and dry. . . . Together we discuss the news. In Europe war is coming. Out of consideration for me, perhaps too out of love for France, they assume downcast expressions.

"Do you think many will die, Gabriel?"

But a positivist is a positivist. All wars have the power to stimulate markets for raw materials, including rubber. So I often catch them gesturing in anticipatory glee—involuntary reflexes, suddenly and vigorously rubbing their hands together, for instance. Or smiling, their eyes gazing out at nothing, like me when I am remembering Room 212. You might be surprised by this choice of the floating Café Byron as a meeting place for members of the Land Registry Society. Such surprise would imply ignorance of the history of Romanticism in Amazonia.

Around 1820, when fevers, sudden pallors, and trembling sleepless nights became fashionable in Europe, the young people of the tropics exclaimed (with a hint of superiority), These symptoms—why, we know them well! Your *mal du siècle* is merely a benign version of malaria. Welcome to the club. And the youthful literati of Bombay, Havana, and Belém threw themselves upon the mist-shrouded texts of the north—Ossian, Chateaubriand, Musset, Byron—and themselves began to write; listen to us, they cried, do not ignore our yearnings; we too deserve to call ourselves Romantics. But Europe was deaf to their pleas. The south would never produce anything but slaves, spices, and brown sugar. Tropical manuscripts rotted in the archives of temperate-zone publishing houses. . . . Mortified by such indifference, these young people began to cast about for something to die for, convinced that this was the entry fee to the Romantic club. Nor did they want for a model—the attempt by George Gordon, Lord Byron, between March 1823 and April 19, 1824, to liberate Greece. They merely had to wait for an opportunity to present itself. It was a long wait. European Romanticism had already been dead a good many years when in March 1899 the American man-of-war *Wilmington* steamed up the Amazon without so much as a by-your-leave. Could this be our long-awaited chance, the Romantics asked themselves? In June a Spanish adventurer, Luis Galvez Rodrigues de Arias, an employee of the Bolivian Consulate in Belém, sold to the newspaper *Provincia do Pará* the text of the secret agreement between La Paz and Washington, in which the United States betrayed Brazil and supported Bolivia's claim to the province of Acre, a huge chunk of Amazonia at the foot of the Andes. The hearts of Brazil's Romantics beat fast. Would they be called upon to confront, via Bolivia, the all-powerful United States of America? They emerged from their smoky chambers, did strenuous calisthenics, swam, and marched, just in case. In July, Luis Galvez proclaimed himself emperor of the independent State of Acre. The Brazilian Romantics almost died of disappointment. Could they have missed their opportunity? Could the adventure have been stolen from them by a vulgar emigré journalist? In September, when a thousand Bolivian soldiers invaded Acre, they breathed again. The hour of the poets had come. They must speed to the defense of Emperor Galvez. They embraced their wives, their mothers, their sweethearts. They embarked from a floating landing stage at the very spot where the Café Byron would be moored the following November. They whiled away the time sailing up the Rio Purus reading *Childe Harold* and reproaching one another for not alerting the major newspapers of Europe. There were 132 of them. They were slaughtered to the last man.

Three months after the horror, on page four of *The Times* and page six of *Le Figaro*, identical paragraphs appeared under the heading: DOES RUBBER DRIVE MEN MAD? VIOLENT SKIRMISHES BETWEEN RIVAL TRIBES IN THE JUNGLE: 132 DEAD.

I like Europe, the president said to me, but there are times when . . . He had founded an Association to Commemorate the Poets of

Acre. Every year, toward the equinox, a group of women throw flowers into the black river just across from the café.

## *July 27*

A gift from the president: The Great Positivist Calendar.

"Establishment of an Amazonian Land Registry is a useful, indeed an essential objective, Gabriel. But compared with our true plans it is the tiniest of steps. The Christian calendar, with its haphazard jumble of saints and Christian names, is now meaningless. We must replace it if we are to give men a deep-seated awareness of daily progress. In our calendar you will find Byron Day, for example, on the twenty-seventh day of the eighth month. You see, France is not alone in her crusade for Reason."

## *Which Date?*

How can we date dreams? Do dreams exist in a time scale such as ours, with months of July, numbered days, leap years? Or do they come from elsewhere, from another galaxy, without clocks, without labels around their necks?

Gabriel, long white robe, stands before a jury, the positivist general staff gowned in red and wigged like English judges. He has come to negotiate an amendment to the Great Calendar. Dare I ask you, Senhor President, to substitute Knight, Markus, for the musician Sacchini, Clara for Santa Pulquéria, and Ann (you know, my very young wife's sister) for Cromwell? The president and his colleagues confer endlessly together. Walid the Syrian appears to be the most recalcitrant. They finally agree, nodding their heads as if a mighty wind had taken them from the rear. The sound of the goose quill scratching out the final clause rouses me from sleep. . . .

## *August*

Green, the color of hope. We have penetrated the world's biggest repository of the color of hope.

Our captain is an impatient soul. He rejects roundabout courses: "Don't worry, I know a shortcut."

# CALENDÁRIO

## PARA UM ANO

OU

## QUADRO CONCRÉTO

| | | PRIMEIRO MÊS<br>MOIZÉS<br>A TEOCRACIA INICIAL | SEGUNDO MÊS<br>HOMÉRO<br>A POEZIA ANTIGA | TERCEIRO MÊS<br>ARISTÓTELES<br>A FILOZOFIA ANTIGA |
|---|---|---|---|---|
| Lunedia | 1 | Prometeu *Cadm* | Heziodo | Anaximandro |
| Martedia | 2 | Hércules *Tezeu* | Tirteu *Safo* | Anaximenes |
| Mercuridia | 3 | Orfeu *Tirézias* | Anacreonte | Heráclito |
| Jovedia | 4 | Ulisses | Pindaro | Anaxágoras |
| Venerdia | 5 | Licurgo | Sófocles *Euripedes* | Demócrito *Leucipo* |
| Sábado | 6 | Rômulo | Teócrito *Longo* | Heródoto |
| Domingo | 7 | **Numa** | **Esquilo** | **Tales** |
| | 8 | Bel *Semiramis* | Escópas | Solon |
| | 9 | Sezóstris | Zeuxis | Xenófanes |
| | 10 | Manú | Ictino | Empédocles |
| | 11 | Ciro | Praxiteles | Tucidides |
| | 12 | Zoroastro | Lisipo | Arquitas *Filolaus* |
| | 13 | Os Druidas *Ossian* | Apéles | Apolônio de Tiane |
| | 14 | **Buda** | **Fidias** | **Pitogóras** |
| | 15 | Fu-Hi | Esopo *Pilpai* | Aristipo |
| | 16 | Lau-Tseu | Plauto | Antistenes |
| | 17 | Meng-Tseu | Terêncio *Menandro* | Zeno |
| | 18 | Os teocratas do Tibéto | Pédro | Cicero *Plinio Junior* |
| | 19 | Os teocratas do Japão | Juvenal | Epitéto *Arriano* |
| | 20 | Manco-Capac *Tamcamêa* | Luciano | Tácito |
| | 21 | **Confúcio** | **Aristófanes** | **Sócrates** |
| | 22 | Abrahão *Joel* | Ênio | Xénócrates |
| | 23 | Samuel | Lucrécio | Filon de Alexandria |
| | 24 | Salomão *Davi* | Horácio | S. João Evangelista |
| | 25 | Izaias | Tibulo | S. Justino *Santo Irineu* |
| | 26 | S. João Batista | Ovidio | S. Clemente de Alexandria |
| | 27 | Arun-al Rachid *Abdarâman III* | Lucano | Origenes *Tertuliano* |
| | 28 | **Mahomé** | **Virgilio** | **Platão** |

| | | OITAVO MÊS<br>DANTE<br>A EPOPÉIA MODERNA | NONO MÊS<br>GUTENBERG<br>A INDÚSTRIA MODÉRNA | DÉCIMO MÊS<br>SHAKESPEARE<br>O DRAMA MODÉRNO |
|---|---|---|---|---|
| Lunedia | 1 | Os Trovadores | Marco-Pólo *Chardan* | Lópe de Vega *Montalvan* |
| Martedia | 2 | Bocácio *Chaucer* | Diogo Cœur *Orescham* | Moreto *Guillen de Castro* |
| Mercuridia | 3 | Rabelais *Swift* | Gama *Magalhães* | Rójas *Guevara* |
| Jovedia | 4 | Cervantes | Napier *Briggs* | Otway |
| Venerdia | 5 | Lafontaine *Robérto Burns* | Lacaille *Delambre* | Lessing |
| Sábado | 6 | Defoe *Goldsmith* | Cook *Tasman* | Goethe |
| Domingo | 7 | **Arioste** | **Colombo** | **Calderon** |
| | 8 | Leonardo de Vinci *Ticiano* | Benevenuto Cellini | Tirso |
| | 9 | Miguel Angelo *Paulo Veronese* | Amontons *Wheatstone* | Vondel |
| | 10 | Holbein *Rembrandt* | Harrison *P. Leroy* | Racine |
| | 11 | Poussin *Lesueur* | Dollond *Graham* | Voltaire |
| | 12 | Velásquez *Murilo* | Arkwright *Jacquart* | Metastácio *Alfieri* |
| | 13 | Teniers *Rubens* | Conté | Schiller |
| | 14 | **Rafael** | **Vaucanson** | **Corneille** |
| | 15 | Froissart *Joinville* | Stevin *Toricelli* | Alarcon |
| | 16 | Camões *Spencer* | Mariotte *Boyle* | M[me] de Motteville *M[me] Roland* |
| | 17 | Os Romanceiros espanhois | Papin *Worcester* | M[me] de Sevigné *Lady Montague* |
| | 18 | Chateaubriand | Black | Lesage *Sterne* |
| | 19 | Walter Scott *Fen. Cooper* | Jouffroy *Fulton* | M[me] de Staal *Miss Edgeworth* |
| | 20 | Manzoni | Dalton *Thilorier* | Fielding *Richardson* |
| | 21 | **Tasso** | **Watt** | **Molière** |
| | 22 | Petrarca *Bunyan* | Bernardo de Palissy | Pergoleso *Palestrina* |
| | 23 | Tomás de Kempis *Luis de Granada* | Guglielmini *Riquet* | Sacchini *Gretry* |
| | 24 | M[me] de Lafayette *M[me] de Stael* | Duhamel du Monceau *Bourgelat* | Gluck *Lulli* |
| | 25 | Fenelon *S. Francisco de Sales* | Saussure *Bouguer* | Beethoven *Handel* |
| | 26 | Klopstoch *Gessner* | Coulomb *Borda* | Rossini *Weber* |
| | 27 | Byron *Eliza Mercœur e Shelley* | Carnot *Vauban* | Bellini *Donizetti* |
| | 28 | **Milton** | **Montgolfier** | **Mozart** |

**POZITIVISTA**

**QUALQUÉR**

# DA PREPARAÇÃO HUMANA

| QUARTO MÊS<br>ARQUIMÉDES<br>A SIÊNCIA ANTIGA | QUINTO MÊS<br>CÉZAR<br>A CIVILIZAÇÃO MILITAR | SESTO MÊS<br>SÃO PAULO<br>O CATOLICISMO | SÉTIMO MÊS<br>CARLOS MAGNO<br>A CIVILIZAÇÃO FEUDAL |
|---|---|---|---|
| Teofrasto<br>Herófilo<br>Erazistrato<br>Célso<br>Galeno<br>Avicenó *Averrois*<br>**Hipócrates** | Milciades<br>Leônidas<br>Aristides<br>Cimon<br>Xenofonte<br>Focion *Epaminondas*<br>**Temistocles** | S. Lucas *S. Tiago*<br>S. Cipriano<br>Santo Atanázio<br>S. Jerônimo<br>Santo Ambrózio<br>Santa Mônica<br>**Santo Agostinho** | Teodorico Magno<br>Pelágio<br>Otão, o Grande *Henrique o Passarinheiro*<br>Santo Henrique<br>Villiers *La Valette*<br>D. João de Lepanto *João Sobieski*<br>**Alfredo** |
| Euclides<br>Aristeu<br>Teodózio de Bitinia<br>Heron *Ctezíbio*<br>Papus<br>Diofante<br>**Apolônio** | Péricles<br>Filipe<br>Demóstenes<br>Tolomeu Lago<br>Filopêmen<br>Polibio<br>**Alexandre** | Constantino<br>Teodózio<br>S. Crizóstomo *S. Bazilio*<br>Santa Pulquéria *Marciano*<br>Santa Genovéva de Paris<br>S. Gregório Magno<br>**Hildebrando** | Carlos Martel<br>O Cid *Tancredo*<br>Ricardo *Saladino*<br>Joana d'Arco *Marina*<br>Albuquérque *Walter Raleigh*<br>Bayard<br>**Godofredo** |
| Eudóxo *Arato*<br>Piteas *Nearco*<br>Aristarco *Beroso*<br>Erastotenes *Sozigenes*<br>Ptolomeu<br>Albatênio *Nassir-Edin*<br>**Hiparco** | Júnio Bruto<br>Camilo *Cincinato*<br>Fabricio *Régulo*<br>Anibal<br>Paulo Emilio<br>Mário *Os Gracos*<br>**Sipião** | S. Bento *Santo Antônio*<br>S. Bonifácio *Santo Austino*<br>Santo Izidóro de Sevilha *S. Bruno*<br>Lanfranc *Santo Anselmo*<br>Eloiza *Beatris*<br>Arquitétos da Idade-Média *S Benezet*<br>**S. Bernardo** | S. Leão o Grande *Leão IV*<br>Gerbert *P. Damião*<br>Pedro, o Eremita<br>Suger *Santo Elói*<br>Alexandre III *Tomaz Becket*<br>S. Francisco de Assis *S. Domingos*<br>**Inocencio III** |
| Varrão<br>Columéla<br>Vitrúvio<br>Estrabão<br>Frontino<br>Plutarco<br>**Plínio, o Vélho** | Augusto *Mecenas*<br>Vespaziano *Tito*<br>Adriano *Nérva*<br>Antonino *Marco-Aurélio*<br>Papiniano *Ulpiano*<br>Alexandre Sevéro *Aécio*<br>**Trajano** | S. Francisco Xavier *Inácio de Loióla*<br>S. Carlos Borromeu *Fred.co Borromeu*<br>St.ª Tereza *S. Catarina de Siena*<br>S. Vicente de Paula *O. P.e Del'Epée*<br>Bourdaloue *Cláudio Fleury*<br>G. Penn *J. Fox*<br>**Bossuet** | Santa Clotilde<br>Santa Batilde *Matilde de Toscana*<br>Santo Estêvão da Ungria<br>St.ª Izabel de Ungria *Mateus Corvino*<br>Branca de Castéla<br>S. Fernando III *Afonso X*<br>**São Luis** |
| UNDÉCIMO MÊS<br>DESCARTES<br>A FILOZOFIA MODÉRNA | DUODÉCIMO MÊS<br>FREDERICO<br>A POLITICA MODÉRNA | DÉCIMO TERCEIRO MÊS<br>BICHAT<br>A SIÊNCIA MODÉRNA | |
| Alberto, o Grande *João de Salisbury*<br>Rogério Bacon *Raimundo Lulio*<br>S Boaventura *Joaquim*<br>Ramus *O Cardeal de Cuza*<br>Montaigne *Erasmo*<br>Campanéla *Morus*<br>**S. Tomás de Aquino** | Maria de Molina<br>Cósme de Médicis, o Velho<br>Filipe de Comines *Guicciardini*<br>Izabel de Castéla<br>Carlos V *Sisto V*<br>Henrique IV<br>**Luis XI** | Copérnico *Tycho-Brahe*<br>Kepler *Halley*<br>Huyghens *Varignon*<br>Diogo Bernoulli *J. Bernoulli*<br>Bradley *Roëmer*<br>Volta *Sauveur*<br>**Galileu** | Dia complementar. . . Fésta universal dos MÓRTOS<br>Dia bissesto . . . . Fésta geral das SANTAS MULHÉRES |
| Hobbes *Espinóza*<br>Pascal *J. Bruno*<br>Locke *Malebranche*<br>Vauvenargues *M.me de Lambert*<br>Diderot *Duclos*<br>Cabanis *Jorge Leroy*<br>**Bacon** | L'Hôpital<br>Barneveldt<br>Gustavo Adolfo<br>Witt<br>Ruyter<br>Guilhérme III<br>**Guilhérme, O Taciturno** | Viete *Harriott*<br>Wallis *Fermat*<br>Clairaut *Poinsot*<br>Euler *Monge*<br>D'Alembert *Daniel Bernoulli*<br>Lagrange *José Fourier*<br>**Newton** | |
| Grócio *Cujácio*<br>Fontenelle *Maupertuis*<br>Vico *Herder*<br>Freret *Winckelmann*<br>Montesquieu *d'Aguesseau*<br>Buffon *Oken*<br>**Leibnitz** | Ximenes<br>Sully *Oxenstierna*<br>Mazarino *Walpole*<br>Colbert *Luis XIV*<br>Aranda *Pombal*<br>Turgot *Campomanes*<br>**Richelieu** | Bergman *Scheele*<br>Priestley *Davy*<br>Cavendish<br>Guyton-Morveau *Geoffroy*<br>Berthollet<br>Berzelius *Ritter*<br>**Lavoisier** | |
| Robertson *Gibbon*<br>Adão Smith *Dunoyer*<br>Kant *Fichte*<br>Condorcet *Fergusson*<br>José de Maistre *De Bonald*<br>Hegel *Sofia Germain*<br>**Hume** | Sidney *Lambert*<br>Franklin *Hampden*<br>Washington *Kosciusko*<br>Jefferson *Madison*<br>Bolivar *Toussaint-Louverture*<br>Francia<br>**Cromwell** | Harvey *C. Bell*<br>Boerhaave *Stahl e Barthez*<br>Lineu *B. de Jussieu*<br>Haller *Vicq-d'Azyr*<br>Lamarck *Blainville*<br>Broussais *Morgagni*<br>**Gall** | |

As soon as we were clear of the bank he swung the rudder hard to port. And the miniature *gaïola* steamboat, taking advantage of the rising floodwater, left the river and headed straight for the forest, crashing like a bolting deer through ramparts of foliage and creepers. Since then it has been all shadow, vegetable chaos, a blue-green universe, stagnant waters, giant mosses and water lilies, wisps of fog clinging to branches, floating insects. We thread our way between partially submerged trees just beneath the topmost boughs where unseen monkeys fight and howl. Without a sign, without a gesture, villagers who have been flooded out of their homes watch us pass by: mulattoes waist-deep in the water in front of their houses, vegetable growers in craft half awash in mud, children tucked away in what look like storks' nests. Tawny-hued cattle dipping their heads underwater to rip up grasses from the bottom, then swimming back to their raft stables; a priest standing alone on a tiny hillock, saying mass to a flotilla of dugout canoes; a floating grass island on which two egrets and a colony of spoonbills forage.

At night it is wise to keep your ears tightly covered. The jungle screams in terror. It trembles in every limb, groaning, teeth chattering. The denizens of the world beneath the forest canopy have lost their daytime arrogance. Creatures never seen during the day, thousands of species—animal, insect, reptile, spotted felines, rodents, red macaws, the concealed, the threatening—all compete at the top of their lungs, each in its own language, croaking, piping, roaring, doing their utmost to drive the ghosts away. Suddenly all goes quiet as they catch their breath. A dreamlike silence ensues, broken only by the sound of trickling water, by the infantile suck of a surfacing fish, long bird whistles, a nearby cooing, a beak rapping against a trunk. And then fear returns, stronger than before, a tidal wave of baying, of high-pitched screams; somewhere murder is taking place, wings are ripped off, the world is torn apart . . . creatures in naked panic. The forest shows its true colors, much more frightened at night than frightening by day. You long to comfort it. But where could you find the words, the lullabies to soothe Amazonia?

By morning all is quiet again.

Spiders have been spinning all night long and the steamer is shrouded in gossamer; your slightest movement tears asunder curtain upon translucent curtain. Life, already motionless, is now muffled and even slower moving. Not until afternoon do the blue and gold butterflies erupt in their hundreds. Like a vast shifting sombrero they swarm about the captain's head, then fly away. The captain draws himself up, smiles.

"It's a sign, *seu* Gabriel, we have chosen the right shortcut."

At one point, the steamer heaves to in the middle of a kind of clearing. The water is so pure and transparent that you can see the forest floor, a fallen tree, a tangle of roots twenty-five or thirty feet beneath the surface.

"Listen, listen." The lover of shortcuts has leaned his head down below the railing. We hear whispers that seem to come from the water.

He is reaching down to worlds far below. According to him, the submerged villages go on living—hens cluck, dogs bark—listen, you just have to listen.

But no one aboard is interested in the worlds below. All day long a gigantic German stands motionless, binoculars glued to his eyes. From time to time he leaps up, pointing at a spot hidden among the fronds. He is watching for wild orchids, epiphytes, the kind that grow in the treetops and can be auctioned off for a fortune at Christie's or Sotheby's in London. At each discovery he wants the steamer to change course. The captain refuses: a shortcut is a shortcut.

The two other passengers are Englishmen, specialists in primitive religions (Christ College), collectors of cosmic myths.

> a. Tupan begets the sun, who begets earth.
>
> b. Tupan breathes upon earth, scattering her into infinity.
>
> c. The sun, anxious not to be separated from his daughter, begs Tupan not to send her too far.
>
> d. The God agrees and orders earth to stop where she is.
>
> e. Earth, daughter of the sun, is made of fire. Tupan therefore causes it to rain upon her for a thousand years in order to cool her. Then asks the sun to shine upon her, for twelve hours out of every twenty-four, in order to warm her. . . .

All day long the Englishmen file their index cards, shut away in their cabin and emerging only in the evenings to call on me for confirmation.

"There is nothing so wonderful as a creation, don't you agree, Monsieur Gabriel?"

*August 12*

Suddenly a white ship straight ahead of us through the trees. Hailing. Cabin boy Zé Alphonso rings the bell. Without success. With no other response than the beating of wings, a great cacophony of birds. Cautiously, we approach the ship. She lies quite still, aground on a hilltop. Herons and scarlet ibis do us the honors, standing faultlessly to attention on the rigging. The captain's comment: You can't expect too much from shortcuts.

*August 14*

Fourteenth day of watery green submersion. Retribution for all women, mothers and grandmothers who so reproach the masculine species for not loving the vegetable kingdom enough. Every shade of green, from brilliant to dull, from emerald green to goose droppings, everything is green or seems born of green: tree trunks, creepers, floating plants, mushrooms, insects, abandoned canoes. The water is no more than a great dark sodden leaf that closes again as soon as the ship cuts through it, and the very air is wet as though water, determined to show its mettle, were climbing heavenward in imitation of the trees. Green, indigestion, the nausea of green, the terror of green. The captain is familiar with the madness that grips travelers in this part of the world; he tries to calm us as best he can, tirelessly drawing our attention to other colors—Oh, look at that bed of blue hyacinths; oh, that red macaw—but by the time you raise your eyes they have vanished. Green has devoured them; the glaucous curtain has fallen back into place. And the flower hunter is getting nervous. He no longer watches for orchids through his binoculars but scans the undergrowth for tunnels, for passages, for potential waterways. He pesters the poor captain with a barrage of questions, shaking him by the lapels of his threadbare uniform: How much farther is your shortcut taking us? I'll make you swallow your damned shortcut!

The Englishmen on the other hand are ecstatic. They think they are in the Bible. " 'And the Spirit of God moved upon the face of the waters. . . . And God . . . divided the waters which were under the firmament from the waters which were above the firmament.' What do you think, Gabriel, this is Genesis, isn't it? We are in the very heart of Genesis. 'Let the waters under the heaven be gathered together unto one place, and let the dry land appear.' No, Amazonia is before even Genesis. . . . What would you say, Wolseley, to writing a preface to Genesis?" And they clap their hands, shut themselves in their cabin, and celebrate the event with rejoicings of a decidedly pagan nature (from what I could hear).

I share their enthusiasm. But I am not in the Bible, I am in the womb. The forest is a womb. I listen to this womb's pulse, I listen to the ferocious mating of plants and waters to bring forth birth, birth, always birth. I am in the earth's loins; I feel her very long, very gentle contractions, the contractions of an old and patient being permanently giving birth. I long to stay there, where there is no more death, just life, where death is but one of life's faces, where life goes on and on and on.

*August 16*

Absence is green. Absence is like the forest. Absence is a form of decomposition. As green as Amazonia. As obscenely fecund. Dreams of resting from life. Dreams of total, complete death, *useless* death, a death that would feed nothing, not even a maggot. The green womb's dream of death.

*August 17*

In the middle of the night, I came upon the captain kneeling on the bridge: Saint Christopher Columbus, help me.

*August 18*

Prayer granted. Harsh return to the light, the double light of the river: the gray-white of the sky from which the heat descends, the pink-ocher of the waters with heat rising from them. The top and bottom of the oven.

The captain leaves the helm and asks us to join hands. "Thank you, Lord. Until next year, then."

He never attempts more than one shortcut per year. We are approaching my first plantation. I feel naked, and despite the extreme heat I shiver. I have not stayed long enough in the green, where things and beings beget one another and where resurrections brew. The sky is empty, the river is empty. I still need creations. I spend my last day shut away in my cabin, my ear glued to the partition that separates me from the Englishmen. And I listen. I listen and my courage returns.

The Moon and the Sun were two benevolent twins who rectified the imperfections of the Universe and protected creatures from the jests of the Creator. His favorite caprice was to thrust his wand (an extremely sharp rod in the form of a serpent) into every human orifice within reach. The Moon and the Sun, according to the specialists in the cabin next door, ventured to uproot these accursed serpents from the ground and graft them you know where, the place you so love to suck, Wolseley; don't be vulgar, William. Thus was born the dangling virile appendage.

I consider my sex with new interest. Such brave beginnings!

From this point Gabriel's notes abruptly forsake lyricism. From the end of August until December, they are no more than the gloomy report of an engineer crushed by figures, by production tonnages computed plantation by plantation* and month by month, by the accumulated debt (enormous) of the *seringueiros* (including sums owed by the dead or by fugitives: we knew their home villages in the Nordeste, and the company might consider taxing them collectively), by warehouse inventories, by profit forecasts based on rubber prices. . . .

Dryness, accuracy. As though Gabriel, having reached the heart of his profession, rubber, sought to protect himself. Or else had begun taking himself seriously. Had abandoned the human condition for that of Efficiency.

Hence all these soulless reams of writing with never a word about the men uprooted from their coastal homes in the early days of the

*Can you give the name "plantation" to something planted by God alone?

boom—Fortaleza, Pernambuco, São Luis—and prisoners of the green ever since. Not a word about their green lives. Four hours on foot every night to slash the trunks, four hours on foot every morning to tap the latex, four hours standing in your hut to smoke the gum, with only debt to look forward to at the end of the day, debt that expanded and imprisoned you because of course you had to buy machetes, alcohol, and fish hooks at the company store . . . and because the price of these items kept rising while the price of the gum fell. . . .

Nothing about the local Breton managers, Nedelec, Cleuziat, Corlouer. Yet they welcomed Gabriel like a messiah. It's been two years, each one told him, since I was last in town. . . . They showed him their finds, a bookkeeping trick, a small herb garden kept cool enough to grow turnips. . . . So, they asked, eyes shining, we're closing shop, when can I go back to France?

Gabriel did not answer. Simply entered in his notebook that evening: *Gustave Eiffel Plantation. Director Nedelec, Loïc. Appraisal: defeatist.*

Nothing, either, about the hevea, the monarch of rubber trees, with its gray bole and far-flung foliage, *the* rubber tree, the wounded tree, the tree whose red gashes are reopened every day by man so that the milk will flow.

I blush for Gabriel. I remember it all. They were waiting for one word. It did not come. I confess this to you, but no one else will know. I have burned the whole "efficient" chapter.

Then suddenly, on January 12, 1915, I can't say why (doubtless he considered his inspection complete), Gabriel rediscovered his soul. He at once abandoned his figures and returned to the forest.

### *January 12, 1915*

Everything rots in the forest. Everything. Leaves, branches, trunks, vines. Even the epiphytic orchids in the forest canopy. You would think their eternal communion with the sun would shield them from earthly malediction. But I find more and more of them fallen to the forest floor, where mildew consumes them.

*January 17*

Completed study of birds: they also rot. Including the most fragile of them, the scarlet ibis, the rainbow-hued araras unas pitangas gubas. They seem to consist only of feathers, bright colors, and wind. As soon as they fall they are like all the others. They stink.

*February 1*

This morning Zé Alphonso killed an ocelot. Before it was completely dead its spots were obliterated by swarms of flies.

*February 3*

Closed the file on snakes; their cunning can't save them, quite the contrary: beetles and ants fight inside their corpses.

*February 5*

Fish hold the record. I calculate that it takes less than ten hours for a *piracuru* trapped by a tree root to rot completely.

*February 6*

Major find: the very stones, eroded by moss, crumble and turn to sand. And then the sand itself, permanently immersed in water and deprived of sunlight, rots. So much for those mocking little crystals that give themselves such airs and graces.

*February 9*

Yesterday I left some blankets on the ground as an experiment. By this morning they had already begun to rust, to unravel. You cannot leave anything lying around.*

*The smallest object (perhaps even the smallest idea) will be borne away as if on a moving sidewalk, already far away, already transformed, by the time you return.

*February 13*

Despite appearances, a forest will intoxicate you with its speed if you only know how to look. Life spurts forth, blooms, wilts, ends, and starts again. Spectacular event follows spectacular event, with the same backdrops, the same characters. Or rather they are born of each other, the way kings beget kings. The way dreams beget dreams in Cervantes.

*February 14*

Time itself seems stricken. Seconds are endlessly protracted, and suddenly hours have gone by without leaving a trace. Is this not a symptom of fever in the metabolism of time? I am sure of it now. Even chronology is vulnerable to contagion.

*February 17*

Yes, everything rots. I hadn't even thought about light. Still limpid in the morning, it decays little by little as hours pile on hours. Green, blue-green, then black. And night, night is not merely another color but the very seat of fermentation, the source of those unceasing noises in the dark, those suckings, those endless lappings.

*February 20*

I am even beginning to believe that sadness (Clara's letter: *I am not leaving you, Gabriel*) is a part of the empire of decay. Slow decay, quiet decay, scarcely a teardrop, a little verdigris around the heart. Modest decay, but decay just the same.

It did no good to wall up that painful memory *(I am not leaving you, Gabriel)* with cold; it did no good to heap ice blocks around my dead love, a particularly difficult undertaking in these climes. All attempts at cooling are powerless against the might of the forest; ice thaws, and I sense that my love has resumed life as a corpse, fermenting and swelling before rebirth. Yes, Clara is returning in strength. Because of the forest.

*February 27*

All forests are hotbeds of decay. But there are degrees, ranging from those least abundant in decay (the temperate zones) to those most richly endowed (tropical and equatorial zones). And this hierarchy precisely reflects the prevalence of rubber. I refer only, of course, to wild rubber. As a result of my observations and the botany classes we took at Clermont, I am in a position to draw up the following table; it summarizes the state of my knowledge to date:

| *Type of forest* | *Degree of decay* | *Prevalence of rubber* |
|---|---|---|
| Temperate | Average | Nil |
| Equatorial and standard tropical | Substantial | Moderate (lianas, shrubs) |
| Amazonian | Extreme | High: hevea |

*February 28*

Why this connection between rubber and decay?

*March 2*

*Idem.* Why?

*March 5*

I shall attempt an explanation. What is rubber, if not the *rebounding force?* Which is to say, the principle vital to the process of decay, the process that transforms death into life. Therefore would not rubber be the purest form of decay, the very essence of decay, *clean decay,* as the whiteness of latex seems to attest? And would not Amazonia alone be so far gone in decay as to engender *that essence* which is rubber? Let us pursue the argument. Without Amazonia, there would be no rebounding force on earth, and therefore no rebounding: once struck down, no being would rise again. Stories, like journeys or loves, would have once-and-for-all endings.

Amazonia is the driving force of the planet.

## *March 22*

When I awoke this morning there was a slip of paper lying against my teacup, a quote from Quevedo's *Dreams:* "And what you call dying is the end of your dying, and what you call birth is the beginning of your dying, and what you call living is dying while living."

Who left me this invaluable message: Father Pettorelli, who is my host here in Porto Velho, or Father Carpentier (another Breton)? I have not met him, but I know he was in the house.

## *April 8*

The return trail. Dawn. First a translucence, the air gradually leeched of blackness, banks emerging, foliage etching itself against the sky, trees coming one by one into view as if returning from a journey. Then the whole river is bathed in light, suddenly buttercup yellow, and the whole forest reverberates, celebrating the light and shouting its joy as the sun bursts forth, an orange mass above the trees like a great round ship escorted by birds.

I should stop at Manaus, thank all my friends, and give the promised talk, "Time and Latitude." I don't feel up to it. The time for nostalgia is over. I will bypass the city. I will bid them all farewell from afar: attorney Guilherme, the bachelor pediatrician, the president with no first name, Walid, all the Francophiles, the members of the Land Registry Society. . . . I see them crossing the bobbing pontoons toward the Café Byron. They are no longer in the flower of youth. They stop when boats go by, clinging to barrels and buoys and great bales of rubber, waiting for the waves to die down. There are more than just trees and animals in jungles. Might I suggest human beings, among the most moving products of Creation?

# 8

# *Futebol*

In Belém marketplace nothing had changed. Not the sixty varieties of orange, not the red-bordered nail files made from the scales of the giant *piracuru* fish, not the aphrodisiac roots, not the hemp hammocks in which you could prove the efficacy of the aphrodisiac roots.

It was thus with carefree steps, if with overheated body (it's about time I had a real sex life at my age), that Gabriel came ashore and entered the Hôtel de Paris.

"Ah, dear friend, ah, dear friend, here you are at last; we've been trying to get in touch with you for ages."

And using dishes and glasses to represent whole army corps, General Manager Abel described in detail the shameful month of August, the glorious month of September, the German dash for the sea, the nation standing its ground, in short, the start of the Great War.

Gabriel listened bewildered, mumbling, "How can this be? I heard nothing. How is it that a world war makes no sound in Brazil?" He sat bolt upright. "But Clara, but Ann, Louis, my two families . . . ?"

"Now stay calm: They've written; it's a good sign."

And General Manager Abel handed him his mail.

Gabriel,

You were right, you and your father. What is the point of building an empire without either Alsace or Lorraine? But perhaps now is the time to revive the idea for which Maximilian and your grandfather gave their lives: the creation of a powerful and Catholic Mexico to counter American dominion. Anyway, I leave you to judge. You are the man on the spot. And then, an engineer like you knows what he is about.

With kisses.
Marguerite

. . . What would be the point in worrying?

Clara

Oh, Gabriel, I hear that your body is overheated. And my brother tells me the Argonne clay is cold. So please, for our sakes, stay where you are. Marie-Ghislaine

Choose whichever war you please, Gabriel, provided your own life be long.

Ann

. . . And I left, Gabriel, because it seemed to me that my fear comforted you. And stayed gone (can one say "stayed gone"?) because your sadness did not comfort me.

Clara

All across Europe, a terrible Asiatic flu, much worse than tropical diseases, and I am a nurse, I know what I'm talking about.

Your Martine in white

Gabriel had never known a Martine, or a Marie-Ghislaine, or an Odile, or a Jeanne, or any of these ladies who had been writing him day after day since general mobilization had been decreed. It took him a short while to piece it together. Clara was Clara. Ann was Ann. But Martine, she was Louis. And Marie-Ghislaine, she was Louis. He must have been worried about the censors. Masked the trail after his fashion. Once decoded, the messages were plain: *Stay where you are. Please don't come into the war.*

An order impossible to follow, and the time lag merely accentuated worry. Gabriel returned to his arithmetic:

Nine P.M. to 6 A.M. (French time): night. Chance of a lull in the fighting.

Between 3 P.M. and midnight (Belém time), he therefore felt a relative calm. His heart beat less quickly, hope was reborn; perhaps I'll really see all my loved ones again.

But later, just after sunrise in France (dead of night in Belém), he couldn't stand still, he besieged the post office in order to reach Paris (without success, Brazilian postal workers were asleep like everyone else), he paced the hotel's (deserted) lobby, about-faced at the potted plants in the reception area. He had switched on all the lights in an effort to dispel the pictures: Louis inert under the barbed wire, a shell obliterating the Washington and Albany.

And when the general manager finally came down from his room (7 A.M. in Belém, 1 P.M. in Paris—let us hope, yes, let us hope that by lunchtime they will be killing one another less over there)—Gabriel leapt on him: I must leave, I must leave.

"I have already told you, Gabriel, you will have a ship in a week, not before. You will be attending the Society luncheon, I trust?"

Let us face facts. Not everyone in Belém was an admirer of Victor Hugo and Jean Racine during the year 1915. Many Brazilians openly preferred Goethe and Wagner for pleasure and the Brazilianische Bank für Deutschland for business. As for Auguste Comte, certain people alleged, not unreasonably, that Germanic society was a model of positivism: serious, concrete, industrious. Could the same be said of France? In short, the German colony was powerful. It paraded through town on the smallest pretext: a half mile won at Ypres, the Bulgarian takeover of Macedonia.

The Hôtel de Paris was a haven for Francophiles, and it was there that Gabriel gained a better understanding of this curious breed.

Take for example Major Febronio de Brito, who wore two watches, one showing tropical time and the other the time in Paris, rue Mouffetard, where he had once lived.

Take for example that immensely prolific family whose children had been christened Cosette, Valjoão, Quasimoda, Esmeralda, Napoleão-the-Lesser, Marius, Javerto, Boozinho, and Jerimadeth.

But the keenest Francophile of all was without a doubt the engineer Carlos Drumond, one of the builders of the legendary railway that would shortly link Rio Mamoré to Rio Madeira in the depths of the jungle. I met him on the eve of my departure. He seemed exhausted.

"Woof, that's that, I've just sealed up my latest exam form. Since you're leaving tomorrow, could you take it to France for me? I think I did well this time."

Every year Mr. Drumond took the entrance exam for the École

Polytechnique. Had them cable the questions to him. And went to work under the eye of a proctor. As soon as he had finished writing, he sent his answers in a sealed envelope to the school headquarters, Montagne-Sainte-Geneviève, Paris (France).

"I am graded without any allowance being made, believe me. I twice came close to being accepted, in 1908 and in 1910. This year I'm very hopeful. . . . Assuming that the mail gets through. Tell me, since you are French: there's been talk of a change of syllabus; you haven't heard anything, have you? So much the better, but I don't trust them, they're quite capable of changing everything without warning. . . . If I pass I'll be off like a shot. Do you think I can get there in time for the orals? What a dream it would be for me. The École Polytechnique. It's the pinnacle of French Reason, isn't it, the pinnacle?"

The Francophile atmosphere proved stifling in the long run. Particularly when all these friends of France began casting strange looks at Gabriel. What is he doing here among us, this young Frenchman who should be defending his country? And what kind of war is this if it doesn't boost rubber prices? Perhaps the taxis of the Marne don't need to change tires, could that be it? And if Europe is stupid enough to commit suicide, perhaps the hour of retribution has struck for us, the American and Latin Americas?

So he left the hotel, braving the German colony, and strolled around the city, from the river to the Teatro da Paz Opera House, from the market to the Castelo fort, and from church to church, from Baroque to Jesuit to even more Baroque. . . .

As he strolled, Gabriel bounced his rubber ball up and down. Put yourself in his place. His youth slipping away (thirty-two years old). His wife absent, his country at war, his Amazonia asleep, his father almost certainly drafted, his mother unknown, his grandmother an empire fanatic. . . . Hardly a propitious inventory. More than ever, he needed bounce. No writer of pulp romances would contradict me.

It was at this precise juncture, not far from the port, that his magical ball struck something uneven (a pebble? a crushed fruit? a mislaid wallet?). It shot off to the right. Ricocheted off the polished shoe of a photographer whose body was concealed beneath the familiar black hood, and landed against the bare right foot of a street urchin shelling *maracujas;* the boy at once kicked it across to his neighbor, who irritatedly (for he had for some moments been following the hand movements of a young Negress who for want of anything better to do was polishing a pewter vase with that artless guile typical of the Negresses of Belém do Pará, Brazil)—this neighbor, then, irritatedly sent the red ball high into the air where, at the end of a short arc, it lodged in the upper right-hand corner of the porch of the church of Nuestro Senhor-das-Merces.

In relating this episode, Gabriel has no intention of claiming for himself the signal honor of introducing the game of *futebol* to Brazil.

Once again, he simply presents you with the facts:

1. Before this episode, Belém was futebolistically speaking a wasteland.

2. After it, the very next day, all over the city, beneath mango trees, in front of warehouses, between market stalls, human beings of the masculine sex were kicking balls similar to his own from foot to foot; witnesses too numerous to count would confirm it (if the matter interests you, make haste, some of them must still be alive).

On the morning of October 20, on the breakfast table between the moist mango slice (after the war, you must think seriously about your sex life, Gabriel) and the orange juice so full of pulp it was almost solid (first take vitamins, Gabriel), Gabriel found the exculpatory note.

> I, the undersigned, Petraglia Abel, unofficial French consul in Belém, State of Pará, Brazil, certify that M. Orsenna Gabriel is absolutely unable to return to his regiment due to the isolation of Amazonia and the dearth of ships destined for Europe.

Gabriel ran to the kitchens to embrace General Manager Abel and to thank him for the note and for the rest (everything). Clara, how could I refuse him when he asked me for your letters at the moment of my departure, so beautiful, Clara, the letter severing our relations and the other one, the one that explains everything, *and I went away because it seemed to me that my fear comforted you?* How to refuse a man who despised (and I agree with him) the practice of the visitor's book but who dreamed of opening a museum, a museum of love, where the bread oven stood?

"With all the items people leave behind in my rooms, believe me, I'll have a lot to choose from. But I promise you that your correspondence, together with a piece of your magic *Swann in Love* book, will have the place of honor."

I do not know if he ever carried out his plan. If he did, will you please forgive me,* Clara, for my indiscretion?†

*Forgiveness granted. Delighted with my tropical fame. Excuse me, equatorial. *(Signed) Clara.*

†On due reflection, I regret it. For they did indeed dwell on our fears, the fears we had at that time, and it's hard to remember fears if you no longer possess the letters, fears are so easily forgotten, so I do regret it. But I understand. *(Signed) Clara.*

## 9

# *Memories of War and of Armistice*

MEMORIES LOVE WORLD WARS. We tell them again and again that they shouldn't, that other periods are more compassionate, but it's no use; they return to flutter about those years like lovesick butterflies. I recall Clermont-Ferrand, those hours and hours we spent designing tires to navigate the terrible mud at the front. I recall that world of men stooped over wheels, those women all around them who had invaded the factory to replace their conscripted brothers or husbands. I recall all those faces that were not Knight faces: not Clara, not Ann, not Elisabeth. I recall those sad absences. Clara wasn't there, but no one is ever there during a war. I recall letters from Louis, serving as number two aircraft spotter on Suresnes hill. From dawn to dusk, binoculars glued to his eyes, he scanned the Paris skies for enemy planes and chatted with his comrades about women.

"War was invented in order to die, certainly, but also to allow men to talk about women, peacefully, without being disturbed. You should visit the battery more often, Gabriel." "The lads tell me I should change careers. They claim that bookstores and all the dreams that go along with them are booby-trapped, and that women who read are the hardest of all women to handle, what do you think, Gabriel?" I recall his attempts to mend his fences with the nation's thermal establishments, the pamphlets he published.

I recall the war years as if they had been my only years of peace. In spite of all the dead, the trainloads of mutilated men. . . . Years of reprieve: I was no longer fighting for my impossible double love; life rolled tranquilly on day by day, week by week. I am ashamed of my memory. I sense its readiness to breed still more recollections of war, peaceful, almost pleasurable. Stop. Contraception. Who will invent contraceptives for the memory? I move straight to the Armistice.

# THE MINERAL WATERS OF FRANCE
## ARE SUPERIOR
## TO THOSE OF GERMANY AND AUSTRIA

*The table below, which came to light accidentally and whose author is an anonymous Englishman, accurately states the case for the superiority of French mineral waters over those of Germany and Austria. We have added the names of several French spas overlooked by the author.*

| GO TO | | INSTEAD OF |
|---|---|---|
| Vichy, Pougues, Royat, Le Boulou, Châtelguyon, Plombières, Vals | *For Stomach Ailments* | Neuenahr, Karlsbad, Marienbad, Homburg, Kissingen, Ems |
| Châtelguyon, Plombières, Brides, Vichy, Aulus | *For Intestinal Disorders* | Karlsbad, Marienbad, Kissingen, Miers, Kreuzenach |
| Vichy, Pougues, Le Boulou, Châtelguyon, Vals, Contrexéville, Vittel, Martigny, Thonon, Évian, Brides | *For Liver Complaints* | Karlsbad, Marienbad, Homburg, Miers |
| Vichy, Châtelguyon, La Bourboule, Le Boulou, Vals | *For Malaria and Tropical Fevers* | Karlsbad, Marienbad, Homburg |
| Aix-les-Bains, Dax, Luchon, Bourbon-l'Archambault, Bourbon-Lancy, Lamalou, Saint-Amand, Barbotan, Préchacq, Bourbonne-les-Bains, Néris, Eaux-Chaudes, Ax, Saint-Honoré, Bagnères-de-Bigorre, Plombières, Luxeuil, Vernet, Saint-Nectaire, Royat | *For Rheumatism* | Karlsbad, Marienbad, Franzesbad, Baden-Baden, Nauheim, Teplitz, Aix-la-Chapelle, Badenweiler, Nenndorf, Wiesbaden, Johannisbad, Elster |
| Biarritz, Salies-de-Béarn, Salies-du-Salat, Salins-du-Jura, La Mouillière (de Besançon), Salins-Moutiers, Balaruc, La Bourboule, Bourbonne-les-Bains, Bourbon-l'Archambault, Dax, Luchon, Eaux-Bonnes, Amélie, Uriage, Cauterets, Aix-les-Bains, Saint-Nectaire | *For Scrofula and Inflammation of the Lymph Glands* | Kreuznach, Nauheim, Homburg, Wiesbaden, Baden-Baden, Reichenhall, Aix-la-Chapelle, Ischl, Ems |

# FRAUDULENT CLAIMS
## OF
# AUSTRO-GERMAN
# SPAS

The Unquestionable Superiority of our French Thermo-Mineral Waters.

Austro-Hun Spas are sheer Bosh.

. . . German Mineral Muds. Superiority of French Mud, rich in Medicaments, over Teutonic Slush . . . . . . . . . . . . . . .

Waters Rich in Salts. Overwhelming Superiority of Our Waters—Health-Enhancing French Table Waters . . . .

The Case for a Boycott of their Mineral Waters . . . . . . . . . . . . . . . . . . . . . . . . . . . .

Medical Commercialism of the Boche.

Down with Germanic Pharmaceutical Products! . . . . . . . . . . . . . . . . . . . . . . . . . .

etc., etc., etc.

With a Preface by

ONÉSIME RECLUS


**By DOCTORS CHARLES & LOUIS LAVIELLE**

**Medical Director and Assistant Medical Director**

**"BAIGNOTS" THERMAL ESTABLISHMENT**

**DAX**

**1916**

**PARIS—A. MALOINE Publishing Company**

25-27 Rue de l'École de Médecine

## MY WAR

*by Clara, née Knight*

Remembering is a contagious disease. It's no good Gabriel shutting himself in the room next door, never raising his voice, barely murmuring; I hear his pages turning. The fact is, old age is a porous condition. Doors don't close properly. So I too, yes, me, Clara, I feel the past inching back.

I recall Markus as a refugee in New York, the unlikely artistic adviser to the "Foundation for Allied Music," whose aim was to prove that the powers aligned against us had no monopoly on musical genius, that Edward MacDowell (1860–1908) was fully equal, for example, to Brahms, and that the conductors of Cincinnati and Chicago were not serving the just cause by offering up an exclusive diet of Beethoven and Mozart.

To console him in this lost cause, I used to accompany him on his walks, his ritual tour of Manhattan, sometimes heading west to the piers, sometimes strolling the waterfront across from Brooklyn before diving in among the blacks to the north.

He talked to me about me.

He refused to believe that human fear was suitable raw material for a true profession.

"You're earning your living on the backs of ghosts, Clara."

"Well, what about music, what about rubber, do you consider them true professions?"

"Gabriel was a very nice husband."

He always had a weakness for you, Gabriel; he believed that I was losing precious time being separated from you.

"For you will come together again, Clara, I am totally convinced, and it will be too late. Married life is already distasteful enough when one is young, intimate noises, odors, but you must have memories and long periods of turning a blind eye to tolerate the proximity of old age. I do not like your attitude toward Gabriel, Clara. It's the attitude of someone who will grow old alone."

I recall Elisabeth's smiles, her uncertain surreptitious smiles, the smiles of a little girl believing herself unobserved as she dips her finger in the jam; smiles that said, Thank you, war, I have Markus all to myself.

I recall my job in France later on, in the psychiatry department of the hospital. With the increasing horror of battle came corresponding increases in the number of shellshock victims as well as true malingerers. How could we tell them apart? My superiors, Professors Hesnard and Dumas, had devised a classification system and a series of simple tests to get malingerers to reveal themselves. With the help of Thierry, an intern with a voice so gentle that patients fell blissfully asleep, thumbs in mouths, the second he began to speak, I was responsible for presenting these academic findings in the most practical possible form to the army doctor at the base. Were we successful?

"For clinical purposes all malingerers can be divided into three main groups:

"1). Those who display decreased function, in particular *stupor,* mutism, or deaf-mutism. Simple diagnosis: the subject possesses none of the features of true melancholia, neither anxiety, nor rejection of food (at least over a long period), nor psychic pain, nor coolness of the extremities.

"2). Those who display more or less *agitated,* uncontrollable, or disorderly behavior. Simple diagnosis: the malingerer's agitation has one distinguishing feature: it ceases at night.

"3). And finally, those who exhibit *absurd* behavior (in words, absurd actions, eccentricities), Ganser's syndrome. Tricky diagnosis. Should be referred to psychiatric centers. Such syndromes, which at first sight seem obvious to the layman, are often in fact the ones that give experts the most trouble."

Every Wednesday morning we went off on our "torpedo run." This was the official name for the operation. All four of us left for Ville-Évrard, the two celebrities, M. Thierry, and me, Clara, the novice in such matters. A laboratory had been set up, a rather terrifying room festooned with copper wires, dials, and solenoids; this equipment, said the doctors, was in itself highly therapeutic.

Then they brought a patient in, usually a mute who rolled terrified eyes at the therapeutic fittings.

A nurse had him lie down on the marble table and glued rubber pads to his shoulder, his arms, and his throat, at the spot where words are made.

"Now don't you worry, dearie, this is going to hurt a little, but you want to get well, don't you?"

Power on. A simple downward pressure on a lever.

"Oh! Oh! Oh! Oh!" bellowed the patient.

"See, you're not mute at all, you pronounced the letter *O!*"

The two doctors, Hesnard and Dumas, took turns; from time to time M. Thierry joined in.

"Yes, well, now say *A* or we'll start all over again."

"Why pretend, dearie, since you're already cured? Come on, do what the doctor tells you."

"That's right, don't force me to—"

"You're an intelligent lad, don't make us raise the voltage. . . ."

*"A,"* the mute finally answered.

"And now *E, I, U,* and you're cured, go on, *E, I, U."*

*"E, I, U,"* the mute finally mumbled.

"Wonderful, yet another miracle cure!"

The nurse extricated him from his tangle of wires.

After the sessions we usually made a brief inspection of the communal wards, abuzz with conversation from one bed to another.

"Just listen to them," Hesnard and Dumas said to us. "All former mutes only this morning!"

We also achieved some success with the deaf, the paralyzed, and the permanently stooped, men unable to stand upright again after picking up a fallen comrade. But in the latter cases success was less certain, only 30 to 40 percent to be frank. Our German counterparts, with whom we corresponded via Switzerland, were amazed at our success rates and extended sincere congratulations; roll on the armistice so that we can all convene to further the cause of Science.

I recall the select committee that recommended recruiting soldiers from among the insane, the unstable, and various other misfits. They would be led by French colonial officers from Africa, "used to dealing with abnormal types." A good dozen "shock battalions" could thus be thrown together, the committee's report suggested.

I recall the sinister Dr. L'Ogre (sic) who listed no fewer than six categories of "pathological retreat from the enemy" in the *Neurological Review* of 1916.

I recall the neutral delegates. Two men and a woman, always the same ones, all of them fair-haired (if you'll forgive me, Gabriel), wearing red crosses on the lapels of their white coats and constantly consulting the blue folders clutched in their hands. They were the arbiters of the Geneva Convention. They came every three months to visit our hospital and make sure the carnage conformed to the rules. Our orders were to make them welcome and to keep the more grotesquely maimed cases out of sight. The high command was concerned that the neutral delegates might report such cases to the United States. It was felt that the United States would agree to intervene only in a legal war. These delegates knew the ropes. They could tell at first glance whether a wound was of an authorized variety; they nodded: appalling, appalling, but permissible. They bent over the mouths of inert men, sniffed, made a face: no, this mustard gas is forbidden.

We invariably ended up with self-inflicted wounds. And I used to wonder: how would a neutral feel about self-inflicted wound cases? First and foremost a certain basic empathy (those who inflict wounds on themselves hate war, just like the neutrals): but no, there was an immediate distance between them, a degree of contempt, a determination to underline the difference. You refuse to fight out of cowardice. I, a neutral, refuse on principle. The neutrals inspected self-inflicted wounds the way you visit your home village after making your fortune in the big city; your nostrils quiver: barnyards, cow dung, perhaps they're contagious. . . . Madame, monsieur, the sufferer would plead, look at my wound, would I have done such a thing to myself, on my own? They showed their stumps, whistled through the holes in their lungs; they knew this was their last chance, that only a veto from the Geneva Convention would save them from the firing squad. . . . From time to time the neutrals would burst into private laughter in Scandinavian accents. The medical colonel escorting them would enter into the spirit of things.

"I agree with you. Not one of your brighter self-inflicted cases, this one; he could have faked it more convincingly."

Will these recollections suffice, Gabriel, to remind you of what war is?

## I TOO LIVED THROUGH THE GREAT WAR

*by Ann, still Knight*

Since everyone else is remembering, I feel obliged to add my own contribution.

One afternoon in 1915 or 1916 (anyway, the newspapers reported bitter fighting; I can still see the black splash of the headlines without being able to make out the words: Verdun, Ypres, Chemin des Dames?) I went to that big café on the corner of the place de l'Opéra and boulevard des Capucines. Picked a seat. With the usual fuss you find so exasperating, Gabriel, but you must admit, and this particular occasion was no exception to the rule, that restaurant booths in Paris are *always* littered with crumbs. Sat down. Arrival of waiter. Order placed for a hot chocolate, the kind that takes exactly a quarter hour to cool, just the time I needed to kill before a (bank) appointment. All of which distracted me. At last I raised my eyes and looked about me. And who did I see through the steam rising from the chocolate? You, Gabriel. A false Gabriel. The real one was at the other end of the café. But through the miracle of mirrors and optical laws, there was your reflection in front of me. As is well known, reflections have no eyes. So I was able to examine you at leisure. I had not seen you since your famous leave-it-to-chance wedding (heads or tails, Ann or Clara). You had changed very little, your cheeks were as chubby as ever, your eyes as blue. Only around the temples were there some lighter streaks: real white hair, or a mirror's flattery? In any case, you kept glancing anxiously at your watch, as if you could feel yourself growing older. Finally the man you were waiting for arrived, a wounded soldier, a tall man, his head swaddled in cream-colored bandages. My God! you stammered. For a second conversation in the café died down. The wounded hero sat down at your table, hiding your reflection from me.

"Don't look so worried, Gabriel!"

"What's happened to you?"

"Don't look so worried, I said. Your old Louis is doing fine."

The sound of your conversation was reaching me from behind (optics and acoustics obey different laws).

"What's wrong with your head?"

Then wounded hero Louis explained to Gabriel that he was not severely wounded or even slightly hurt, that he was in fact in the pink of condition, that he was simply taking advantage of the war to cure his baldness once and for all. "You understand, Gabriel, in peacetime I'd never have the nerve to go around with all these dressings on my head. But the bandages keep the ointment in contact with my scalp, and this constant contact is essential to the treatment's success. . . ."

"Be quiet," said Gabriel. "People can hear us."

Gabriel was right. Once again conversation had stopped. Ears were straining toward your table. At a neighboring table sat pilots, real fighting men these, in fur-lined cloaks and sporting the Croix de Guerre with palm leaves. But the counterfeit wounded hero Louis carried on talking, and the lower he spoke the deeper his bass rumbled and the better he could be heard. Your father is physiologically incapable of whispering, am I not right, Gabriel?

"So how's that for an idea, Gabriel, taking advantage of the war? By the armistice I should be ready for my new life with a head of hair like a teenager's."

It all ended very badly. The fighter-pilots challenged him, ripping off his turban. Only the terrible stench it gave off, sulfur and petroleum, saved him. The true fighting men fell back in disgust. Luckily you seized your chance and fled.

So I fully understand your wish, Gabriel, to draw a veil over the Orsennas' war and push on as quickly as possible to the armistice.

*Since you never come to see me, there are times when I tell myself I should speak only to my attorney. Attorneys at least make appointments. And keep those appointments. And listen attentively to their clients' lives. And find excuses for them, however grievous the offense. The opposite of sons who heap their fathers with blame over trifles.*

*There are times when I tell myself a son is worthless. Far better in all instances to consult an attorney. Yes, long live attorneys! Paying your attorney is the sweetest and most gratifying of expenditures. Whereas raising a son is at best subsidizing his absence.*

*Forgive me this display of temper, but the work of remembering can sometimes be a dreary business. Forgive me, it is up to me to make you want to come. So I'll tell you a little about the wonderful place where I am preparing for my trial. Besides, as my attorney (from Nice) sagely observes while viewing our pictures, "The background in such cases is all-important." You climb avenue Wester Wemys, no. 13, Cannes-la-Bocca, and you come to a little fortress surrounded by high walls, almost battlements, and overlooking the sea, but at a bit of an angle, like the sidelong glance of a married woman. Its walls are the red ocher so cherished by the Italian sun. Its impressive bulk harks back to the golden age of families when the low cost of domesticity went hand in hand with the fertility of Catholic wives. It sits in a big garden surrounded by native trees: pine, laurel, eucalyptus, and several aloes whose stems stand proud and then tail off into stunted limbs, a heartrending cycle common to every virile spe-*

*cies on the planet. Note too the big terracotta pots of flowering geraniums and nasturtiums, and the white boxes on wheels bearing orange trees (alas, the oranges are sour) and lemon trees (alas, the lemons are obstinately tasteless, despite our annual attempts at grafting). In overall shape, the house is a* U. *From left to right: the sunset wing, where we live, the horizontal connecting segment (library on the second floor, summer dining room below), and the dawn wing, where the owners live.*

*Who are seldom here, apparently kept away by the furious pace of their Parisian preoccupations. On the morning of their arrival we are awakened by the clink of cups against saucers, of knives on butter dishes. . . . For it is their habit, as soon as they get in on the night train, to breakfast in the courtyard, whatever the weather, and to exclaim wonderingly, What balmy air, what light, what folly to be living in Paris!*

*Then they go back into their apartment, settling in across from us on the other side of the* U.

*This proximity is not without its charm, for many and good-natured are the smiles we exchange from window to window. Nevertheless it has forced me to adopt new working stations. For in fact, the female half of our two landlords, a most amiable-looking woman possessing one of those half-rough, half-musical accents that closely approximate the stridulation of cicadas in the Auch region, is a handwriting expert.*

*A terrifying proximity for the kind of man Gabriel is, doubly vulnerable both as a writer and as a defendant. I was on to her tricks, the little glances she darted in my direction, from the very first day. She wants to rob me of my privacy. That is certain. Just one line of my writing (rounded, obsessive, tiny), and she will know all my secrets. I believe her to be skilled, even a virtuoso, at her craft. Able to identify my lettering from my hand movements alone, to discern my personal style of sexuality from the aggressive slash of my "d's." So I keep out of sight. Like any good student during a Latin test I write behind a bastion of books. All she sees of me is my head, a rather anxious head, for graphology is not the only form of larceny. I know experts who can deduce personal strengths and weaknesses from the shape of the skull. Vigilance! Perhaps she possesses this skill as well. It would be wiser to work with shutters closed and curtains tightly drawn. But as he prepares his case Gabriel desperately needs the sky. From time to time he gazes at it. And its mere presence beyond the roof, gray or blue or red depending on the hour, reminds him not to lie too much, to stick to the truth. Who knows what our Gabriel might dream up in a hermetically sealed room?*

*I have fewer fears about our landlord. His clothes, several sizes too large, flap reassuringly about him. There is a dream in this man, a dream in quest of fulfillment. Circumnavigating the globe in a sailboat? Founding a theater? One day we will trade our experiences. We will go off together without a word to anyone. The restaurants of old Cannes all have discreet tables, naturally, what with the festival. The two of us will sit there chatting at great length, to the fury of our wives, who will be calling across to one another from their windows. Have you seen my husband? No, madame, and have you seen our Gabriel? Well, no, that's why I was wondering. . . . First anxious, then furious. And there's nothing like a woman's fury to cement friendship between men. I'll tell him all about rubber, and he'll initiate me into the secrets of paper, since that's his field. And then he'll reveal his dream to me, the dream for which he's preparing, the dream for which he wears such oversized trousers, pullovers, and blazers.*

*Enough, back to work. Try to come and see us, your mothers and me, one of these days. I must soldier on.*

The armistice, then.

Forced to travel constantly between the front and the Works, I had decided to live in a hotel. The establishment I selected, between the cathedral and place de Jaude, was most often empty (wars do not encourage tourism). Sometimes a general would drop in to throw his weight around. The high command could not understand why French vehicles continued to stick in the mud; the army is bogged down because of you, they complained. It was my job to calm our visitor, to outline the complexities of the problem to him. I took him on a tour of our pride and joy, our testing grounds, every conceivable kind of terrain, between two and three acres apiece and watered with gardening hoses on days when it didn't rain hard enough. The general and I would sit side by side on folding chairs. The guinea-pig trucks would drive up and down in front of us, shod with XL-12 tires, then with A-14 tires, then with 17-B tires. A wearisome display of skidding and sliding, generally culminating in mired vehicles.

"I see your point, sergeant" (that was my rank), the general would say, mopping red and brown splotches from his face. "I see your point, no excuse for throwing in the towel of course, but tires are a complicated business."

And that night he would invite me to dinner in the vast deserted dining room, its walls hung with hunting trophies (the small deer of Auvergne).

"I too used to hunt before the war," he would confide.

Apart from the generals, the hotelkeeper and I had the place to ourselves. She was named Mme. Haeberlin after a husband who had run away (with a hussy from Chaise-Dieu) just a few days (as it turned out) before war was declared and had therefore been recaptured by general mobilization. And had since died. So that after one or two glasses of plum brandy, Mme. Haeberlin had no difficulty seeing herself as a war widow rather than a deserted wife. Moreover, she could appreciate her blessings: War isn't all bad, you know.... That was her personal refrain, her own brand of optimism. She would wink and blush faintly. I had grown used to the mole on her upper lip, to her short-cropped gray hair. We chatted together in the dining room for hours, with her standing against my table, a plate in her hand, and me sitting over the carcasses of my crayfish. For in the absence of real meat she served crayfish with every meal. I would suggest that she sit down. She would pretend not to hear.

The most unpleasant thing was to sleep surrounded by empty rooms. I would suddenly start awake with the feeling that a desert was on the march all around me. Luckily, the Grand Hôtel de Lyon made comforting noises. The rumble of the heating system, Mme. Haeberlin's constant comings and goings, the creak of the front door, first for the milkman and then for the mailman (still nothing, Mme. Haeberlin), and even that moment of utter silence between the shattering of a breakfast cup and the sounds of busy scrubbing. All these noises were a substitute for my own family.

November 12, 1918. I was still half asleep. Not that I had been out late celebrating victory, but I felt as if I were on vacation. And then, too, on the day after an armistice, peace reclaims its rights and you remember former fears, you find you are suffering from serious diseases. I rose to retrieve the newspaper that had been slipped under my door. On page nine Apollinaire was dead. They had apparently strewn the road outside his house with straw and drawn the curtains tight to spare him the clatter of passing carriages and the happy singing outside. I heard women's voices, and Mme. Haeberlin's "I'm coming, I'm coming." And then my name:

"Monsieur Orsenna"—in a questioning tone—"this is where he lives, is it not?"

I lost what followed.

"But who are you ladies?" Mme. Haeberlin had raised her voice. As it happened, my room, number 4, was at the top of the stairs, so there was no need to strain my ears.

A whispered reply.

"In that case, then . . ."

There was laughter and giggling and a great rustling of dresses. Every stair on the staircase creaked. Then my door opened.

Years later I saw Mme. Haeberlin again, doubtfully consulting the map at the Madeleine stop in the Metro. She was in Paris for a funeral. Standing there between trains, she confessed to me that she still thought back to the answer the two unknown women with flushed cheeks and glittering eyes had given that morning.

" 'We are Gabriel Orsenna's wife.' Yes, those were their very words: 'We are Gabriel Orsenna's wife.' If it hadn't been for the armistice I would have called the police."

Mme. Haeberlin would have liked to prolong our conversation. Would have liked me to explain the exact meaning of those words. But it wasn't the right place, standing on a platform at the heart of rush hour with a train going by every four minutes. I was a little abrupt with her. "Goodbye, Mme. Haeberlin, how glad I am to see you again and in such good health. Enjoy your stay in Paris."

"And what about you?"

The gaze she directed at me held few illusions. I reassured her by lying a little. "Oh, everything is fine, Mme. Haeberlin, I am very happy." And I pointed her in the right direction—"Change at Concorde for Montparnasse; after that it's direct"—and I plunged whistling into my own itinerary.

One of the reasons I wanted so much to have a son was in order to evoke for you, my grand and glorious boy, memories like the one that follows. I could talk about my life to many people, to a woman met by chance, to a garlic-breathing priest in the confessional, to a jury. But with the flesh of my flesh, contact is closer. A mighty river flows through me, born high upstream, flowing far downstream: Gabriel Orsenna, son of Louis Orsenna, handing down to his son X Orsenna (I prefer not to reveal your first name so soon) the philosopher's stone, the secret of happiness.

And now wouldn't you like to know, my dear son? You itch for details. You would like them to be spicy, yet you are also a little apprehensive; after all, we're talking about your mother and your aunt. I picture your forehead turning pink, your palms growing moist, as you prepare to turn the page, abandoning this one, utterly innocent, but a harbinger of the next, so much more promising. Like every adolescent in the world engrossed in a smutty passage, you keep one ear open and are ready to toss the compromising work into a drawer at the slightest suspicious sound. You are straining your ears the way I strained mine as they came up the stairs, as I recognized their voices, Clara's first: "Let's watch him sleep"; then Ann: "Don't be silly, he's already up, dressed, shaved, happy, and expecting us."

Calm yourself, dear boy, I'm going on, I'm going on.

Old age in any case confers impunity. Old folk like me can say anything. People will let them tell all kinds of stories, even the truth. And then advanced age is a kind of incognito, a pseudonym; the people you mention are dead or hardly recognizable. Looking at them now, Clara and Ann, so dignified and respectable, looking at their wrinkled hands, who would believe them capable of the caresses they lavished on me that morning? Believe me, you can advance into time past as boldly as into a desert, for it is generally uninhabited.

Giggling, then, they knocked at my door.

"Come in, Mme. Haeberlin," said your father, his wits still about him despite the rapid heartbeat that overwhelmed him.

And as if diving from the heights of almost four years of absence, they hurled themselves into the bachelor's bedroom. First Ann, plum-colored suit, flared skirt (doubtless an American invention), followed by Clara, nurse's cape, long navy-blue silhouette. Cried out, "Gabriel, oh, Gabriel!" Pulled a face at the hollyhock-pattern wallpaper. Smiled at the photo sitting on the rickety bedside table: four Knights lined up on a sidewalk beneath a sign in giant letters, WASHINGTON AND ALBANY. And they kissed Gabriel and kissed Gabriel and kissed Gabriel again.

"How cold it is here, Gabriel!"

(I had left the window open all night long, the better to savor the armistice.)

And at once slipped beneath the covers, Clara on the left (Well, here I am, Gabriel) and Ann on the other side (Do you like your job?).

"And how is Markus?" asked Gabriel.

"Oh, Papa still adores you, if that's what you want to know."

"Adoptive life volume two," said Ann.

You have two choices, my son.

Either you intend to store your life in sealed compartments, carefully isolated from one another: love / family / friendship / job / sex / travel / sports / hobbies / nostalgia / fear of death. This is your right. You would not be the first or the last. I would merely remind you that the *Titanic,* constructed on this very principle, sank.

Or else you prefer to give battle along an unbroken front and not divide your forces. In this case, select two sisters and never leave them. Try not to.

For two sisters represent at once love, family, friendship, sex (tracking down their echoes and affinities revives you much more effectively than ginseng root), travel (particularly when they are as nomadic as the Knights), sport (exhausting), hobbies (if you have any time left over for hobbies, which I doubt: statistical tables turn up no stamp collectors among men passionately in love with two sisters), nostalgia, and fear of death (cf. above, sex and affinities).

So there you are, my dear son, you need know nothing more. I've excited you enough. A son should not witness his father's frolics. Such activity might shock or disappoint him or, worse, fill him with admiration and envy, stunting forever his own future initiatives.

Believe me, my son, don't hold it against me but leave me sandwiched between the two sisters in my hotel on this post-armistice morning. Go away, go back into your own life; it would be better for both of us, believe me. If you like, just take this one detail along for the trip: Ann wanted it standing up, Clara didn't. That's it, time to say goodbye. Don't lean out of your window. A big hug, Gabriel.

You won't leave? Not yet? Very well. Then stop giving me that scared-child look, a naughty child afraid of the dark, and I'll go on.

They were so high-spirited that morning, even serious Clara, the navy-blue nurse with the chestnut braids, as they sat on the edge of the bed and clapped their hands. "Do you realize, Gabriel, the war is over and we are not dead? Oh, long live life, real live life! Elisabeth and Markus will be back from New York on the first available ship out, and we'll go and meet them together. Markus will be so glad to see you, yes, here's to life!" and they kissed me all over my chubby cheeks, while Ann of the golden braids lay beside me in her heavy flared skirt. "Remember, Gabriel," Ann murmured into my ear, "I told you so, life is long, long, here we are together again. . . ." And they laughed, they couldn't stop laughing; I was the solemn one—"But why the long face, Gabriel, aren't you glad to see us?"—and laughed and laughed.

You'll find out, there are days, extremely rare days, when bedrooms go away, uproot themselves from their hotel and leave, drifting down fast-flowing rivers and heading out to sea. It was high spirits that led us from one act to the next, yes, Gabriel, the women you love have knees, and thighs, what a schoolboy he is, our blushing Gabriel, faster, faster, soon they were all out of breath, even earnest Clara, even distant Ann.

You refuse to go?

I knew it. So much the worse for you. It's hard to live with a grotesque image of your father within you, but you've asked for it. So I'll go on. I'll describe the insane ambition that suddenly seized me while I should simply have been savoring this miracle: Ann and Clara in my bed on November 12, 1918, and ready for anything—for anything, do you hear?—anything to give me a happy armistice. Yes, an ambition came to me, and don't start muttering, What an idiot, really, what an engineer my father is, for this ambition directly concerns you. With the eternally solemn Clara bestriding me, and with Ann whispering unbelievable propositions into my ear, I said to myself, And what if we seized this opportunity to create a child, all three of us? What if we took advantage of the circumstances (the new world arising out of a world war) to shatter genetic laws? Those excessively binary laws: one man + one woman = one child.

So I altered my rhythm, I rushed them, I became at once frenzied and calculating, an acrobat and a sharer, scarcely loving one before leaping upon the other, tacking port and starboard, switching my line of attack; I'm all yours, my beauties, I'm the woman now, make a son for me.

They looked at me, at first surprised and full of admiration—Well, well, Gabriel, you the shy one, these last four years have changed you; my word, what energy!—and then they were alarmed. Slow down, Gabriel, what's going on? Perhaps even disgusted. They realized I had left off just being happy. They sensed effort, repugnant effort. And that was that. The bedroom became a bedroom again and they got dressed. And since they are now dressed the sight holds no more interest for you, and you can leave without regrets.

For to recall a scene like the one that follows, ingrate, it would be better to have no son. Even though a father's amorous failures are always of some comfort to his son, I have no wish to comfort anyone. Nevertheless, Gabriel will describe the catastrophic lunch that followed, course by course.

First a tomato salad, pale unpeeled winter tomatoes, their pink skins dappled with dewy little bubbles of oil wherever they emerged from the nasty mixture of chopped onions and parsley they swam in. Just imagine a human body going outside at first light and stretching out in the grass: would it be bathed in dew like the rest of Creation? Neither Clara nor Ann had any reply to this first attempt of mine to steer the conversation along rather poetic lines.

Next, somewhat limp chicken breasts ringed by the inevitable crayfish. Did you know that during the war these creatures took advantage of the lull to invade all our streams? One more year and they would have taken our armies from the rear. What do you conclude from that? asked Clara.

Then blue cheese from Auvergne, with its miniature caverns fuzzy with the faintest of down, not unlike—"What are you thinking, Gabriel," asked Ann. "Personally I have always found this cheese rather revolting," said Clara.

And then the crowning touch, an offering from the widow Haeberlin, a huge chocolate-flavored éclair, pinkish rather than brown, clear proof of a serious cocoa shortage. "I didn't know they had ovens big enough," said Clara. "This time I know what you're thinking," said Ann. And, in the noise and bustle surrounding this victory dessert, her fingers lightly (and in final settlement?) brushed the once and future bachelor Gabriel.

That red, white, blue, and disastrous menu takes up a disproportionate (an enormous) place in Gabriel's memory. For years and years it was the first thing he thought of when he awoke. It was no good forcing himself to think of other things—a sunny beach, a painting by Piero di Cosimo—or to go on dozing as long as he could, the menu always returned, taking its own sweet time: first the tomato salad, then the limp chicken breasts. . . .

Coffee was served in white cups with blue stripes. So the two sisters raised the white cups with blue stripes to their lips. They did not move. They gazed at Gabriel across the thin wisp of steam that floats up from coffee. They gazed at Gabriel and reflected one last time: Let us think, will we be able to live with this Gabriel sitting here before us? Who was at this moment acting the part of quite another Gabriel, a devil-may-care Gabriel, a Gabriel who had not had merely two sisters in his life but many, an armada of sisters, in fact you probably ran across one or two of them on your way here . . . a seducer of a Gabriel. Seducers are people who do not feel obliged to talk of love when the subject is love. So Gabriel strove to talk of other things. But those other things concealed themselves, as they always do at such times. Gabriel saw only his love, and absolutely nothing else. He therefore spoke about what he saw, his love. And was utterly boring. Suffocatingly. Unforgivably.

It was Ann who called for the bill—"Yes, yes, we insist"—and Clara who pronounced sentence. A predictable division of tasks, given their respective professions.

"Well, Gabriel, we've given this a lot of thought, and we hope, from the bottom of our hearts, Gabriel, that you will be happy."

"Oh, every hour on the hour, or very nearly," Mme. Haeberlin replied when Ann asked her about trains to Paris.

Gabriel would like to take the opportunity afforded by this preparation for his imminent trial to acquit himself of his debt to Clermont-Ferrand and to Auvergne, which had done so much for him, which had tried so hard to heal him.

But the sight of slumbering volcanoes was not enough to cure him of his craving for sisters.

It was the first real postwar Sunday, the first one o'clock luncheon for four years, a return to old habits. Two of the waiters had been there before the war. People hugged them. Flags and bunting on the walls, *Honor to our fighting men* painted on windowpanes, a few threadbare VIVE LA FRANCE signs; it had been a whole week now since the signing of the armistice at Rethondes. And the restaurant was turning people away. Every table was taken, mothers and eldest sons, hungry-looking blondes of the wartime godmother variety, reunions of regimental chums, tearful lovers, sad ladies seated side by side, crippled youths who never stopped laughing, every possible combination of the human species. . . . And everywhere, wherever you turned, the same stories, those unending stories of battle: I had the devil's luck, and poor old X . . . as if they wanted to relive it all so that the horror too would end all over again. At several tables people were proposing penalties, a two-franc fine for anyone who mentioned the front. But no one could resist. The slightest gesture, the merest bottle—My God, that reminds me of a night alert—and the ball of yarn would unwind: Douaumont, Chemin des Dames, the Dardanelles, there was no stopping it. And always returning to the same question: What are we going to do now? Now? The instant war ended, peace had set in. Many people would have been grateful for a transition, an intermission, neither peace nor war, a lazy morning dozing under the bedclothes.

At last Louis arrived.

He had changed, his hair whiter, his skin paler. With age, men begin to look like paper rubbed too hard and too long with an eraser; you can see through them without quite being able to identify what you see, perhaps something taking its leave.

Father and son stood and embraced. Gabriel closed his eyes. He preferred to listen: Louis's voice was unchanged, the same old joy of battle.

"This is it, Gabriel, I believe the time is ripe."

The headwaiter stood ready for their order, pad in hand.

"Oh! I'm sorry, how is your pâté today?"

And could the wine be brought just a tiny bit earlier? Gabriel had never seen him in such festive spirits. His years as an aircraft spotter, no doubt. Waiting must have given him a taste for things. Constantly busy until now, busy beginning his life over and over again, he had never really taken the time.

"I'll show you the plans later. But the whole planet has now given me permission to organize a Universal Exposition."

A newsboy walked by with the morning papers: PRESIDENT WILSON PROPOSES INTERNATIONAL TREATY.

"Just watch, we're going to be flooded with recipes for peace. Nothing wrong with that, nothing wrong at all. But what we need is a rebirth of confidence; we need to know what we human beings are capable of. . . . Global stocktaking. . . ."

He had extracted a small blueprint from a shopping basket. "What do you think? The Universal Exposition. It could be set up on the Champs-Élysées all the way from the Rond-Point to the Carrousel, with the Louvre as a backdrop. . . . I don't mind telling you they're already fighting over it like cats and dogs. . . . Of course a lot of people favor the traditional Invalides–Trocadéro hub."

The 1913 Pauillac had oxidized. I was a bit bored—as so often when faced with other people's enthusiasm. Louis noticed.

"And what about you? You don't look well. Still your two princesses?"

That's what he called Ann and Clara. For him princesses were a breed apart, with clearly defined characteristics: long limbs, amused-smile-even-during-the-act-of-love; someone else's women no matter what you did, even if you became that someone else yourself; always poised to be off.

"I warned you. Princesses are a curse. I raised you badly. The only useful thing a father can teach his son is to prefer women who stay. Gabriel?"

"Yes."

"If you can't do without princesses, at least change cities. Clermont-Ferrand isn't their style. Gabriel?"

"Yes."

"Trust me, stop being so stubborn about it, you're no longer young, you know. You'll see, there comes a time when you realize you won't have fingers, a body, or smiles for very much longer. The lack of a woman is a luxury you can afford only in youth. Please listen to me. Pick a real woman, Gabriel, a truly real one. And you'll see how much warmer life will be."

A lady with a mass of piled-up golden hair stood at their table. Of Nordic or Slavic type, large rather than tall. Too healthy-looking. Absorbed in his fatherly counsels, Louis had not noticed the real woman's arrival.

"Good afternoon, Louis, are you going to introduce me to your son?"

A good sign for Gabriel's father's continued happiness, her accent wasn't very strong. The irritable and pedantic Louis could not long have endured a too-pronounced rolling of *r*'s or excessively modulated vowels. A good sign for Gabriel's father's future, the tone in which she had framed her opening remarks; Good-afternoon-Louis-are-you-going-to-introduce-me-to-your-son meant that she intended to take matters into her own hands.

A good sign for love in general: the present liaison was starting off on the right foot.

Bad news for Gabriel: the two Orsennas were no longer alone in the world.

Louis jumped to his feet. "Oh, forgive me!" Her first name was Wladislawa, from Sopot (a suburb of Gdansk), and she was an interpreter by profession (hence the lack of accent).

"Wladislawa," said Louis (he must have practiced for hours and hours behind the closed doors of his library to be able to pronounce it so Polishly), "Wladislawa is here for the international conferences that will be starting soon."

"It's a job where you need something solid to hold on to," she said, looking Gabriel straight in the eye.

Message received. Change of subject. Return to Louis's big plans.

"Granted, the Eiffel Tower seemed quite novel for the exposition of 1889, but admit it looks garish now. . . ."

Exposition fever had again seized Louis. One problem obsessed him: how best to present the tropics.

"You know the colonies, Gabriel—or Brazil, anyway—what would you say to a gigantic greenhouse down Avenue Marigny? Would you be willing to take care of rare plants?"

"I don't know if I'll have time. It doesn't look as though peace is going to leave us much leisure."

"What can you possibly have to do that would be more important than the Universal Exposition?"

Louis did not understand, nor did Wladislawa. They looked at him in amazement. Lack of ambition, fair enough. But when someone has offered you an ambition, a vast one, an ambition in which you can spend your whole life, when they slow the parade down for you, when they open the door for you and all you have to do is hop aboard and take the seat awaiting you in that warm ambition, a cozy little window seat . . . would Gabriel Orsenna remain standing on the platform, arms folded? They stared at Gabriel Orsenna, not daring even to ask him what he intended to do, or what he thought was more worth doing than a Universal Exposition. They were afraid he might be a creature bereft of preferences, as they themselves had been before the blossoming of their love, merely an indecision, a haziness of the soul.

Finally Louis said, "Very well, just as you wish. But you'll come around, just wait and see."

The real woman and the two Orsennas ate dessert. Bourdaloue pears were the rage. With powdered sugar that rose in tiny puffs from your lips at every teaspoonful, like talking in winter.

Louis the bespoken looked around the dining room: what fun they were all having! In celebration of victory the women had brought out all their ostrich plumes, their boas, their fox furs, and since they were all (or almost all) dressed in black, you could have sworn it was the fashion and not mourning. Dreams refused to die. People talked louder and louder. Nobody left the tables. The waiting list grew longer, dozens of customers who had overslept or had just got in off the train. We were sitting by the door. We heard the headwaiter say, Come back in half an hour, then later, Come back in an hour, and then finally, Don't bother to come back. I don't understand what's going on; no one wants to finish.

Louis was explaining his son to Wladislawa. "Would you believe it, ever since he was a little boy Gabriel has had a genuine passion for a raw material, for rubber?"

He had seized my forearm and was smiling tenderly at me.

"But the fact is he showed me the way. . . . The essential truth of vocations . . ."

He was crying out for help. Because of Wladislawa. Too great an estrangement between father and son might frighten her, as if it represented some genetic flaw. And perhaps he was also trying to send me a message, an all-important message: a three-way conversation is often the very best way for two people to talk. He stressed his point.

"He and I are just the same; we lead life exactly the way you lead a horse."

This comparison seemed to please Wladislawa enormously. Her hand never left that of her French betrothed. Our family locomotive was hungry. I fueled it.

"But you too had a calling, Louis. A bookstore is already a Universal Exposition. A little less obvious, a little slower, that's all."

Louis beamed.

"That's true. I hadn't thought of that, Gabriel. Visiting the Expo will be like reading a thousand books. I won't be betraying anything. I'll simply be moving into higher gear. Come, we must celebrate all this," said Louis. "Yes, celebrate; you see, I was right to make a fresh start. I was right. Come, celebrate with me"—he leaned closer—"and forget your princesses; trust me, leave princesses to their faraway destinies."

He called for liqueurs and announced his forthcoming marriage. The climate was suddenly light, Viennese, like a triumphant evening at the theater or music hall. You could have spent your whole life there basking in the encores.

The restaurant made up its mind: the lunchers would stay on for dinner. They simply added stickers to the menus: no more orders taken after 11 P.M.

Outside, where peace had replaced war, night fell.

# PART

# TWO

# 10

# *The Motor-Racing Stage*

## I

UNDERSTAND THIS: these were years turned inside out, an unbelievable upheaval of time; youth and age shuffled, cut, and dealt like cards. The young died, the old lived.

At any moment the secretary might poke her head through the door.

"More bad news, I'm afraid, monsieur."

"Don't say it!"

"It's Monsieur Georges . . . the bookkeeper . . . the day before yesterday . . . outside Bapaume."

"The idiot!"

Being personnel manager is not an easy job. Particularly during world wars.

He would rise, take his eraser, and banish yet another name from the company rolls. I was one of the few remaining who had joined the firm before 1914. Every time our paths crossed he gripped my shoulder.

"You at least are a survivor, Gabriel. So, what are your peacetime plans? We need to know, Gabriel. Let's talk about it later, when we have a little more time, the sooner the better. We can have lunch if you like."

His name was Michel Charton, I remember, a roguish, portly man with an eager look and gaudy bright suspenders even in those days of bereavement, and an Arts et Métiers graduate to boot. He took me to one of those neighborhood restaurants where tables touch and conversations overlap. You rapidly lost the thread. You were tempted to pick up the conversation where the customer to your left had finished off. . . .

"First of all, Gabriel, you can rest assured. We are cutting our losses in Brazil."

M. Charton looked me straight in the eye. Twenty years as personnel manager had taught him how to polish off a dish of lentils in oil and vinegar without once shifting his gaze from his table companion's pupils.

"Finances are not your cup of tea. Fine. At present you're in charge of military vehicles, but that can't last forever. So what are you planning to do for us?"

What did he mean by "us"? His forces had been decimated by the war. You felt that he drew new hope from lunching with someone still alive and kicking. But from time to time a suspicion shot through him: What if this one too disappears? Whence, no doubt, his passion for garlic; he must somehow have confused ghosts with vampires. He constantly ordered extra, by the whole clove or chopped, to go with his lentils, with his stuffed cabbage, with cheese.

"What are the options?"

"There's room for everyone. But first, which do you prefer: the colonies or France?"

Careers always begin with such a moment, a moment to be savored above all others: someone riffling before your very eyes through the catalogue of your potential existences. You lean back and picture yourself in one role after another.

"What kind of job would I do in the colonies?"

"Well, you could manage a plantation, or head a marketing network, or supervise transportation, or represent us at the Bank of Indochina. What appeals to you?"

I should have liked him to be more specific; after all, we were discussing Gabriel's potential destinies. And a destiny, even a potential one, has to be rolled lingeringly around the tongue.

"Well, what's it to be, can I put you down for Indochina?"

My mind was already made up. I was still angry with Asia for stealing Brazil's rubber trees. And my own rubber was the wild variety, not the domesticated. I could not see myself as a planter. . . . Would M. Charton have understood such reasoning?

In answering: no, I do not want to go, I have a family to support, I clearly saw the steamer receding in the direction of Port Said. And I had to restrain myself from waving my handkerchief. Across the hot apple pie we had both ordered for dessert.

The personnel manager said nothing. His lips twitched in a fleeting grimace. Clearly I had disappointed him.

"Very well, France, then. I can offer you a solid job in our Racing department. How does that sound? Splendid! I'll put you down as an assistant researcher to begin with. But in research it's never the boss who does the real research work. I'm sure you'll acquit yourself with honor. If what they tell me is true, there's a kind of love affair between you and rubber, isn't that so?"

The personnel manager shook hands with me long and carefully and even patted me on the cheek. I understood why. He wanted to make sure one last time that Gabriel Orsenna really belonged to the land of the living. Reassured, satisfied that he had routed the armies of ghosts, he went off with sprightly steps, stinking of garlic.

Months went by, peace was signed, the guns fell silent. The days flapped about you like clothes several sizes too large. War had taken up all the available space. Armistice brought gaps and war-surplus dumps, whole acres of green camouflage-painted trucks. Nobody wanted them. It was no good trying to auction them off, even when we started the bidding at rock bottom. What is to be done with them? asked the press.

Tires were more successful. We piled them up into eerie black mountain ranges; on weekends families came to view them, rummaging for hours through the rubber to find a complete set of tires and bearing them away in wheelbarrows at nightfall.

"Now we'll be all set when we get a car," the husband would say to the wife.

The wife would nod. Where dreams are concerned, women are highly amenable.

Keeping an eye on these stockpiles was one of Gabriel's tasks. Every morning he called for the price lists:

Used car tires, smooth . . . . . . . . . . . . . . . . . 53 francs
Used small car tires, smooth . . . . . . . . . . . . . 40 francs

| | |
|---|---|
| Used car tires, steel-belted | 23 francs |
| Used bicycle tires, smooth | 14 francs |
| Used car tires, bald | 40 francs |
| Used bicycle tires, red | 280 francs |
| Used bicycle tires, gray | 280 francs |

These secondhand mountains flattened the market for new equipment. It would have been better to burn them all, but for fear of the press no one dared. The same press that had grown so fat on war: for want of anything better it had come up with a new refrain, postwar scandals, the crime of waste. And then, too, burning rubber smells awful!

So the company was working at half speed, at a ghost's pace, as Personnel Manager Charton liked to say. Time hung heavy in every department, but particularly in the Racing division after we received this directive from the automobile manufacturers' federation:

> In view of the urgent and daunting challenges facing the French automobile industry in its efforts to return to peacetime production norms, and in view of uncertain future prospects, it would at present be premature to envisage automobile competition of any kind, including racing, *concours d'élégance,* etc.
>
> It has therefore been decided to ask all automobile clubs, racing organizations, etc., to suspend any plans for automobile contests of any kind whatsoever.

"What do you think of this?" our department head asked me when we received this notice. "I'm in favor of marking time."

Jean Arnoult was my boss, a stout man with gentle, dreamy eyes. Every morning he wound a tape measure around his middle. To his vast disappointment, he was rapidly reverting to his pre-1914 girth.

"Yes, I'm in favor of marking time. How can you design tires without knowing what kind of cars will be using them? But let's take advantage of this delay to woo the sports world. That way, once racing picks up again we'll already have a foot in the door. Believe me, in racing winning isn't enough, you need to have the press in your pocket."

And so it was that we spent the year 1919 "wooing the sports world."

* * *

The first phase of our courtship was the world wrestling championships. I failed to see the connection with motor racing.

"You don't understand the science of public relations, Gabriel, it's all a matter of indirect approaches, of seemingly aimless moves . . . and then, just when you least expect it, bingo! A locker-room acquaintance or a racetrack friendship saves your bacon. This wrestling, for instance. If you go there just once, you're merely doing the fashionable thing; the press turns up its nose. Go twice and it means you've had a fight with your wife; the reporters feel sorry for you. But go back every night and you're one of them. Your reputation is established. Gabriel Orsenna? Oh-yes-the-sports-fan. And that will be that: as soon as racing comes back, all the good stories will be about us; the press will be on our side. There's no magic involved."

So for two weeks we spent our evenings at the Folies-Bergère where the bouts (Dubonnet Cup) took place; all the prewar stars were back, Constant-le-Marin, a 253-pound Belgian, Joe Polte the doughboy, Louis Lemaire, champion of the North. But there were newcomers with large followings too: Gaumont-le-Frappeur, Raoul Saint-Mars and the formidable Italian Gianni Raffaelli, Black Ellio, the Estonian Walter Rentel. . . . The experts traded bets: had the war upset the pecking order? At long last we were going to set the record straight.

Gabriel had trouble keeping up with Jean Arnoult as he forged his way through the crowd shaking hands, dozens of hands, hundreds of hands, breaking off only to clap.

"A few more evenings like this and I'll know everybody," he would tell me as we went home along the rue du Faubourg-Montmartre and rue Vivienne.

That was his goal in life: to know everybody some day.

We began our days combing through the papers. We spent all morning at it. "Don't think we're wasting time, Gabriel. Now you'll be able to quote our reporter friends back to them at the drop of a hat. People who work on dailies are very conscious of the things you remember." Gabriel still recalls how some of the reports began.

> Constant-le-Marin! Hiltman! What a titanic struggle these two waged last night! What fire and ferocity the Swiss displayed, but with what cool mastery the world champion countered his moves! And if the champion's counterattacks were sometimes energetic enough to warn

his adversary that there were limits not to be overstepped, it was always in a spirit of courtesy and fair play.

And then the report on the final:

> Suddenly the Italian champion applied a hammerlock and sank to his knees. Constant-le-Marin followed through on the fall, squirmed in midair, turned, and caught his opponent in an unbreakable scissors.

We all celebrated his victory together at the Café de Paris, presided over by Henri Desgranges and the whole reporting staff of *L'Auto* magazine.

After this initial success we had to select a theater for our next offensive.

"What do you suggest, Gabriel? Let's see how you're coming along in public relations."

"One thing is certain, we should change sports. At least with cycling we'd see a little of the countryside. And bikes use tires, don't they?"

"Conclusion?"

"The postwar resumption of Paris–Roubaix, April twentieth."

"I have a much better idea: the Tour of the Battlefields. Three points in its favor. One: the patriotic angle. The race starts in Strasbourg, only recently in enemy hands. Then on to Luxembourg, Brussels, Amiens, Paris, Bar-le-Duc, and back to Strasbourg. We have to be seen, we absolutely have to be seen, on this pilgrimage. Two: sphere of influence. If you kept up to date on these things you'd know that *Le Petit Journal* is organizing the race. Do I have to spell it out for you? Wrestling championships with *L'Auto,* cycling with *Le Petit Journal;* we'll be extending our range. Three: personal contacts. In one week, particularly evenings outside Paris where there are few distractions, we'll build a whole network of relationships."

And that was how Gabriel came to visit the ruins, the skeletal villages, the yawning churches, the leavings of battle. It was June, but there was not a blade of green in sight. A naked landscape, brown rolling hillocks planted with black stakes as far as the eye could see. "That was once a forest, Gabriel, only grass will cover it now. We have to replant a giant meadow all the way from Lorraine to the sea. Yes, Gabriel, replant. . . ."

Their cars picked their way amid ditches, shell holes, craters. Sometimes a whole piece of wall and a half-open window still stood. You could see sky on the other side even though the curtains were drawn. The inhabitants had come back, for they were there cheering on the racers. But where could they be living? The rain hammered relentlessly on the mud.

"Rain is good for the grass," Jean kept saying.

Every now and then a sign among the stones pointed the way to Querrain, Bapaume, Albert, proof that we were indeed making headway.

This spring bereft of green stabbed our hearts. Inside the cars people stopped talking. One by one, without exchanging a word, the drivers accelerated. Leaving the racers behind to face the past alone.

At Amiens they all waited in a fever of impatience on boulevard Beauville. In the nearby café, Le Palais, the Paris telephone never stopped ringing. It was the sports desks.

"We're going to press in half an hour. Anything?"

"Nothing."

At nightfall the ghosts appeared. Well ahead of the cyclists. The crowd's gaze was focused on the far end of the boulevard, where the racers were expected to appear. But rain, darkness, and ruins conjure up ghosts. A spectator gave a shout. Then another. . . .

"Look, look, it's Marcel!—or Ferdinand, or Georges"—"I knew he'd be back."

The ghosts would come no closer. They remained huddled there in the gloom in the middle of boulevard Beauville, just at the beginning of the final straight.

"Sssh! Be quiet!"

It was vital not to frighten them away. There was not a sound, not a murmur, just the jangling of the phone. They had closed Le Palais's doors, yet it went on ringing. Probably a small window left open somewhere. Perhaps it was this noise that discouraged the ghosts from drawing nearer. . . .

Gabriel, who had no ghosts in his life, only wandering women, was embarrassed.

Now Jean Arnoult was chanting, half in words and half in music, five unchanging syllables, Marc-Alain-Willy, the names of his three sons killed fighting for France. He had seen them ("I swear I did, Gabriel, right over there") beside the bleachers. "See that street lamp? Just a bit farther on. Marc-Alain-Willy. . . ."

Gabriel put his arms around him. Jean Arnoult's teeth were chattering. A chill had overcome him, the chill of fathers without sons. Just before midnight the winner, Deruyter, arrived after eighteen hours' riding. He too was weeping, like everyone else.

The applause was sparse and full of bitterness. Nobody was glad to see him. They would have preferred the ghosts. Deruyter should have waited for them, persuaded them to come forward.

"And what about the others, your racing pals? Did you leave them behind in the war too, did you leave them back there?"

Shaken with sobs, Deruyter said nothing.

There was no sequel to this Tour of the Battlefields, a brainstorm for which cycling circles are reluctant to take credit. Ask them about it today and they'll answer, Really, are you sure? Never heard of it myself. But Gabriel's memory will vouch for it. And his memory's ally, that august publication *L'Auto,* will confirm it, the big special edition with its red spine and its yellowed pages, spring 1919. Check it if you don't believe me.

I lost Jean Arnoult a few months later, in November, after the Targa Florio. It was the big postwar return to automobile racing, the race no one could afford to lose.

On our return from Sicily we made ourselves as inconspicuous as possible. We came in very early, lost in the incoming flood of workers. A sandwich in the office for lunch. We left late, after nightfall. Nobody could have said for certain that we were back from Palermo.

Except M. Charton, our personnel manager and acting head of the marketing division. He waited patiently. We were beginning to breathe again, to raise our heads, to come to work just a little bit later when, on December 4, on the stroke of noon, he summoned us.

"Do you read the papers, Monsieur Jean?"

"Yes, sir, it's part of my job."

He did not address me. I was there merely as a recorder, a witness.

"And nothing struck you about today's, Monsieur Arnoult?"

"I don't think so," stammered Jean.

"Nothing at all, eh?"

Then the personnel manager handed us page 3 of *L'Auto:* from top to bottom, spread across four columns:

A. Boillot<br>on<br>Pirelli Tires<br>wins<br>the Tenth Targa Florio

"Pirelli tires, It-tal-ian tires. . . . It is just as I feared. You appear to have lost interest in the fortunes of the M Corporation. These things happen. Let us separate on amicable terms. Here is what you are due, Monsieur Arnoult, and good luck in your new life. I hope one awaits you, I sincerely hope so, Monsieur Arnoult."

He escorted Jean Arnoult to the door without giving him a chance to bid me farewell. We watched him walk away, past every office door, down the stairs, across the courtyard, and out through the gate without once looking back. Jean Arnoult, public-relations wizard, left without shaking a single hand, not even mine.

"Now to business," said Charton. "Management has agreed to wipe the slate clean. It should have been our concern, my concern, to get to know you better. Promotion is not among your gifts, nor publicity. You are more of a research type, am I not right, Monsieur Orsenna? Good. You and your beloved rubber are about to renew acquaintance. I want cars that hold the road no matter what their speed. The party is over, Gabriel, and so is Pirelli. Are we agreed?"

Gabriel replied with dozens of affirmative nods, so many that he did not think of Jean Arnoult again for years, not until the glorious episode of the Eiffel Tower.

I had not lost sight of him. Indeed, how could I unless I left Paris for good or lived with my eyes permanently fixed on the ground?

A car manufacturer had immediately hired him for its advertising department. Of course the aforementioned manufacturer took credit for the ensuing stroke of genius: CITROËN, in capital letters, in letters of flame, running up and down all four sides of the Eiffel Tower. But the little world of advertising and public relations at once recognized the creative spirit, the imprint, of Jean Arnoult.

And up there he lived out the end of his career.

He ordered a camp bed in a spare room by the elevator on the third floor. Claiming that he needed to be able to check the state of the bulbs at all hours, day or night.

## II

Place de la Concorde. Just right of the Crillon Hotel.

All racing's memories are there.

This time Gabriel addresses himself to you, monsieur, esteemed counselor, since my son most decidedly never comes to see me. Would a son who is unconcerned with his father's here and now be concerned with his past? Whereas to you, dear monsieur, distinguished attorney, all this is just a job. Should you therefore need further information for your dossier, here is the address: the Automobile Club, place de la Concorde, a stone's throw from the Crillon Hotel. You can't miss it.

Before you take your first steps down its paneled halls (brass wall lamps, red hangings), know that this is your last chance; everything about the old days, the grand old days of motor racing, is enshrined here. Elsewhere, not a trace of that heroic era remains.

I do not think they will admit you to the swimming pool. First of all because you are not a member. But mainly because you are clearly (one look at you is enough) the kind of man, still young, who flaunts his physical fitness at the drop of a hat, pectoral muscles braced, scalp thick-maned, scrotum swollen with sap, the impetuous kind who immediately dives into the water without so much as a glance at his extraordinary surroundings, dives in and swims a hundred yards in barely a minute at a sizzling crawl, then explodes from pool to poolside and instantly engages you in conversation to show he isn't winded. I don't hold it against you. It is your nature, and attorneys are meant to be fighters. But this kind never goes down well with Automobile Club regulars. For instance that brisk toss of your hair (I can see it now), flicking your raven locks back into place as you emerge from the pool. The regulars—well, yes, often bald—would never forgive you for it.

A pity. A pity for you, honorable counselor. What stories they might have told you in their deceptively offhand way, what highly instructive stories, sitting there with their feet dangling in the water, naked as the day they were born and leafing through *Le Figaro*'s two full pages of gossip.

You will therefore have no choice but to fall back on the bridge players behind their frosted-glass door on the ground floor. And perhaps they will serve your purpose better, for they are even older than the bathers and will thus be more fully informed about the period that interests you. Watch them play, and try not to sneer; they have elected to await death in fours, cards in hand, a way of waiting no less intelligent than any other.

Sooner or later no doubt one of them will rise. Curb your impatience. Do not importune him at once. Wait a moment or two, let him get back from the men's room, and, please, approach him politely.

"Orsenna? Wait a minute, wait a minute, that name rings a bell; wait a minute, it's all so long ago. . . ."

And here you must hold your tongue, believe me, don't rush him, for a man reentering his past is like a sleepwalker; arousing him too suddenly might destroy him. At the very most, murmur one word, *tires,* one date, *the twenties,* no more, then go back to listening and be sure to smile; smiling opens all doors, 50 percent your own youth, 50 percent his nostalgia.

"So you're interested in all that ancient history?" the old gentleman will ask, deeply touched and raising his unclouded gaze to yours. "Ah, yes, it's coming back to me. Orsenna, Gabriel, a conscientious lad, inventive, and—what's the word?—roly-poly. Yes, that's it, inventive and roly-poly. In fact that was his nickname, Roly-Poly Gabriel. A real wizard with rubber. No one could put tires on a car like Gabriel Orsenna. His life, you say? His personal life? There you're asking a lot. Let me think back, now. But of course, that's it, how stupid of me. A very beautiful woman, Jewish, wasn't she? In any case, tall, dark-haired. With looks like that we wondered—well, that's something else again—anyway, the perfect couple. Always together during races. . . ."

At this point his partners will call him: Come on, Georges, what are you doing? I went down one trick; you aren't dummy any more, come back.

But Georges will be off and running.

You will have no idea how lucky you are to have met someone who remembers Gabriel Orsenna. For in motor-racing circles people tend to remember only engine displacements, Bugatti radiator grilles, maximum speeds on the Hunaudières straight, drivers; they forget all about tires and tiremakers even though no automotive feat would be possible without them.

"Yes, the perfect couple. Never any question of other women with him, or of hanky-panky with the drivers on her part, even though we were a pretty rip-roaring bunch, believe me, in motor racing back then."

The partners are getting impatient, the cards have been dealt. Georges, I bid one no trump, what about you?

"As you see, I must go. . . ."

Somewhat dazed, the old gentleman takes his leave; travel is tiring, especially so dizzying a round trip through time. He walks like a bear on its hind legs, rolling, legs splayed, like a man who has forgotten to shake himself off after urinating because of a nagging question from the past.

And you (since youth and obsession with time have taken the place of human warmth within you), you merely say to yourself, Wonderful, thank you, bridge game, for sparing me his endless meanderings; old people are hard to get started but once they're off there's no stopping them. . . .

As you leave (without so much as a look at the tasteful pink clouds sailing over the National Assembly on this particular morning), you shoot a glance at your wrist. Your watch is the only thing you have eyes for. Then you leap into a taxi, saying to yourself, Well, reconstructing the professional and conjugal existences of this Orsenna turned out to be quite easy. Let us now move on to more serious matters, his dealings during the Second World War and his little trip to Indochina.

* * *

Now that the lawyer has gone to pursue his chopped-meat destiny, chopped by appointments, themselves chopped by the ringing of the phone, Gabriel will address himself to the truth.

But with a heavy heart. Truth is never sweet in the telling. It scrapes the mouth raw as it emerges. Gabriel speaks not for the benefit of his son (who never comes to see him and on whom he has declared war—provisional duration of estrangement: one month). Nor for the benefit of his defender: truth is slow, sometimes endless; people pressed for time, as all attorneys are, overtake it without even noticing. Nor does he speak up for his country's justice, which takes too little interest in ancient history. Once sentence is pronounced, the dossiers are tossed into a cellar, a crawl space. Who today could put his hands on the Stavisky file? Who could say which of Stavisky's teeth were gold, a detail of crucial importance to anyone wishing to understand charm, and through charm the art of the confidence trick?

No. If Gabriel is now willing to divulge his memories of love, it is out of respect for the Automobile Club.

An institution that has stored in its memory the name of the Count De Dion's Abyssinian chauffeur (Zélélé), and many other things besides, deserves respect and a scrupulous account of the facts.

## III

### The Perfect Couple

One first thing is certain: Gabriel's wife appeared.

A second thing is certain: Gabriel's wife disappeared.

The conclusion is less certain: does such intermittent attendance justify our calling them "the perfect couple"?

Clara always appeared at the same time, on Sunday morning after our last-minute testing was over, with the track once again empty and the cars sitting in orderly motionless rows in front of the stadium, most of them with mechanics still diving into their yawning bellies. Every now and then an engine thundered, then was still. Someone tested the loudspeakers. *Un, deux, trois,* one, two, three, *ein, zwei* . . . depending on the country you were in. Through our own smells, hot oil, high-octane gasoline, rose the powerful smells of the crowd: frying fat, beer, skewers of pork, burnt onions. They were beginning to fill the stands. This was the moment of truth for Gabriel. He stroked the tires, smooth and treaded, hard compounds and soft, and he scanned the heavens; was it going to rain?

Then Alsina, our team's fanatic junior member whose job it was to keep us supplied with sandwiches and to keep the curious at bay, Alsina would come charging up.

"Monsieur Gabriel, Monsieur Gabriel, your wife, she's here, you're so lucky she's a racing fan, believe me, because Janine and I . . ."

Gabriel didn't answer. Without realizing it he had twice consulted his watch; he knew it was time. His heart, as always, was pounding, and the air had suddenly taken on a different complexion, pale, flat, featureless, like a whitewashed interior.

And there she was, regal Clara. "Thank you, Alsina, my, what a big crowd today.

"Hello, Maurice, it's going to be a difficult race, I think, but I have confidence in you.

"Hello, Georges, I hope I'm not in your way. I know what it's like, last-minute adjustments, handing out smiles and handshakes, pretending to consult the stopwatches, three-thirty-one; well, well, there won't be any dawdling this afternoon!

"Hello, Gabriel, aren't you glad to see me?" Her long figure approaching me, dark skirt, light blouse, cropped hair, a curious tomboy look: a fashion that did not suit her, I seized on these mistakes, these small flaws, too-bright raspberry lipstick, a bitter little line at the corner of her mouth, on the left side; oh, if I could stop loving her. Ridiculous barricades that never held for more than a second or two. A woman leans against me. "Aren't you going to kiss me, Gabriel? Will it rain, do you think?"

Why always and only on Sundays? Her day off? Did she find Gabriel more attractive on Sundays?

Sunday, a good day for seeing Gabriel, the way you say, My left profile is better than my right? I have wondered about it for years.

In fact, she came looking for fear.

Her motives were scientific, professional: fear, the soul specialist's raw material. Psychologists are on this earth to calm fears. And how can you calm them without first knowing them?

With hindsight everything is clear.

Her excitement (she was normally so cool, so self-contained), her way of ferreting about, of peeping into every corner, of drawing near, then stepping back—"The last thing I want to do is get in your way, Gabriel"—nose quivering, nostrils palpitating like beating wings, temples slightly moist. . . . For a long time Gabriel was taken in, but this was not love. Love was there, perhaps, but remote, trailing far behind, overtaken by that passion for fear, by her conviction that she was plumbing the depths of human nature, the place where tremblings begin.

The closer we came to the starter's flag, the closer she stuck to the drivers, following them like their own shadows, the ones who cracked jokes right up to the last minute, surrounded by admirers; the ones that strolled solitary and devil-may-care in front of the stands, helmet straps already buckled, racing gloves already pulled on; and the ones who sat on the ground, backs to the stadium wall, like children in a schoolyard the day after vacation ends, lost, turned to stone. She stood there devouring them so hungrily with her eyes that on some Sundays Alsina would try to comfort Gabriel: It doesn't matter, believe me, they're all in love with the drivers, take my word for it, it's much worse when they don't even like racing. She went with them right up to the toilet doors, stood guard, didn't take notes, didn't dare, but you guessed from her furrowed brow that she was storing it all away.

Later on, once the race was under way, she would briefly join our competitors' lady friends. They followed the action with their hearts in their mouths, turning pale whenever they heard the roars of the crowd above the terrible din of the engines. Then she would return to me. "I'm not in your way, am I, Gabriel?" We would lean out over the track as one, eyes riveted on the end of the final bend. "Number 24 hasn't come by for a while; ah, there he is, not this time then; are you scared too?" Clara would shout into my ear, and as Etancelin overtook Caracciola I felt her tremble against me. It was generally at this point that it started to rain. Or else it was announced that there had been an oil spill at the end of the straight, just where the drivers began to brake; what kind of tire would grip on an oily track? We would remain side by side until the end, counting the laps, only seven to go, only six, until the checkered flag fell. "To think they'll be doing it all over again next Sunday," Clara murmured. "That's the craziest part of all, doing it all over again. . . ."

Clara always disappeared at the same time and always in the same way: on Sunday evenings, after the awards ceremony.

The winners had received their cups, the speeches were over, and it was time to feast. Once again applause filled the vast dining room of the big white hotel where Grand Prix trophies were always handed out. As the cold lobster and mayonnaise appeared, Clara would slip away. Followed by Gabriel.

"Leaving already?" friends called out.

"We couldn't have won without you!"

"Our tire wizard!"

"Well, we understand; love and all that. . . ."

"What love?" the Grand Prix camp followers would ask, blinking, torn for a moment from their daydreams (which of the surviving drivers will I be spending the night with?).

"Good luck, Gabriel."

"A roadholder like Gabriel doesn't need luck in bed or on the track."

Gabriel would hear the din of celebration fading behind him and the *click, click* of Clara's footsteps on the marble floor. So she's still following me, I daren't turn around to make sure. He drew himself up to his fullest height. Only the tall and aloof truly belong in palaces; only they have the right to cross the bright ocean of the hotel lobby and approach the dark-wood cliffs of the reception area.

The roly-poly are barely tolerated there. At a nod from the all-powerful manager they are thrown out into the cold.

A red and blue porter was already opening the door. Forgive me, Gabriel. (They heard behind them the distant sound of applause.) You must give me time, Gabriel.

He would focus on the mauve placard with gray lettering, WAGNER ROOM (or VICTORIA, or GARIBALDI, all depending on the country): *Nine o'clock, Grand Prix Auto Racing (private reception)*. "Gabriel, please, don't look so sad, I need time. . . . A taxi?" asked Clara.

"Five minutes at most, madame."

Then Gabriel would lend his hand to the disappearance. That is to say, he would walk Clara down the front steps.

Another doorman held the umbrella, and the taxi pulled away: "What luck, just in time for the Paris train; have a pleasant week, Gabriel." The two red taillights faded into the night, out there where time was surely to be found, time which produces such perfect couples.

## The Real World over Lunch

A lofty label, chosen by Louis: I feel more and more responsible for you as a father, Gabriel; our lunches must be of help to you. You must heal, you must be liberated.

The setting, one of those restaurants in the second or third *arrondissement* where, in deference to the French provinces, the food is always heavy, very heavy: goose and duck conserves, garlic mayonnaise, boiled beef in onion sauce, pig knuckles, *tablier de sapeur* (tripe, beaten eggs, snail butter), the finest physic for what ails you, Gabriel. Come, have another helping, that's right, eat hearty.

The date: every Monday, the day after Sunday.

So it was a sorry-looking Gabriel, a pallid Gabriel, with trembling hands and a weak smile on his lips, who slid into the seat across from his father.

"Ah, Gabriel, things aren't going so well, by the look of you. Still your princesses?"

"Please—"

"And how long has this wretched business been going on?"

"Louis, please—"

"Hush! When will you understand that there are other women, millions of other women, real ones, kind, caring, restorative? That's what you need, a woman who's restorative, like this splendid mutton stew."

"Let's change the subject, please. Just for once let's spend Monday talking about something else."

"What else is there for a father to talk about if not his wretch of a son? You remind me of King Midas; all that he touched turned to gold, and he starved to death. That's how you are with women, Gabriel. A blundering King Midas."

"And what about you, do you love Wladislawa?"

"Most assuredly, my poor Gabriel. . . . She stays, doesn't she? Don't you understand that? I get on with my life and she stays."

"How is Marguerite?"

"Still the same. America, nothing but America. She's just like you with your princesses. I forbid you to visit her. You're both such dreamers, you'll end up egging each other on."

And here he generally fell silent until the real world lunch was over, merely muttering the occasional "What a family!" between mouthfuls, or else, "Re-stor-a-tive, yes, re-stor-a-tive. Why don't you pay the bill this time, Gabriel? You really are too stupid; at least that's something your princesses won't get their claws on."

Another Monday.

As we came up for air between the *lapin en crépine* (only so-so, too much fat), and the Reblochon cheese (the whole gamut, extra runny, runny, creamy, or firm, a specialty of the house): "Gabriel? Yes, Gabriel, what I have to tell you is going to hurt."

Louis rummaged about in his black corduroy suit. One pocket, a second, a third. At last he found it in his fob pocket. "Here it is. It's for you, Gabriel." A rather crumpled visiting card, schoolteacher's copperplate, still blue, elegant downstrokes and upstrokes.

*Luc Grévenynghe*
*2 Louvois Place*
*(basement)*

"That's him, Gabriel."

"Who?"

"Clara, or at least her man. Monday and Wednesday evenings. For the last three years. A businessman. Princesses have their needs, believe it or not. Gabriel?"

"Yes."

"I hated having to tell you. Now, Ann. No way of knowing, unable to tail her, too international. Benefit of the doubt. You aren't angry with me, Gabriel? I don't like this, but as a father I have certain responsibilities. Forget your princesses, I beg you. Make me happy. Find a woman who stays."

Another Monday.

La Coupole.

Strange odor.

"Do you smell anything, Louis?"

"No, no, not I."

A dank smell, seaweed at low tide.

"Are you hungry, Gabriel?"

I was not alone in noticing the smell. Two women sitting nearby, in their thirties, attractive, discussing the merits of the École Alsacienne, threw startled glances in our direction and blushed, both of them, almost simultaneously.

I looked at Louis, I breathed in deeply, I dared to breathe in deeply.

My father smelled of sex.

Almost certainly a new educational gambit on Louis's part, that smell. The message was clear: a man, a real man, should have a sex life, Gabriel.

But did it really happen, that redolent Monday afternoon?

How to be certain after all these years? How to track down our two lunchtime neighbors and ask of the old ladies they have become whether, truly, that odor . . . you're absolutely sure?

## IV

### The Perfect Couple (continued)

Ann was my sister-in-law. She was also my friend.

But it must be clearly understood that in our friendship bodies held the monopoly.

And monopolies stand alone in this world.

At each of their meetings Ann would say to herself and Gabriel would promise himself, now, this time we will talk to each other, this time we will converse, get to know each other, exchange gossip about our careers, we've been friends so long. But the monopoly was ever watchful, and the same force that threw them into each other's arms, that same force, equally implacable, that tore them from their daily routine no matter where they might be and sent them running to a bedroom, that same force imposed silence once their bodies were slaked.

"I'm sorry," Ann would say, "an appointment. . . ."

"Excuse me," Gabriel would say, "I must leave. . . ."

And once more they would go their separate ways without managing to exchange the slightest word.

Not that boredom set in, quite the contrary, not that their encounters were brief (they were known to last up to four days and nights, without breaks), but the monopoly, the arrogant monopoly of the body held absolute sway.

We never spoke at all, or else very rapidly, disguising our voices the way kidnappers call about ransoms, swallowing their sentences and speeding up their delivery so as not to be recognized, so that the identity of the caller will remain forever a mystery.

Another unusual aspect of their friendship was Ann's long-standing stipulation: that we do it upright.

In the beginning, in their first years, it exasperated Gabriel.

"Come on, Ann, all women lie down."

"Perhaps. Or rather, precisely. In any case, I don't."

And little by little he began to understand: Ann had at least three reasons for not wanting to lie down.

1. She was a woman, and in recent years a small storm had been gathering, the voices of women demanding a measure of freedom. And Gabriel, thanks to his line of work, realized that a great victory, at Le Mans for example, is always the result of repeated and extremely domestic attentions: giving the driver a cup of coffee at just the right moment, telling him again and again that he is the greatest so he won't be intimidated by his leading rival. For Ann, not lying down must be one of the prerequisites of victory. Why not?

2. She was a businesswoman and businesspeople, men or women, must never lie down.

3. At all times, even in the middle of the day and despite a most strenuous life, her fair-haired face retained that very slight puffiness

all women have on waking. And (just to keep the Automobile Club apprised of the smallest detail) if I may strike an even more intimate note, her lovemaking was neither greedy nor distant but trusting, sweet, without violence, almost childlike. The childlike quality of a woman sleeping. Knowing her body to be already predisposed to sleep, Ann refused it further concessions. Thus her refusal to lie down. *Sleeping Beauty* strikes fear in the hearts of more little girls than one would think.

That strange stipulation: that I stand up. At first Gabriel had merely accepted it. Now he loved it. And when he thought of this woman, he no longer called her Ann but She-Who-Always-Stands. And he regretted not being a Sioux or a Guarani, one of those sage peoples who differentiate human beings not by commonplace generic names but with roundabout phrases. Have you seen She-Who-Always-Stands? Good night, She-Who-Always-Stands.

Let me add, in passing, that an upright partner is among the most stimulating of constraints. Like rhyme in poetry. You can do so many things with a standing woman; positions and approaches can be varied almost infinitely. A word of advice, however: never trust hotel furniture. At best, hotel managers make sure their beds are solid. But their chairs and their tables creak and shake and fall apart as soon as you subject them to the slightest familiarity.

Either (you will protest) Gabriel is exaggerating the duration of certain of these interviews (four days and four nights without a break, come now!) or else you must have rested, and in the latter case did Ann sleep standing up the way horses are said to do, or did she finally consent to lie down?

To this question (intended to be subtle but in fact betraying a rather unhealthy interest in our friendship), Gabriel answers with all the assurance in the world. Like everyone else we would rest after each assault, but each on his own side of the bed. And if Ann did lie down (which of course did happen), she never neglected to warn me.

"If you touch me lying down, you will never see me again. Never."

I believed her. The Underworld is not the only place where Orpheus can lose Eurydice.

So it was alone, every man for himself, and not intertwined like most of the world's friends, that we rested from our labors.

And a few quarter hours later, it was two new separate beings, new to themselves, new to each other, who resumed their upright sport.

Yet I must acknowledge one lapse in our double vow of silence and separate repose: it was during one of our recuperative phases, as each clung to opposite edges of the mattress to keep from rolling down together into the central trough. It was at such a moment, amid the very relative silence of hotels (gurgling toilet systems, buses stopping just beneath the window, the hum of vacuum cleaners), that Ann's rare voice was heard.

"My parents are organizing a little party for Markus's birthday. And I think he will be awarded the Legion of Honor. He would love it if you could be there. Just like the good old days."

Gabriel arrived late.

The day's tests had gone on and on. They were trying to determine the different possible causes of overheating in tires. Too much friction on the treads and repeated bending of the tire walls. The engineers had devised a particularly cunning system they called the "flytrap": by means of cables placed in perpendicular arches at the edge of the rim, you could study the inner tube at work within the tire and make appropriate corrections.

In spite of the importance of these experiments, crucial to our drivers' safety, Gabriel could not contain his impatience. The second they were finished he was out and racing to the Knights' Parisian pied-à-terre on the rue Louvois.

The guests had already left, the Legion of Honor was already bestowed. The white and gold star and red ribbon gleamed beneath Markus's smile.

"Ah, Gabriel, a man who truly appreciates decorations. Welcome!"

They handed me champagne and lady fingers.

Since there were just the five of us, the good old days returned without much prodding. Perhaps they had simply been waiting for the chance?

"So, Gabriel," asked Markus, "how goes the racing?"

"So, Gabriel," asked Elisabeth, "are you happy?"

(Of course Gabriel is now paraphrasing. The questions they asked him were neither so stupid nor so cruel.)

Staring fixedly into their glasses, the two sisters watched the bubbles and every so often, with the flawless regularity of metronomes, laughed nervously and protested: Come now, Papa, come now, Mama, leave Gabriel alone.

Suddenly Elisabeth took my arm. I have something to say to you, Gabriel. And she led me into the bedroom, the pied-à-terre's second and only other room.

"Please, Mama," said Clara.

"This is ridiculous," said Ann.

Markus said nothing.

Once the door was closed: "Gabriel, listen to me, Markus and I have had our own storms. So many to choose from. The 1911 storm, or 1917, or the redhead with the perfect ear, so she claimed. I'll just tell you about the last one and how it ended. To cheer you up as well as to tease you a little. Here it is. It was the first of February, our one hundred and thirty-fourth day of separation. For we were separated at the time, Gabriel, separated. We too! Well, anyway, big concert at Carnegie Hall. All New York in attendance, myself included, escorted by Gerald, in his forties, a very charming man and a banker as well, who had appeared in my life at exactly the right moment. Bankers are quite skillful at exploiting separations. Look how they manage bankruptcies. I spotted Markus. In a better seat than mine, naturally, close to the stage. Beside him was a tall blonde, the female equivalent of a banker. Nothing to say. The score was even. And suddenly, at the beginning of the andante . . ."

The bedroom door would not close properly. This is often the case with pieds-à-terre. Gabriel heard the two sisters loudly protesting—I'm leaving, so am I, this is grotesque—Markus begging them to stay.

"Are you listening to me, Gabriel? At the beginning of the andante, Markus stood up. And almost immediately there were murmurs, angry murmurs: 'This is insufferable! Sit down! What's wrong with the man?' I didn't understand the anger. Usually concertgoers are more tolerant, especially toward the old. After all, you can be both a music lover and incontinent, more especially as Markus was bent over like a Sioux tracking his foe, toe and heel, like a man attempting stealth. I didn't understand until the very last moment, as he drew nearer. He was wearing his yellow shoes, and his redskin gait made them crackle like pine logs in the fireplace. Up on stage the pianist continued to play as if nothing had happened. But his notes were clonking and heavy; they had lost their airy quality. It would not have taken much for them to come tumbling to the ground and scuttle across the floor to be squashed by the yellow clogs. And that was what Markus wanted. You follow me, Gabriel? He wanted the symbol to be clear. Then he leaned over me. The banker was ready to spring to my defense, the way bankers always spring to your defense, blustering, See here, now see here, sir! Markus took my hand and together we left the concert, without the tall blonde, amid general reproval and the creaking of the yellow shoes. All this is to tell you, Gabriel, that a woman has the right, do you understand me, the right to want to be preferred. Even to music. Now hurry, let's get back, they will be getting impatient."

Ann and Clara had already pulled on their coats. They could scarcely bring themselves to bid me farewell, coldly, perfunctorily, when they left.

Markus walked me home.

"She told you about the yellow shoes? Good. Don't let it scare you. With men, preferences are never total. Take me, for instance, I've never been able to stop humming."

Gabriel could have kissed him.

"Even during?"

"Yes, even during."

Gabriel did kiss him.

## V

### The Perfect Couple (final installment)

They were not happy times. As anyone at all will tell you, women in partial eclipse make you suffer much more than those who disappear outright. And yet . . . in spite of what has to be called sadness, Gabriel now admits that those twelve or thirteen years were something like a golden age for him, the golden age of his sexuality.

What inspired this sudden epiphany? Had sorrow lined his face? Had he progressed from roly-poly to gaunt?

No.

To comprehend the incomprehensible, you must first be willing to broaden your acquaintance with motor-racing circles.

On Grand Prix evenings there were never enough drivers to go around. The women who wanted one (a driver) for the night belonged to two categories: the locals, whether official guests or clever gate-crashers, and the internationals, who followed the circuit from Grand Prix to Grand Prix, some legitimate, some just temporary. To be absolutely accurate, we should further distinguish between two subcategories of legitimate mates: the pluriannual (those whose love endured) and the seasonal (those who declared eternal love anew every spring, usually around May, just after Monaco). In short, and regardless of classification, local or international, women demanded drivers. Whence the shortage: on certain Sunday nights a supply of thirty or so drivers to meet a demand for more than two hundred.

The circuit devised a solution. To satisfy our clientele we minted counterfeit coin. Every man jack of us was dubbed a driver, even mechanics no lady would ever want (because of their black fingernails and oily smell, but above all because they never risked their lives, because what the customers really wanted was to swoon and coo over the condemned man, I am his last pleasure on earth, and so forth). Also labeled as drivers were team factotums like Alsina, who fetched sandwiches and shooed onlookers, even the car manufacturer's elder sons, who had just passed their exams and had been invited along as a reward. . . . Drivers all, we addressed one another as my dear fellow driver. It was easy to fool them; faces are unrecognizable beneath racing helmets. The locals fell for the ruse, and the internationals kept the secret as long as their own territory remained inviolate.

And Gabriel, standing well back from it all, watched through a screen of green plants.

He could quite easily have taken advantage of the windfall, tire wizards being drivers like everyone else.

But Clara, as was her habit, would have just that moment left. This departure, although by now regular and utterly predictable (oh, how predictable!), was nevertheless devastating. He watched the sport without ever taking part in it.

No, it was in Paris, only in Paris, in the bosom of the Paris racing crowd, that his sexuality blossomed.

Readers unfamiliar with the period can have no idea. The Maillot-Champerret quarter was a kingdom, a genuine kingdom, with coronations and anointings, with drivers for kings, mechanics for wizards, Boussacs and Staviskys for bankers, tire experts for court jesters, and hack reporters for heralds.

Today all that has faded, the bars are closing; little by little they are butchering that enchanted kingdom, the western end of the seventeenth *arrondissement,* disemboweling it, piercing it through and through in the name of unclogging traffic jams. . . . You'll see, traffic will be the end of racing, you'll see.

It's the same way with onions: the only way not to cry is to press memories hard against your eyes. And the old days return. The days of the ratodrome, boulevard de Verdun, a fenced-in track where we began by unleashing the rodents, a black, strong-smelling swarm. The lady spectators shuddered. Then the owner would take bets on the dogs, intelligent mongrels specially trained for this kind of hunt. The best of them could rip a rat's throat open every three seconds. The black swarm would turn red. The lady fans would scream, but there was always an aficionado to console them afterward in one of the Porte Maillot's little hotels.

The days of Lunapark, with its Lilliputian Village, a favorite spot for children, and its Voyage to the Moon, more for the parents, with its epic itinerary, tilting stairways, backward-moving sidewalks, and myriads of fan vents to test the mettle of girls wearing panties under their skirts. The days of Marius the colossus, breaker of chains, who could push a Rosengart car in full throttle back to the starting blocks.

The days of the Ballon des Ternes, Bartholdi's tribute to Gambetta, a lovely monument melted down by the Germans in 1940.

And then the drivers, all the drivers: Etancelin with his helmet worn back-to-front, Chiron and his red-spotted scarf, Nuvolari with his little golden tortoise pendant, Caracciola the German, who drove his fastest in fog, André Dubonnet, who could never decide between racing and aperitifs, Ralph de Palm, the American, and Varzi and Sénéchal and Djordjaze. . . . All mortals but more than mortal, spellbinding, magnetic as wreckers' lanterns. Were they still living or were they already ghosts?

The women wanted to be sure; they never stopped checking, throwing themselves at the drivers' necks, taking their heads in both hands: Are you here, are you still here?

And this is where Gabriel's luck came in.

For every now and then the women wearied of this limbo between life and death. They wanted something solid. And on whom did their eyes fall? Awaiting his moment, for once distending belly and cheeks, renouncing his gaunt ambitions, showing all the outward signs of the bon vivant: Gabriel. So at the bar or in the dining room they discreetly changed places to say hello to our roly-poly friend. And little by little their fingers would discover the advantages, yes, the advantages inherent in a roly-poly lover: broad surfaces, unexpected areas of resistance, elastic material, reassuring bulk, memories of childhood. Then, too, that start of surprise without which there is no complete sexual experience, those gurglings they make when they are at their most intimate, their most probing: well, well, my goodness, roly-poly men aren't exactly small . . . or soft . . . my, my. . . .

And so, no matter where, cloakroom, automobile, stairway in hotel or home, Room number 9, 14, 28 or conjugal bed, no matter, Gabriel was overjoyed to be paid such attention, intoxicated by all that adjacent hunger (oh, you really exist, they said; oh, you are really you!). He was conscious of his ambassadorial mandate to uphold the honor of roly-poly men everywhere and (if he proved himself worthy) to open up whole new prospects for them (through the medium of hairdressing salons, erotic reputations travel like lightning). And so, gritting his teeth, digging deep into his reserves when he felt himself flag, and murmuring the occasional "I do this for you, my roly-poly brothers, hang on, the fashion in lovers will soon be changing, out of our way you army of skeletons." Oh, yes, speak to me, they said, and so, speaking of things only the roly-poly know, roly-poly Gabriel fornicated and fornicated and fornicated again.

And too bad if, at daybreak, his clients went away without leaving an address and instantly swooned all over again for some gaunt and commonplace swain.

And too bad if, running into Gabriel at the track or in a bar, their eyes betrayed no recognition, those blond women's eyes that even brunettes possess, flickering past you to focus elsewhere. . . .

Too bad for them.

And so much the better for Gabriel, for in this way they preserved his anonymity. They protected his reputation as the only faithful husband in the "racing crowd." Along with, perhaps, Philippe Etancelin, whose wife was never more than a hairsbreadth from his side (never a good sign).

It being our task to paint a comprehensive portrait of our hero's sensuality, we should also mention his trade and his very personal way of practicing it.

On the day of a race, Gabriel would arrive at the track with the dawn.

And his extraordinary consultation with the track would begin. Yard by yard he would question it, caress it, note its bumps, its ruts, the condition of the joins between its concrete slabs, the dangerous areas where gravel would accumulate as the laps rolled by. At bends he would lie flat on the ground to check inclines and gauge probable trajectories, to weigh the risks of running water or of puddles in case it rained; then he would rise, pull out his red ball, and bounce it endlessly, here, there, and everywhere, like someone searching for treasure. Little by little the tracks answered, each in its own way: Montlhéry candidly, Nürburgring grudgingly, Brooklands ironically. . . . But all in the end yielded up their secrets. None was proof against his blandishments. The tracks would warn Gabriel: Be careful here at the end of the straight, the surface is deteriorating; beware of the reverse bank at Farmhouse Corner. And the tracks were always doubly moved, first by Gabriel's courtesy—he always thanked them, the way you stroke a horse's coat with your fingertips—and second by his perplexity as he walked slowly back to the stands juggling various types of tire in his mind.

Hard compound? Moves fast, with very little wear, but doesn't hold the track well.

Soft compound? Sticks to the track like glue but finishes up on rims.

Is it going to rain? Then deep treads. With two possible choices: lateral openings, to expel water, or deep longitudinal grooves with unbroken walls to hold the water in the treads.

Dry surface? Should we take a chance on the smooth tire?

As starting time approached, Gabriel (most unwillingly) left the reassuring technical sphere to enter those shifting zones where only magicians and politicians are at ease, for the perfect choice of tire depends on clairvoyance (will there be a downpour?) and on compromise (like those carefully balanced cabinet appointments that make for a stable administration).

Gabriel will provide just one example: Francorchamps, 1930, Belgian Grand Prix, winner Chiron, mounted by me as follows:

Right front: soft compound (for holding)
Left front: medium hard (for longer wear)
Right rear: medium soft
Left rear: regular hard

Once upon a time there was Gabriel, a tire expert but in no sense a militant antifascist, who, while questioning the German earth of Nürburgring, heard it rumble far beneath him, deep deep down. And who told himself before the race, They can race around clockwise to their heart's content at Le Mans, in Belgium, in Sicily, in England; they can turn the screw tighter and tighter, they can tighten every screw in Europe; but it will do no good: the continent is disintegrating, the breakup is at hand.

## Dream

A town hall. Gabriel goes in beneath the red, white, and blue flag. Inside, plans for the war memorial are pinned to the bulletin board among other public announcements (building permits, marriages, water cutoffs). A blueprint painstakingly drawn in India ink, with a handwritten *N.B.* appended: *The two angels and the soldiers' helmets will be in bronze.* He climbs to the second floor, unpainted wooden stairway, nasty disinfectant smell (since Brazil, Gabriel's dreams have involved odors). Opens a door, asks to see the appropriate clerk. Line of black-clad women with hushed voices: Will the lettering be big enough? Should first names be written out in full? "Silence, please!" cries the clerk. "And write legibly. Then you'll have no reason to complain to the sculptor about spelling mistakes." The war widows apply themselves to their task, make timid inquiries: Can you tell me where he will go? "Name?" Perron. "From L to P will be facing west, according to current plans. Next!"

"Knight, Clara and Ann."

"I'm sorry, monsieur, the memorial is not open to women. Do you have other dead?"

"Yes, Orsenna, Gabriel."

"Your relation to the deceased?"

"I am he."

The clerk rises, the war widows fall silent; the memorial is for the dead, yes, for dead men, the clerk calls for help; the war widows, the pale faces of the war widows surround Gabriel. With a huge effort he pushes through the circle, breaks free of the black and white, tumbles down the stairway with its disinfectant smell. Someone shouts after him, "The Republic is not responsible for your broken heart!" Gabriel wakes, arms pushing against the wall.

## VI

By this time the Porte Champerret area had its own following, like Montmartre for striptease or Montparnasse for bohemians. Whole families arm in arm, provincials nudging one another, a few loners with wandering hands. . . . A large crowd gathered every day, pretending to admire the cars and show interest in the engines . . . but nobody was fooled. Everyone was there for death. They came to sniff the air of probable passings. They looked around wide-eyed, committing every sight to memory.

"Take a good look at him, that's Chiron. You may be seeing him for the last time."

"Yes, considering the way he drives."

"And that one, there, Fagioli, how much longer will he last?"

"War wasn't enough for men like them."

"At least they chose their fates."

"Do you think drivers are superstitious?"

All the aficionados of death would meet there, like horse lovers at Longchamp and old soldiers at the place de l'Étoile. Paris is a breeding ground of clubs. They would prowl among the cars. Without so much as a by-your-leave they would lie down in the road flat on their backs to examine an engine.

"Move along, move along," policemen sang out, but it did no good. They had scarcely turned their backs before the fans were back again under the engine block, evaluating its chances.

"Hunaudières, two-mile straight . . . with brakes like these he'll never stop in time. Let's make sure we're there next Sunday."

Clara had stopped leaving me on Sunday nights. She stayed in my little apartment on boulevard de l'Yser. I had never known her so sedentary. The racing crowd kept avid track of our married life. "We suspected all along that you had problems. All couples have rough patches, even the best. But now everything seems to be running smoothly again, am I right?"

My friends counted (as did I): the lady has been there twenty-one, twenty-two, twenty-three nights. . . . Like all sportsmen, they loved records; they invented their own rules for me.

"After twenty days they stick."

"Do you think so?"

They watched over me as though I were pregnant.

"Go on home, Gabriel, I'll take care of clearing up. At the start you have to be punctual."

"Well, this isn't exactly the start."

"Even so."

And Gabriel started all over again.

Starting all over again with a woman is full-time work. Or rather, it is never-ending work, not unlike a lineman in a railway yard (endlessly hitching cars that endlessly have to be unhitched), or a castle dweller (endlessly raising drawbridges that endlessly have to be lowered). Not to mention your main task, which is to drop anchors throughout the day so that the lady will not leave again. And then mealtimes, face-to-face encounters, twice a day, day after day.

How can I be sure not to bore her this evening? What subject should I choose, tenderness, wit, physical desire?

Gabriel rehearsed it all ahead of time, foraging in his memory or elsewhere, keeping his ears open for funny stories, lines of verse. Before coming to table he studied his notes. To anchor her today I shall be brilliant, brilliant and tender, for brilliance will not be enough. . . .

She would notice my efforts and gently stroke my cheek. "Don't worry, Gabriel, all is well."

I could have killed her for her offhandedness; it reminded me of those men who sit down to dinner when everything is ready and call in the direction of the kitchen, "Come on, dear, let's eat before it gets cold."

Now that it is all so long ago, Gabriel can afford to be frank: She was not staying for him. A different ambition inhabited her.

By 9 A.M. she was out in the square with the first arrivals. She would stay there until nightfall, busily harvesting.

"This Champerret is a gold mine. . . ."

She would kiss me on the way in or out, a quick peck on the forehead. "Thank you, Gabriel"—not breaking off her scribbling in her little sepia notebook—"thank you, Gabriel, for respecting my work. I think we are going to last, you and I. Oh, look at that boy over there measuring the wheelbase of that Voisin. . . ."

She would rush over to interview the young fanatic: Is your mother living? How old were you when you first fell in love with cars? The urchin would answer in monosyllabic grunts, but Clara's little shrieks, her private eurekas, went on unabated.

"You see, in children it's still a pure passion, still unadulterated by affective substitution."

Gabriel would nod. By now he was used to such jargon. In any case, starting all over again demands countless compromises. In hopes of keeping her he acquiesced in everything she proposed; she would not encounter the slightest obstacle in Gabriel, not the slightest; he put all his hopes in his docility. And then, too, this meticulous interest in children seemed to be a good omen.

They now came in greater numbers than the adults, on Fridays and Sundays but also in midweek, besieging the mechanics of Levallois and Champerret, roaming from garage to garage the way all children do, stuffing things into their pockets.

They came from nearby schools, Carnot, Chaptal, private institutions in Neuilly; they no longer went home after classes. At around

9 P.M. parents would call every bar in the neighborhood: Have you seen a little boy, brown hair, answers to the name of Albert? The cops chased them down on bicycles. Later, sheepish fathers would appear at the police station, I promise you, officer, this will never happen again. But no sooner had they been dragged home than they escaped. In summer you saw them flitting from tree to tree in bright pajamas, playing cowboys and Indians between visits to the garages. They would take advantage of the dark to sit in the racing cars for a few moments and then return home to bed, moving a little like sleepwalkers.

Clara had pinned a crowded chart on the flowered wallpaper between the peasant wardrobe from Lorraine and the single window overlooking the boulevard; on it only the two words BIRTH (near the top) and DEATH (near the bottom) were legible, the rest was all arrows, boxes, letters, columns, graphs, sketches.

"I know this seems mysterious, Gabriel, but I'm planning a surprise."

She spent whole days in front of the crowded chart, erasing a hieroglyph here, replacing one there, giving little clucks, sometimes of anger, sometimes of satisfaction, like any extrovert artist at his easel.

From time to time she would drop her pencils. "Quick, relax me, my muscles are all knotted up." Gabriel carefully kneaded her shoulders, first the right, then the left. "There, that's enough, I'm untied now, thank you, Gabriel. Whatever would I do without you?"

But the instant the massaging hand began to drift southward, the woman of science would rise to her feet again.

"How can you think of such a thing, Gabriel? I must focus all my energies on my work. Later on, in Vienna, I promise."

So Gabriel would go out and stroll from Péreire to Champerret. He walked along the tracks and watched the trains go by. He kicked imaginary balls into the air, and the sky was full of them.

"There's nothing so unhappy as an unhappy man," the neighborhood concierges observed as they called their cats indoors.

If ever your path crosses a writer's (of whatever kind: novelist, essayist, freelance reporter, thesis writer), remember that a calendar always makes a highly suitable gift.

For we must understand people who write. The ideas and the characters they manipulate are at once fleeting and fixed. Whereas days are both definite and pliable. You can shift them around, add them, subtract them.

So Gabriel regularly slipped beneath Clara's door one of those big cards on which the whole year is printed, six months on one side, six months on the other.

"Oh, thank you," she would say, "thank you."

And he would hear her murmuring. "Tomorrow, the seventeenth, I'll begin the writing proper; by the twentieth I should have completed the introduction; that'll be the hardest part. Then on Sunday the twenty-first I'll think about section one, perhaps even Monday the twenty-second as well; in any case, by Friday evening, June twenty-fifth, I must have it finished, or at least twenty-five pages; now, should I give myself two days off before tackling section two? That will depend. . . ."

And then suddenly, in the middle of the night, she knocked against the dividing wall.

"I've finished," she said. "Come."

The thesis sat on the table, a solid inch-thick block of paper. Clara had risen and, with a triumphant smile on her lips, was removing the hieroglyph-cluttered chart from the wall. Then she locked the original idea away in a briefcase.

"I want to go for a walk, Gabriel."

"But Clara, it's the middle of the night!"

"So?"

We walked as far as the Bois de Boulogne. She kept a tight grip on the briefcase. On our way back, with the sky turning pale at the far end of the avenue de Villiers, she raised her arms heavenward in an unbelievable gesture, a gesture typical of intellectuals, timid by nature but periodically drunk with immeasurable pride: she raised her arms toward the pallor slowly spreading above the rooftops and said, "See that light? It's thanks to me, Gabriel, yes, thanks to me!"

I had naïvely supposed she would be content with presenting the original idea to her French colleagues. Since the war I had come to know all those soul specialists, those famed deep-sea divers of the ego: Édouard Pichon, shortsighted, round glasses, always hunched in his rheumatic's wheelchair; René Laforgue, mustachioed ruddy Alsatian visage; or the Polish woman Eugénie Sokolnicka, Gide's friend, who spoke every language under the sun. . . .

"Vienna," she told me. "I want to submit it to Him in person. We leave next Monday."

"You don't think it would be wise to discuss it first? Here, with your colleagues?"

"So they can steal my ideas? Or garble them to Him? No, thank you."

"But, after all, your observations have been confined to France. To Porte Champerret—Levallois, even. How will He understand?"

"Are you going to be like the press and the politicians? Listen, Gabriel, if He is nothing to you but a minor regional thinker, tell me right away so I'll know who I'm dealing with. And we need have nothing further to do with each other."

We stayed a month in Vienna, having found rooms in a very old hotel, the Ungarische Krone, chosen for one reason alone: Never did a single colleague of Clara's set foot in it, unlike the Bristol, where Marie Bonaparte stayed, or the Zita, where Lou Salomé lived.

As soon as we arrived, Clara dropped off a copy of the original idea at His residence. ("Nineteen Berggasse, Gabriel, a most curious building, very classical at ground level, then more and more florid and rococo as you get nearer to the roof, with lions, wreaths, heroic busts. I met His maid. Such piercing eyes! You sensed right away that she knew human nature. I mean really, He wouldn't hire just anyone as a maid! Her name was Paula.")

And we waited.

Clara never wanted to leave the room ("What if He were to call me this instant; what can you be thinking of, Gabriel?"). I spent my days strolling. From time to time I would sit at a table in a café, often the Kapuziner; I would ask for paper and would describe this capital of the former two-headed empire to Louis. I would list Vienna's dimensions, the size of its houses, of the Ring, of the Volksgarten, of the Prater (4,229 acres), of its pastry shops, of St. Stephen's Cathedral, of the Imperial Palace, of the Opera (2,350 seats), of the Maria Theresa monument (more than twenty feet high, Louis).

I knew all these figures would reassure him about my health. "We are alike, you and I, Gabriel: we love facts."

In the evenings Clara, ever tenser as the days went by without a word from Him, talked on and on about her original idea. "What do you think of it, Gabriel? Tell me."

She would sit on her bed, motioning me to sit opposite her, on my own bed, and stare into my eyes from across the bedside bearskin rug and explain at great length that the human psyche had changed in the twentieth century (of course, Clara, undeniably), that our machine environment had aroused new feelings in us (how could it be otherwise, Clara?), that the Romans, for example, who did not have the automobile, were ignorant of some of our most intense emotions (who would dare to disagree, Clara?). She would look severely at me. "I want you to think, Gabriel, not to love me." She gave me pages from her thesis to read.

> With the advent of adolescence man enters a *motor-racing stage* that ends only with death, when the hearse stops by the grave in the silence of the churchyard and the delectable titillation and vague pleasures occasioned by every journey in a wheeled vehicle come forever to an end.
>
> The passion aroused in some people by skidding tires is clearly of a substitutive nature: their taste for rough-textured roads masks a hidden yearning for mucous membranes. And are not roads themselves the mucous passageways of the Earth?
>
> By analogy it is possible to pinpoint distinct erogenous zones for the planet, such as Mount Ventoux, the Hunaudières straight, the Nürburgring track. . . .
>
> Thus, after the oral and anal stages, and interspersed with periods of remission, we perceive a motor-racing stage more intricate than its predecessors, for its speed permits it to stimulate three bodily zones at one and the same time: the eyes, which drink in the world; the palms, which prickle with fear; and the lumbar regions, which thrust back against the driver's seat in a desperate appeal for help.

"So? What do you think of it? Gabriel, be honest. Give me a real opinion, instead of gaping at me like a village idiot. A woman is a person, Gabriel, with a right to be listened to, not just smiled at. . . . A woman is more than just a decoration, Gabriel."

* * *

Clara refused to leave the hotel until their last week, and then only after doling out large sums to the clerks at the reception desk: "Don't fall asleep, now; be careful to make a note of every message. . . ."

With a little store, Tabak-Trafik, as our starting point, we made wide circular sweeps via St. Stephen's Cathedral, the Opera, and Parliament, as well as tight little circles along the Graben, Schoffengasse, and Kohlmarkt. As long as we stayed in the vicinity of the tobacconist's, said Clara, we could not miss Him. And despite the city and the deafening roar of high civilization all around us, we felt like hunters waiting for game by a pond where of necessity He would come to slake His thirst.

"He smokes twenty *trabuco* cigars a day, Gabriel. . . . Mathematically speaking, He has to run out any day now. And luckily for us, you see, He comes here to buy them alone, unescorted."

Louis, in Paris, was growing impatient.

WHY STAYING SO LONG IN STUPID VIENNA STOP WHEN LUCKY ENOUGH POSSESS TRUE EMPIRE STOP EUROPEAN STOP NOT TROPICAL STOP WHY REMAIN BOGGED IN JOINT POSSESSION STOP WHAT DO YOU THINK STOP AUSTRIA STUPID STOP HUNGARY ALSO STOP SIGNED LOUIS.

We finally did run into Him. Once. A stroller, already old, with a round beard and a long fur-lined coat. He was talking to a yellow chow, the kind that pulls sleds. He noticed us, probably because of the little veil Clara wore out of mistrust of her colleagues. She gripped my arm with such force my hand went numb. He glanced at us with gentle, faintly surprised eyes, then followed in the chow's wake.

"Do you think He recognized me?" Clara stammered. "Do you think He guessed that 'The Motor-Racing Stage' was mine? He runs into so many people in the streets. If He looks at someone, imagine what that might mean! That was an encouraging look, wouldn't you say, Gabriel? He's shy. That's what everyone says. He didn't dare speak to me in the street. But after such an outburst of feeling I wouldn't be surprised if our phone were to ring at the hotel today!

That's how it always is with Him, you know. Between Him and certain women sparks suddenly fly, yes, true sparks that augur lasting friendship, a total and transparent commingling of souls. You realize, Gabriel, He puts much more trust in women. It is up to us not to disappoint Him."

We waited another five days without leaving the room. "Stay near me, Gabriel; you don't mind, do you?"

Every three hours a dark-haired aloof-looking chambermaid—doubtless unable to fathom how we could remain so long indoors, a man and a woman, both fully dressed and occupying separate beds—as I was saying, a rather haughty chambermaid brought us steaming, creamy cups of chocolate, sometimes with *Apfelstrudel,* sometimes with *Mehlspeise.*

"These are His favorite pastries, you know," said Clara every time.

She outlined for me in tenderest (and most irritating) detail the course of His daily life. "That's what He has taught us, Gabriel; the slightest detail can be meaningful. For example, He adores wild strawberries."

"Oh, yes?"

"And to reach His sister-in-law Minna's room you have to cross Their bedroom, where He sleeps with Martha."

It was precisely at this point that Gabriel first began to trust Freud. He has not read all of the great man's books, far from it. Nor has he understood all he did read. But a man who can live with two sisters for forty years can hardly be faulted.

One night Clara roused Gabriel. "Come." She was ready, cloak pulled around her, briefcase in hand, standing motionless by the bed. "Come along, we're leaving." Now? "Now." It proved necessary to dress in the dark. "Don't turn on the lights, Gabriel!" It proved necessary to shake the reception clerk at the Ungarische Krone into wakefulness so he could prepare their bill. It proved necessary to walk all the way to Vienna station, as all the cabdrivers were asleep. It proved necessary to request that the waiting room be unlocked, to step into that smell of stale tobacco. It proved necessary to ask Clara repeatedly to sit down. It proved necessary to position himself before her and take her icy hands and to find within Gabriel enough warmth to thaw them, but there was not much warmth in Gabriel, because of Clara's eyes, which stared at him without seeing.

Later on it was day and our train was on its way. Clara asked me to throw away the original idea.

"Now?"

"Now."

"But . . . you mean through the window?"

"Yes."

So the obedient Gabriel heaved with all his might on the two brass handles and managed to lower the window. Smoky billows flooded the compartment. The train, the sad homeward-bound train, was just entering the region of hills and dales known as Bavaria, and the engine was panting for breath.

"Please, Gabriel, you'll choke us; not here!"

So Gabriel took the original idea; it was from another car that he accomplished his destructive mission. He tactfully selected a downwind window so that the sight of papers whirling in the Bavarian breeze should not wound Clara's eyes. Alas, aerodynamics are complex. As their railbound convoy clove the air it created numerous crosscurrents—so many that for a moment, a long cruel moment, Clara was besieged and taunted by dozens of white birds, fluttering fragments of the original idea.

It would take Clara years to leave Vienna.

And not without a painful struggle: living underground is damp but comfortable.

She returned only gradually to the surface.

She kept me informed of her progress. "Come along, Gabriel, and I'll show you."

We would go walking. Arm in arm we strolled along the elevated tracks beside the avenue de Breteuil. Looking like convalescents.

"Do you see what I see?" Clara would ask.

"Yes, children on roller skates."

"No, higher up."

"Their mothers (or Breton women) looking after them."

"No, no, higher. Those are trees, aren't they?"

"Why, certainly. Chestnut trees, in fact. And they will soon be in flower."

"Well, Gabriel, once I would have seen only phalluses there. But all that is over now."

I kissed her. I teased her a little and kissed her. I sensed that her emergence, coming out from backstage and facing life head on, without the aid of symbols or a user's manual, was not easy. I kissed her so hard beside the elevated tracks on the avenue de Breteuil that she felt against her belly the very shaft she used to see (before her cure) in place of innocent chestnut trees.

"Oh!" Clara cried.

And pushing the insensitive beast violently away she fled down boulevard Garibaldi.

After three or four months of penitence, I was called back. "You will be nice?" I swear. "Then come, I've made more progress."

I thus witnessed her complete recovery.

She was waiting for me on a bench on avenue de Saxe in front of the Pasteur monument, abundant in cattle and youthful male figures.

"Do you notice anything?"

What was there in particular to notice in a Clara whose whole person you adored?

"No, nothing."

"You simply don't know how to look. What am I holding in my hand?"

A small rectangular black box, its upper half resembling an eye topped with four silvery buttons and a visor. Gabriel later learned its name: Leica, Leica I, model B, Compur shutter.

"What profession concerns itself solely with surfaces? The surface aspect of objects and living things?"

"Tiremaking."

"Cars aren't the only thing on this earth, Gabriel! Who concern themselves with landscapes, still lifes, faces?"

"I don't know."

"Photographers, idiot!"

Vienna and her exploration of the depths were forgotten. Clara was on the threshold of a new life, the life of the *superficial*. And once again, Gabriel was ecstatic. Once again, roly-poly incorrigibly optimistic Gabriel saw in this professional proximity (photographer and tire expert) the promise of conjugality he had so long awaited.

She raised the camera.

"How old am I, Gabriel?"

"I don't know."

"Good. Forty. Take that look off your face. Now, how do you like me best? With"—the black box hid her eyes, her nose, half of her forehead—"or without?"

"Without, of course."

"It shall be with. You will have to get used to it."

She had decided to hide her growing older behind the Leica.

But these are not things an optimist ever guesses. Or not until much later, when he is thinking back to the old days: avenue de Breteuil, the Pasteur monument. He becomes more perceptive. Memory has no time for optimism.

## VII

Ann again.

I remember women's clothes. They help me pinpoint dates. For example 1925, the tiniest of innovations, the schoolboy style evolving toward the schoolgirl, leg revealed to the knee. Or 1928, the dawn of the Schiaparelli era, when skirts were pleated and hairstyles lengthened. "You see, Gabriel, I was quite right not to cut mine." Fashions are my hourglass. I watch them change, detail by small detail, until they are completely new, and I know that time has gone by.

Ann crossing the hotel lobby in a red jersey dress: "Forgive me, Gabriel, businesswomen are always in a hurry." Ann in a raw silk jumper, sea-green jacket slung over her shoulder: "Whew, Gabriel, my God, it's hot this afternoon; do you really imagine that in this heat . . . ?"

And half of a suit, the most vivid picture of all, intact after I don't know how many years, the urge to reach out again, to leap out of bed and catch her. Ann would first undress below the waist and then pace up and down the bedroom floor, often for several minutes: "I'm sorry, Gabriel, it's the job; I need to unwind." Can you imagine?

Following a skirtless woman with your eyes for any length of time, up and down, up and down? Men have gone mad for less. Afterward Ann would put her clothes back on, beginning with her skirt. And then would pace again, pace and comb, pace and blond hair, before she put the rest back on. Who could have resisted? "Oh, come now, Gabriel, please, Gabriel, I'm a working woman." Oh, how Gabriel could love working women!

That kind of thing is generally little known, the part dress styles can play in a man's life. I don't know who started them. Chanel? The Irishman Molyneux? Maggy Rouff? Someone else in a dim and distant past? Historians would tell us that already in Upper Egypt, where women worked hard, the fashions changed periodically. Whoever it was, to him or to her, the inventor of different styles, my heartfelt thanks.

# 11

# *The Colonial Exposition*

THIRTY-FOUR MILLION VISITORS.

Rabbit hunters dreaming of big game, armchair travelers pretending to be explorers, deserted husbands wistfully dreaming of slavery, married women yearning for climates warmer than wedlock, failures looking for vindication, fat little white men despising long thin black men, Paul Bourget getting a whiff of Kipling, royalists recalling Louis XIV, republicans remembering the Italian campaign. Small boys seeing themselves as missionaries, little girls as martyrs.

Thirty-four million, the most successful public extravaganza, wars excepted, in all French history.

And Louis, because he was not a government employee, almost missed the boat. He scurried from office to office offering his services—Foreign Affairs on the quai d'Orsay; Colonies on the rue Oudinot; Armed Forces on the boulevard Saint-Germain; Education on the rue de Grenelle—but everywhere he went he faced the same question: Are you a government employee? followed by the same pity: Alas, are you quite sure? Not even for a brief spell in your youth that you've forgotten about? Officials appalled at this state of affairs (not being a government employee) moved heaven and earth to help him. On his behalf they consulted lists of former employees, thumbed through new regulations governing direct entry to public office, looked into the possibility of freelance contracts, roundabout routes.

After the exchange of many smiles and much innuendo, a blonde in one office even murmured across the sepia counter, "My name is Mylène, I'm sure we could find something for you to do that you'd be good at."

But after checking the matter in a small hotel on the rue du Louvre: "No, none," she said, "I must have been mistaken. And don't insist, please, I have three children, and a real position."

Louis refused to be dissuaded. He was the first to arrive on the rue Oudinot next morning, waiting outside for the office to open.

"Your lover's back, Mylène." Her colleagues snickered.

She threatened to call the police.

But Louis dug in his heels; all day long he sat in the office's only chair beneath a poster extolling French Equatorial Africa, its wide-open spaces, its flora, its fauna. The office workers soon appreciated the positive side to his persistence: seeing someone constantly waiting there, their superiors might well conclude that the staff was up to its ears in work.

Every two hours someone called out, "Still there, Monsieur Orsenna?"

"I wish to see the Minister," my father replied.

It was evening, just before they turned on the lights. French Equatorial Africa was almost lost in the gloom. A white smock opened the door, a woman's voice called out:

"Anybody else?"

Louis rose.

"Oh, I didn't see you! Well, you aren't exactly conspicuous, are you? You must learn to be more assertive, monsieur. If I have to start making the rounds of every office. . . . Not afraid of injections, are you?"

She took his arm and led him into a small windowless room.

"Put your clothes on that chair. The doctor is in there."

She motioned to a door plastered with warnings about malaria, amoebic dysentery, sleeping sickness. Louis had trouble controlling his rapid heart rate (an Orsenna tic on all momentous occasions): he consulted his pulse, took deep breaths, counted at top speed; his pulse continued to race. What if they withheld permanent positions from hearts that beat too fast?

"Well now," said the doctor. "Previous illnesses, childhood diseases, surgery? Come come, my friend, speak up, it will be night soon. What part of the world are you leaving for?"

"I'm staying here," said Louis. "I want to work at the Exposition."

"Like me, eh, scared of traveling? Let me make a small confession. I may be a doctor but you'd have to kill me before I agreed to go. If you only saw what I see when they come back—particularly the livers and intestines—it really puts you off the colonies. I prefer our home-grown diseases, even the fatal ones. If you have to die, you might as well die on familiar ground, don't you think?"

And they talked about tropical diseases. At such great length that they were the last people left in the Ministry, alone in the depths of the Finance department.

"Do you know the way out?" asked the doctor.

"I haven't the slightest idea," Louis replied.

"I must say, you really seem made for public office; once inside, you stay inside. Yes, indeed, leave it to me. I'll help you. But now I would really like to get home. Let's pool our resources."

In total darkness (the power had been cut off, doubtless as part of an economy drive: the Finance department had to set an example), they wandered along endless corridors, shouting for help without getting the slightest response. From time to time they blundered into heaps of folders whose titles Louis made out with the help of his lighter: "Look, here we are in the Collections department."

"Fat lot of good that does us," grumbled the doctor.

At long last, pushing through a concealed door, they emerged onto the sinister Cour Napoléon which led to the rue de Rivoli.

"Please excuse me," said the doctor. "I must dash, my dear friend, but you can count on me. Let's talk again. Admit it, though; you *are* a doctor, aren't you? Oh, if only all my colleagues knew as much about amoebic dysentery as you. . . ."

Two days later Louis was summoned by a Ministry aide.

"I've heard good things about you. Let's see whether I can be of help. What was it you wanted? Oh, yes! a permanent position, like everyone else. I'll be frank, it won't be easy. The problem is which branch of the service to choose. Let me see, let me see, what might I suggest? Curator? Are you a lover of art objects?"

Louis pulled a face.

"A pity, but you really have to be passionate about art objects to be a curator. Librarian, then? Perfect! You are passionate about books. Oh, but wait a minute, the Colonial Exposition has nothing to do with libraries. I'm sorry, it's not for want of trying, but I don't see what branch to put you in. And without a branch you have no chance of a permanent position, do you see? On the other hand, we could always sign you up on a contractual basis . . . renewable, of course. And, let's face it, this damned exposition's been gestating so long . . . eight years now . . . a truly elephantine pregnancy. Look."

He pointed to a gray wall, folders heaped on folders leaning against the wire-mesh covering of the cabinet.

"At the moment it's scheduled for 1931. If it ever sees the light of day! Well, one thing's certain, the exposition needs people like you, real enthusiasts, people willing to grasp the nettle."

The aide, discouraged at the start of the interview, seemed to be perking up.

"Wait, I can use you, I think I can use you. We're going to need someone to help run the new committee. You wouldn't know this of course, but I'm going to let you in on it: Monsieur Angoulvant was too simple a solution for them. So farewell, Angoulvant! And hail Marshal Lyautey! I've nothing against the marshal, but now we're going to have to replace half the committee; the marshal has his own funny little ways. That can be your first job. . . ."

"So when may I begin?" asked Louis shyly, hands clenched on his hat brim.

"Why, tomorrow—no, at once; ask my secretary for an office. Or settle down in the waiting room. With all the time this business has taken, the waiting room is just the place! No, no, I was joking, you will have a real office and a real contract . . . renewable, of course. Well, congratulations then, and welcome to the exposition!"

Now began what Louis later called "the happiest years of my life." He trotted from one end of Paris to the other. To the Land Registry Office to make sure the Vincennes site had a clear title. To see contractors, who received him with a certain coolness.

"So you political hacks have finally stopped squabbling. Ready to start work?"

"Um . . . well, actually I came to tell you there may be a slight delay."

"In that case I demand a penalty payment."

"But don't you realize we have an entire empire to put on display?"

"I don't give a damn. What am I supposed to have my workers do? They were scheduled to start on the Chinese pagoda tomorrow. What are they going to do now, huh?"

"Take another look at the order. It isn't a pagoda but a Cambodian temple."

"This is no time for word games!"

Politely, Louis took his leave, bewildered by so much hostility, as if the Exposition were some run-of-the-mill building project! They had read too much Genesis, these small-time contractors; they believed everything could be created in six days and they could rest on the seventh. Someone should explain to them the metaphoric—yes, gentlemen, *metaphoric*—nature of those six days of creation.

And he returned to the Ministry haloed in the insults he had borne.

Moreover, the small-time contractors called back next day, all sweetness and light. The effects of the American Depression were starting to be felt. It was said in well-informed circles that things might get worse. So an order—even a deferred order—for a Khmer temple was not to be sneezed at.

"Right! Now, don't dilly-dally, Orsenna, off you go and talk to Rosengart."

Rosengart was a well-known car manufacturer at that time. He had proposed making little golf carts to ferry visitors from one pavilion to the next, from West Africa to Asia. People who like the colonies may not necessarily like walking, isn't that so, Monsieur Orsenna?

And there, not far from the Levallois ratodrome, Louis was in familiar territory.

"I am Gabriel's father—"

"The tire expert, of course, of course."

"So, how are we coming along this month, Monsieur Rosengart?"

"You'll see for yourself in just a few moments. The prototype is on its way back from a road test in the suburbs. You'll have a drink?"

M. Rosengart ordered two glasses of Suze, sweeping papers aside to clear a space on his desk: "our newest creations, Monsieur Orsenna." They might almost have been discussing high fashion.

"So you used to know Levallois?"

"Yes, a little," Louis mumbled.

"Well, then, you certainly remember the golden age of the custom-made car. Look down there. Do you find assembly lines attractive? I've never been able to get used to them."

A large picture window looked out onto the workshops. Cars took shape piece by piece before their eyes. Rosengart and my father raised their glasses: to craftsmanship!

"Don't let me delay you," said M. Rosengart. "I know how much time it takes to put an exposition together. Don't you worry, everything will be ready in time. In any case I'll drive the prototype around to the Ministry tomorrow. If only to set your mind at ease."

The prototype never arrived. You watched for it, you listened for it in vain.

"Luckily we have the circular track and the electrocars," the organizers comforted one another. "But don't relax your grip, Orsenna, go back there as often as you have to, Rosengart gave his word, and he must stick to it."

Louis preferred the Rosengart file to the human-rights case. The League of that name had protested about rickshaws; in its view, such forms of transportation degraded the human species. It was threatening to take the case to The Hague, the Court of Justice, even the pope, although the League itself tended to be of secular, not to say Masonic, persuasion. Perhaps their bluff should have been called; the dialogue between Lodge and Holy See would certainly not have lacked spice.

"No matter what, keep them talking," the Minister told him. "Without rickshaws the Exposition will lose all its flavor."

Louis defended the Minister's position to lawyers who were overworked but at the same time deeply committed to the issue at hand.

"Surely a little exoticism never did anyone any harm?"

"Such exoticism is an insult to the human race."

The telephone on the lawyer's desk rang incessantly. "Forgive me, this won't take a second." And Louis was abruptly immersed in endless legal squabbles, divorces, bankruptcies, inheritances.

Exhausted, the lawyer replaced the receiver. Sighed. Looked slowly up at Louis.

"Yes? What is it? Oh! Forgive me, but you see how hectic life is in the legal profession. Yes, rickshaws. . . ."

Some evenings Louis asked me to drop by. Wladislawa would let me in, her features icy: He's going to talk to you about that disgraceful business of his again.

"Now, Gabriel, be frank," said Louis. "What do you think of rickshaws?"

We agreed they were not a matter for pride.

"But tell me, Gabriel, does an exposition have the right to make its own selections from real life, to show only the bright side of things? Gabriel, from the bottom of your heart now, from a purely deontological point of view, are we not morally obliged to exhibit rickshaws *as well?*"

When it came to hypocrisy, Louis was absolutely unbeatable.

I was almost forgetting the intracolonial wars. They were fought out on the map pinned to the wall showing the rectangle formed by avenue Daumesnil, Highway 38 from Paris to Charenton, avenue de Gravelle, and avenue du Château. The "Africans" threatened to walk out if sub-Saharan Africa were not allotted more space. Very well, retorted the "Indochinese," in that case take the whole of Vincennes; we'll put Angkor on somewhere else and we'll see which the French like better, our temples or your huts—

"Gentlemen, gentlemen, calm yourselves! The exposition grounds are big enough for everyone."

But the colonials were deaf to reason.

"Africa deserves more."

"Savages, scarcely out of the trees!"

"Too much slant-eyed sadism and the children won't want to come."

"Sadism, perhaps—but a real civilization! How many cities like Hué have you Bantus built?"

Night fell. Their insults could be heard out in the street.

Fortunately such outbursts were rare. Exhibitionists are gentle creatures; the shyest of all educators, they cannot bear direct contact with their students. They lovingly set out their wares and step back. Visitors could draw their own conclusions. Inside this touchy world, Louis made useful contacts. He told people he lived in the sixth or seventh *arrondissement,* where public servants dwell. He saw career employees home. After meetings he walked slowly beside them through deserted streets. He listened to long speeches about civilization, about the smallness of our country, about the urgent need for Empire, isn't that so, Orsenna?

In the darkness Louis agreed.

The most talkative of these strollers were Hirsch, vice-president of the Greater France Association, and Labbé, chief engineer on the projected Djibouti–Addis Ababa railroad.

"Have you ever visited these countries, Orsenna?"

"No, Monsieur le Président," Louis answered. "No, Monsieur l'Ingénieur en Chef."

"Then why this devotion to the Exposition?"

"I detest cramped living."

They would gladly have embraced him. At their doorsteps they had a few more words to say about the wide-open spaces.

"One of these days you'll go there yourself. Then you'll understand. But it's getting late."

In vain Louis took every possible precaution, climbing over walls instead of negotiating the squeaky front gate, avoiding crunchy gravel walks, and, once inside, leaping over sections of the wooden floor he knew to be sensitive; it never worked. Just as he finished undressing in total silence his name floated up in the night.

"Louis?"

"Yes."

"More colonial rubbish?"

Wladislawa never put the lights on. She got up and threw the shutters open. She looked out at the city, the lights, the sky just beginning to turn pale.

"When I think of what we might have built together, Louis, together, instead of pulling in opposite directions! For I too love the influence of French culture; every Pole loves the influence of French culture, and myself more than most Poles. Look at the Aragons, Louis, you and he have the same first name; look at them. Day by day every breath they take, every gesture they make reaches toward the same goal: communism. Do you appreciate the extent of their love? If there were as much love in our home as at the Aragons', if we added, Louis, if we multiplied, instead of subtracting ourselves, we would set a better example than the Aragons. Think about it, Louis, while we still have time."

And she began to sob, one single, endless sob, broken only by references to the Aragons.

"Where are they at this hour, Louis? Side by side, snug, hand in hand, perhaps still making love! And it is not because they are younger than we are, Louis, don't try to use that as an excuse; we too could muster enough desire to embark on love the whole night long. I came from Poland for that, just for that, for a true love. But you have squandered it all, Louis, you have to poke your nose into everything, no matter how small, you blow everything out of proportion, everything except the size of our love—"

Wladislawa's broad back shook convulsively, and her fair head jolted against the telescope she used to spy on the Aragons.

"Oh, no! I've thrown it off course again. What's their address? I get so lost in Paris. Which way should I turn it? I have to keep my eye on them"—her voice turned thin and hateful—"because their love is dangerous for Poland. The more they love one another, the more communism prevails. And what's good for communism is good for Russia and therefore bad for Poland. Can you imagine what might have happened, Louis, if our own love and not theirs had occupied center stage? Louis, what would communism then have to offer to tempt the world with, radiant tomorrows? Liquidation of the kulaks? Oh, Louis, how irresponsible of you not to love me enough; what a calamity to let communism have a monopoly on Great Love! Oh, Louis! If anything happens to Poland it will be your fault and I shall say so; yes, Louis, no matter what the consequences I shall say so. Oh, Louis, what a terribly destructive destiny yours has been. Terrible, oh, terrible. . . ."

And on these words—terrible, oh, terrible—Louis would leave; they faded from his hearing the closer he came to Paris and the Ministry. He was in his office before anyone else, just in time to receive Marguerite's call: "Louis, it's me. I wanted to wish you a happy day. I am proud of you; not too many problems, I hope? Opening day still unchanged? Long live France, Louis, I am proud of you." He replaced the receiver.

He had had no sleep, or hardly any. But he was not in the least tired. He was back again, all of him, at the Exposition. When you live in a dream you have no need for sleep.

Impressed by his zeal, the Ministry finally admitted him to its holy of holies, to the womb of its loftiest ideas, to the place where the goals of the Exposition were slowly and carefully formulated, every word sifted, every clause weighed.

"France is no longer just a corner of Europe. Whether in North Africa, where a sturdy branch of the race has been grafted; whether in Indochina, West Africa, Equatorial Africa, or Madagascar, where armies of Frenchmen are building our new Empire; whether in the West Indies, where faded eighteenth-century charm and manners live on among the descendants of the first settlers in their three-cornered hats and powdered wigs—no matter where, it is all France, tirelessly re-creating herself in near and faroff lands, lands now thriving segments of her ever-expanding territory."

Endless negotiations, constant disputes over procedure:

"Don't you think we should prepare an official statement? Let's ask the École Normale. They write well over there on the rue d'Ulm."

"No, no, my dear fellow, the committee and only the committee is responsible for that task. We are not entitled to delegate."

"We're marking time, and the hour draws near."

A sour note had entered the debate.

"Now, now, gentlemen, settle down," said department head Chadeau-Zylber.

"Oh, you, why don't you settle your own marital problems?"

"I demand an apology!"

"All right, I apologize, I apologize," cried Alazard, director of the Algiers museum.

"Well, Crouzet, it's a long time since you said anything."

"I still believe that this repetition of the phrase 'whether in' is infelicitous. 'Whether in North Africa,' 'whether in Indochina': it's cumbersome at best."

"Don't forget that our aim is educational, Crouzet. You of all people, a school inspector, should understand that!"

"Let's not confuse educational with pedantic. Which is why I have so far held my tongue."

And there were others who were there to champion just one sentence: the ideal (in their view) verbal distillation of the colonial adventure. Thus Gruvel, professor at the Natural History Museum and laboratory director of Colonial Fisheries and Livestock. He had befriended Louis. He outlined his conception of Letters to him:

"No need for a novel, Orsenna, or even a short story; I am the author of a few terse words. 'A well-ordered chaos of plant, animal, and human life.' Answer me frankly. Is that, or is it not, the very definition of a colonial exposition?"

He tried to have his chaos adopted at every meeting.

"Later, Gruvel," Chadeau-Zylber would tell him. "This isn't the right moment."

At last the right moment came.

"Whereas, in the case of every citizen of the United Kingdom, the notion of the 'British Empire' is something tangible, concrete, in France the idea of a colonial empire, far from being familiar to the man in the street, has never been adequately expressed even at official levels."

The department head proposed a description of the Palace of Colonies.

"Behind the clean sweeping lines of its colonnade, the soaring façade is a vast stone fresco throbbing with life—"

Louis leaned toward Gruvel. "Perhaps this is the right moment for your chaos."

"You are right."

And Gruvel finished the department head's sentence for him:

". . . a well-ordered chaos of plant, animal, and human life, capturing forever in the immobility of stone our young Empire's exuberant spirit, bubbling over with wealth and strength."

"That seems to strike exactly the right note," said Chadeau-Zylber. "Does the committee approve? Splendid. Excellent meeting. A few more sessions like this, and we'll be nearing our goal."

As they left, Gruvel seized Louis's arm.

"My dear fellow, I shall never forget your help. The Education Ministry would probably take you on if it's tenure you're after. I can't get you tenure in Colonial Fisheries, but I could put your name down for contract assignments."

"Alas, I am too old."

"Then I'm terribly sorry. Contract work can solve many problems, but it can do nothing about age. Well, I'm sure you will find something else. A pity all the same." Whistling, the proud author went off in the direction of the Seine.

Louis had no friends at this point. Not enough time. His life had been a succession of stages: each time a small pool of light with a woman at its center. He barely had time to develop habits (for instance a Pernod at the corner café before going up to see her, or the ritual Sunday afternoon chat with his prospective father-in-law) before the light went out and the woman vanished. The train left the station. You had to forget faces, neighborhoods, addresses.

Admittedly, the Wladislawa period endured. But a great love is not conducive to the furthering of friendships. As for Chadeau-Zylber—caution and clear thinking in all dealings with one's superiors!

The department head often came to sit in the nontenured employee's small gray office: "I'm not disturbing you, am I, Orsenna?" He waited until nightfall. Everyone had left for the day. Then he would tell of his woes, a post in Cameroon, a runaway wife, a bachelor raising two children—"It's hardest on Sundays, believe me, Orsenna"—a man on his own and two children in an apartment on the rue Boulard: "It's hard after Cameroon, and suddenly here's my wife wanting to steal them back from me, Pauline and Jean-Baptiste." Louis sympathized but was not taken in: friendship and the need to pour out one's soul should never be confused.

And then came that story in *L'Auto*.

Summer. Rue Oudinot. The temperature rose rapidly after 10 A.M. People queried colleagues who had held overseas posts.

"Yes," they said, "yes. It's about as hot here as it was there."

People asked them about ways to combat the heat. There are none, replied the colonials.

And silence fell on the rue Oudinot, on the corridor housing the Directorate of African Affairs, Sub-Directorate for French West Africa, Senegal office, Guinea office, Ivory Coast office, Dahomey office, Togo office . . . almost the whole length of the coast (except for a few German or Portuguese enclaves) as far south as Namibia.

Conversation flagged. Even gossip ran itself into the ground. The terrible boredom of office life in summer when time stands still, seeming to stick in the air the way shoes stick to molten asphalt.

"You should take a look at this," said a colleague, handing him a copy of *L'Auto*. "You should really take a look at this."

Thus it was that the sports press entered Louis's life.

And he realized quickly that sports magazines help life run more smoothly. . . .

Very soon he was immersed in a world as teeming and abundant as a tropical market, feeling that sense of intoxication so well known to all of us followers of sport, first a quick glance at the sculling section—oops, a small setback there, the Rowing Club didn't make the head of the river—a short visit to the tennis pages: the winners of the Wimbledon mixed doubles have refused to play together again. A permanent rift? To be continued. A moment of (feigned) fellow feeling for the competitors in the Los Angeles Marathon (a warm-up for the Games): Will the Frenchman El-Ouafi repeat his Amsterdam victory? With a name like that, he must be used to heat waves. Louis was sucked into that interminable soap opera that fed you all day long: victories, defeats, loyalties, betrayals, travel, medicine, techniques, torn muscles, human drama, not to mention the daily larger-than-life drama of the Tour de France.

When it was over (won by Dewaele, Belgium), Louis contemplated the void ahead. Late July is the worst time for sports fans. Like a family vacation when you love another.

So he was moved beyond belief by an article on August 1:

WHAT ABOUT A YEAR-ROUND TOUR DE FRANCE?

The plaudits fade, the Parc des Princes is closed, yellow jersey tucked away, Izoard forgotten . . . how can we go on living?

The author's answer set him seething with excitement:

What if we carried the Tour de France over into a Tour de l'Empire?

That very morning he dashed off a letter to the author, a certain Dekaerkove, first initial E. Élie? Émile?

They arranged to meet at a small Auvergnat restaurant near the newspaper offices, the Puy-de-Dôme, patronized exclusively by sports fans. Louis always suffered from stage fright before entering a new world. His hand on the doorknob, he hesitated at the threshold. Here he was, barely ensconced in public office, abandoning it for sport. There was still time to change his mind.

"Ah, you must be the colonial!"

The whole restaurant turned to stare at the newcomer.

Those who often change worlds, jobs, or women are good at taking their courage in both hands. Louis took a deep breath and approached the "sportsman" who had spoken. Past his fifties, already bald, a round face above a violet bow tie, gentle shortsighted eyes. How did he ever manage to tell the riders apart when they bunched to sprint?

The conversation around them had resumed. Louis relaxed. There, the anxious part of the journey was over. Now came that heady feeling of settling into a new world.

The "sportsman" studied him.

"So you're interested in the Tour de France?"

He had to shout at the top of his lungs because of all the conversations around them.

"Couldn't we find a quieter place?" asked Louis.

"Impossible, they always have to know where to find me to give me the results. If a world record is broken, for instance. It's a bit hot, but you never know down in the southern hemisphere. . . ."

From time to time someone yelled, really yelled, from right across the room: "Well, Dekaerkove, what'll it be next year, Aubisque, Galibier, *and* Izoard?"

Thus Louis learned Dekaerkove's true vocation. His was the most patriotic of journalistic callings: planner for the Tour de France. It was he who mapped out the route every year. He began with major cities, potential overnight stops. He sought out the mayor.

"How would you like your town to be a part of the Tour de France?"

The official blushed and stammered: I would be honored, honored.

Then Dekaerkove would tell him the rates, call in the local hotelkeepers, read them the usual moral strictures, remind them about hygiene, insist on a basic code for bridal suites. And then he had to dream up the course itself, alternating steep inclines with gentler slopes, hairpin descents, flat terrain where you idled before kicking into the final sprint.

Of course he knew the whole of France commune by commune.

"Go on, ask me a question, give me the name of a village, any village."

Louis picked Le Thoureil, a locality on the banks of the Loire we visited with Marguerite just before our abortive departure for the colonies.

"Le Thoureil, let me see now . . . oh, yes! Two houses facing each other over a garden overflowing with hollyhocks. Close to the bathing beach, right? Across the river from a horse farm? And watch out: floodwater can make surfaces treacherous."

"Amazing. I don't believe it. May I try again?"

"By all means."

"Well then, Moernach (Upper Rhine)."

"Wait a second. Yes, yes, the manure pit at the entrance to the village leaks; I remember back in 1926 the tires stank all day long."

I too have met prodigies like Dekaerkove in political circles. They also have France mapped out in their heads, but theirs is an electoral France, district by district, and the results of every vote ever taken in the past hundred years. Dekaerkove's knowledge was more tranquil, less strife-fraught, a vast geographic love.

Every year he returned exhausted from his planning activities, his liver swollen; he slept for a whole week, drank nothing but Saint-Yorre mineral water, and started to think about next year's Tour de France. Such was his trade, a life spent tracing hexagons, his own private hexagons.

"It isn't that I no longer love my country, believe me. But sometimes you have to be able to broaden your horizons."

That was why he had suggested a Tour of the Empire, or at least a tour of sub-Saharan Africa to start with.

"A wonderful idea," said Louis. "I shall bring it up with my department head at the Exposition. Your idea couldn't be more timely; we'll make it the centerpiece of our sports section."

They went on talking far into the afternoon.

"Good Lord!" Louis suddenly cried. "I'm late."

He said goodbye.

"See you tomorrow," the sports fans called out.

"You see, it wasn't so hard. They've adopted you," said Dekaerkove.

"Who stands closer to the heart of France than I do? Tell me that, Marguerite," Louis would say every evening at Levallois. "Tell me who?"

And then, after eating dinner with his mother, he would return with dragging step to his home, where Wladislawa received him more and more acrimoniously.

"What good does it do you to have a Polish woman in your life, Louis, will you tell me that?"

"But you know full well that I too would have preferred a Universal Exposition. Wait a little, Wladi, be patient."

"Do the Aragons wait to make love? Are they patient? Your lack of love is a crime against Poland, Louis."

Chadeau-Zylber now dropped in every evening at closing time to review the situation.

"Is there anything we have overlooked, Orsenna?"

There was silence throughout the Ministry, not a footfall, not the solitary scrape of a chair.

"Sounds as if they've all gone home. Just wait, one day they'll abandon us both. Leaving us holding the baby. By the way, have we kept the children in mind? The Exposition has to attract children. Did I tell you my wife is coming closer? Yesterday she was spying on our apartment from the sidewalk across the street. Yes, Orsenna, we must make sure the Exposition pleases the children."

Louis spent the first part of the year 1931 in specialty stores with manufacturers of pedal cars, electric trains, merry-go-rounds. Together they pondered new and more exotic varieties.

"Instead of these pink pigs going up and down and these outboard motorboats, couldn't you do ostriches and dugout canoes?"

"I'm not sure my workmen are up to that."

Colonial purists balked. "We can't turn the Exposition into a zoo."

But Louis stuck to his guns. And the results were there for everyone to see: here an enchanted Congo; farther on, in the Cameroon enclosure, a safari pavilion with three big dioramas by the painter J. de la Nozière (what a struggle to get his name past the committee!). Between them a pride of five lions sleeping away the heat of the day under a baking sun. On their right, two gorillas in the gloomy depths of the forest, patrolling their domain with ponderous majesty. On the left, a panther about to pounce on a gazelle slaking her thirst at a spring.

Louis brought sketches and plans to the office. Chadeau-Zylber rubbed his hands.

"My children will be pleased as punch! They will adore me forever. And that bitch can go to hell!"

With these words he scowled, gripped the inside of his right elbow with his left hand, and thrust his right fist into the air, a timid man's hasty, furtive gesture of defiance.

*Le Temps* announced opening day: May 6. They might have let us know before they told the press, grumbled the Minister. But he had to suppress his resentment.

"The last nuts and bolts," said Chadeau-Zylber. "I rely on you to tighten them, Orsenna, because with all these characters I have to deal with . . ."

And he fled to his office where the phone was ringing off the hook.

You could hear him reply: "Yes, Monsieur Deputy, of course His Eminence has been invited. . . . There's been a small delay with the invitations. . . . Please remind your ambassador of the time. . . ."

Dark long-standing antagonisms had kept the Quai d'Orsay out of the preparations for the Exposition. So it was sulking. And had sent nobody from protocol. Despite promises and high-level requests.

"You didn't turn him away, by any chance?" they asked Mangin the doorman, a veteran of Verdun.

The doorman mumbled that he might be a cripple but he knew the difference between a Boche and a diplomat.

The protocol expert finally turned up on April 20, a day of sudden downpours. Despite the umbrella his shoes were sodden. But his upper reaches were impeccable: stiff collar, brilliantined hair, gloves held in left hand.

The situation was outlined to him. Immediate verdict.

"The opening ceremony you propose—and how could you have known? Ceremonies are an art—this ceremony, as I was saying, could involve us in at least four wars."

His tone was distressed and gentle rather than contemptuous.

"Well, let's start again from scratch. Has the President of the Republic confirmed that he will attend?"

The Colonial Ministry's rage knew no bounds. This man must be Jewish, a Jew; the Quai d'Orsay had sent them a Jewish protocol expert.

It bore all the hallmarks of the Quai. We'll give them a nice little mix of ethnic minorities. Hebrews and Ubangi should get along like a house on fire. That was undoubtedly what they were saying at the Quai.

Louis called me at all hours of the day and night during that period. It was vain to protest: Louis, I'm at work. Louis, I have Monaco in under a month. Louis, have you ever heard of the Le Mans twenty-four-hour race? He summoned me to Levallois. "Come over right away, Gabriel, I must speak to you." We conferred out on the terrace. Wladislawa had locked herself in her bedroom.

"I think the Colonial Exposition is tearing Wladi and me apart."

"What's the matter, Louis?"

"Look."

He handed me a leaflet. I could make out nothing in the dark, so I went over to a lighted window.

BOYCOTT THE COLONIAL EXPOSITION!

On the eve of May Day, 1931, shortly before the opening of the Colonial Exposition, the Indochinese student Tao was kidnapped by French police.

World opinion protested in vain against the death sentences pronounced on Sacco and Vanzetti. As for Tao, a helpless pawn of arbitrary military justice and mandarin law, we cannot even say for certain that he is still alive. Exactly the curtain-raiser the Vincennes Exposition needed in this year of grace 1931. . . .

That these men, from whom we are set apart if only by reason of our white skins (we colorless men who call other men colored!), that these men were marched to the slaughter in 1914 at the behest of the European metallurgical industry and were rewarded with inglorious mass graves—this entitles us too to inaugurate the Colonial Exposition in our own fashion, and to condemn all supporters of the Vincennes enterprise as beasts of prey. The Lyauteys, the Dumesnils, and the Doumers who ruled the roost throughout the Roaring Twenties will be presiding over a carnival of skeletons. . . .

The dogma of French territorial integrity, so piously advanced in moral justification of the massacres we perpetrate, is a semantic fraud; it blinds no one to the fact that not a week goes by without someone being killed in the colonies. The presence at the Exposition opening of the President of the Republic, of the Emperor of Annam, of the cardinal-archbishop of Paris, and of assorted governors and roughnecks cheek by jowl with the missionary pavilions and the Citroën and Renault stands, clearly marks the complicity of the bourgeoisie in the birth of a new and particularly loathsome concept, the notion of Greater France. It was to implant this larcenous notion that the pavilions were built for the Vincennes Exposition. For of course we must imbue our citizens with the requisite landlord mentality if they are to bear the sound of distant gunfire without flinching. To the foot of our flawless French landscape, already lavishly celebrated before the war in a song about a bamboo hut, we must now tack on a vista of minarets and pagodas.

And we have not forgotten that splendid colonial-army recruiting poster: an easy life, Negresses with big tits, the elegant linen-suited NCO taking the air in a rickshaw pulled by a native man—adventure, quick promotion.

Whether the corrupt Socialist Party and the Jesuitical League of Human Rights like it or not, we believe it is pointless to try to distinguish between good and bad kinds of colonialism. The champions of capitalist-style national defense, with the unspeakable Boncour at their head, can be proud of their fun fair at Vincennes. . . .

Answer their speeches and their executions by insisting on the immediate evacuation of our colonies and the arraignment of the generals and officials responsible for the massacres in Annam, in Lebanon, in Morocco, and in Central Africa.

And it was signed:

André Breton, Paul Éluard, Benjamin Péret, Georges Sadoul, Pierre Urik, André Thirion, René Crevel, Aragon, René Char, Maxime Alexandre, Yves Tanguy, Georges Malkine

"What should I do, Gabriel? Wladislawa shoved this under my nose and now she's packing her bags."

I had given him so much advice in the past. He had so often done the opposite. And the opposite had brought so many calamities in its wake that I now held my peace.

"You're asleep, Gabriel, you're asleep just when your father needs you most!"

The light in Wladislawa's bedroom went on and off and on again above our heads.

"See that, Gabriel? Wladislawa is nothing like you, she can't get to sleep. Clearly you know nothing about love. I most decidedly don't have the son I hoped for, someone I could lean on. . . ."

"This protocol business is an absolute nightmare, Orsenna. Tell me, could you answer this kind of question? Does a bey take precedence over an ambassador? El Glaoui over the Primate of the Gauls? And these are minor examples, mere binary problems. Just imagine having to organize the parade, allocate seats in the viewing stands. . . . No, believe me, I'm very happy to be relieved of the burden. Now I can concentrate on the last nuts and bolts. You haven't forgotten our children?"

On the eve of the great day the weather was the sole topic of conversaton. The whole Ministry eyed the sky through the windows.

"Think it's going to rain?"

Chadeau-Zylber dropped in on Louis at a late hour.

"Come with me, Orsenna, we must check the lighting."

They parked the Ministry Renault at Porte Dorée.

The exposition site was in a fever, ghostly figures wielding flashlights and jostling one another as they shoved and tugged at light or dark shapes unidentifiable in the gloom amid construction-site smells: plaster, wet cement, sawn timber. A climate dark with invective. More to the right, dammit, that totem pole's tilting. Well, are you ever going to get that lion in place? A truck heaped with raffia masks asked for directions: The Dutch East Indies pavilion, please. Delivered at long last, the Rosengart golf carts lined up one by one on the front parking lot, while rare plants moved forward, their foliage trailing on the ground: gangway, up ahead! watch your step behind! A whole forest advancing on little wheels, squeaking and rustling, the rattle of porters' handcarts and the sighing of wind in palm fronds.

And suddenly the lamps came on, red, white, and blue, the whole length of the avenue des Colonies, from Madagascar to the two missionary pavilions. Workers put the last touches to the reliefs along Angkor's façades. At the very top of the Colonial Forces Tower a tiny black dot (probably a Chasseur Alpin) unfurled the French flag.

The whole Empire was there—the Empire minus its defects. Minus its climate, for instance. But with huts, temples, the army, huge trees.

"A pity," said the department head. "This would have been a good time to bring the children."

Then the spell was broken. Electricians scurried about replacing defective bulbs; plasterers resumed their work on Angkor. The corps of artisans was putting the finishing touches to the Empire.

"Come on, Orsenna, hop in the car and we'll check the nuts and bolts one last time."

So all night long they drove up and down the avenue and alleyways. "Well, Pierrotin, no problems with Saint-Pierre-et-Miquelon, I trust? What's up, Linton, you look worried. Is anything wrong with Senegal? Spitz, please do me a favor and check French West Africa's plumbing system."

At dawn, at long last satisfied, the department head called a halt. "I think our Exposition is a success. Now I can go and wake the children."

## More of the Real World over Lunch

Months after the Exposition closed, the sad tale of his department head, the only boss he had ever had, continued to torment Louis. In the middle of lunch he would glance left and right in case of spies, then lean across the table.

"You know, Gabriel, there are times when I just can't go on. Every time I enter my bedroom I feel as if I'm in a factory. A factory where Wladislawa is manufacturing our relationship. Gabriel, it's exhausting to live with a manufacturer of love! But when I think of poor old Chadeau-Zylber . . ."

And once again he described how Mme. Chadeau-Zylber had burst into the Cameroon pavilion, how the children had rushed into her arms, much preferring her to the lions in the diorama, and how she had left with long, somewhat shaky strides, like a shepherd in the Landes marshes perched high on his stilts, a bizarre animal, a most handsome woman in a black dress with a child clinging to each leg.

"And there you are, yet another cruel princess. You see, Gabriel, we are very similar, Chadeau-Zylber and I. Princesses have robbed us of our children. If you had met real women, not princesses, I would have grandsons by now."

For some mysterious reason, perhaps the responsibilities Chadeau-Zylber had vested in him, perhaps the educational aura surrounding every colonial adventure (blacks are of course overgrown children), the Exposition had left Louis with one obsession: to become a grandfather. He filled his glass, sighed, refilled his glass, and in his mounting self-pity gradually got fuddled.

"Gabriel: give me a grandson, Gabriel."

"But Louis," I replied, "if I had a son he might be my best friend, and then you and I would no longer be alone in the world."

He would have none of it. "Gabriel, you are my best friend in all the world; we love each other, don't we?"

He turned to the maître d': "Well, monsieur-know-it-all-headwaiter-with-your-little-pad-in-your-hand, tell me why fathers and sons who get on well (for Gabriel and I get on well, we get along famously for a father and son), tell me why we can't make a son together, Gabriel and I his father, without having to trouble ourselves with princesses like yours, Gabriel, or manufacturers like mine; come on, tell me, I'm waiting for your answer!"

"But monsieur, but monsieur," answered the headwaiter, and on the following Monday we changed restaurants.

*The doorbell rang.*

*It wasn't you.*

*Just my young attorney, somewhat at sea in the details of my case (how I sympathize with him) and seeking clarification.*

*"Well now, 1931 to 1938, what did you do then? Can we say it was then you discovered Marxism?"*

*Almost terrified, he studies the three of us: Ann, who has briefly abandoned Monaco and her financial schemes; Clara, trotting around us like an old woman with a duster, her features masked by the Leica as she seeks the best light; and myself, Gabriel, the official storyteller, compiler of all these pages, sitting just now on a rather wobbly coffee table. And the four others, absent by reason of death but nonetheless present on the wall above the piano, thanks to Clara's photos: Elisabeth in a long gown and Markus in a dinner jacket, his hand resting on her shoulder, in her hand a sheet of white paper, a concert program no doubt. They are smiling. It must have been after a performance, for Markus (stage fright) never smiled before one. As for Marguerite, she is waving a handkerchief from the upper deck of her steamship as she sets off for America. And Louis, very young, tossing a flower into a grave.*

*The lawyer studies us all one by one, all seven, the three live ones and the four photos.*

*"What a family!" he sighs.*

*Our family memorabilia clearly mean little to him.*

*At such times he always seems discouraged. He would so much prefer a more traditional case, more political and more traditional, with real Fascists and real Communists instead of all this rambling about botany, expositions, raw materials. He slumps into his seat, one of those creaky wicker chairs just as appropriate (or so their advocates claim) in winter living rooms as on summer terraces.*

*I offer him some more of the Rivesaltes muscatel.*

*"Just a drop," he says.*

*But he quickly recovers his aplomb.*

*"You must admit that you're not very clear-cut, any of you. But I'll get there, don't you worry; I'll defend you in spite of yourselves. The law requires it. One thing I understand already: you were mad about empires but unenthusiastic about colonies, which you will allow is contradictory. But I see your point."*

*And off he goes, rubbing his hands, his own, instead of shaking ours, highly satisfied with his intelligent remark.*

# 12

# *The Fontanel*

AGE OF COURSE padded ever closer on wolf's paws. It nosed through the door into Gabriel's room, into Ann's, into Clara's, and began its work.

*Don't look at me, I'm so ugly today:* this was now the two sisters' refrain, their bitter refrain.

For Gabriel there was no pain in this invasion. He welcomed age's intrusion as you might a lodger you can talk to when you are too much alone. He listened for age's footsteps, its footsteps within him; he noted its habits, the times when age dozes and for a year or two seems to forget its mission, and the other times—much shorter ones, sometimes a lost summer or just one night—when age serves double helpings and you grow old overnight, as they say. People who have never been able to accept their own faces welcome age with relief, with hesitant complicity.

To tell the truth, Gabriel found age somewhat lackadaisical. He would have preferred swifter, more momentous upheavals within himself. It had been drummed into him since childhood: after forty, a man has the face he deserves. His fiftieth year was upon him, and Gabriel was still the same, his face plump and barely lined (he had so hoped for wrinkles, believing that a wrinkled man was as good as a gaunt one), his eyes too bright, his hair yellow (he yearned for touches of gray, even a few bald patches). Faster, faster, he murmured to age, making sure he was not overheard. Clara and Ann would have called him a madman. They were resisting the invader. Growing rigid. "Hands off, Gabriel, and calm that animal down; just because I'm getting old doesn't mean you're going to find it any easier to make love to me" (Clara). "Old or not, I remain standing; you're going to have to muster the energy somehow" (Ann). Scrutinizing themselves, faces almost touching the mirror, fingertips roaming over forehead, neck, temples, murmuring: My God! Or: Already! Or: Oh, hell! Seeking out flattering light: You know I hate sitting in that chair. Suddenly disappearing: I'll be back in a minute. What were those minutes for? And where?

Seeing them thus lost, thus stricken, whereas he felt so comfortable in age, he whispered to himself: Victory, cheerless victory. The way you welcome travelers to a rainy spot where you have preceded them by a few days—Welcome, welcome; alas, the gutter drips at night and when the wind blows the shutters will bang; there's nothing you can do about it.

Gabriel kept no log of this inexorable passage. A pity. Such rememberings would have been as good as others. The same woman, described year after year, noting what vanishes and what endures. . . .

All he can do is record his reaction when something, some slight detail, changed in the woman he loved, in that zone between cheekbones and eyebrows where age always launches its first attack on women. Temples radiating lines, like two half-suns, the expression less intense, warier, less teasing, quicker to laugh, the eyes themselves haloed by tiny wrinkles to remind them to be modest, lids bluer and more transparent: "I don't know why, Gabriel, but I don't sleep as well as I used to." And more and more often, shadows beneath the eyes like a second gaze monitoring the first, graver, more naked: "Stop staring at me, Gabriel." But Gabriel could not stop. Always enormously curious about women's bodies, he had discovered that after thirty or thirty-five women develop a vulnerable soft spot, a baby's fontanel, in the strategic zone between cheekbones and eyebrows. You had only to look closely to see it there, pulsing with life.

What luck! Gabriel then thought to himself. What luck; they are growing old! Or: What's this, a new season? Or: No doubt about it, age (along with Louis) is my best friend.

And through a further beneficent working of age, they traded characters: Ann became strained, less arrogant these days, whereas Clara, who had discovered in photography irrefutable proof of the existence of things, had drawn confidence from it. This double evolution, Ann toward Clara and Clara toward Ann, came at just the right time. When you love two sisters it is best that they grow to resemble each other. This spares you the need for wild leaps, leaps that become more and more arthritic with the passage of the years. Gabriel was optimistic. And why not? Was not everything for the best in the best of worlds, the best of possible old worlds?

*Don't look at me, I'm so ugly today.* The fools! They were never more beautiful.

# 13

# *Into the Jaws of the Wolf*

## I

GABRIEL HAS NOTHING to be ashamed of. He sounded the alarm as often, as long, and as noisily as he could.

But they refused to hear him.

They even stole his job.

Once upon a time there was disgrace.

French cars were no longer winning.

And who was to blame?

French drivers, French engine designers? What an idea, striking at the very heart of French industry at a time of rising international tension!

The conceivers and manufacturers of single-seaters? Come now, not while we still boasted the elegant Bugatti, the aristocratic Delahaye, the fiery Talbot!

French mechanics? Beyond reproach. Engines ran virtually without a hitch.

Who else was there? Why, tire experts, of course, and foremost among them (until now) Gabriel Orsenna.

Disgrace is always heralded by a request to move to a different office. The former favorite is switched to quarters no one else wants: a large glass box on the first floor of corporate headquarters exposed to all eyes.

Another mark of a fall from grace: it is announced in the press. Whereas in the world of honor and glory you summon the golden boy discreetly; you let him in on the secret, the glittering promotion: "You'll keep this to yourself, won't you; I don't want the press to get wind of it until the show."

Gabriel learned of his fall from two articles, the first in *Le Figaro:*

PAINFUL DECISION AT THE EUROPEAN TIRE CORPORATION

In the little world of motor racing Gabriel Orsenna built himself an enviable reputation as a tire expert. He wedded cars to tracks with consummate skill; the tires he slipped on the four fingers of his racing machines were so many engagement rings, so many pledges of faithful conjugal life. . . . But in the past few months the spell has apparently been broken. . . . Mindful of its responsibilities to the nation, the European Tire Corporation yesterday took the decision (painful from a human standpoint, perhaps, but unquestionably necessary) to appoint a new manager to its Racing division. The new man is Yves Flamand, twenty-nine, married with three children, a graduate of the engineering department of the École Centrale. All racing fans, as well as the nation's automobile industry, wish him success.

*L'Action Française* was rather more radical:

NO MORE JEWISH TIRE EXPERTS!

When cars could move no faster than 60 mph there was still no harm in allowing Jews to select their tires; after all, their age-old habit of prostration has given the Jews an instinctive feel for dirt and dust. But now that speed has arrived the Jews must go! Who believes for a moment that our Bugattis don't measure up to the Mercedes of the Hun? Perhaps someone will object that Gabriel Orsenna is not Jewish. What of it? Is he not the very image of the contaminated race? Does he not share with the Jew a temperament too craven to devise ambitious tires, proud tires, in short, victorious tires? At the European Tire Corporation . . .

Gabriel Orsenna might have responded, reacted. He had a knapsackful of good arguments. For instance, the lovely Bugatti type 60, darling of collectors, favorite racing machine of homeward-bound Lotharios (those who preferred gastronomic rallies to the Hunaudières straight), in other words the pride of France, delivered a mere 285 horsepower (Gabriel had carefully measured it) against the 400 and even 500 horsepower of its German and Italian rivals. And the French racing car known as SEFAC, financed by national subscription (no less), was so badly designed that it never once left the starting line in any race, however piddling. But Gabriel, preferring not to force a fresh apple of discord down France's throat, said nothing. Let us admit too that after thirty-five years in the tire business he was somewhat travel-worn.

Yes, Gabriel tried to make his voice heard. It was an original, down-to-earth voice, perhaps a better way of jogging French minds than soaring flights of lyricism.

And the intellectuals dismissed him as a negligible quantity unworthy of the right to speak.

Just one example: June 21, 1935. The opening of the International Writers' Congress. It was hot as an oven inside the Mutualité conference hall. All the leading lights had removed their coats, even Gide, even Huxley, even Martin Du Gard. Gabriel would like to go on record as having kept his on, out of respect for the audience. So no one can claim he was spurned for being improperly dressed.

What is more, he was polite and circumspect. A tire expert is not, properly speaking, a writer, although there are several similarities between the two fields: a shared sense of the soil, a blend of knowledge and of intuition, awareness of the imminence of death, and the like.

He considered himself a guest and behaved accordingly. He listened to Malraux: "Communism restores man's fertility." He listened without the slightest interruption as Aragon fought to keep the Victor Serge case off the agenda. He listened again to Malraux: "Each and every one of us must restore sight to these blind statues; from hope to determination, from revolt to revolution, we must remold the human conscience with all the immemorial suffering of humankind."

Superb stuff, superb: like everyone else, he applauded. He did not raise his hand until after Pasternak's address, which seemed to him the most fitting of introductions: "Poetry will always be in a state of germination. It is and always will be the organic function of a happy being, nurturing afresh the joy of language that lies curled like a newborn leaf within the human heart! The greater the number of happy men on this earth, the more poets there will be."

On the heels of these botanical observations, Gabriel felt free to raise the question closest to his own heart.

And so, conquering his shyness, Gabriel raised his hand in the great Mutualité hall, and to compensate for his small stature he even climbed onto a wobbly folding chair; one slip would have sliced his legs off at the knees.

And this, articulated as clearly as he was able, is what he tried to say:

Ladies and gentlemen, for the last two years Germany has been substituting synthetic for natural rubber. This change implies two things. First, Germany's determination to be self-sufficient from the rest of the world. Second, invasion plans. Ladies and gentlemen, this is my conviction, based on my experience as a tire expert: With the help of synthetic rubber, Germany is making ready to invade Europe. Thank you.

Gabriel had carefully worked out the length of this declaration beforehand: thirty seconds.

A conservative estimate, for due to stage fright he apparently swallowed half his words.

Might those thirty seconds have changed the course of history? Might a government strategist, buried in the audience and hearing this all-important piece of information, have redirected our armament program in the direction of tanks and away from the Maginot Line?

Being modest by nature, Gabriel would never make such a claim.

But the hypothesis is a valid one, particularly since those thirty seconds were denied him. The Communists shouted him down: This little man, they said, was attempting to revive the Victor Serge affair. And the others wanted Malraux, more and still more Malraux. Nothing but Malraux.

For a few moments Gabriel stood his ground. This was understandable. He had never before felt the intoxication of towering over even the smallest of gatherings. Then he dismounted, calmly heard the debates through to the end, and returned home to write an article for *Le Temps* ("The Case for Rubber Rearmament") which never saw the light of day.

* * *

Nor can it be said that Gabriel was helped by his family in his quest for truth.

Louis had immediately plunged into another exposition (universal this time) scheduled to open between the Eiffel Tower and Trocadéro toward the middle of the year 1937 (nothing will be ready on time, Gabriel, we shall be the laughingstock of the planet). He held fast to his illusions: in his view exhibitions, the encyclopedic depiction of diversity, were still the only way to avoid war.

Louis spent his leisure hours, his endless leisure hours, with the cycling crowd he had been introduced to by his friend Dekaerkove, organizer of the Tour de France, my rival. The man who was stealing my father from me little by little.

On Sunday mornings, like all true aficionados, they met at Longchamp and cycled tirelessly round and round the track.

"You don't get bored pedaling like that all day?"

"No doubt about it, Gabriel, you know nothing about the human body."

In July—his rendezvous with the Tour de France—he disappeared, and in March or April as well, depending on the years, for the long-distance trials at Grenelle.

"No problem if you need to see me, Gabriel. I'll be there the entire Six Days."

He was one of the diehards who stayed all night until the track closed at 6 A.M. and were back at the 10 A.M. opening, the intervening four hours allowing just enough time for a stop at home (everything all right?) and breakfast, always at the same bistro on the rue Nélaton because the owner brewed strong coffee.

Louis had decreed that his birthday should fall at midpoint in the Six Day race no matter what that date might be, a movable birthday to which he always invited me, although our relations were now strained. That was how Gabriel became acquainted with the vast black barn of the Vélodrome d'Hiver, the Winter Velodrome, the air inside it blue with smoke, its lights hanging from invisible wires, the sand-colored track, the restaurant on the green, and the cheap crowded seats of the masses who showered taunts, orange peels, and even nuts and bolts on the elegant diners. Louis always reserved the same table, right on top of the action. When he introduced me, my-son-Gabriel-who-works-in-the-motor-trade, I detected dirty looks: the cycling world had nothing but contempt for machines, with the exception of pedal-driven ones. I didn't mind; to each his own.

The characters I met at Grenelle were most colorful: the trainer Ferré, for instance, with his flat cloth cap; Fernand Trignol, the "king of underworld slang" who "looked for suckers to fleece," as he put it, at dice or cards; Bobosse, the former rotary-press operator turned fashionable masseur; an Italian named Cyrano, amateur tenor and professional plasterer, hired to present bouquets to winners or visiting stars, dozens of bouquets, all the Six Day bouquets. . . . And I mustn't forget the racers themselves, Wambot and Lacquehay, hometown favorites, members of the Levallois Cycling Club; shy Alexis Blanc-Garin; and the nicest of them all, Charles Pélissier. They used to sit with us for a few moments—"Well, having a good time? It gets tougher every year"—and then—"Excuse us, gentlemen"—they returned to their treadmill trade.

Every now and then Louis would give me a triumphant wink: See, I too have an adoptive life. It was very odd to see him there in a man's world talking men talk after spending his whole life exclusively in the company of women. They argued about racing, racing, and still more racing, how Piet Van Kempen had jostled Lucien Choury just short of the finish line, or why Guimbretière had lost last year's winning kick. . . .

Every now and then one of them would stare into his glass and solemnly declare, "Wait and see . . . there are hard times ahead . . . in the next few years the bicycle will come back into its own." The seer turned toward me. "Nothing personal, Monsieur Orsenna."

Louis had not heard. He was watching the track. Had forgotten me.

Suddenly, silence. No one spoke. Not a murmur, not a cough. Nothing but that deep dreamlike humming, the whir of the pack pumping around the track.

"Isn't this fantastic?" Louis whispered in my ear.

The blast of a horn. Dream over.

"Ten thousand francs' bonus for five laps from the sponsor, Laughing Cow Cheese," trumpeted Berretot, the announcer.

"Mooooo!" roared the crowd.

I heard my father tell his neighbor, Police Inspector Maizeaud (the one who investigated the killing at the Rat-Mort in Pigalle), "My son is nicer than he looks, it's just that he's a bit of a stuffed shirt, that's all; we don't laugh at the same things. Domestic problems, you know?" Inspector Maizeaud nodded.

Nobody noticed Gabriel's departure. I left without saying good-bye, before the sprints were over, amid the strains of accordions. Once outside, I strolled for a while along the Seine, toward Javel or Issy. I became my old self again, gradually shedding all the names and faces and technical terms, inner-tube pressures, the number of teeth in gear sprockets, all Louis's new toys. I inhaled the air gratefully, a little punch-drunk, like a man crawling out from under an avalanche. On the elevated track behind me trains flashed back and forth. I did not look back. I preferred to forget all that till next year, till the next birthday, to forget Grenelle, Nélaton, the cycling world that had swallowed my father. Past the Bar de la Marine, I turned left along the avenue Émile Zola and La Motte-Picquet, taking a long round-about way home.

In the meantime, Marguerite was cuckolding America. Ever since reading *With the Fascists of Rome* by Paul Herfort (published by the Revue Mondiale), she had joined the France-Italy Committee and dreamed only of going to Rome. Whenever I dropped around she read me extracts from the book: " 'Attired in jodhpurs and riding boots, the leader of the Fascist government has a distinctly Napoleonic air that fits him like a glove. Elbow on desk, chin cradled in hand, he exudes effortless natural strength and good nature eerily reminiscent of the great Corsican. For a few seconds Napoleon's features blur into Mussolini's before my eyes, and I no longer know whether I should say Sire or Your Excellency.' "

"You never knew your grandfather, Gabriel, but I can assure you, if he were not dead, that is how he would be."

She showed me documents proving how right the Duce had been to invade Ethiopia and put a stop to acts of native barbarism.

"Just forget for a moment that I am your grandmother, Gabriel, and look at this photograph through the magnifying glass. See that triumphal archway? Hold the glass closer, Gabriel—there—do you see those little bags hanging from the arch? You have no idea what they are, have you, Gabriel? Well, you can take it from me, they are tokens of *manhood,* the manhood of these poor dear Ethiopians' enemies, preserved by smoking and then whitewashed. When I think that the League of Nations tried to prevent Italy from putting a stop to such horrors!"

Typical Orsenna exchanges, for which my adoptive relations had no time: every step they took brought them closer to the jaws of the wolf.

## II

Elisabeth didn't leave right away. She wasn't the kind to give up easily. Nor did she let herself go like those who, either from laziness or to test the limits of love, begin to neglect themselves the moment they conquer, just to see whether they will go on being loved even if they don't bother to bathe; this was not Elisabeth's way. Every morning at exactly the same time, after her bodily needs but before breakfast, she climbed onto the only reliable scales, the merciless kind with weights you have to manipulate yourself. Doctor's scales. She noted her weight. She had set herself a limit. Beyond it, I shall cease to inflict myself on Markus. And she fought.

Markus was back on the road. Blazing a trail through town and village, all ears. And his wife looked distressed when you asked her if Mr. Knight would soon be home. But deep down she was grateful for this respite. She hoped that by the time her loved one returned she would be down to her former size, the size she had been the night of the famous concert when Markus had preferred her to music.

At that time, in New York as in Paris, the female body was all the rage. Subtly at first, then more and more vociferously, advertisements told women: Smooth away your wrinkles, have dazzling teeth, bid your corsets farewell. There is nothing I do not know of that period. Elisabeth recorded the progress of the disease in a daily log, noting her appointments with healers and pasting prescriptions on the left, results on the right. I may one day reveal to you how this log came into my hands, a strange set of circumstances involving an article about love in a defunct periodical, *Marianne*. The details of this discovery most assuredly deserve to be related; there was a whole chain of coincidences of the kind that make us say it's a small world, when in reality all you have to do is listen to what people say and reconstruct the chain.

This particular time period was the true debut of the budding cosmetic industry. A spate of new products was launched: anti-aging creams, lotions, cucumber masks. Compare the before-and-after photos. Essential to rub down with a horsehair mitten each morning. Essential to sleep with a chin strap at night. It was the first rising of stars soon to be famous: Elizabeth Arden, Gaylord Hauser. After dinner or at theater intermissions, as the men drew on their cigars, the ladies went off into huddles to trade beauty secrets. Such a climate made it all so much easier. Elisabeth sought *her* personal regimen, the perfect blend of liquid and solid, which would first restore her looks and second (although not promising eternal youth) would at least guarantee that until the very end she would never look her age.

But finding her regimen took time. There were so many advertisements, filling whole pages of the newspapers. I picture the heap of daily papers on her bed in the hotel each morning. How did she choose? Did she underline them with a fat pencil, or did she snip them out? I have no idea. In any case she tried everything: drinking only water for thirty-six hours at a stretch, then eating only grapefruit, then giving up salt or sugar, then jumping rope for fifty minutes morning and night wearing three sweaters, then ingesting as many hard-boiled eggs as she could in one weekend, then steaming everything. She tried sauna, intensive therapy complete with flagellation (the sauna was at the other end of Manhattan, and she spent her whole life in taxis). Then downing appetite suppressants, an innovation back then (they gave you an overpowering urge to vomit). Then signing up for massage in the Grand Central area; after thirty sessions, her blind masseur assured her, you will have melted away—but whatever you do, don't stop in mid-treatment, fat takes cruel revenge. And of course the usual rules: no more alcohol, no more bread, and as little bed as possible, I mean for sleeping. At night she walked around and around the park to vanquish temptation, battling (oh, how she battled!) eyelids that weighed ever heavier. And then there were the humiliating get-togethers with her overweight sisters at the Seventeenth Street club where you paid three dollars a month for the privilege of having accusing fingers pointed at you, where last week's and today's weight—three large and very legible figures—were worn like a locket around your neck. So many regimens tried and rejected, eternally switching from one program to the next the way you switch subway cars when someone is following you. All that money thrown away for nothing, constantly on the alert for Markus's return: oh, please let him stay away long enough for the new diet to start working, this impresario who never let her know when he would be back. Sudden footsteps in the hallway: oh, if only he won't turn on the light; oh, if only he's a little bit tight!

One morning she stepped on the scales, and its graduated arm still did not balance even after she slid the little weight past the limit she had set herself. Then, but only then, and of this particular war her family never knew a thing (and Gabriel, you may depend on him, will not tell, even at the trial), then she disappeared.

It was what she wanted. That was clear from her diary.

*In case of suicide, the husband has to identify the body. But I've changed so much, would he be able to identify me? And if he could identify me—what a horrible thought!*

His wife's disappearance made scarcely a dent in Markus's routine. Outwardly his life went on unchanged. He no longer returned to New York or Paris for a few months of the year, that was all. Spouse untraceable: return pointless. Every now and then he called the reception desk at the Algonquin or the Washington and Albany: "Any news, Georges?" (That is what he called all hotel receptionists, but they are used to such shorthand.) I'm afraid not, monsieur. "Well, keep a lookout, will you? And Georges, don't bet it all on the races." Oh, monsieur . . . ! "See you next month." Goodbye, Monsieur Knight. "Goodbye, Georges."

We never know about other men's grief. So Gabriel will make no attempt to depict Markus alone in his hotel room, slowly and carefully wiping his spectacle lenses, one and then the other. What can be said is that Elisabeth's disappearance was in a small way counterbalanced for Markus by the reappearance of the world. Since his wife had taken care of everything he had allowed his own eyes to rest, using them only for reading scores or dodging lampposts in the nick of time. Hearing had been his life. When your wife disappears, a wife you love in your own way (but who does not have his own way of loving?), when your wife vanishes into thin air, you are always on the alert. Almost without knowing it you scan your surroundings: could that have been Elisabeth, that fleeting form that just disappeared behind the scarlet post office van? That gray mink jacket in the cloakroom of the Opéra, being crushed by dozens and dozens of anonymous coats, fur capes, cloaks; might that not be hers, oh, Elisabeth, who felt cold only above the waist?

Thus, thanks to his wife's disappearance, Markus discovered well past the age of sixty-five that the real (that is, the nonmusical) world existed.

And although (given the tragic circumstances) he never admitted it, it gave him a degree of pleasure. Particularly marketplaces, where the amazing diversity of species populating the universe met openly and brazenly. An example? Ripe swollen eggplants lustrous as mirrors hefted in a middle-aged housewife's doubtful palm before reluctantly vanishing into the greenish depths of her shopping bag. Or the sight, so heartrending it seemed like music, of old couples strolling at dusk along Europe's riverbanks.

Had he not acquired this novel faculty of sight, had he not possessed the neophyte's enthusiasm for things seen, would he have noticed the presence of that hybrid entity across the street? A woman to judge from its clothes, a robot judging by its lack of face, which was replaced by a black metal rectangle with one feature, a nose or eye, in its center.

Most unlikely.

That day the impresario was combing the streets of Leopoldstadt, the Jewish quarter of Vienna. Music was there for the taking, he had been told. Because of street fights and police raids, no recruiter of talent dared go there any more.

"So," said his informant, "you are sure to find bargains there; after all, whether you harvest them or not, violinists grow, do they not, dear friend?"

So he combed. People offered him apples, bagels, Russian-language gardening almanacs, spare parts for horse-drawn carriages, oil lamps, herrings, a map of the Promised Land, iron hoops for the left wheels of carts, a *shtreimel* hat with its thirteen sable braids (for thirteen is a holy number denoting belief in one God), a secondhand prayer shawl, and egg *challas* for the Sabbath . . . in short, everything ever offered you in a ghetto.

But he slowed his pace only at stalls hung with shoe leather, soles without uppers, uppers without soles. And the shoemakers' philosophy struck him as irrefutable. Irrefutable in its logic and its despair.

"You will agree, mein Herr, that without soles nobody exists, neither market porters nor human beings. We even need soles on our shoes for going to the temple. And you must tramp the streets just to feed your family. Everyone needs soles. And that is the whole trouble with trade, particularly the shoemaker's trade. To pay me, Jews need money, which means they need shoes. On paving stones like these, leather soles last a mere six weeks. It is hard to be Jewish. Because of shoes. Do you not agree?"

Across the street, the hybrid entity pushed its cylindrical snout close to a window. And its forefinger (a human forefinger, not a robot's) pressed down on a small shiny button on the upper right-hand corner of the black metal rectangle.

Markus waited patiently, not throwing wide his arms and shouting Clara! until she had completed her task, tucked her camera into the pocket of her navy-blue wool jacket, and drawn herself up to her respectable full height. "Clara!"

Hugs. Exchange (skimpy) of family intelligence: "Any news of your mother?" No. "Nor I. And Gabriel?" Markus asked in spite of the fact that he had often sworn that he would not do so. He had even practiced meeting his daughter without mentioning his son-in-law, but: "And Gabriel?" asked Markus.

"It's my life, Papa," replied Clara, but without anger, more with a touch of weariness.

"You are right, it's your life. But may I at least ask what brings this life of yours to Leopoldstadt?"

(Naturally, Gabriel has reconstructed this encounter between father and daughter. He was not present in the shtetl, spying on their reunion from behind the vendors' pushcarts. This being the case, he is unable to state categorically that his name, Gabriel, was brought up by either of the two Knights. But it is a possibility. At all events a possibility dear to my heart and therefore included in the dossier and listed as note 49).

Clara thought for a moment, then smiled at her father. And blushed. Which was her shorthand way of saying: I'm-sorry-but-I'm-going-to-say-something-serious-but-serious-matters-do-exist-don't-they-and-must-be-discussed-so-here-goes.

She motioned to the stream, the crowd bustling by, the shoe leather hanging on the walls, the excitement of children glimpsed through a window, candlelight, dark forms bent over the lighter patches of books, the coming and going of market porters.

"Don't you find all this very ephemeral?"

The impresario agreed. "Yes, in fact I thought the Great War had destroyed it."

"So I take photographs," said Clara. "There are two of us, myself and a Russian born in St. Petersburg and living in Berlin but who must remain nameless, you understand? Just him and me. Not much, for all of Eastern Europe. If you know anyone who might be interested in joining us, even a gentile as long as he has a good eye. . . ."

They spent a few days together in Vienna, a few days without music. At last. "How I hated music!" said Clara.

"I understand, oh, yes, how I understand you! But you must admit that the *vivace* of Beethoven's Seventeenth quartet, opus 135 . . ." replied the incorrigible Markus.

A few days to talk together, father and daughter, with words. Just as lovers never get out of bed, they never left the table. Meals coupled together: lunch, tea, dinner—*Mein Herr, gnädige Frau,* we're about to close—Frankly what you're saying about London . . . but yes, Papa, I assure you. . . . Markus called Clara his Noah, because of the ark, "since you concern yourself with vanishing species." And did not hold her back when she wanted to leave. There were still so many photos to be taken, so many scenes and faces to be frozen for posterity. "I understand, I'm proud of you. I'm sad and I understand."

Clara's destination was sub-Carpathian Ruthenia (today incorporated into the Ukraine, itself swallowed by Russia). She intended first of all to welcome aboard her ark the little hamlet of Vrchni Apsa, whose peasants knew nothing of the twentieth century, nor of the nineteenth, nor of the eighteenth, seventeenth, or sixteenth. Just a few snippets of information had reached them about the fifteenth, a strange period when a goy had passed through the world, a goy with a pretentious goy name (Christopher Columbus), a nonetheless useful goy since he had brought back from one of his voyages (themselves pointless: why voyage when you are persecuted neither by the Czar's Cossacks nor by the people's commissars and when, being a goy, you have no reason for going to Israel?) had brought back the grain known as maize, which they now cultivated. From there she would go on to Mukachevo, where the renowned Rabbi Baruch Rabinowitz taught.

Markus insisted on seeing his daughter off. Long after the train had left he remained standing on the platform, arm raised and fingers moving in a gesture that did not mean goodbye but the exact opposite—Come back, Clara, come back, Elisabeth, please, Ann, stop running; there's more to life than business, don't leave me all alone—a gesture that amused the porters: Look at him; he doesn't understand much about stations, does he?

At that precise moment Elisabeth was living in Paris near the place de la République. From time to time she called her little Gabriel: No, don't come over, I prefer the phone. Do you remember Clermont-Ferrand, Gabriel? Now it's my turn to season myself. She used the formal *vous* with me, as if the phone and the distance between us were not sufficient protection.

Disenchanted with reducing programs, she now sought other solutions; three times a week she went to the rue du Châteaudun, second floor, to see one of Clara's former colleagues, a Hungarian named W who was said to be a good soul specialist. There she talked, talked, and talked about her love, an interminable story interrupted at the end of forty-five minutes by the soul specialist's voice: "Good, good, until next time then." But out on the street she went on, and in her hotel room: numerous versions of the evening when Markus had preferred her to music, recounting the shameful dreams that came to her as she read the terrible news filling the papers (rearmament here, public executions there); oh, if only war broke out, we'd go back to New York; Markus wouldn't be able to travel any more, yes, long live war. "Long live war!" she cried out in the consulting room. "Oh, forgive me, doctor!"

One day, she said, "I have finished."

"That is good," said Dr. W.

"What are my chances?"

"Love less, madame; try to love less. No diet will help. It is this love that feeds you."

"But how can one love less?"

"There's traveling, they say. But look, I am fat too. Goodbye, Madame Knight. Keep your chin up. Would you have any objection if I published your story? Some time in the future. And I would change all the names, of course. Goodbye, Madame Knight. Do as I do: to cure myself of loving I publish. You should publish too, find a beautiful story and write it. Goodbye, Madame Knight."

## III

On some nights in the house on avenue Wester Wemys, Cannes-la-Bocca, Gabriel starts to scream. He stands in the middle of his bedroom, wearing his maroon pajamas with the blue trim, and he screams. Lights go on. The two sisters rush in, take him in their arms, walk him to the library. "There, there, Gabriel, there there, the war is over." And the three of them wait for daylight to come, huddled close on the oldest settee, the one that sags in the middle, the one beneath the rows of art books.

When dawn at long last appears: "Come on," says Ann, "let's get busy; telling the story will soothe your nerves. I'll make us all a cup of coffee."

And this was how Gabriel faced that far-off September, a September much like any other, with storms and with leaves changing color, a quite ordinary September fifteen years earlier, yet a September that still terrifies him in the night. To bolster his spirits he remembers Cuvier: in the evenings, after their Sunday strolls through the woods, families used to bring the scientist small bones they had picked up. A few bones were enough for him to reconstruct the whole dinosaur. That is what I will do, Gabriel says to himself in his maroon pajamas.

This time I will imagine nothing and invent nothing and fill in no blanks. Tell only what I know. Few things, few facts, but all true.

And thanks to me, thanks to Gabriel, thanks to these little truths, some future Cuvier will reconstruct the beast.

Once upon a time there was a September 29.

And it must have been a holiday.

Markus swung into action. Swarms of telegrams, addressed to all those places his daughters were known to frequent: grand hotels for Ann, Jewish groups for Clara. They run around like rabbits, he explained to the woman at the post office, so I have to set snares.

THIS SEPTEMBER 29 1938 KNIGHT FAMILY GATHERING MUNICH STOP NINE P.M. HOF UND NATIONALTHEATER STOP CONCERT MY TASTE ADMITTEDLY STOP BUT GUARANTEE MUSIC NOT DISCUSSED AFTER SUPPER STOP ATTENDANCE COMPULSORY

Good luck, monsieur, said the woman at the post office after sending off the sheaf.

Once upon a time.

Like everything else, swastikas and barbed wire have to begin somewhere.

Once upon a time there was the Hof und Nationaltheater, its doors thrown open to admit the cleaning squad. Through the gloom came the purring of vacuum cleaners, the slosh of mops first in buckets and then on the marble of the ornamental staircase, the swish of brooms on the stage, the rumble of cartloads of soap and towels headed for the dressing rooms and toilets, and the shouts of the supervisor—"Faster! Silence!" (because too many words weigh music down, said the stage manager)—and also the squeak of chamois leather on brass fittings, the tinkling of chandeliers being dusted with tall ceiling brushes, the angry clatter of coat hangers in the cloakrooms, and, a little later, the footsteps of battalions of inspectors coming one by one into the vast lobby with their reports, heels clicking as they snapped to attention.

"Stalls clean!"

"Boxes clean!"

"Upper dress circle clean!"

Around ten they called in the assistant general manager. The cleaners screwed up their eyes; all the lights had to be turned full on for inspections.

A half hour later the assistant stage manager returned and saluted the cleaning supervisor.

"Everything in order!"

"Thank you, Herr assistant stage manager."

The lights went out. As soon as the cleaning squad had marched out, two abreast, the steel grilles and doors and windows slammed shut. A dry breeze blew over Munich, the kind of breeze that raises dust and precedes storms.

Once upon a time there was a businesswoman who gripped her idealist sister's arm as she stepped off the train. Clara was in from the East, one of those journeys she specialized in: exhausting and unpaid. Cameras bumped against her bosom.

"You poor thing! Soon you won't have any breasts left."

Poor Clara, lifting two enormous suitcases with a heartrending sigh.

"And no arms either."

Luckily a porter, summoned by the businesswoman's imperious call, saved the latter portion of Clara's anatomy, one of my favorite portions, those two alabaster arches, doorway to bliss.

"I've checked you into the Russischer Hof. We'll join Markus at the concert. Apparently he's had a good trip: six virtuosos this time."

Once upon a time on the gray airport runway there was Max Theodor Horkheimer, virtuoso violin with the Munich Opera, wondering, as he pushed back a shock of black-dyed hair, the same hair that had so often fallen forward over his eyes during love that most of his memories of frenzy were linked to the sensation of semiblindness (only a few women, two to be exact, had made him lie on his back "so that I can look into your eyes," they had said, imploring him not to move; "I'll take care of everything"), hair once abundant and commanding, a source of pride, but now lank and translucent, not that he was losing his hair but the hair was getting finer and finer, like gossamer. Once upon a time, then, there was Max Theodor Horkheimer, wondering at this precise moment whether or not his life had been a failure. Whether—instead of rocking on his heels out here at the airport today—he should not have been snugly back in his hotel room, eyes half closed, preparing for his concert, since soloists are not expected to serenade visiting politicians even on great occasions such as today's in Munich, September 29, when any old military band would have sufficed to play the national anthems (in view of Daladier's musical knowledge, and Chamberlain's), but there was a point to be made here; these men had to realize the instant they arrived which side civilization was on. A stroke of luck, at all events, that it wasn't raining.

Across the runway, officials chatted away the time. You couldn't hear the words, simply a buzz, a continuous buzz. Amazing how much non-musicians find to say to one another. Model blond German children had been allowed to sit on a corner of the red carpet, holding red, white, and blue flags, some French, some British.

And M. T. Horkheimer was still wondering what had gone wrong with his life for him to end up here, in the third row of an orchestra on a gray airfield, an anonymous string among other strings although he was a man for whom opportunities had not been lacking. The renowned Busch family, for example. One evening when understudies had been urgently needed (the first violin had a sore throat, the second a death in the family): We like your tone, the Busches told him throughout an after-concert supper; switch to the viola and join us. Not to mention plans dreamed up with fellow orchestra members during tedious spells (for instance, during applause directed at the conductor and the first violin), ideal moments for communication; you acknowledged the audience with smiling lips and out of the corner of your mouth counted chickens before they were hatched: Why don't we put together a little four- or five-man ensemble? Splendid idea, let's discuss it tomorrow. The applause faded, you put your instruments away. And so the days went. You lost heart. It was like missing a boat, watching it steam slowly away, still almost within seaplane or fast motorboat range.

And other even more magnificent proposals. A lot of things happen in twenty years of foreign tours, music lovers are so avid for novelty. Hands clasp your arm late at night: in New York for instance the not very well-kept hands of a young man, or in Buenos Aires the hands of a woman who kept her gloves on as long as possible to hide her chewed nails, and so many others and always the same words. "What if I helped you form your *own* orchestra?"

And nothing had ever come of these overtures. And third violin M. T. Horkheimer's fear of dying grew with each passing moment.

You could object that there is safety in anonymity: wrong. The terror of death strikes everyone. The good thing about stage fright is that it blurs the trail, sowing confusion in fear's ranks; as long as you fear the public and the critics you do not think about the ultimate end.

But third violins never have stage fright.

"Please, Gabriel, just this once, stop making things up. I would like our son to have an accurate account of events. Remember Louis's refrain: sons need reality."

"I'm not making things up, Ann. Third-ranking musicians always think about something else while waiting at airports for official visitors. It would be making things up to describe Munich without those thoughts. But perhaps you are right."

Terrified, and ashamed of his terror, Gabriel returned to the facts, the brutal facts of this month of September he would so much rather have concealed behind anecdotes and psychological digressions.

Markus was arrested first, taking tea in the garden of the Victoria Café, 17 Maximilianstrasse. He was surrounded by six child prodigies enjoying themselves and laughing, enchanted to be attending a concert that night for the first time in their lives, overjoyed to be stuffing themselves with sweetmeats rather than eating a proper dinner, six willowy children still unaware that you do not seize a mug of piping hot chocolate in your virtuoso hands, unaware that a burn can have disastrous consequences for the touch; they would have to be taught, taught particularly not to raise their voices so. . . . "Not so loud, please," Markus kept telling them, "not so loud, wait till we've crossed the Atlantic; over there you can be as loud as you like."

The waitress in her lace cap and little white apron went on smiling; she brought napkins to clear away the mess—two glasses spilled, a plate broken in the excitement—she asked if they would like

Black Forest cake (eggs, cream, kirsch, cocoa, cherries in brandy).

She went on smiling when the trenchcoats arrived.

"There they are," she said, not pointing, just making a small motion of the chin under her smile.

"Are you in charge? Where are you taking these children?"

"They are not children, they are virtuosos."

"I said where are you taking them?"

"That's none of your business."

"Do you think Germany doesn't love music enough?"

"I don't think anything."

"Come with us, please."

"Oh, Lord," said Clara as they arrived at the theater, "I've left my photos behind, all my photos spread out on the bed. I have to go back. I'll join you at intermission."

"Don't be silly. German hotels are the safest in the world."

And, one sister leading the other, they reached their seats in the middle of an almost-empty row: six seats for the virtuosos and one for the recruiter-impresario: "Seven, that's right," said business-woman Ann. "Don't worry, they'll be here. Markus is always late for everything except music."

Higher up, safely hidden in the upper circle, Elisabeth was obtaining news of her daughters unobtrusively, as unobtrusively as possible through opera glasses. One of Markus's innumerable telegrams had reached her, informing her of the date and hour of the great Knight reunion. How pale my Clara is! And Ann looks so nervous. Why isn't Markus with them?

At intermission, Clara—who had never hated music more—Clara hunted high and low, jostling, questioning, craning to her full height without seeing anything but skulls, hair, and hats, no sign of a Knight in this forest of music lovers. Elisabeth, who had come down from her upper circle and was following her daughter's frantic passage as best she could, yearned to call out to her, to take her in her arms, but was held back by this stupid question: Does an unsightly mother have the right to force herself on a daughter? The trenchcoats had no such scruples. They surrounded Clara: "No scenes please, *gnädige Frau*." Elisabeth screamed, the trenchcoats turned. Mother and daughter just had time to embrace. Were hauled away in two separate cars.

When Ann returned, after trying to move heaven and earth as only a businesswoman can, when she returned empty-handed, the Hof und Nationaltheater was closed.

"The box office will be open tomorrow," the janitor answered when she knocked at the only window still showing a light.

Once upon a time there was a phone call to Levallois.

"Gabriel, it's Ann. There was nothing I could do."

## IV

Oh, fateful year! Year of apprehension and foreboding! How could a Polish woman possibly say 1939 was the happiest year of her life? But how not to say it when you are Wladislawa in love (with the unreliable Frenchman Louis, admittedly, but also with the truth)? Oh, 1939! Cake with a thousand layers: a layer of joy, unbelievable professional success; a layer of irritation, Louis flapping and leaping like a landed fish the second he heard the gravel crunch on the path outside—"It's Gabriel, it's Gabriel" (as if a son were all life had to offer); a layer of joy, the unbelievable international success of the Commemoration; a layer of anguish, what will happen to Poland?; a layer of joy, Léon Blum's telegram, THANK YOU MADAME FOR YOUR APPRECIATION OF THE EVENTS OF 1789; a layer of terror, the pincers pact, Germania on one side and Sovetia on the other, united to stamp out my country, stamp out my childhood; a layer of ecstasy, sweet ecstasy, crackdown on Communist traitors, the Aragons forced into hiding.

"At last, at long last, Louis, we have the field to ourselves; we'll show people the quality of our model love, easily as fine as the Aragons'; come on, Louis, give the reporters a smile."

By now (with the 1937 Universal Exposition over), Louis was without a job.

Wladislawa hired him.

"You don't understand because you're French, Louis, but France's true glory is the Revolution, liberty, equality, fraternity. Seventeen-eighty-nine blazes out to the four corners of the earth. We're going to celebrate the hundred and fiftieth anniversary. Do you see all these letters?"

Wladislawa corresponded with the whole planet, even Chile, even China.

She received so many letters that stamp collectors fought for her favors. Starting with the mailman. He approached bent under the weight of the mail. May I, madame? he asked, fingers already gripping his scissors. It was all she could do to stop him from snipping off the upper right-hand corners. The neighbors too; they pleaded with her through the front door: I have a nephew with tuberculosis who collects stamps, or an out-of-work husband, or a stamp album I intend to bequeath to the Auteuil orphanage when I die. And even the Levallois parish priest, who should have known from whom all these tiny pictures came (cosmopolitan supporters of the Revolution, at best heretical worshipers of the Supreme Being, at worst champions of the guillotine), yes, even the priest was all smiles, eager to get his hands on her hoard: Why not, madame, I can announce it from the pulpit; we'll offer your collection as first prize in the annual church raffle, the congregation's a little bored with Sèvres chinaware.

But Wladislawa was unmoved.

She steamed the letters open, taking care not to damage either stamps or seals. She had her own plans.

"One day we shall have our own museum, since the French government is so ashamed of its past. We'll call it The French Revolution and the Universe. We'll illustrate its most far-reaching effects. It would be ideal if they lent us part of the Meudun Observatory. Heaven for them, earth for us. What do you think, Louis?"

Louis thought highly of it.

"Fine. Tomorrow we'll talk to the director. And we'll open the exhibit with a big planisphere recording the number of letters sent in from each country. We have to show these forgetful French, you see, that the Revolution of 'Eighty-nine is still very much alive all over the world."

She was right. They came in from all geographical and political points of the compass, from would-be avengers of Marie-Antoinette, offering their services, to disciples of Saint-Just eager to continue his work of purification. A learned society in Rangoon wished to know how to pay homage to the Hébertists. An Australian club sought permission to put on a play about Marat's assassination *(Gentlemen, I have the great honor to request from you particulars about the property rights . . .).* Californian admirers of Lepelletier de Saint-Fargeau wanted details concerning his murder. Dozens of ladies tucked the paper currency of their countries (sols, rupees, yens, marks, dinars) into their letters, they would be so happy to receive a portrait of Charlotte Corday; not to mention the anonymous gifts *(for the triumph of liberty,* postmarked Kyoto, Japan), bequests of property *(my estate is yours on condition you erect a memorial to the Duchess de Lamballe, Córdoba, Argentina).*

I almost forgot the countless invitations to symposia. You could have spent years hopping from one to another. São João del Rey, Brazil (Minas province), June 10–15, 1939: "1792 to 1889, How are Republics Born? The French and Brazilian Models." Bogotá, Colombia, July 1–4, 1939: "Bolivar and Robespierre." Madras, India, July 10–13, 1939: "The Supreme Being and Reincarnation."

Wladislawa even received official thanks from Brazil: Without Revolution, no Napoleon; without Napoleon, no French invasion of Portugal; without French invasion, no flight of the Portuguese court to Rio; without this presence in Rio, no Brazilian independence in 1822. And to think they say the people of the tropics are illogical!

After a few weeks of this toil, a little weary of wrestling with Thermidorean or Girondist subtleties, Louis decided to farm the work out. All it took was a small advertisement pinned to a wall of the Ministry of Education on the rue de Bellechasse at the spot where results of the exams for university teachers are posted. Dozens of professors responded, and not only history instructors but teachers of mathematics, French, and gymnastics, almost as if the Revolution lived on only in the nation's teaching community. They helped Louis answer all these letters, their penmanship full of inspiring upswings and downstrokes, the very bedrock of our educational system. They would gladly have done more. But the government turned a deaf ear.

"They told me this isn't the right time to rekindle civil war among the French," wailed Wladislawa, collapsing into an armchair after a day spent fruitlessly pleading her cause. "They prefer to channel everything into defense spending. What about the battle of Valmy?

Or Arcole? Wasn't France forged there as well? And all those people expecting us all over the world!"

There was only one demonstration worthy of the name: it took place on July 14 itself, on the Trocadéro hill. Wladislawa had bought a camera, intending to send photos to all our foreign friends. But the night was dark and the tricolor searchlight beams were not bright enough. . . . She hugged Louis's arm. It was an awe-inspiring scene. Gallic roosters and fairy-tale characters adorned the two wings of the palace. At center stage, three lofty masts towered over a tricolor cockade.

Thousands of schoolchildren stood guard down the long stairway. Below them two regiments of spahis, sentinels of Empire, looked as if they had just emerged from the trees around the aquarium.

First the fountains spouted red, white, and blue water; then, barely covering the sound of the fountains, exotic music arose, played by six natives specially brought in from the major outposts of Empire, all the way from Algeria to Indochina.

There were loudspeakers everywhere. It was no good changing places, trying to get a different view; there was no getting away from the speechmaking: national unity, the example of our forefathers, long live the Republic . . . the grandiose words rang all around us. After speeches by Lebrun and Reynaud, the whole of France gave tongue. Recordings of distant voices: an Alsatian steelworker, a Lyon silk manufacturer, a vintner from Anjou, and then an Annamite mandarin, a Senegalese marabout, a Tunisian dignitary. . . . Given a little more time, the whole nation might have said its piece.

Wladislawa shuddered: If the government had given us its support, do you realize what a lesson we could have taught the world?

She almost swooned when it was time for a live message from the steamship *Normandie*. The crowd and the musicians fell silent. People sat more tightly in their seats as if to counteract the Atlantic swell. The captain's words rose and then faded as if buffeted by fierce gusts. You could almost see the storm coming up, every porthole glowing, a dance in the first-class saloon and black night all around. "Long live the Fourteenth of July," he said, "and long live France!"

# 14

# *The Winter Velodrome*

*Dear friend and attorney,*

*Resistance worker? Collaborator? I'm sure you are dying to know how Orsenna behaved during the Second World War. I have no intention of hiding anything. Was Gabriel Orsenna a Gaullist? I give my answer in six separate parts, each part corresponding to one of the several means of transport I used in order to rally to the General in London. Then I shall speak from London itself (Swiss Cottage), and you will know everything.*

*Judiciously,*
G.O.

P.S. *Have you ever dealt with a client as conscientious as I?*

P.P.S. *If my son questions you on this matter, please be careful how you reply. There are two kinds of secrets that embarrass children: their father's bedroom behavior and their father's views from 1939 to 1945.*

## *1. Sightseeing Boats*

The General was tall, born in Lille, a lover of Chateaubriand. Gabriel was short, born in Levallois, inclining more toward Stendhal. Nothing predisposed me to Gaullism. Unless you accept that, just as all roads lead to Rome, so all hotel bedrooms communicate with London.

For a clear understanding of what follows, you need to be familiar with hotel policy regarding rooms rented by the day. Rare indeed is the hotel manager (except in specialist establishments) who (as you appear before him blushing slightly and shuffling from one foot to the other) will select a key for you at random: Room 13, Room 14, Room 28.

The vast majority prefer to separate the wheat from the chaff, to segregate couples *in flagrante* from their other guests.

The ground-floor solution is a staple. It has the great advantage of discretion, or at least of visual discretion. You have barely presented yourself at the reception desk before you are whisked off into a small cell between kitchens and stairs: Will this do? In any case you're not concerned about the view, are you?

This seemingly reasonable option has the disadvantage of noise: the sinful couple hears the ruckus of the whole hotel at work (the clatter of dishwashing, the clicking of the hotel switchboard, squabbling in the boiler room). And conversely, the hotel hears the moans, sometimes the shrieks, of the aforementioned sinful pair.

Many hotel managers consequently prefer to stow illicit lovers under the eaves, even at the price of comings and goings on the stairs and the constant creaking of the elevator. Since noises tend to rise, the establishment thus remains silent even through the most abandoned of frenzies.

"You'll feel like teenagers all over again up there," said the manager of the Véga, rue du Mont-Thabor. "Yes, indeed! Any luggage? No, of course not. And if you decide to switch from daily rental to a regular room, please let me know in good time, along with your breakfast order."

It was only 2 P.M. Usually Ann and Gabriel, remembering the Washington and Albany, would be up to their practices the second they were in the elevator. But here it was out of the question, this one being a latticed cage open to all eyes—and God knows Breton chambermaids have sharp vision.

A couple was waiting on the landing. The man (he was nibbling at a pair of gloves) abruptly turned his head away, like one of those marsh birds that seem to twist their necks out of joint at the slightest sign of danger. Perhaps he had practiced contorting his upper vertebrae in this manner ever since he started to lead his double life. His partner, a small redhead, stared both of us straight in the eye.

As soon as she entered hotel bedrooms, Ann compulsively opened windows. For what purpose? To invoke the gods or to scoff at them? Gabriel kept his distance; he was subject to vertigo, and the hind view of a woman bent slightly forward and thus presenting the most inviting of posteriors did nothing to alleviate matters.

This time she had scarcely put her face outside when: "Gabriel, Gabriel, Paris is burning!" She summoned him without turning around.

Gabriel approached her, step by reluctant step, pulse 140 beats per minute, palms moist (an attack of panic, that same old Orsenna affliction).

"Look!"

It was true. Across the Seine, above the houses on the rue de Rivoli and beyond the trees of the Tuileries Gardens, dense smoke climbed from the chimney tops. The smoke of many fires. A most unexpected sight in June. Ann did not know Paris well. She pointed at the largest billows. What's that? Probably the Ministry of the Interior. And beyond it, by the river? The Chamber of Deputies. And that one to the West? Why, the Quai d'Orsay.

"Let's go there!"

Gabriel recalls a cool silky fabric flowing through his fingers. I must have been putting my tie back on as we went down the stairs.

"Is anything the matter?" asked the manager. He scrutinized us both. "Was anything wrong with the room?"

"No, it's fine, we'll be back."

Gabriel plonked down the key and a second tip. We crossed the river at a run.

A crowd had already surrounded the municipal building on the rue de Grenelle, spilling into its forecourt and yelling so loud for information, for someone in authority, that a shirt-sleeved form appeared at a second-floor window.

"The offices will not open until three P.M.," said the form.

Amid jeers, it hastily shut the window again.

"That's France for you!"

"Which of my things should I get rid of?"

"Is it safe to keep my husband's Croix de Guerre?"

"And my Romain Rolland book, better to destroy it?"

"I simply threw away all my books. With the dedications ripped out, of course, so no one can trace them to me."

"How close are they now?"

"Do you think they'll come into our houses looking for anti-German material?"

It was like a huge clucking chicken coop, all questions, no answers.

At 3:01 P.M. an official appeared at the top of the stairs; he was adorned with a tricolor sash, as if for a wedding.

"Please! Ladies and gentlemen, please!"

No one paid any attention. The crowd shouted louder than ever, particularly the women, elegant women with penetrating voices.

"Where can we get gasoline?"

"Are the buses still running?"

"Are the Loire bridges still open?"

"Please, please," begged the tricolor sash.

Jabbing with their elbows, Gabriel and Ann left this deathbed scene.

The seventh *arrondissement* was on the move.

The rue de Bourgogne was black with cars. They sat waiting, doors agape. People were stuffing suitcases, furniture, and children's bicycles into them.

A plump storekeeper, hair disheveled and blue work jacket unbuttoned, was smashing his bottles of Alsace wine one after another against the curb. "Rats, rats, the French are rats!" muttered a stiff-backed old man with the look of a retired cavalryman.

"And what about your husband?" Some of the women were exchanging goodbye hugs. "Isn't he here yet? Well, you'd better wait for him, then."

"Do you think so, do you really think so? I was so hoping you might have room for little Hélène and me."

"No, believe me, in times like these it's best not to go anywhere without a husband."

Mattresses, countless mattresses, were emerging from front doors. People were lashing them to the roofs of the cars. The rue de Bourgogne was one enormous bed.

Ann speaking.

*Then Gabriel seemed to go mad.*

*He will never admit it to you, because what drove him mad is a secret, a secret he keeps hidden in the depths of his small person. But you attorneys need such secrets in order to plead mitigating circumstances, don't you? That's why I'm writing this. My name is Ann, and I was by Gabriel's side when he seemed to go mad.*

*When he saw all those houses spilling their contents, those bedridden elderly brought downstairs seated on cane armchairs, those shopping bags bulging with silverware, those women clutching bundles of letters fastened with pink ribbon, those children crying out for their goldfish, those still lifes gashed in the scramble, those reed baskets overflowing with medicine bottles, eyedroppers, enema bags, all those bottoms of dresser drawers suddenly dumped out defenseless into the harsh light of day . . . the sight of it was too much for him.*

*First he just stared, rooted to the spot, amazed.*

*Then he started running in all directions, asking the refugees, "Have you seen her?" and jostling concierges, going into people's houses—of course the windows were wide open anyway—ferreting about, sniffing like a bloodhound: "I'm sure my mother is here, I'm positive, everyone is leaving today, so she must be too. . . ."*

*I chased after him and had a lot of trouble calming him down. He wouldn't listen to me, didn't even recognize me. "Who are you?" he said. "Let me go." The thing is, I had hardly spoken to him till then, so you see my voice was not familiar to him.*

*It was a long time before he returned to his senses, after perhaps three or four hours of searching. I walked him down to the Seine and urged him to talk about it, to get it off his chest. He launched into tangled recollections, a birth, nuns in white headdresses, a woman leaving. It was as if he had pulled out a plug and his life was gurgling away, a hemorrhage of himself. Put yourself in my shoes. Who could I call on to help handle him in this wild state? Luckily he stopped abruptly and said, "To the Foreign Office!"*

*He was my roly-poly Gabriel again, all of one piece, with no childhood and no secrets.*

At the Quai d'Orsay a line of clerks handed an unbroken stream of cardboard boxes down the ornamental staircases. It was like the Treaty of Versailles in 1919. You could read all the labels: Balkans,

Danzig, Sudetenland, Ethiopia. . . . Small Citroën 11's waited at the foot of the stairs.

"The convoy should have been on its way by now," said a nervous and very pale young man, forefinger stabbing his watch.

"It will leave, it will leave," replied a clerk. "It's not our fault if the Minister insists on taking the whole world with him."

"Now don't forget. Once we're in Bordeaux all the files go into the mayor's office in alphabetical order."

"What if other ministries claim the mayor's office?"

"Throw them out. Wars are foreign affairs, are they not?"

All was chaos and disorder. It was easy for us to get inside.

Every office was wide open, with papers stacked high on either side of every door, like shoes left out to be cleaned in big hotels, and well-tailored people standing in every doorway.

"Is the cart on its way?"

"The cart isn't the problem, counselor. The problem is where to burn it all. Only the corner offices have fireplaces. I've just checked."

We went to take a look at the Political section.

A clutch of young men in flannel suits, their hair faultlessly parted, were on their knees stabbing with pokers.

"Fortunately for us there's no wind today," muttered the section chief, standing a little way back from it all, his elbow on a bookshelf. "You've no idea how quickly it blows the smoke back down."

In the entrance hall the flow of cardboard boxes went on: West Indies, Dardanelles, Annam, Near East. . . . Outside, the air was close under a pale afternoon sky. Many Parisians, like us, were wandering from one shrine of officialdom to another, the National Assembly, the Foreign Office, the Prime Minister's residence. You wondered what could possibly endure amid all this disintegration, what you could possibly cling to. But the shrines just went on with their internal combustion, each of them capped with dense smoke, sometimes snow-white, sometimes black, as if we were no longer very certain whether or not we had a pope.

"What about Clara's photos: you know, the ghettoes?"

"In the safe at my office."

"Quick!"

Ann's employers' headquarters were on the Champs-Élysées.

"Oh, madame," said her spinsterly secretary, "your appointment has left."

"Never mind, Geneviève, you do the same."

The shoemakers of the shtetl had been stored, appropriately enough, in a shoe box. Along with their friends the yeshiva pupils, the bagel vendors, passersby with spit curls.

"We have to put these somewhere safe."

"Yes, so at least they'll be waiting for her when she gets back."

"I have an idea. Let's go back to the Seine."

Two policemen approached us. "Your papers, please. . . . Ah! lucky for you you're French."

Then: "Do you really think this is the right moment?"

The right moment for what? We were arm in arm, the shoe box between us. Ann, who never stopped running, had stopped running. She had slowed to my pace, perhaps even slower. She kept looking all about. She was probably seeking the horizon in order to start running again. But there was no longer any horizon.

She was wearing a sea-green linen dress. Her cheeks were as pink as a little girl's. Every few seconds she rubbed her temples and forehead with the back of her hand. Men turned to stare at her. Since Clara in 1913 I had not really taken walks with a woman, experiencing the world as if on tour with a star, making myself as unobtrusive as possible, an escort who never competes for attention and brings flowers when appropriate. Over Paris that day there hung a sense of being backstage, of watching sets change before your eyes, a grinding of ungreased pulleys.

"Interested in a little trip?"

We had reached the dock near the Eiffel Tower where sightseeing boats tie up. A navy-blue uniform with gold braid doffed its cap.

"I haven't had any passengers since the beginning of the offensive," said the boatman, "but every now and then I weigh anchor just to keep the engines in trim."

We chugged downstream. There was no more smoke from the buildings beyond the elevated track. The fifteenth *arrondissement* had no records to burn.

Our skipper was right. The Seine was empty. No police patrols. Even the firefighting boats were moored along the Quai de Javel, despite all the fires.

"We'll turn back at the Suresnes lock. Aren't you going to try to get away, then? Since early June, people have been trying to requisition my boat. Even people talking about America. As if I was built for the open sea!"

Gabriel told him no. "No, we're staying. But could you possibly keep going as far as Levallois? I would like to say hello to my grandmother."

"Ah, she's still alive then?"

The house was empty. Gabriel hid the photos in the library, a new, unfamiliar library devoted entirely to modern Italy. No one would dream of hunting for the shoe box behind Mussolini's books.

On the way back Gabriel saw Longchamp. You could imagine the roof of the stands behind the trees. Farther on, the waterfall in Saint-Cloud park, splashing down over its rocky grottoes. Had he been with anyone else, Gabriel would have talked about his childhood. With Ann he didn't dare. How could Levallois compete with Central Europe?

"If they draft three more age groups my number is up. Can you see me in the infantry?" Our helmsman added several choice remarks about the government's inability to recognize the skills it needed.

War had depopulated the riverbanks. Not a soul stirred to port or starboard.

Beside him Gabriel heard a tiny voice: "Could we go back?" Ann was ill; her complexion had gone from ashen to yellow.

"I know what's wrong with her. Take her below, monsieur, there's a bunk down there. I can't leave the wheel because of the Île des Cygnes. You'll find sugar cubes and spirit of menthol in the right-hand locker."

The cabin smelled of coal, oil, and wet ropes. Almost exactly the same smell as a certain Channel crossing in December 1900.

"Do you think we'll ever see her again?" Ann murmured to me, her voice faint, almost inaudible, the voice of someone seeking her sister in faraway places.

She would not let go of my hand. I had the feeling I was belaying her, as they say in mountain climbing; she was swinging out over the void. Had Gabriel let go of her that day, the whole Knight family would have disappeared.

"Is she feeling better? Don't spare the spirits!" the captain called down to me from the deck.

It was night by the time we got back. I wondered how many times we had steamed around the Île des Cygnes.

"This often happens," said the skipper. "With seasickness it's best not to tie up right away. It makes more sense to get over it afloat. Landsickness is much worse."

## 2. *Shoe Leather*

Gabriel will say nothing about the Germans. Everyone knows they took Paris. Book after book has described their stay. There will be more such books. It seems a popular subject.

Gabriel would rather stick to his profession, explain the part rubber played in an occupied city, even though it was an inglorious role. You must know everything, significant and trivial, horrifying as well, about this raw material that has done so much for the twentieth century.

Let us begin at the benign (not to say philanthropic) end of the scale. Louis turned down any suggestion that he retire.

"If only I could find a job," he complained to his son as they lunched together. ("Lunch" is a very grand word for those who still remember what rations were like in the year 1941. But anyway, since father and son were separated that day by a table, a checkered tablecloth, two glasses, and two plates, knives, and forks, let us not quibble over the word.)

Louis, then, was chewing on a piece of meat as tough as it was costly. From this point the birth of his brilliant idea was but a logical progression: meat → shoe leather → Gabriel → tires → shoe leather made from car tires.

Gabriel curbed the objections rising within him (you know nothing about shoemaking, you aren't the first to have this idea, what will Wladislawa say?) and loudly applauded.

"Wonderful! These wooden shoes everyone is wearing aren't exactly ideal. You can hardly hear yourself think."

Anything rather than an out-of-work father.

Louis organized everything, hired workers, was successful. People now came to the bookstore to buy shoes. No one was offended. Stores with false fronts were common in those days.

Fashionable women were delighted.

"Where have you been hiding these prewar pumps?"

With the right amount of cutting, gluing, sticking, dyeing, drying, you could manage a fair imitation of leather. There was only one drawback to the paternal product: static electricity. Rubber insulates. On dry days ladies were jolted every now and then by electric shocks. Louis calmed their fears.

"It's because of the fighting. The bombing has damaged the air. Just wait until peacetime and you'll see."

Renewing his clientele in this way, exchanging Colonial Ministry officials for women who were often young and ready for anything, perked up his spirits. I never heard him whistle so cheerily as during those bleak years: Trenet, Sablon, Chevalier ("A shopkeeper has to be jolly, Gabriel, it's the very least you can do for the customers").

*Clippety-clop*. You heard them coming whether their shoes were of oak or ash. It sounded like a peasant uprising, the clacking of clogs, a rustic invasion. But it was only a customer.

"Make yourself comfortable, madame."

Some of them fluttered their distress: All this walking, my feet aren't very pretty, I think they're a little bit swollen.

"No, no, they're fine."

Wladislawa watched him like a hawk, but I am sure he did not always stop at the ankles. There were days when I overheard distinct cooings and the kind of question that left no doubt: But what kind of shoemaker are you to have such gentle hands?

It is not hard to guess at the reason for Wladislawa's departure a few days later. She must have caught Louis redhanded at his shoemaker's practices and refused to forgive him. "Are the Aragons shoemakers, Louis, is this how they nurture their love?" I can almost hear her last words, her perfect interpreter's French that flew to pieces now that she was devastated. "Not deserving love, Louis; you lonely person, Louis . . . too late for me find another great love; you responsible shattering Polish life. . . ."

She was not the kind to leave quietly.

But Louis never answered the questions I was careful never to ask him.

## *3. Bicycles*

From 1940 on they revealed their true guerrilla nature. No sooner had cars fallen silent for want of gasoline than bicycles occupied the city. They overran streets, avenues, and boulevards, piled up at entranceways, blocked corridors, even went upstairs into apartments, so afraid were their owners that they might be stolen. They dominated conversations (guess where I had a flat the other day), they inspired daydreams (how I'd love to have a ten-speed). They brought on backaches, they taught Parisians all over again what calf muscles were for and reminded them that Paris is nothing but hills, Montparnasse is a mountain, avenue Junot one hell of a steep climb. They created aromas, bike-riding makes you sweat, entranceways smelled like locker rooms. Their saddles warmed the female sex and of course crushed the male. They taught people the joys of tinkering and the unpredictable character of Rustine tire patches (sometimes bonding onto thin air, sometimes refusing to stick at all), the usurping nature of Rustine tire patches, gradually taking over the inner tube, preferring their own company—we Rustines are quite capable of keeping the air in all by ourselves, thank you very much. And then there was the swarming buzz that arose whenever a group of cyclists went pedaling past in formation. On the sidewalks aficionados closed their eyes and relived the Six Day Race, the Tour de France.

Yes, beneath their innocent guise of machines designed to move people about, bicycles liked nothing better than war, the economic privations of war, the silence (between explosions) of war, the resourcefulness and the physical fitness engendered by war. It was now that Gabriel first perceived the deep complicity between war and the bicycle. And he was unsurprised later on when the part that bicycles played at Dien Bien Phu was revealed. And General Giap will back him on that score. Don't worry your head about it, counselor, Gabriel will return to the subject, he'll return to it, but for now he'd like to underline the conclusion he came to: yes, bicycles are disturbing creatures.

### *4. Buses*

Now the truth can be told. Gabriel should never have accepted the assignment. In a voice old age has not completely cracked, he firmly reiterates: never.

But it must also be stressed that, just as cancer doesn't save you from catching cold, war doesn't save you from finding a job. You have to live, pay your rent (even though the building is bombed every night) and your electric light bill (even when the power is more off than on). And when your employer asks you to lend a hand to an important customer, just for a few weeks, how can you refuse? But Gabriel also pleads further extenuating circumstances: until June of 1942 the Paris public-transit system (the Régie Autonome des Transports Parisiens, or RATP) seemed the most peaceable of establishments, the most useful, dedicated to filling human needs, to getting Parisians to their places of work or to their lovers' trysts. And then keep in mind that many people—the overweight, those with weak hearts, the unathletic—are not allowed to cycle. Moreover, Gabriel will not conceal the fact that he was proud to be assigned to the RATP. A *useful* job at last, after the folly of a youth spent in motor racing!

He will reveal even more: until that shameful night, he was on the best of terms with the RATP chairman. If we weren't exactly friends, there was at least a bond of fellow feeling between us.

Monsieur de L. was a former naval officer. Indeed, Gabriel noticed that sailors filled many important posts in those days. This fact might seem paradoxical in view of Marshal Pétain's constant refrain: The land does not tell lies. But to endorse this sentiment would be to deny the sense of tradition and discipline—the conservative soul—of seafaring men.

Monsieur de L. retained many of the idiosyncrasies of his former profession, for example calling his vehicles his fleet and having the buses repainted at the drop of a hat whenever they were confined to port (the bus depot) more than one day, which, given the gasoline shortage, happened with increasing frequency. Monsieur de L. personally preferred white, but war made darker shades more appropriate: gray, or possibly forest green. No matter; a fleet has to keep shipshape even in port, he was fond of saying. Which did wonders to revive the flagging enthusiasm of the painters in the sheds.

He told us of his secret dream: a solemn mass on the Esplanade des Invalides to bless the assembled buses, bright with bunting.

It was not Gabriel's fault. Not his fault.

One July day they asked him to inspect all the bus tires. All of them? All of them!

So he inspected, and then submitted an unvarnished report which must still exist somewhere in the RATP's records. Its conclusions were dire: the tires were worn down to nothing.

Next day, still a July day, he received orders to act rapidly and decisively. This is war, Orsenna, get moving! The fleet had to be ready to weigh anchor just before midnight. He went to work. Conscientiously. Constantly mindful, believe me, of the passengers' safety. Discarding tires that threatened disaster. Assembling usable sets of tires. To do this effectively, he needed precise information. He asked for the fleet's projected itinerary. Secret, they told him. He insisted: If they're going to be making more right turns than left, monsieur, then I'll fit the less-worn tires on the left wheels. They finally handed him a piece of paper. And Gabriel, fool that he was, tried to figure it out. Apart from the rue des Rosiers, the rue du Temple, the rue des Écouffes, the rue du Trésor (how on earth will the buses negotiate such narrow winding streets, monsieur?), apart from the Marais, the addresses they had given him were scattered far and wide: 5 rue de Villersexel (third floor), 78 rue de Miromesnil (fourth), 19 rue d'Alésia (second, facing elevator). No logic to it. A most random route. Nothing to help a tire expert carry out his mission.

"Then I see only one solution," said the fool (that efficient fool!) Gabriel. "We'll mount the best tires diagonally. Left rear, right front. But I don't like this. I can make no promises."

He gave instructions. More lights were turned on, all available jacks put to use. Each bus rose gently in the July night and then knelt slowly to one side as if rocked by the most sluggish of seas.

"They look as if they're at anchor, don't they?" said the old seadog. He was visibly moved.

Gabriel still remembers the smells of that night, the smell of rain on hot streets, the musty smell of rooms through open windows, the smell of chestnut blossoms strewing the sidewalks, the smell of summer in cities, the smell of July.

We stood for a few moments contemplating the armada.

Then: "Good Lord," said the chairman, "what about the other depots?" We jumped into the service Delahaye and drove toward Vaugirard. Every few minutes patrolmen stopped us, blinded us with flashlights, their gun barrels menacing, and snatched our safe-conducts from us, studied them, scrutinized us.

"On your way."

And so it was that every bus in the city that night was beset with a peculiar nautical motion, pitching, rolling, rear left, forward right . . . rear right, forward left, southwest, northeast, southeast, northwest. Calculating the prevailing winds would have been a mathematician's nightmare.

"Do you think they'll manage?" asked the chairman.

"It all depends on the weather. Our biggest worry is sudden cloudbursts. Bald tires don't stand a chance with rain."

"Of course, of course. It would have been better to wait for a less variable weather report, but there you are; neither you nor I have the final say. We do our job, that's all."

He drove me home, to my pied-à-terre for nights when I was too lazy to go all the way back to Levallois, or when I wanted Louis to think my sex life had caught fire: a tiny studio on the rue de Sèvres.

"It's a pleasure to work with such a conscientious technician. We need skilled men, not prima donnas, for this job, don't we, Orsenna?"

"Aren't you going home tonight?"

"No. I have to issue sailing orders. And I need to be on the spot tomorrow. One has to expect the unexpected in this game. But you get a good night's sleep and take the morning off; you've earned it."

I thanked him. He gave me his hand. In retrospect I am sorry I wasn't wearing gloves. The Delahaye left for Grenelle. For a moment I thought he was sporting a green light to port, a red one to starboard. Whatever the circumstances, I have always managed to end my day with a lovely picture, the kind that lulls you to sleep.

Gabriel woke late. For some time the sense of being alone had kept him asleep. (A depopulated world is silent.) He at once began to wonder what yesterday's commotion had been about. Had the war started up again? Were they transporting troops? A glance at the street calmed his fears. Women in print dresses trudged along the sidewalks as they always trudge on hot days. The only place you could hope to be moderately cool was under the chestnut trees. In short, it was summer.

At the depot they were hosing the buses down. Inside and out. The yard was already flooded. A Senegalese was digging drainage channels.

"That's enough, that's enough!" shouted the foreman.

But the cleaning squads paid no attention. Inside and out. Water sloshing, brooms swishing.

"That's enough, get them lined up!"

They went on washing, scrubbing floors, swabbing windows. There were stains on them, long trailing fingermarks as if someone had fallen. And stubborn little round spots, the fog you leave when you push your nose very hard against glass.

When it was time for a bus to leave, time for it to accomplish its so useful public service, it literally had to be wrenched from the hands of the cleaners.

And such, my dear attorney, and such, ladies and gentlemen of the jury, was Gabriel Orsenna's contribution, ordered (I would remind you) by his employer to assist an important customer, the RATP; such was his technical contribution to the roundup of the Jews and their overnight incarceration in the Winter Velodrome.

These are the facts. Let the courts decide what was right. If right exists in such matters.

## 5. *A Ketch Without a Spanker*

### Heroism: Act One

Two German soldiers checking papers at the foot of a gangway. Two olive-green forms stamping their feet to keep warm on a pink granite wharf. And Gabriel was making a most deafening din. This is one of the horrors of age: your body makes noises. Digestion, respiration, creaking joints. Your insides in an uproar. Whistling, gurgling, crepitating. And on top of everything a racing heartbeat. Gabriel stepped forward amid this earsplitting racket. Luckily the gulls were squawking. Old people should live among gulls.

"Electrician. *Ach!* Very useful. Often breakdowns on other side."

The soldiers wished them a good crossing.

The air smelled of iodine, of that brownish tincture you dab on scraped knees.

I shall not dwell on the Île de Bréhat. I know you are waiting for London and my meeting with the General.

Know only that the island, a former pirates' lair, was now a vacation resort.

The Reich sent its wounded to convalesce there. Caressed by ocean breezes, their bodies built up by milk from the local black-and-white cattle, rejuvenated by the honey-sweet aroma of heather and broom, they were soon brought back to health. Too soon. Once their recovery was official, their next assignment was automatic: the Eastern front.

And so, understandably, they fought off recovery, tried to catch some really lasting illness, their favorite tactic being midnight soaks in icy water.

The islanders loved to watch. On favorable (very cold) nights the local inhabitants peered from behind reeds and sparse remnants of heather as our invaders arrived in furtive groups of two or three. They undressed down to their white shorts and stood motionless, chests exposed to the wind. Feet sunk in the icy sludge below their long white shorts, they stood at rigid attention. Soon the coughing began. They wanted to make sure it had taken. Some of them lasted the whole war with the same case of bronchitis, lovingly stoked, always on the verge of pneumonia, a permanent fever of 100.5 degrees Fahrenheit. Others, less careful, coughed blood. They were taken away, deathly pale. Sea air is fatal to galloping consumption. Cavities form in the lungs and are filled with fluid. You die swept away, as if by the tide.

I stayed at the Hôtel des Rocs, on the left as you go up. Open, according to the sign; closed, according to the shutters. A row of deck chairs sat out on the terrace. How long had they waited there? Since '39 or '40? They had assumed strange, distorted shapes. Deck chairs too suffer from rheumatism.

When you saw the damp patches on the flowered walls of Room

7 you felt sorry for those poor chairs. How they must have suffered in winter!

Every morning Gabriel opened the window. And summer came in. Meaningless wartime summer. The sea was empty, not a sail in sight even when the sky was blue. Around the bay lay deserted gardens: former flower beds, clumps of hydrangeas choked by long grass. Which might explain how a thought took up residence inside his head, like a catchy tune: At the Liberation why don't I become a gardener? At the Liberation there'll be a desperate need for gardeners.

But this was merely a preliminary glimmer, the forerunner of a real dream: to settle here bag and baggage with Ann and Clara (but which would be bag, and which baggage?) as soon as the war was over.

These offshore islands were created as a haven for the less than handsome. This observation is based on common sense. Anyone doubting it has only to visit Bréhat and make the acquaintance of its dogs. Knock-kneed, one-eyed, drab coats, all shapes and all sizes, half-basset-half-setter, quarter-cocker-quarter-boxer-quarter-terrier-quarter-spaniel; these were common mixes. Would they have had any hope of finding romance on the mainland? Yet here their lovemaking never ceased. Every new moon produced a new litter.

Once the last boat left, Gabriel felt safe for the night. A woman, even Ann, does not leave a man by swimming away (Clara is too fearful even to think of trying).

I shall spare you a recital of my blunders. How on my first day, at the Chardon Bleu café in the square in Bourg, I encountered a man who turned out to be a Breton Home Rule militant (the breed who believed for over six years that the Germans were of Celtic blood and vice versa) and mistook him for a Free Frenchman.

"What?" he roared when I put my question. Luckily the place was jammed with the pre-dinner drinking crowd. He had not heard me. I made my getaway without further incident.

No. Gabriel will spare you all that. Let us simply pay tribute in passing to a real Resistance worker, Rémi, a young ex-sailor whose teeth had been knocked out (decay? a swinging boom?) and replaced with gold ones. They were an emblem of his courage; who could long survive underground with such a gleaming, metallic smile? Anyway, he had taken charge of my escape plans and would let me know as soon as it was time.

Let us salute Gilles, the translator, who lived on the northern half of the island. So invaded by cats that he didn't notice the Germans.

"Translators from English have a lot to learn from the company of cats," he told me.

I agreed, despite the sour latrine smell and the fur, gray, russet, black, white, milling around our feet.

He had one ambition: to tackle a book by the Irishman Joyce. "*Finnegan's Wake,* the translator's Everest, Gabriel."

Meanwhile he was cutting his teeth on a slim book, *The Real Life of Sebastian Knight*. "An author worth watching," he said, "a native of St. Petersburg who writes in Russian, German, French, and now English."

He showed me some pages.

"So far it's easy going, he's being straightforward. But with a polyglot of his kind I wouldn't be surprised if it turns out to be an enigma even more nightmarish than *Finnegan.*"

He refreshed my knowledge of English, well and truly lost after the passage of forty years.

Well be with you = *Bonjour*.

How does your honor for this many a day? = *Comment allez-vous?*

I was vaguely aware that he was not teaching me the most up-to-the-minute English.

That's how translators are. I had memories of a simpler English. But can you trust your memory after forty years?

At last the hour struck.

## HEROISM: ACT TWO

The German soldiers were back from their medical examination and celebrating their stay of execution. You could hear them singing in their citadel. The seashore would be empty.

Rémi and Gilles took me down to the water's edge. A boat lay on its keel on the wrack-strewn shore.

"Just let the ebb carry you out. The meeting place is the bell buoy.

Don't worry about the boat. When the tide turns she'll come back on her own."

We embraced, murmured "Long live France."

"Take it from me, Gilles, a man who has learned to live with fifty-two cats"—"fifty-three, Gabriel"—"Sorry Gilles, fifty-three, such a man has cleared the highest hurdle. You can translate any book, even *Finnegan's Wake.*"

And I drifted out. The last picture I took away with me from France was the metallic glint, head high in the gloom, of Rémi's smile.

By the buoy a more substantial craft awaited me, half cutter, half ketch; in other words she had been designed to carry a spanker aft of the rudder post, but it had not been mounted. Her helmsman, David Birkin, was British. He went back and forth across the Channel for the Cause: the Channel with its storms fierce enough to uproot every windmill in Guernsey, the Channel with its patrols of supremely evil German knights. David Birkin was Don Quixote de La Mancha. I think you'll recognize him in spite of his alias. . . . At about that time one of his passengers was François Mitterrand, our present Minister of the Interior. I never saw David Birkin's face, just his long thin figure, the figure of the man of La Mancha. My roly-poly form must have disgusted him; he immediately showed me to the cabin and shut me in. Later, in '47 or '48, by the most incredible of flukes, I happened to learn that he had had a daughter, first name Jane. I sent him my congratulations, via the Royal Navy. Perhaps the address on the envelope was not specific enough? No reply. Let's wait for my trial. All the publicity around the case. . . . Many old friends will come forward out of the shadows.

To return to heroism: apart from some choppy seas off Dover Rocks it was an uneventful crossing. Lying on my bunk, eyes riveted to a long needle attached to a paper cylinder and held prisoner inside a glass-fronted case called a barometer, I thought back to the last phrase the translator had taught me:

"The bald little prompter shuts his book, as the light gently fades" *(Le petit souffleur chauve ferme son livre, tandis que doucement la lumière s'éteint).*

And I wondered if such phrases would come in handy in London. Perhaps on leaving a place, instead of saying bye-bye?

# 15
# *Swiss Cottage*

## I

FREE FRENCHMAN ORSENNA was most surprised to find two policemen waiting for him when he came ashore on a Penzance pier.

"Would you mind coming with us, sir?"

Gabriel (English soil was rocking so wildly he had trouble keeping his footing) complied.

He was led to a train, shut into a compartment smelling of stale cigar smoke, and taken to London, Victoria Station.

"Would you mind coming with us, sir?" two other policemen asked him.

To give fresh proof of his goodwill as a Free Frenchman, he at once consented and thus arrived at Camberwell College. On these vast and sinister premises, rechristened the Patriotic School, surrounded by high walls and guarded by countless soldiers, the Intelligence Service strove to separate the wheat from the chaff: on one side true Free Frenchmen, on the other side spies.

Gabriel waited three weeks to be interrogated. Every morning he went in search of the sergeant: an Irishman, and therefore a lover of France.

"Sorry, sir. It was all much quicker in 1940. But since our victory at Stalingrad there's been a stampede to join. So it's taking a long time to get applicants sorted out. The whole of Europe's in London, sir, looking for Allied credentials."

"What do they do with fake Free French?"

"Shoot 'em, by Saint Paddy!"

Gabriel spent his days strolling under the trees in a greenish gloom conducive to introspection: All things considered, has mine been the life of a Free Frenchman?

At last he was led into what had once been a classroom. He sat down at a front-row desk. After a while an old young man appeared. Towering, stooped, with hair that might have been gray or fair, clad for the most part in a kind of sweater: a coarse woolen pullover with holes at the elbows and sagging almost to his knees.

"George Cornwell," he said, pulling a chair onto the platform just in front of Gabriel and beginning at the beginning. "So your name is Gabriel Orsenna?"

"Yes."

"Born in Levallois-Perret?"

"Yes."

"Name two perfume manufacturers in Levallois."

"Oriza, Cosmédor, Marcérou wax, Holstein candles—"

"Just answer my questions."

George Cornwell did not look at Gabriel. He stared at a point somewhere at the back of the classroom, probably the dingy wall where a few portraits of English heroes had been pinned up: Shakespeare, Lord Byron, and a lady dressed in a way no longer fashionable, probably Elizabeth I.

He frequently rose to consult one of the works piled on the table behind him: phone books, yearbooks, maps, catalogues, every possible kind of spy trap.

"What race did the Trotting Club organize in 1893?"

"Buffalo Bill versus Meyer."

"What's the shipyard's name?"

"Cavé."

On a stupid impulse (a childhood memory immediately translated into action), Gabriel felt to see if the inkwell sunk in the desktop was full. It was. Whence his convulsive attempts to dry his violet little finger on his pants where it wouldn't show (back of the knee).

"Is anything wrong?" asked his inquisitor.

"No, no, everything's fine," answered Gabriel.

This first session lasted until nightfall. The old young man seemed satisfied. "One thing's certain, seems to me: you really were born in Levallois. I don't often find myself on such firm ground."

But happiest of all was Gabriel. It's true, it's true, he said to himself, my life began at Levallois. Proof that I exist. Of late he had not been so sure. He regularly consulted clocks. But an ever-rising pile of hours does not necessarily add up to a life.

His dormitory mates sympathized with him.

"Cornwell's the worst of the lot, he won't let go."

"Cornwell's a civilian, commissioned just for the duration. They're the toughest. They want to show they have what it takes, see."

"Cornwell? Just a second. I believe he used to restore paintings. No, a tax inspector. In any case obsessed with detail. You'd better be patient. He won't let you get away with a thing. I hope you don't have anything on your conscience."

"At your age, watch out. He's the type to go on interrogating you even after you're dead."

"Know how many soldiers there are in a firing squad?" No. "Twelve. Know why?" No. "Because a spy has at least twelve lives; you need a bullet for each of them. Ha, ha, ha!"

The atmosphere at the Patriotic School was scarcely fraternal. The real heroes were chafing at the bit. The fakes were shaking in their boots. Nearly all of them were beginning to be sorry they had chosen England.

But Gabriel let the scoffers scoff. Every day he congratulated himself more on the inquisitorial attentions of gray- or fair-haired Cornwell.

"Wasn't there a woman behind the renowned impresario Knight?"

"Of course, Elisabeth."

"Please pay attention, I said a woman, not a wife."

"Oh, wait a moment, yes, perhaps. I remember now, at the Washington and Albany: auburn, at the next table; she was always asking for the salt or the sugar."

"Precisely. You had me worried for a moment. Well, she was his mistress. She followed him everywhere without ever getting found out. Scribner's published her memoirs just before the war. *A Discreet Love*. You should read it. After all, it's closer to your life than mine. Now tell me, when you reached Portsmouth for the first time, was it high or low tide?"

While Gabriel thought about it, Cornwell leafed through tide tables, sighing as if overwhelmed by all these figures.

"I can't remember."

"You have me worried again, Mr. Orsenna."

"Wait . . . yes, very low . . . yes, that's right, so low that the gangway climbed straight up from the ship to the sky, like a ladder. I could see Clara's white ankle socks just above my head. And clouds sailing above; I've never seen clouds like them."

"Spare me your erotic impressions. Intelligence is concerned only with the facts. Which are accurate, by the way. On the eighteenth of December 1900, low water was five P.M. Great Scott! A record-breaking low tide. Must have made for a nasty lop at the mouth of the Solent. You certainly had dirty weather that day, didn't you?"

After a certain age, life, like coarse woolen pullovers, is full of holes. Cornwell forced me to darn myself. I thank him.

We broke off for tea, brought in by a young soldier whose chin fascinated me. Pitted with acne and sown with sparse needle-sharp blond whiskers, a pitiable attempt at a beard devoured by white pimples.

On the tray, between cup and sugar, there was often a slip of paper folded in two.

"Message for you, sir!" barked the acne victim, bringing his heels together with a click.

Cornwell read, smiled.

"The colonel wonders yet again when I expect to be done with you. He's getting impatient. Apparently I'm the slowest sorter in the Patriotic School. Poor Orsenna, falling into my hands!"

At these moments, and only at these moments, he would look at me. Exhausted. Visibly harassed: all these lives waiting to be verified made him dizzy. He sighed, twice, and removed a flask of Scotch from beneath the coarse woolen pullover.

"Care for some? It's good for you. Tea doesn't loosen tongues enough."

And so it was he began to confide in me.

" 'Let's see now, Cornwell, you're in publishing, you must know all kinds of stories, adventures, high-flown yarns, and all that kind of mumbo-jumbo. You can sort out overseas arrivals.' That's what Intelligence said to me in 'forty. Such are the quirks of fate, Orsenna!"

G. Cornwell entered publishing via the index pages. Cambridge University Press had been looking for someone to compile an index for its 21-volume leatherbound *Dickens*. Looking and looking, but without success. Yet it was a simple enough project: an alphabetical listing of all the author's characters with their dates of birth and death, along with the high points of their fictional lives. Ten lines at most for each entry: a Who's Who in Dickens Land. The first attempts had been disastrous, full of omissions, spelling mistakes, confusion over ages, geographical errors, misguided notions of what the "high points" had been. And it must be admitted that the task, a herculean one, was wretchedly paid.

Then came G. Cornwell, whence or how nobody knew.

"I can do your index," he told the astonished receptionist, but by the time she had called personnel on the fourth floor the rare pearl had vanished.

Three months later a bulky parcel arrived in the mail, Dickens's whole exhaustive universe listed and filed.

In the meantime the leatherbound project had been canceled. But young G. Cornwell, until then a junior French master at Harrow School, was immediately taken on by the publisher as an assistant editor, then quickly promoted to reader, then to literary adviser in charge of "blockbuster" novels. For slim works did not even exist in his eyes. He had to heft at least two manuscript pounds before he began to be impressed, unlike his fellow editors, who, at sight of such a monster, thought only of their briefcases (all that weight to lug home at night) and whose inclination was just to dip into books: ten pages early on, ten in the middle, and ten at the end, following this with the comment "verbose."

G. Cornwell, on the other hand, was sated only after three hundred thousand words. Every publishing house was after him. Can you imagine, someone actually willing to read these interminable manuscripts, always ready to go over them again, to pinpoint inconsistencies between pages 3 and 842!

Gabriel found all this out later at a half-baked symposium he attended with Clara in Frankfurt. She wanted to take pictures of German authors (Is the guilt of the Holocaust stamped on their faces?). The subject was the future of books. On the dais a sociologist sought to establish rules: modernity = speed = small books = easier division of property after divorce (statistically more and more frequent).

"So you knew Cornwell?" the great Rowohlt, king of publishers across the Rhine, said to me. (I forget how the name George Cornwell had come up. I believe it was at the cocktail party that closed the symposium; everyone was delighted to be done with sociologists and literary sociology and to be getting back to books.) "Ah, Cornwell, a fascinating personage." (Rowohlt mixed up French and English a little: character, *personnage*, personage.) "After 1945 he founded some kind of cult, didn't you hear about it? Yes, a cult, the worship of fat books, agoraphilia, the love of crowds. . . . Devotees corresponded with one another, sent each other indexes, appendices, family trees. First all over England, then far and wide, from one end of the planet to the other, they alerted one another to the existence of Chinese novelists who although quite unknown were veritable volcanoes of fertility, the creators of thousands of protagonists. There are still people like that, you know. To them the world is nothing more than an enormous novel and human beings too lazy to write it out in full." Every now and then Rowohlt held out his empty glass, and the butler, looking sour, wordlessly refilled it for him. "In his declining years Cornwell had a dream: to incorporate the novel in the Constitution. For him democracy was the offspring of the novel, of stories, of the limitless diversity of men's lives and of the necessity for dissimilar people to live together in harmony. It's not such a stupid idea. What do you think? Why not include the novel in national mottoes: All for One (one novel)? Or Liberty, Equality, Fraternity, Novel. If people wrote only novels (and never essays), there would be no dictators. Dictatorships are based on concrete ideas. As soon as characters appeared, there'd be no point anymore; you'd never be able to establish certainties. Essays should be permitted only in very old and skeptical societies protected once and for all (but how can one be sure?) against the assaults of the arbitrary. Don't you think?"

Everyone else had long since left; there were only the two of us there, Rowohlt and Gabriel, plus Clara curled up asleep on an orange bench—that orange color that Frankfurt believes enlivens hotel reception rooms.

"Really, he came up with the healthiest proposal for the postwar world. He asked his authors to work overtime. He believed writers should make up for all the war dead by creating characters. A literary baby boom, so to speak. So you knew him? And he interrogated you?

That means you can't be alone in life. He never wasted his time on loners."

One fine day, one fine gloomy day, the interrogation was over.

"Know where you'll be staying?" asked Cornwell. "You don't, do you? Heroes never worry about where they'll be staying."

The hero Gabriel stammered no; like his fellow heroes, he did not know—

"Splendid. May I suggest a family boardinghouse just behind Baker Street, a little eccentric perhaps, run by a Polishwoman. So liquor and peace and quiet are guaranteed. You're the intellectual kind that needs peace and quiet to wage a good war. Am I right? Here's the address: Three Adamson Road. The Polishwoman is Hanna Lifshutz. In Swiss Cottage. Away you go. Next!"

"May I ask a question?" said Gabriel.

"This is wartime, questions are rationed. Just one."

"Is there a Winter Velodrome in London?"

"I don't think so. Wait a second. No, not even Crystal Palace. Good luck, Mr. Orsenna."

## II

Swiss Cottage. A Swiss cottage actually stood there in the heart of North London, complete with carved wooden balconies and painted columns.

Only daffodils were missing, and a lake in the background mirroring the Jungfrau. The Polish woman lived a mere step away. She greeted Gabriel resignedly.

"Another hero? Fine. You can have number seven, on the second floor. It's my last room. I won't give you any advice. Heroes never listen to advice."

She sat down again, gray eyes, white hair, a violet shawl over her shoulders. Massive and grumpy. She went back to her knitting, sitting on her folding chair among the empty milk bottles at the front door.

One glance at the knitting, one at the sky. She had watched the first Battle of Britain, English fighters against Nazi bombers, and had been so thrilled by it she did not want to miss the second. After the reverses suffered by her poor Poland, Mrs. Lifshutz had basically transferred her allegiance to the heavens: all day long she kept a lookout for aerial dogfights; at night you heard her prayers, endless strings of Ave Marias. Not mumbled at top speed the way people usually go through their devotions, but clearly articulated, and very loud, as if the Black Virgin of Czestochowa, either from old age or a too-rapid assumption, had become hard of hearing.

## III

I met Him.

One morning in September 1942.

I put in two weeks of meticulous preparation. I stationed myself outside the Connaught Hotel in order to get used to His—how shall I put it?—*unique* physical appearance. I regularly read the daily paper *France,* listened to Maurice Schumann on the BBC. I even interviewed His personal secretary, François Coulet. ("Tell me about Him. What does He like?" "Librarians. He told me one day, but this is confidential: 'The best job in the world is to be a librarian. A public library in a small town in Brittany. . . . You find yourself 60 years old, and suddenly you sit down and write an 80-page monograph: Did Madame de Sévigny ever visit Pontivy? After that you become frenzied: you send stinging letters to the parson for challenging a date.' ")

This information gave me the courage I needed to approach Carlton Gardens. Marguerite Orsenna, bookseller; Louis Orsenna, bookseller. When booksellers make as little money as the Orsennas, surely they can be classified as librarians. I had planned out our whole conversation and rehearsed it to myself as I climbed the four front steps. Preamble: libraries and librarians. First part: France. Second part: Gabriel Orsenna's pro-French role. End: lively discussion of literature; but be very very careful never to mention Paul Morand.

Gabriel rang and entered. Gabriel was not alone. A sullen throng of Free French waited in the hall. They looked at their watches, loudly telling the butler, "I have a noon appointment!"

Everyone had a noon appointment.

"You should have come in 'forty," said a passing secretary, mouth set disapprovingly. "You would have had Him all to yourself."

At long last He appeared on the landing and began to descend the stairs. And, contrary to the universal laws of perspective, the lower He came the taller he got. His aide was with Him. One by one the Free French introduced themselves. And when it was my turn:

"Orsenna, Gabriel," said Gabriel Orsenna, craning his neck to look the General in the eye.

"Orsenna, Orsenna, is that Italian?"

"Mexican, General!"

"Monsieur Orsenna is in rubber," said the aide, who was François Coulet, my informant.

"Every trade has its value," observed the General before turning to the next in line.

At that moment and at that remark, a nature quick to take offense might have turned anti-Gaullist. Not Gabriel. He saw merely an example of that reserve so characteristic of natives of Lille, reinforced by British understatement. "Every trade has its value" meant "the finest profession in the world," every bit as good as a librarian's.

And Gabriel left Carlton Gardens with his heart beating a tattoo that refused to be calmed by the sight of the ducks on Saint James's pond; they reminded him too vividly of the coming landings.

## IV

Gabriel spent his whole world war on the phone. The International Rubber Fund had offices in the City, 8 Friday Street, smack in the heart of the financial district. With our less-striped shirts and our less-svelte waistlines, we traders were a bit out of place in the rarefied atmosphere of the bankers. Yet we were doing the same thing; money is merely one among many raw materials, after all. Yes, I remained on the phone until the end of the war, in a large room with no view at all, not even the smallest stretch of the Thames. Yet all you had to do to travel was close your eyes and listen. We telephoned the whole world, the most out-of-the-way places, just as long as there were rubber trees there.

"You have rubber? How much? What grade?"

We no longer even consulted the atlas. You quickly learn the names of towns and villages.

Every week generals dropped around, choleric or conciliatory. "Now then, lads, couldn't you get things sorted out a bit quicker? The army's waiting."

Some bellowed. "It's your fault the war's dragging on and men are dying! You, you!" They poked their swagger sticks at us and tossed stacks of photos onto the table, photos of vehicles, of whole fields of aircraft, of jeeps, of trucks, sitting on tireless rims, their wheels embedded in the ground: petrified machinery.

"Well, what about those damned tires? Is it that you want the Nazis to win?"

They uttered the direst threats: "Even you, the Frenchman. Especially you. Court-martial, firing squad, you're a saboteur!" But the high command had little power over us. Phones are a medium all their own, and rubber a world unto itself.

It was these photos that alerted my young associates to the importance of our task. At first they had no inkling. They placed their orders the way you might order just about anything: copper, tungsten. But seeing those motionless armies, drained of strength, paralyzed, they realized that the guiding force, the essence, the miracle that raised your feet off the ground and at the same time gripped the ground, thus fostering mobility, was rubber.

All the youngsters nodded: John, James, Mark, Peter. "It's true, it's true!" they said. "Rubber is pure gold, it's all-important!" They asked questions, just like children. Like a grandfather, Gabriel answered them. He took advantage of rare lulls in the work to explain the science of tires to them; he dredged up old memories. All those conversations with Brazil (Hello, Manaus, Santarém; hello, Porto Velho) gave him the feeling he was chatting with his youth, with his new young bride, Clara *(I am not leaving you, Gabriel),* with the general manager of the Hôtel de France in Belém, the expert on love, with all his friends in the Land Registry Society, the regulars at the Café Byron. . . .

I remembered them all, each and every one. In Brazil, sons often have the same first names as their fathers: I felt I was among old friends. As if, thirty years later, nothing had changed, as if the forest's slumber had preserved things and people.

"Hello, Aristides; hello, Eugenio, how are you? I'm calling from the United States." (I was lying, but tropic dwellers can imagine America much more readily than England.) "America, America!" they said. They treated me like an old friend.

"Yes, yes, hello, speak a little louder, please."

"This is Gabriel Orsenna. You know, the man whose wife left, the lovesick Frenchman."

"Yes! *Si!* My father talked about you."

"Well, what are you up to these days?"

"Making deals. . . ."

Money does not exist in these regions. Yet it circulates. That is the miracle of the tropics, their philosopher's stone: the quicker it passes from hand to hand, the more money there is. Like the Indian method of making fire.

"Do you have any rubber?"

We had to shout into the receiver, the connection was so bad, and we had to manufacture background noise: a radio turned up full blast, an anthem played on the phonograph during each call, words like "baseball" and "Coca-Cola." We re-created the United States in the studio. And everyone was taken in, even the most cautious and suspicious of Brazilians.

Sometimes conversations spread themselves over several days.

"Yes, we were cut off. So what about the rubber industry?"

"You know as well as I do, Senhor Gabriel, it's dead. Asia killed us."

"But the trees are still there?"

"Of course, of course."

"Then start all over again. The Japanese have invaded Asia. They've avenged you. Europe needs latex. Good luck, good luck. I'll buy everything you have. I'll call you next month. Yes, at the same hour. Long live Brazil. We'll take care of the shipping end."

The man at the other end lowered his voice. "Are you sure? Are you sure?"

You could almost see the Amazonian, excited, ear glued to the receiver, eyes darting about to make sure no one was there to overhear, no one to guess the news and steal from him the best opportunity since the turn of the century.

Still speaking in hushed tones, he sought to negotiate.

"A month isn't enough. We need time, Senhor Gabriel, to hire *seringueros*, reopen the old trails. Everything is dead, you know that."

"The Allied forces can't wait."

"I'll manage somehow, count on me. But please, for the sake of my father who was very fond of you, give me exclusive rights for the area—"

Their whispers trailed off. Some even neglected to hang up. You could hear their footsteps on the floor, women's voices: "Who was that?" Nobody, nobody. . . .

It took only four or five calls, to Belém, Santarém, Manaus, to set the fever racing as it had forty years before. Gabriel Orsenna can claim without fear of contradiction that he brought Amazonia back to life. Thousands, hundreds of thousands of books have been published on the 1939–1945 war. Which of them even touches on this matter of crucial importance?

I loved it when it was my turn to have telephone duty, on Sundays or at night. I remained on my feet the whole time, standing amid the phones. And as soon as someone rang I was back again among the trees beside the ocher river. My young colleagues were puzzled. They listened to my calls but it did no good, they had no memories. . . . I don't know where they are now. I don't know if they ever dared confess to their children how they spent the war, in rubber.

We looked for rubber all over the world. At random. Spurred by increasingly urgent need. The Normandy landings would soon take place. How could they land without tires?

Thus I got Trinidad on the phone.

A very polite gentleman with an Indian accent answered. He thought I was calling about the carnival.

"There's not a room to be had. Not even a mattress. I can reserve you the back seat of a car. De Soto? Pontiac? In any case you won't get any sleep—"

And I heard him yelling, "Be quiet, I have America on the line." In the background a band was rehearsing. Syncopated music, the kind that jolts even paraplegics into motion, much better than the little mirror they hold under your nostrils to see if you're still alive; when a human being no longer reacts to that rhythm it means he's dead. Seeing me tap my toe and snap my fingers, my young associates snatched the receiver from me and despite the static began to beat time to the music, deaf to the secretaries' shouts of "Stop that, for goodness' sake, stop!" We might have gone on dancing for the whole of carnival, not unlike a rugby team suddenly swept up in mid-scrimmage by a pulsating Caribbean rhythm, but the other phones resumed their jangling. The Allied army was waiting for us. Gabriel had to break off the concert. And a little later he was forced to be the cause of a rude awakening when he caught a dreamy look in a fellow worker's eyes, a slight swaying of the torso, a blank blissful smile, all the symptoms of a rubber dealer in a trance.

"John?"

"Yes, sir."

And John hung up with a sigh. I would prowl among them with ears pricked up. "It is forbidden, do you understand, forbidden to call Trinidad. The first hint of music and it's curtains for you; this is war, for heaven's sake." They promised but could not keep their promises. Trinidad, St. Lucia, St. Vincent. Carnival lasts a long time in those parts, particularly when you include rehearsals, preparations, the four days of festivities, and the aftermath, inertia: a body in motion tends to remain in motion for weeks on end before reluctantly slowing to a halt. . . . No one in the islands was cut out for rubber.

"Call back later," they would say. "In June. Or July."

Gabriel relented and permitted his team these interludes of relaxation only after air-raid alerts, those hours of waiting in the Underground corridors, on platforms and escalators, while aboveground, bombs exploded and houses fell in ruins. As soon as his young colleagues were back in the fresh air they stampeded to Friday Street, fought for the phones: "Hello, get me Grenada (or St. Barthélemy)."

"Do you have any rubber trees?"

"Who is this? What do you want?" a voice from the far end of the trade winds would reply, the accent each time a new blend of the most unpredictable cadences. Dazzling white sand, painful to the eyes, the turquoise sea, restful to the eyes, a shallow boat pulled high and dry on the shore, the roaring of surf on coral reefs. At such times how could you believe in war? And this notion (the unreality of war) was like a vacation day, a morning spent lazing in bed.

Gabriel swears it on the bones of his impossible double love: they called there so often the phones smelled of rum.

I had this idea: Once the war is over, I shall invite Louis and Marguerite to London. I shall settle them down for the day in the Underground, at Leicester Square station or Baker Street. I'll say to them, "Since you're so fond of Empire, take a good look."

I know them well. They will widen their eyes in surprise. They will say, "This is too much, Gabriel, this is going too far." But they will be delighted, as rapt as kids around a Christmas tree. Despite their age they'll clap their hands. I'll hire an old ex-colonial to help them distinguish between Tamils and Sikhs, Mau-Maus and Zulus. For you need to have spent a whole lifetime in the tropics to tell one dusky skin from another, for instance an Indian from Madras and an Indian from the West Indies.

I ran into them every day, all these men and women of various shades. They stood motionless on the platform, waiting for some imaginary ark. Or else you saw them whisked away, crammed together, sealed in by the doors, impassive behind the glass, all sizes and types, essence of human race already boxed and ready for delivery.

In '43 and '44 I spent endless hours in the London Underground. I can hear Gabriel's enemies sneer: Aha! he was afraid of the bombs. Not at all. Suddenly Gabriel might decide to follow a tall black man, sticking close to his heels down the long corridors, changing at Green Park, changing at Charing Cross, and getting off right behind him at Colliers Wood. Gabriel would stop only at the foot of the last stairway, the one leading to open air. Then the tall black man would disappear from view, returning to his own country, for this much Gabriel knew: Colliers Wood was nothing more than a code name imposed by those in counterespionage. At the top of the stairway at Colliers Wood station was Kenya. Like Trinidad (code name Ealing

Broadway), Belize (West Ruislip), or Rangoon (renamed Dagenham East for reasons of national security). That was why traveling through London took so long between stops. It takes time, after all, to cross oceans and make long overland journeys.

Thanks to its Underground, London was still the hub of the world. Having foreseen hard times ahead, England had dug long subterranean tunnels. Did such a farsighted and persevering nation deserve to lose the war?

Heartfelt thanks to Miss Fitzpatrick, long-distance phone operator at the central post office, auburn, she claimed, and thirtyish by the sound of her voice: heartfelt thanks and clusters of medals pinned to her chest.

For without her how would I ever have reached the four rubbery corners of tropical America? How indeed? At a time when waiting for a call to go through could drag on for hours, even days, when wrong numbers were the rule and you suddenly found yourself conversing with a Sacramento butcher instead of a Santarém rubber trader, and oh, the time wasted ironing out misunderstandings caused by constant static on the line and by disconnections that always occurred at key moments! Without her, how could we have noted delivery dates, names of ports, the flag the ship was sailing under (changed every month to confuse the shipwrecking enemy)? How indeed?

"Could you get me eight in Óbidos, please, miss?"

"Hold the line."

In her makeup there was something of the motorbike cop escorting a procession of dignitaries. She liked to clear a path through the stickiest of jams. As soon as you gave her an assignment you heard her ordering the crowd to make way, eliminating the competition: "Your time is up, sir, call back tomorrow . . . all lines are busy; out of the question, all overseas circuits are down . . . well, there's a war on, isn't there . . . yes, of course, direct your complaints to Room Ten-oh-four. . . ."

And how she berated her tropical counterparts!

"Have you any idea of the consequences of not taking a call from Great, Very Great, Britain? I have your name, and I intend to report you to the international federation."

"Oh, no, please don't!" the terrorized girl would reply. "I believe Senhor Pereira is by the river. I'll send for him."

"I should think so!" Miss Fitzpatrick observed severely.

I took advantage of these brief delays to get to know her.

"I chose this job to meet people," she told me.

She spoke softly, so as not to be overheard by her fellow operators. I did likewise, because of my young staff.

"You aren't married?"

"A dedicated operator hasn't the time."

I would have liked her to talk more about her life, about her career in telephones (by now you will have noticed that Gabriel is a great collector of careers). But scarcely had she described her first telephone to me, a black wall phone with a crank in her parents' villa in Buxton (Derbyshire), scarcely had she fluttered, "I don't know whether I should be telling you all this," than Senhor Pereira, a little out of breath, returned from his Amazonian riverbank.

"Your party is on the line."

And I heard the click as she hung up.

Miss Fitzpatrick was the only switchboard operator in the world who did not listen in. "I sleep so badly as it is," she told me, "with all those voices in my ear." I pictured her little flat near Paddington, filled with fragile knickknacks sitting on lace doilies. . . . Knickknacks also have voices, but domesticated voices, like dogs or cats, a silent language, the language of companionship. She refused to believe my life was devoted to rubber.

"You're not telling me the whole story, Mr. Orsenna."

Miss Fitzpatrick was a romantic. She was convinced I was really searching for my lost love from island to island, from clearing to clearing. She even suggested places to call. "Cartagena, for instance, or Curaçao, your girlfriend could easily be living there." I knew no rubber tree had ever taken root in those places, but I yielded to her suggestions nonetheless, so as not to bruise her romantic soul. I probably called every single number from north to south, east to west, from Miami to São Luis do Maranho, from Cartagena to Baton Rouge.

"You'll find her, Mr. Orsenna. A love as deep as yours is bound to triumph in the end."

On the day of the landings I would invite her to join us. I had two bottles of Château Brazzaville Bordeaux. She did not come. We thought of waiting for her outside the central post office at the end of the day, but how could we have recognized her? The switchboard operators left the building in swarms. And auburn was in fashion at the time. On the streets of London one woman in two had hair neither blond nor brown, yet not quite all the way red.

## V

Since business is business and the show must go on, war or no war, Ann often passed through London. She called Gabriel. "No, monsieur, I'm afraid I have no rubber. Still negotiating deals, monsieur? In the final analysis, our jobs are similar. See you at five this evening, usual place."

In the hotel lobby they kissed, then pushed apart, looked at each other, drank each other in. Their bodies were no longer greedy, no longer bold. They had become diffident bodies, which no longer dared make demands. Beyond shyly proposing a walk.

London in October is nothing but leaves. They take over sidewalks, come into people's houses. A London autumn is one of the world's most assertive seasons. When you walk there in autumn, you stumble over autumn. "Notice it's autumn?" autumn keeps saying.

Children dart along the streets disguised as vampires, as skeletons, as witches, chanting as they go:

> On my Jack o'lantern
> I will put great eyes,
> They will be so big and round
> He'll look very wise.

"What's going on?" asked Ann. Nothing. It was life going on. The children were celebrating Halloween, October's little carnival.

Then Ann took Gabriel's arm. And squeezed. And Gabriel answered. "Yes, Clara, we wish you a happy autumn day, the best possible day. Have a good Halloween, Clara, wherever you may be."

## VI

Gabriel is ashamed.

Never again will he dare set foot in Great Britain. When he sees an Englishman these days, and God knows they are thick on the ground on the Côte d'Azur, Gabriel lowers his head and hurriedly crosses the street.

For Gabriel misbehaved toward the United Kingdom.

Here was a country which, after doing a little checking on his identity, had opened its pubs to him, its cellarsful of claret, its Underground to shelter him during the blitz, its gardens where he could walk his fear of the blitz away. Here was a country that had stood up to bombs, thousands of bombs, whereas we, France, were already retreating south across the Loire by the time the first shrapnel ricocheted off the first tree in the Ardennes forest. Here was a country that had had faith in him, had entrusted him with important responsibilities, even global responsibilities, and how had he, Gabriel, behaved in return?

Unspeakably.

Do you mean he was a traitor, that he yielded to Germanophile tendencies?

No, in this respect our Gabriel's comportment was beyond reproach.

He was involved in underhand dealings, then, he tried to contaminate Great Britain with the well-known Latin mania for the black market?

No, not that either.

The problem was (since I must tell the whole truth before the court) the problem was impropriety in his private life.

Gabriel pleads guilty. You must decide for yourself whether the circumstances he is about to relate exonerate him.

All big cities are cruel to the lonely. But London distills its own very particular brand of cruelty.

Its houses are low, two or three floors, and its curtains often remain open to admit the meager English light. So when you walk its streets you would have to keep your eyes closed to miss the sight of families at home on the other side of the windows. All those daily rituals that break a bachelor's heart: children in green school caps eating their porridge, the father most likely hidden behind his newspaper, the mother fussing over them in her light-blue dressing gown, and the eldest daughter suddenly emerging from the front door, eyes still full of sleep, mouth already sulky. And then those overstuffed armchairs with floral slipcovers, the same floral pattern as on the lampshade. And the window frames and doorframes, all painted the same dazzling shade of white no matter what neighborhood you might be visiting.

Like a store window displaying family life for all exiles to see, all those who like Gabriel had a bed but no home in London.

But hardest of all was nightfall, when dark shutters dropped one by one over every window. And in the blackout London itself became black as night. Then Gabriel would walk on between rows of blind house fronts. People's lives had disappeared. Gabriel walked alone.

There was only one place to look: upward. The searchlights were on, slowly sweeping the sky. Gabriel had nothing against civil defense, nothing against antiaircraft guns. It's just that these things were no substitute for daily life. And Gabriel reflected that this was indeed what he'd been missing: daily life.

Of course he could have joined one of the countless societies that proliferate in England, one of the three hundred churches, offshoots of Protestantism, or the Kennel Club, or the Anti-Vivisection League, or the disciples of Swedenborg. But he felt he was being watched. The slightest slip and dear old Cornwell would have him out in the Channel in a boat without a paddle. No. The only time he was ever tempted to join something was when he saw this notice taped to the window of an antique shop in Westbourne Grove:

*The*
*Ephemera Society's*
*Piccadilly Special*
*Britain's Greatest*
*Ephemera Fair*
*featuring*
*printed papers of every description*
*prints, maps, posters, pamphlets*

*greeting cards, old catalogues*
*share certificates*
*Park Lane Hotel*
*22nd February 1943*
*6 P.M.*

He turned up at the right place, but one day late, February 23, and as its name suggested, the society in question was short-lived.

Then Indian cooking took a hand; without it Gabriel might never have behaved so unlike himself.

On the first occasion Gabriel took his seat trustingly, in all innocence. Ordered. His companion, a colleague celebrating his birthday, followed suit. And here was what they chose. I record it faithfully to forewarn all those who wish to be forearmed.

*Peshawari Murg Tikka* (cubes of chicken marinated in spices and stewed in a casserole).

*Kahari Gosht* (lamb slices browned in oil and Punjabi spices, sautéed together in a kind of warming pan and served in a Singhalese hot sauce).

*Bateer-e-Khas* (an Uttar Pradesh specialty: quail very lightly cooked in curry).

*Malai Kofta* (fried eggplant, fresh cream, tomato sauce).

*Chutney Podina* (crème de menthe, lemon juice, assorted seeds, dried mango).

How I wish I could have offered you this gift, you, Marguerite, and you, Louis, who both love the Empire so: a week in Notting Hill Gate. Lunching and dining together, we could have visited every Indian restaurant, sampled all the dishes, all the specialties, state by state. It would have gingered up your taste buds quite considerably. One mouthful of fire, one mouthful of cream, one mouthful of sunlight, one mouthful of snow. . . .

Summer arrived in Gabriel at just about the same time as the quail from Uttar Pradesh. A kind of personal heat wave, born somewhere deep within his rib cage. Of course, certain burning sensations in the palate and throat had been a hint. But once you were accustomed to it, summer no longer hurt. Ardor set in. Gabriel was ardent.

Gabriel's stomach, mouth, hands, and male part were all ardent.

So intense was this ardor that there was no longer any question of enjoying a quiet dinner with his colleague. Gabriel rose, thanked his companion and wished him a happy birthday, made extremely polite farewells, left the Bombay Tandoori, asked a passerby the way to Soho, turned right up Wardour Street (still accompanied by this unbelievable summer night), and looked up. At the first red light (No. 17) he went upstairs to the second floor. Her name, her working name anyway, was Marie-Françoise. A native of Meaux (Seine-et-Marne), well-rounded and a receptive audience. "My you're going strong, Monsieur Gabriel, now that's what I call a landing!"

Since the end of the Twenties, since those mad days when the flappers had suddenly discovered the charms of roly-poly men, Gabriel had not fornicated so vigorously or so deeply.

"You wouldn't have a friend, would you?"

"For tonight?"

"For tonight," the ardent one confirmed.

Stunned, Marie-Françoise stammered "Bernadette, an Irish girl, just a few steps away at 38 Greek Street."

Such, fanned by summer, the summer of Indian cooking, was the first hot night of Gabriel the Free Frenchman.

It was followed by others, by a host of others. Hot nights gave way to hot nights. It was no good going home exhausted on the stroke of 4 A.M. to sleeping Swiss Cottage, no good swearing to himself as he softly, oh, so softly, turned the key in the lock. This is the very last time I'll ever do this; he was off again that very evening. Despite his age (sixty), his fatigue (two and a half hours' sleep), and the ringing in his ears (those long days on the phone), he returned to the attack after a brief halt in India.

For Gabriel was now assailed by that most irresistible of human itches: to fornicate with them all, systematically, starting with the ones who worked near the stations (Victoria, Waterloo) or the port (Whitechapel, Surrey Docks).

A fear had taken hold of him, a fear we must consider somewhat unfounded: What if the landings, just for once, were entrusted to women? What if they all upped and left one fine day for France, and only men remained behind in England?

Haunted by this nightmare, Gabriel plunged back into the race.

"Hello, darling, want to come upstairs with me?" Yes, yes!

Before long they all recognized him. They applauded as he came back downstairs.

These women were light and easy. Gabriel sorely needed the cure they offered. Physically there was nothing light about them at all. Heavy is what they were, heavy-breasted, heavy-buttocked, heavy-thighed. But they registered so lightly on your memory that you forgot them the moment you left; just the opposite of the Misses Knight, the parasitical Misses Knight, just the opposite of two sisters who had taken permanent root in his life.

They were incomparably light and easy. "Bye-bye, big boy." They called Gabriel big boy—very tactful of them, wouldn't you agree, Misses Knight? They were so insubstantial they scarcely existed at all: the briefest of springtimes, even the most Junoesque of them. They did not insist on lodging in his memory, they just fastened their mauve peignoirs. "Bye-bye, big boy." It was like summer, like chasing butterflies, big overscented butterflies that dissolved in the night.

The straitlaced in the General's entourage were shocked at the sorry example Gabriel was setting for the English.

"We must deal severely with him," insisted Massigli, among others.

But on what grounds? A Free Frenchman was free, provided he paid these ladies without a squabble (Gabriel did) and did not disembowel any of them (in fact they all testified to the roly-poly one's good if somewhat rushed manners).

Carlton Gardens was not obliged to intervene until May 1944.

That spring Gabriel really went too far.

The first time was a health matter. Due to assiduous frequentation of undeniably public places Gabriel naturally contracted a small and in the final analysis benign infection, known to the English as clap or the French disease. So far nothing very reprehensible. Gabriel had merely to visit the justly renowned specialists at Charing Cross Hospital and postpone his nocturnal prowling while they gave him a series of painful silver nitrate injections. Unfortunately, as a result of three influences—the interval of abstinence, the Indian food he was forced to consume in increasingly greater doses every week just to maintain his burning condition, and the imminence of the landings (nobody spoke of anything but Them, even in the Underground)—Gabriel's frenzy intensified. Not content with paid company, he laid siege to the clientele of the very elegant Petit Club Français, owned by the formidable spinster Alwin Vaughan, a place where you could run into Joseph Kessel every evening, for instance, or Romain Gary, or the two "hero" parachutists, Colonel Bourgoin, missing an arm, and Boissoudy, missing a leg. . . . In his fevered state, Gabriel on one particularly drunken evening seduced a certain Kathy, a distant Welsh cousin of a token girlfriend of Claude Dauphin. And the Welshwoman, discovering a problem three days later, thanked Gabriel publicly and in ringing tones for his "gift, so typical of you filthy French sons of bitches," and then broke a pint of beer over his head.

Still Carlton Gardens hesitated to intervene.

To be frank, he was the first Free Frenchman to suffer this doubly distressing ordeal: infection plus retribution.

However, Carlton Gardens could not overlook the next episode, Gabriel's bout of exhibitionism. Louis will undoubtedly feel guilty. Louis will fret about it. But it was no fault of his. At that time a narrow but frequently stormy sea, the Channel, separated father and son. And was it the father's fault if the son carried that lazy form of love known as imitation to the point of caricature? Since the start of his misfortunes Gabriel had kept his organ under constant scrutiny. He would stop off in any old restaurant on his way to the office and ask for the gents; he even went into office buildings on Fleet Street, took the elevator, pressed the button for the topmost floor, turned his back to the door, and then and there, lowering his trousers, cast a pitying look at the small finger of flesh from which a whitish discharge permanently oozed. Absentmindedly, he sometimes neglected to rebutton his fly.

Up to this point any attorney could put forward a not-guilty plea. But one day, smack in the middle of the telephone room, amid the ringing, the usual yells, place names, tonnages—Rio Branco, 5,000; Leticia, 10,000—Gabriel abruptly acted as though he had caught on fire. A huge smile spread across his features. With one leap he was on the table, trampling order slips underfoot and spilling two cups of tea. With terrifying speed he undressed. Brandishing his organ, he called out, "I'm a rubber tree, I'm a rubber tree. Look, I'm dripping!"

After a second or two of very understandable amazement, his colleagues closed in. They knew that air raids eventually wear down the nerves. They tried to soothe Gabriel, patted him on the shoulder: "It's all right, old fellow, the war will soon be over." But Gabriel escaped them. And for more than an hour, it seems (I remember nothing), he capered from tables to chairs still chanting, "I'm a rubber tree, I'm a rubber tree!" Then his associates, at their wits' end, exceedingly embarrassed (the bankers across the way on Friday Street had gathered at their windows to watch the deplorable scene), decided to notify the policemen standing guard at the front door of the building. The latter grasped the situation at a glance and called their chief, who got in touch with Carlton Gardens.

A few minutes later a squad of French marines, strapping lads under Savary's command, gently but firmly removed the roly-poly one in his raincoat, put him into a Hotchkiss, and drove him to the Lake District, to an establishment specializing in jungle fever and other nervous disorders. Let us not forget that the United Kingdom was then a true imperial power, undaunted by the sudden bouts of madness colonials are prey to. The remedy was well known. Green, lots of green; that's what these poor devils need: fields, foliage, fairways, and lukewarm rain, lots of rain, on the face, and most important of all no animal whose shape or call might remind the patient of colonial wildlife.

After two months of this green cure, Gabriel was pronounced whole again and returned to work without having to endure the slightest remark or sneer from his colleagues.

All power to the English, who understand that madness sooner or later visits us all.

Gabriel apologizes to the people of the Balkans. If he had collected a little more rubber, the Allied armies might have advanced more rapidly and denied East Germany and Czechoslovakia to the Communists. Hungary too, perhaps, and Yugoslavia. . . . But he did his best, he swears it. He got his hands on all the rubber available. Tire producers will confirm it.

Victory found Gabriel asleep, worn out, among the telephones. Before taking the boat train from Victoria he paid a final call on No. 4 Carlton Gardens, on No. 10 Duke Street, on Alwin Vaughan's Petit

Club Français, the place where a woman had punished him. What for? He couldn't even recall. But all these shrines were deserted, Gabriel was the last Free Frenchman left in London. No band to greet him at Dieppe. He hesitated for some time before walking down the gangway. I'm sixty-two, he reminded himself. Does the world still have any use for a roly-poly man?

And later, in January 1946, when the list of nominees for Companion of the Liberation was announced, he raced around to the Hôtel Matignon and insisted on seeing the official document. He read the names with pounding heart, like an examination candidate, an old candidate for a monumental examination.

He read it and reread it, turning over all the possibilities—perhaps the General put a silent *H* in front of my name, or else he thought Orsenna was my first name—but there was nothing. One thousand and thirty men, eighteen combat units, six women, five cities (Île-de-Sein, Grenoble, Nantes, Paris, Vassieux-en-Vercors), but no Gabriel Orsenna.

Once upon a time there was Gabriel Orsenna, standing stock-still outside 54 rue de Varenne, asking himself Why, why was I left out?

"Move along!" said a police officer.

Then Gabriel removed from his pocket his old, his ancient and faded red rubber ball and moved off in a westerly direction, toward the boulevard des Invalides, slowly, very slowly, cautiously bouncing his ball.

The officer watched him leave, then looked questioningly at a colleague, who shook his head. There was no law against bouncing on the rue de Varenne.

End of the Second World War.

# PART THREE

Once upon a time there were the Liberation, peace, the disease of hope.

Once upon a time there were countless dead and no corpses.

Once upon a time there were the Île de la Jatte and America, the Lutétia Hotel and photography, the Île Séguin and four-horsepower Renaults.

Once upon a time there was a nocturnal recital at the Gare de l'Est.

Once upon a time there was rubber.

Once upon a time there were the Terres Rouges.

Once upon a time there were the bicycles of Saigon, the Cao Dai sect that worshiped Victor Hugo, the royal tombs of Hué, Hanoi airport.

Once upon a time there was Bao Dai.

Once upon a time there was the free world's last line of defense on the Mekong.

Once upon a time there was a colonial exposition and Summer Velodrome on the Laotian border: Dien Bien Phu.

Once upon a time there was reincarnation.

Once upon a time there was the Cannes Festival (springtime every year).

Once upon a time there was America (repeat).

# 16

# *The Disease of Hope*

## I

August 25, 1944? Louis told me all about it. Parisians love French history and dining by the Seine. Cafés on the Île de la Jatte were full and turning people away. As Leclerc and his troops pushed across Boulogne not far to the south, tables blossomed in riverside gardens toward the end of the afternoon. Then came chairs, tablecloths, blue and pink Vichyware glasses, silverware brought out for the first time since prewar weddings, and good bottles put away for the day when . . . And despite the late hour it was still light. As soon as they were brought up from the cellars, the fine vintages were slipped into anglers' nets, and even the most hallowed Bordeaux sank to the river bottom at the end of a string, it was so hot that day. The riverbanks were one gigantic restaurant, the longest restaurant in the world, with endless laughing, singing, chuckling, boasting, scared children, all come together as if for myriad overlapping wedding feasts. . . .

"Any tables left?" late arrivals asked.

"Sorry. You should have come earlier."

They showed their armbands—Forces Françaises de l'Intérieur, Francs Tireurs Populaires.

"Oh, very well, we'll squeeze you in."

"That's more like it," said the heroes.

Louis had struggled out with the Mexican pedestal table. Marguerite, light green dress with white polka dots, lace collar around her neck, followed him with the plates.

The couple who owned that excellent restaurant Les Pieds dans l'Eau (only yesterday a favorite with the enemy), were in a whirlwind of activity. People watched them with cynical amusement: Monsieur

Marcel, so snooty these past five years, and his wife, known as Leatherneck. They were serving double helpings to please their customers. They were buying forgiveness.

"Madame Orsenna, would you mind if I set up a few tables on your terrace?"

"What's that?" Marguerite shouted back, playing deaf. "Would you say that again? You can speak up, the Germans have left."

A very earnest and rather ugly girl changed the records and kept the gramophone wound up. Songs from the radio came out into the open, Sablon, Trenet, Chevalier: "Miss Emily, cher ange, Ah! l'envie me démange."

Every now and then, music and conversations would stop simultaneously.

All you heard was the river. Paris was being liberated in silence.

Around midnight the first Americans appeared, with new records and with cigarettes.

Marguerite embraced them all, even the black ones, to loud cheers.

Since the invasion her love for America had repossessed her. The Germans had sorely disappointed her. They lost too many battles. And the Germans disdained the tropics, they were interested only in Europe. As if empires could be built without colonies!

By nightfall Marguerite was three sheets to the wind. In advanced old age there is not much meat left on your bones, and alcohol and its whims quickly get the upper hand.

"Long live America," she kept saying. "Long live America."

And later, as explosions of laughter and ecstatic sighs floated down the stairs (Will you lend me a bedroom or two, just for tonight, the landlord of Les Pieds dans l'Eau had asked), she assumed a solemn expression, a disturbing expression.

"Sh! Can't you hear it, Louis, under your feet?"

"No. Don't you think you should go to bed?"

"The Île de la Jatte . . . the Île de la Jatte is moving. We're drifting out to sea, Louis, bring me my cardigan. . . . They say it gets very cold . . . out at sea."

And she fell suddenly asleep, her face in her plate—can you imagine, Gabriel?—right in the middle of her strawberries and cream.

* * *

As soon as he was back in France, Gabriel was required to use the contacts he had made in London. He besieged the American authorities at the Ritz or the rue Saint-Florentin. He put on his most candid, his most appealing air.

"My grandmother is determined to die in your country!"

Every evening she demanded a progress report.

"They're doing their best," Gabriel replied. "They promise that in a few weeks—"

"Be quick, hurry! It's obvious you're not old!"

Reporters from Washington got wind of the matter and came to the Île de la Jatte to take photos of Marguerite, hundred-year-old Frenchwoman, soon to be our oldest immigrant. The couple at Les Pieds dans l'Eau took advantage of their visits to further embellish their patriotic credentials, offering round after round on the house, solicitously inquiring after President Roosevelt's health.

Marguerite left on one of the first ships out. She kissed us only once, at the Gare Saint-Lazare. "Goodbye, Louis, and this time try to get married properly. Goodbye, Gabriel, try to have a child with one or the other of your sisters, I don't mind which." And then nothing more. She did not answer a single one of our questions for the whole of the three-hour train ride. She was smiling at something that was not us. A reception committee awaited her at the station with flowers. She went through customs like a star, amid popping flash bulbs, without once looking back.

We watched as she nimbly climbed the gangplank and disappeared into the belly of the Liberty ship. It was our last sight of Marguerite, a small light-green figure surrounded by sturdy navy-blue seamen.

The night before she had warned us: "From now on I am American."

## II

A little later two books came out, two handsome twin books. One Italian, one French; one desert (Tartar), one shore (the Syrtean). In each of these twin books (which one came out first? no matter), a young man waits for the enemy. And the enemy does not come. Life continues, imbued with tremulous maidenly expectation: will he come? oh, heavens, the horizon is shaking. The heat was premonitory, no doubt about it. . . . Curious indeed, after the Liberation, after so many dramas, this compulsion to be frightened all over again, to tell yourself the enemy was coming when he had just left, this need for thrills, this disappointment that the horror had been cut short.

## III

Ladies and gentlemen of the jury, my dear son, you see before you a connoisseur of the Bon Marché department store.

He paced all its aisles, scanned all its display shelves, the skimpy displays of the year '45, stationery department with no colored pencils, photography section with no film, pet section festooned with leashes but bare of aquariums; perfumes with ersatz smells, shoes with soles made from wood flooring, mismatched sets of underwear, unelastic girdles; he inspected every floor, drove every saleslady mad: Would you mind not bouncing that red ball, monsieur, the sound makes the cases rattle and you're making stains on the linoleum. He met countless priests and nuns (for the Bon Marché is a favorite with the faithful). As they went by he bent his head respectfully and they blessed him. He followed nuns in cornets who looked tiny but who purchased enormous undergarments. He tried (and failed) to console a girl with huge eyes who came in every day to ask for watercolors.

"I'm so sorry, Mademoiselle Catherine," the saleswoman told her, "we are still out of stock."

Gabriel understood her distress: with eyes like hers, you had to paint. Otherwise they would shrink. He fed on all these small secrets, he filled up on confidences. Twice he hid in a fitting room to call out "Clara, Clara, Clara," in low tones, Clara did not answer, and he resumed his rounds. The advantage such places have over cafés is peace and quiet. You can spend whole days there without buying anything.

At night, just before closing time, he climbed to the top floor and leaned out, stomach pressed against the rail, as if he were about to plummet headfirst. Out of breath, he feasted his eyes on all those things below: all those fabrics, all those clothes, all the paraphernalia of real life. Endless wedding gifts to be bought and returned. He told himself all these essential items were proof, tangible proof, incontrovertible and variegated proof, certain proof that they would return, Clara, Markus, and Elisabeth. This faith helped him get through the night.

Gabriel would like to take this opportunity to offer official thanks to the Bon Marché for taking him in at a difficult time.

Gabriel and Ann waited outside the Hôtel Lutétia. They had waited there so often and so fruitlessly, waiting and unable to endure the voices of the crowd another second.

"They must have a list somewhere."

"This isn't like exam results, you know."

"The government should have written to us."

"How would they know our address?"

"Why are the hotel shutters closed?"

"Maybe they're resting."

"Never let prisoner of war survivors close their eyes; you have to keep them awake, see, and only feed them slowly, one small mouthful at a time."

"And make them drink."

"Very little."

"On the contrary."

"Do you mind, I'm a doctor!"

Ann and Gabriel preferred to seek refuge in the nearby Bon Marché rather than poke their fingers in their ears. Ann charmed the head of the glassware department, M. Michel, into letting her use his phone. Telephones are oxygen to business people. M. Michel borrowed a stopwatch from the clock department; clucking his tongue, he surreptitiously timed her calls.

# IV

"What do you call a human being without a body?"

"A soul."

"Thank you."

Before Gabriel's eyes was Clara's soul, a soul with protruding bones and lidless eyes, a soul that flinched if you drew near or made the slightest move. A fragile, flaming soul a breath might have extinguished, a bodiless human being reduced to its simplest expression: terror. Its body was not there. Clara's body refused to return. Nothing helped, not changing doctors nor changing treatments. Nor Bach's music. Nor whole days spent by her side promising her it was all over, that the world had changed, that the dogs were hardly eating anyone anymore, that she could come home now, that the creaking on the other side of the door was only the elevator. She looked very gently at you, utterly terrified, so sorry to be causing you all this trouble; she shook her head from left to right without saying a word, an infinitely slow no; she preferred to leave her body far away.

It was Ann, undisputed expert on the Real, who had the bright idea of fetching the old Leica. At first Clara needed help, you had to hold the camera for her, even press down on her finger as it rested weightlessly on the button, shield her eyes when the light was too strong.

Later Clara managed it on her own. She photographed everything. Everything she could see from her bed: the chestnut tree in the courtyard, the two armchairs, Ann's and Gabriel's, the medicine on the night table, the little Chagall canvas, the radio with its small green eyepiece, the Empire lampstand, the curtain loops, the window handle, every smallest detail. . . .

As soon as she had finished a roll we dashed off to get it developed on the rue Villersexel.

"Forgive my curiosity," the man behind the counter finally said, "but is this for some kind of inventory?"

Clara spread her photos on the bed. Picked them up one by one, studied them, lined them up, sought similarities, put them together in series. I believe that is how she regained her confidence. In any case, her body returned.

First her hands, then her cheeks, then the rest. Her color came back, she stopped being gray. Her return journey lasted two years.

Two long years. The time it took us to admit that Elisabeth and Markus were no more.

There was no religious ceremony, for Markus's true beliefs were unknown and Elisabeth's faith in a one God (Markus) was not officially recognized.

There was simply a recital one night.

The piano arrived first, aboard a large yellow Calberson moving van.

It was a black Steinway grand, an exact replica of the one which thirty years earlier, in the cruel city of New York, had emitted the notes trampled underfoot by Markus to prove his love. With infinite care the black Steinway was lowered to the sidewalk outside the Gare de l'Est. The three movers were barbaric-looking giants with the precise gestures of Swiss nurses.

The black Steinway followed a complex route, for it had to bypass stairways. You heard it even though you did not see it. Corridors echoed to the squeal of casters. At long last it heaved into view, an enormous gleaming whalelike bulk. We stood waiting beneath the arrivals and departures board facing the empty tracks, a depleted family indeed: Clara, Ann, and Gabriel.

"Which platform?" asked the giants.

"Number Three," Ann replied.

The incoming Warsaw-Berlin-Cologne-Paris line.

Our small procession got under way. First the Steinway and its escort, the moving men. Then the depleted family.

We walked down the platform as far east as possible, at least three hundred yards, past shuttered sandwich kiosks, all the way to the end where the platform abruptly dropped down to the tracks.

Markus's former young protegé and now established virtuoso François Samson did not keep us waiting more than half an hour. He arrived at a run, a tall somber figure, his scarf like a white hangman's noose.

Moreover, he apologized: curtain calls at the Salle Gaveau.

He seemed agitated, still vibrating to the applause. But the second he sat on the stool it was as if he had suddenly taken leave of this world. He was entering memory. He began to weep.

He played Schumann's *Carnaval,* not particularly well, much too loudly. He wanted the whole East to hear.

As soon as he had finished he said goodbye to us.

"I'm flying to Madrid at first light."

The black Steinway followed him, escorted by the three giants from the Calberson company.

We remained behind gazing at the gleaming tracks, the web of points. . . .

In the distance beams of light swayed, red ones, white ones, as if something were sweeping past. Probably cars crossing the bridge over the rue Lafayette.

## DREAM

Markus and Elisabeth came back.

Gabriel stood alone in the Gare de l'Est in the middle of the night to greet them, stood alone with a bunch of flowers beneath the arrivals and departures board, which announced only the next day's trains.

They came back, Markus and Elisabeth, followed by all the others, the whole six million.

"Let's get something to eat," said Gabriel.

And he opened up every Paris restaurant, the great ones and the small ones, the Tour d'Argent, the Chez Georges, the Chez Germaine, the Rendez-vous des Pêcheurs, all of them. Were there enough seats in Paris, enough plates, enough cutlery, enough breadbaskets for six million people?

Gabriel moved from table to table, making sure nothing was missing, murmuring, This is the finest and greatest meal in the world. He almost felt like dancing. He was proud of his city. He had forgotten the Winter Velodrome. No one else spoke. The sound of his voice, in the silence of the six million, woke him.

## V

Louis caught the prevailing bug.

Life could be changed. Human misfortunes were not eternal. The day was coming when revolution would transform human existence. And that day was just below the horizon, ready, waiting to dawn. You had only to topple the last remaining obstacles, slash the last moorings, for the great day to rise like a luminous balloon, an immense sun created by men, a sun powerful enough—"Stop sniggering, Gabriel"—powerful enough to transform life. Thus spake Louis, and many others like him, in those days.

It was a pernicious disease characterized by bursts of warmth, the urge to embrace people in the street, by sudden surges of affection for gray sky and morning mist (if they only knew they would soon disappear and be replaced by sparkling weather), by terrible hatreds directed against those still attached to the past, against those too frightened to pack their bags even though the new life was right there, within spitting distance. You could hear the flow of the river—"Well, then, you really are deaf, Gabriel; don't you hear anything, can't you feel us moving forward? Come on, get on the train, History's train."

Such was the disease of the time, the disease of hope. A disease everyone caught: young people, for after all they had to feed the yapping pack of days ahead of them; old people, because they had to fill the hole gaping before them somehow. Not since 1789 had the disease hit harder. Never had the epidemic spread wider!

At first Gabriel tried ministering to Louis, bringing him sedatives, placebos. But everything he said fell on deaf ears. All his arguments (life doesn't change just like that, Louis; life is heavy, Louis) and all his reasoning were merely fuel for the flames of hope. So Gabriel stopped talking. He just stood on the edge. And watched. Watched the progress of the disease. Watched this infection without microbes get worse, this disease propagated by humans, kindled, tended, exacerbated, pushed to its limits (to death itself) by humans, and then suddenly cut short by humans. Humans are an improvement over bacteria in that they are visible to the naked eye and talkative; you had simply to listen if you wished to know their plans.

It was a disease that created new jobs.

The *gold panners:* they filtered time and retained from the flow of time only its golden specks, the kind of golden speck that kept hope alive in the toiling masses.

The *gilders:* they sheathed the commonplace in gold leaf. They were a little like housepainters. Like Éluard and Aragon, the gilders-in-chief: Éluard who sang liberty, which gave the air its transparency, Aragon who would gladly have made all humankind sign contracts of love. If not of mad love, at least of faithful love. Or mad precisely because it was faithful.

And then the *fanners* of embers: they walked the city with cheeks puffed out as they blew upon men to ignite them, stirring their emotions with a terrible music played without instruments.

And the *excommunicators:* they ejected from hope the doubters, the questioners.

And Louis asked his son, "Well, Gabriel?"

And Gabriel was tempted to go along, to let himself be carried by the current and swept on into hope. Perhaps what held him back was the marchers, who seemed like puppets on a string. Their parades reminded him of lumps of raw material bobbing along on a conveyor belt.

Nor did Louis reproach Gabriel. He invented all kinds of excuses for him.

"I understand, Gabriel, it's your sadness. I understand, Gabriel, it's your rubber disease. But just wait, one day you will come to feel it too."

And Gabriel realized that the rubber disease was the antithesis of the disease of hope. There is no hope in rubber; there is a fear of snapping, a gentle but irresistible preference for original forms. Just as there is no hope in democracy, merely a preference for the natural order. A man always remains a man. The same with a country. You can pull it, stretch it, enlarge it, and France will always return to its original size: not an empire but a simple hexagon, an average power.

Hope was a tropical disease, rubber a temperate disease.

It was an aggressive hope that came very close to certainty. The very quality of the air had changed, no longer light, no longer free, but fenced in, structured. It was forbidden to take idle strolls or roundabout approaches. The air led you by the hand; up ahead lay the future. . . .

Louis had not moved into communism itself but into its suburbs. The Party was wary of his enthusiasms and particularly of his exhibitionist tendencies. For Louis was still the same Louis, ready to organize an exposition at the drop of a hat: universal communism (all nations won over one by one to the truth and to the radiant morrows that follow), a definitive biography of Stalin (the step-by-step portrayal of a glorious destiny).

"You'll see, comrades, the lessons of a properly planned exposition enter the very blood, carry whole families along."

But the Party preferred to camouflage hope's advance. And it was suspicious of the references to Comte that studded Louis's speech.

"The positivists are welcome to march by our side. We too need friends on the outside."

So Louis belonged to that heterogeneous species known as fellow travelers.

As for Gabriel, he was classified as belonging to another world, the world of "objective allies." Because of rubber.

The people's car then being designed had to have small wheels requiring tires to match.

"Gabriel Orsenna, one of the team tackling the four-horsepower Renault project, cannot be considered totally hostile to the working class."

They looked on him as a kind of Léon Blum, that bourgeois Socialist who despite his countless acts of treachery had nevertheless invented annual vacations. Gabriel Orsenna helped make vacation travel possible. So they tolerated him, but with distaste. All democrats made them retch: can't live with them, can't live without them.

On Saturday evenings Louis took a break. He went off to have a drink with my rival Dekaerkove, organizer of the Tour de France, who was waiting for him at the Grand Zinc bar on boulevard Poissonnière.

They ordered two beers and watched the postwar era go by.

The same crowd as before the war sauntered aimlessly along as if on an ocean boardwalk, the same self-absorbed couples, the same gleeful groups, the same brunettes with blond hair, the same fly-by-night street vendors, the same neckties sporting naked women, the same jeweled watches on the same tattooed arms. Stores were reopening one after the other, with new owners or old ones standing all smiles on their doorsteps, a great tide of commercial warmth enveloping them all. Everyone had lost his place and was now trying to find it again. And people you had given up for dead kept turning up.

"Look, it's Edmond!" shouted Dekaerkove. "Come over and celebrate!"

And as Edmond approached, the Tour de France organizer gave Louis a thumbnail sketch of this Edmond, former typesetter at the paper, bachelor, Resistance fighter.

"So, where have you been?"

"The Francs Tireurs Populaires. They just disarmed us. Feels strange not to have a gun. . . ."

And they spent their evenings with Edmonds and Marcels and Renés, fresh from the Resistance or just liberated from the false ceilings in the Passage des Panoramas where some of these returning ghosts had been in hiding. Élie, for instance, a dealer in fake furs from the rue Bergère, who had spent so long listening for sounds that he now suffered from unremitting earache.

There were also others, all the others, barroom pals, Six Day Race acquaintances, who had disappeared for good. Louis and Gabriel's rival tried to remember their names. But it is difficult to keep an accurate tally of the dead.

They talked sports. They talked journalism.

Dekaerkove's viewpoint was simple: postwar eras were a golden opportunity for sports reporting.

"As soon as peace is signed people get bored. Mark my words, Louis, readers nowadays demand more. They've become addicted to thrilling competition, incredible upsets: Stalingrad, Monte Cassino, El Alamein. Some piddling little sprint at the end of the Paris–Vimoutiers race won't satisfy them anymore."

Louis nodded agreement. "You're right. We're going to have to come up with something new. I see sports reporting as the essential complement of communism. While waiting for the big night, men are going to need a host of happenings to keep their mornings busy."

The two friends called for paper napkins.

"If you wish to have dinner, messieurs, please move to the restaurant."

"Tonight my friend and I are dining on napkins alone, aren't we, Louis?"

And they scribbled out their plans between refills, the same old plans except that the names had changed, the Tour de la Libération des Peuples (formerly the Tour de l'Empire), the Trophée de l'Emancipation (a Paris–Tamanrasset–Timbuktu–Dakar auto rally, formerly the René Caillé Cup).

"Closing time, messieurs."

In the Metro they embraced after having their tickets punched. See you tomorrow, Longchamp, nine o'clock as usual? Dekaerkove went off to the Porte d'Italie (change at République station), my father to Levallois (via Havre-Caumartin). Like all truly jealous people, Gabriel has checked the maps and reconstructed itineraries.

Which of the two first hit on the idea, the very bad idea, of Asia?

## VI

"Well now, one of these days we shall have to think about dying. How do you feel about it, Gabriel?"

"Are you scared?"

"Yes."

Orsenna habits had changed since the end of the war. For instance, our real world lunches were no longer a movable feast. La Coupole had been settled upon once and for all because of the big black in a red fez who brewed coffee in a transparent globe Louis swore was a crystal ball. "I get the strangest feeling when I look at him, Gabriel. I'm sure that one of these days he's going to tell us the future, and at the same time he reminds me of our imperial past, remember?"

Another innovation: father and son no longer spoke exclusively of women. We kept a place for them, though. One by one, dark or fair, they came back to sit at our table, the sweethearts from Levallois, the married woman from Alésia, and dark-haired Nathalie during the war, the one who tried her hand at trout farming. . . . There they sat, somewhat shy, each with her own perfume, her way of pushing her hair back from her face, her own style of dress, some who wore nothing but bright colors, others always in shades of autumn. Brushed by these memories as if by wings and hues of butterflies, father and son wore sweet smiles. But the women's monopoly had been challenged. Another character, also feminine, had insinuated herself and was gaining ground with each passing week.

"What do you think of death, Gabriel?

"Living is all very well, Gabriel, but so far we've given very little thought to death.

"Tell me, Gabriel, how are we going to solve this last problem?

"And you can drop that unconcerned look, Gabriel. At your age it's your problem as much as mine. More, perhaps. I have Longchamp to keep me in trim."

Whereupon the Orsennas systematically (the reader will already have noted their love of systems) reviewed peaceful ways of dying, the solace offered by every religion, not to forget secular sources of inspiration—for example, Jean Moulin, Pierre Brossolette, Haut-Brion 1929, Bach's *Passions*—and as might be expected we came up with no real answer. The net yield of these real world lunches:

"Are you still scared?"

"Yes."

"So am I."

After taking leave of Louis on these occasions ("Are you all right?"; "I'm all right"), Gabriel had trouble going to sleep.

He took his red ball out of his pocket and with its help gradually bounced back.

All this bouncing made noise.

His downstairs neighbor might well have been resentful. Particularly as this neighbor—although his was a normal and even an honorable calling (publishing)—had embarked on a bizarre aesthetic campaign to publish only novels lacking plot and characters. In short, lacking bounciness.

But no. This peculiar publisher merely tapped on his ceiling (my floor) with a broom, bristle end up (and not with the handle in the violent manner most men would have chosen). And no sarcastic remark when he met me on the stairs next morning; he merely murmured good day and went off to his singular calling, novels that were non-novels.

Gabriel should have seen it coming: Louis talked more and more often of the Far East, reincarnation, the transmigration of souls; and he had conceived a passion for mushrooms which, he explained, need only rain to quicken them into life, which are born again every autumn, which are an example to us, which prove that Buddhism is inherent in nature (and so on). . . .

Gabriel listened sorrowfully to these ideas (Could my father be approaching senility?) and accompanied Louis on his walks in the Forest of Rambouillet only from a sense of duty, not pleasure, one eye on his watch, a superior smile on his lips (when you have known the Amazon, Belém, Manaus, what are Saint-Arnoult and Rochefort-en-Yvelines?).

As soon as they were out of the car and in the forest undergrowth, Louis bent over and was lost to everything but boletes, chanterelles, and *Lactarius deliciosus*.

His getup was appropriate. Moving from top to bottom: floppy fly fisherman's hat of brown tweed, sleeveless tan vest bulging with countless pockets, stout beige corduroy pants with leather knee patches, shapeless high-top boots, flat-bottomed wicker basket, magnifying glass, three Opinel knives of different sizes, and an illustrated Hachette guide to the mushrooms of Europe.

An intelligent Gabriel would have guessed the end was near and gone off side by side with his father in pursuit of this last will-o'-the-wisp, vegetable Buddhism. After all, was not rubber too a substance that changes form without dying?

But despite the efforts of his red ball, our Gabriel was weary, felt old, unequal to the challenge of packing his bags for yet another paternal escapade. For once he was like all the sons in the world, unworthy sons. He took the lazy way out, believed or pretended to believe that Louis was falling into second childhood. So Gabriel settled down on a bench in some central part of the forest and let Louis run off to play as if he were a child.

"Will you be able to find your way back to me?"

"Of course, Gabriel."

"Enjoy yourself then."

And while Louis devoted himself to his new multicolored friends (to whose number we should add the honey-colored *Armillaria* and *Amanita vaginata*), his son immersed himself in a British book by Elizabeth Goudge, Daphne du Maurier, or Aldous Huxley. Just like an overworked mother who has had enough of her children.

Minutes later, Louis had a surge of joy, his last, his very last. That burst of joy was a white Orsenna boat gliding slowly alongside the quai.

And Gabriel let this white boat pass by without the least effort to hop aboard, without the smallest sign, without a smile, without even waving a handkerchief. Except after, long after, when it was too late.

"Come look, Gabriel, over here!" Louis was shouting, Louis was ecstatic.

His son put down his British novel, but only with reluctance.

Thrusting upward from the moss was a giant *Cortinarius,* rigid, purple, its shaft slightly twisted, its cap a paler lilac, more phallic than the real thing, more turgescent.

Louis was helpless with laughter.

"Look! Look!" He had the hiccups. "Oh, to be young again!"

Gabriel shrugged. Poor Louis, poor old Louis going soft in the head; what a burden our parents' old age can be! Such were the thoughts buzzing just then in Gabriel's head, a swarm of ordinary unworthy thoughts from an ordinary unworthy son; then Gabriel returned to his bench where Daphne du Maurier *(Rebecca)* was waiting, a storyteller rather effective at dispelling swarms.

Later Louis came up to him.

"Please, Gabriel, cover your eyes and count to a hundred."

"Very well, but don't get too far away. We must go home soon."

Without even looking up at his father, Gabriel complied. He began to count out loud. One, two, three . . . he'll like hearing me count . . . eighteen, nineteen, twenty . . . old people don't just have sexual obsessions, they go through phases . . . ninety-nine, one hundred!

When he lowered his hands and opened his eyes, when the little stars that blur the vision after such compression had faded, Gabriel was alone.

The new orphan shouted, hunted, combed the trails, beat the bushes, enlisted the help of forest wardens and innocent hikers. In vain.

Nothing next day either.

On the third day, scoffing comments from police at the Bureau of Missing Persons.

"We don't even have the manpower to find youngsters. So anyone else . . ."

"I don't deny there's a white slave trade, my friend. But do you really believe there's a geriatric trade?"

Merely a letter, two days later, postmarked rue du Louvre:

Thanks for *really* counting to a hundred
I hate goodbyes
It's better this way
Long live *Cortinarius violaceus!*

Thus did my father Louis vanish.

Thus was our partnership dissolved, seventy years of sharing life.

"Calm down," said Ann. "Calm down, I know where Louis is; he's gone to Indochina with his friend Dekaerkove to start a bicycle business. You should have seen the two of them in my office, nervous, shaking all over, almost holding hands, and dressed in cycling gear, can you picture it? Brown knickerbockers and red stockings, both of them, twins, identical twins, they must have been on their way back from Longchamp; can you imagine what my colleagues thought? Come on now, Gabriel, cheer up. Louis isn't the only thing in life. It isn't very flattering for us to have you pulling such a long face. And leave Louis alone. He just wanted to disappear before the wreckage, like Elisabeth. You have to respect these things. Kiss me, Gabriel."

M. Gabriel Orsenna
Tire Expert
~~Clermont~~
~~Auvergne~~
~~Levallois~~
~~Île de la Jatte~~
~~Seine~~
13 avenue Wester Wemys
Cannes-la-Bocca

French stamp, postmarked twelfth *arrondissement*. Three addresses, two of them scratched out. The moving van that brought us to Cannes had barely left when the persistent little rectangle of white paper arrived on March 30, 1954. Gabriel snatched it from the mailman's hands ("Well, well, well, what have we here, Monsieur le Parisien? Still in love at your age?"). Gabriel ran with the letter to a secluded corner of the garden behind the tubs of geraniums, while behind him the whole house reverberated with Ann's orders, the rumble of furniture being dragged over floor tiles, Clara's sighs, the brisk footsteps of Mme. L., our formidable landlady: brisk footsteps are her way of protesting against human inefficiency.

November 1, 1953

Investment bankers are Queen Victorias. More powerful even, Gabriel.

And their premises as discreet as brothels.

Naturally enough: people go to both places to make their fantasies come true.

So I went with my chum Dekaerkove to the address we had been given, not far from the Saint-Honoré market (Italian specialties, fresh vegetables all year round, red-cheeked mangoes . . .).

I was obviously expected. We were barely inside when a doorman approached, bowed, "Good morning, Monsieur Orsenna," in a bank voice, a low murmur, but not obsequious, Gabriel, a voice that immediately let you know it could crush an outsider straying absentmindedly into the club; "would you follow me?" He led us past some very tall, very emaciated young people, as you will be in your next life, Gabriel. These were future movers and shakers of the financial world, who, busy though they were, greeted me with deference. We finally emerged under a glass roof, as spacious as a railway station but obviously without trains or porters, as yellow, calm, and clean as the city of Florence, an enormous winter garden with gray carpeting and clumps of orange trees in the corners.

And there I waited, Gabriel, under one of the little trees, thinking of our future lives, yours and mine.

Not for long.

For soon a door opened and a lady came forward. As she approached, walking and walking (for this yellow waiting room was vast,

Gabriel), I found it hard to believe but I had the feeling this lady was coming toward me. I guessed correctly. Proof that although inexperienced I have an instinct for banking. As soon as she was within communicating range, she smiled at me. About fifty, silk blouse, tweed skirt, dedication from head to toe, total mastery of her nerves even during her period; I would stake my life on it. That's what secretaries are like in High Finance.

After another walk, chatting as we went, for secretaries at this level talk to you, take an interest in you, make you feel welcome (time enough to notice that all the engravings on the walls were English, hunting, sailing, steeplechasing), the double doors ahead were thrown open. And with a creak of old parquet flooring (a noise as restful to the spirit as the crackling of a fireplace), Ann stood up, came around her desk, and sat down in a Return-from-Egypt chair (sphinx heads on the ends of the arms, in case you didn't know, Gabriel!), motioning me to its twin.

"I am so pleased to meet you at last, Monsieur Orsenna. And your friend is . . . Monsieur Dekaerkove? What a wonderful Belgian name! We have excellent relations with Belgium."

We talked a lot about you, Gabriel. She is like me. She does not understand why you chose rubber. Money is so much more flexible, so much stronger, creates the opportunity for so many more bounces.

I'm not making this up, these were her exact words: "Money is a basic commodity; don't ever forget it: money is the most important of all basic commodities. Noah didn't have to take all those bulky animals onto his ark, a letter of credit would have sufficed."

On this last point she may have gone too far. But enthusiasm calls for a little exaggeration. What a sister-in-law you have there, Gabriel! And how right she is! Why didn't you become a financier?

We would surely have remained until nightfall chatting about my son in that wonderful setting. But an incredible mythological sculpture of gilded Dianas, light-footed Mercurys and bow-wielding Cupids* suddenly emitted multiple chimes.

"Good Lord, four o'clock already!" said your lady friend.

And in order not to waste any more of her Queen Victoria time, your father brought up the reason for his visit: business. He spoke quickly. Important people prefer rapid speech, have you noticed?

*Merely a bank clock *(note from Ann)*.

Our plan intrigued her. But she sweetly explained to me that death was not yet marketable. Not that she dismissed the idea, quite the contrary.

"I'll mention it to one of our clients, a tent manufacturer who wants to create canvas villages all around the Mediterranean. Perhaps when he returns from holiday he'll be interested in death. It's a revolutionary idea. Yes, indeed! Offering people a chance to die in Asia, the land of reincarnation. . . . In a few years I'm sure there will be a market. But not yet, Monsieur Orsenna, and keep in mind that the worst failures stem from good ideas launched before their time. No, really, it would be quite impossible for me to commit this bank to your proposal for deathbed vacations."

Believe me, her refusal hurt her more than it did me. She searched for some way to console me. I saw her eyes sweep from the ceiling down to her bare wrist, unadorned by watch or jewelry. And it was Dekaerkove, even more intimidated than I was, who came up with the brilliant idea of bicycles, investing in bicycles.

"Splendid! They say the Vietnamese are crazy about bicycles these days. Why don't you go and find out whether the craze will last? If yes, I'll take out majority shares in Manufrance. With an option on China, of course."

She pressed a button.

The refined secretary returned.

"Geneviève, would you make arrangements for Messieurs Orsenna and Dekaerkove to leave on a fact-finding mission to Indochina?"

"Certainly, madame."

She turned back to me: "That's my role as a banker. Seizing opportunities, laying foundations so that the future—"

At that moment she really had Queen Victoria's look. Just the look. The rest was so golden-haired, so slender. How old is she, Gabriel? Fifty? More? What kind of pact have blondes signed with time to persuade it to spare them? I would dearly love to know. The very thought makes me shiver.

And we kissed on both cheeks, very simply, in that great solemn room where the marriage contract between Napoleon and Josephine had been negotiated. Abruptly, she forgot business and fixed sad eyes on me. "Come now, Monsieur Orsenna, what in heaven's name were you thinking of? Get rid of all this nonsense about death! Try bicycles! There's nothing like them for your health."

I smiled at her. I thanked her for this mission. I kissed her hand. As one should if one is well-mannered, Gabriel, which is not always the case with you, alas. In my next life I'll not be so lax about your upbringing. And I guessed from various signs (I have an instinct—will you grant me that, Gabriel?—a useless instinct at my age), I recognized in her a woman who likes it standing up. Am I correct?

But the impression I got that was most typical of banking came after, immediately after, when the red-leather double doors closed behind me.

The doorman stiffened to attention. Seeing me emerge from the holy of holies, an up-and-coming plastered-down young banker who chanced to be passing at that moment almost stopped short and tried to inject his whole soul into the look he threw me (I-am-lighthearted-but-made-of-strong-stuff-when-necessary-and-in-excellent-health-and-loyal-and-I-did-not-have-exactly-the-father-I-deserved-and-I-graduated-from-the-Hautes-Études-Commerciales-and-how-is-it-that-I-do-not-know-you-I-who-attend-all-the-fashionable-parties-the-Opéra-the-Racing-Club-and-I-am-learning-how-to-read-faces-so-as-not-to-be-caught-out-by-someone-influential-incognito). Whereupon other future hopes of the financial world, alerted by a sixth sense (one of their dear friends and mortal enemies was forging an acquaintance that might ultimately prove fruitful), emerged en masse from their offices (single doors) and, with folders tucked under their arms, walked down the corridor past the spot where I stood. I understood the message they were sending out: We too are capable, don't forget, of performing quiet and efficient services for you.

And thus it was your father took his leave of this all-powerful establishment—causing a stir that was clearly not customary. Shall he confess too that he made three exits in all, turning back each time to ask a question of the doorman? "Oh, yes! I knew there was something else," running the risk of lowering myself somewhat in the doorman's eyes, but oh, the pleasure I got from the looks of envy and awe on the faces of passersby on seeing me leave such a powerful establishment!

Long live banking!

This time I'm really off. Goodbye, Gabriel.

Fathers without sons are writers, Gabriel; here we are barely separated and I have a pen in my hand. By the way, a query about language. Fatherless sons are orphans. But fathers without sons, what do you call them? Just "writers," or is there another word?

Gabriel folded the letter and walked slowly back to his bedroom.

The landlord's voice could be heard in the other wing. A business discussion on the phone, paper, always paper.

"Frankly, I think the Swedes could be more accommodating about payment dates. Twenty thousand tons of raw two-ply wrapping paper is not something to be sneezed at! . . .

"Now hold on there. Korsnas-Marma is coming on just a bit too strong! . . ."

Our landlord spoke only between long silences (doubtless Korsnas-Marma's rejoinders).

"And when can we expect delivery of the crimped? Are the claims they make for it true—sturdy, nonporous, durable gloss?"

Our landlord's voice grew wearier by the minute, his speech more and more technical. Gabriel would have liked to help him in his paper battles, but what aid could he offer? Rubber and paper are such different fields of expertise!

# 17

# *The Cannes Film Festival*

FORMATION OF THE EUROPEAN Coal and Steel Pool, creation of the Théâtre National Populaire, the Korean War, the success of *Casque d'Or* (Jacques Becker). . . . As for Gabriel, he lived between two sisters. Like Freud. In fact he would have loved to discuss the experience with the great Viennese. In this area too Freud was unsurpassed: forty-three years of shared living with the two Misses Bernays—Martha, his wife, and Minna, her sister, whom he brought along sometimes to visit Rome or take the waters at Badgastein and who had to cross the Freuds' bedroom to get to her own. Yes, the man must have many interesting things to say about resemblances, about the echoes that haunt you, about the adoptive family that binds you, about that searing sense that nothing ever cuts so deep or so sharp as incest. Alas, Freud was dead. A shame, a great shame, not least because the Viennese was fond not only of sisters but of mushrooms. The proof? This letter dated 1899. Gabriel came across it while reading during one of his interminable bouts of insomnia:

> We pick mushrooms every day. On the very first day of the rains I shall go to Salzburg, where on my last visit I unearthed some old Egyptian pieces. They bolster my spirits and remind me of distant times and places.

No doubt about it: Egypt apart, this Freud had distinctly Orsenna-ish qualities.

They were there.

During the day they disappeared, consumed by their careers:

money in the case of one of them (Monaco, Geneva, tax havens, property transactions), photography for the other (Saint-Paul-de-Vence from all angles, or the painter Nicholas de Staël against the light on the terrace at Antibes); but they were there for dinner, then for the night, then in the morning. Ann and Clara, providing Gabriel with the thing he had always wanted: a daily life. In other words something natural, unhurried, flowing. Gabriel had no desire for the hunt, the accumulation of hours bagged like trophies one by one, the whiff of gunpowder that comes over the solitary man when he turns off the light, and that stays with him deep into the night.

I've won, sang gullible Gabriel, I've won! and he forced himself to substitute a few grave looks for his perpetual smile (be on your guard; complacency drives women away), and he refrained from applauding each passing minute (excessive clapping is said to blotch the hands; look at music lovers).

These tricks fooled no one, were mildly irritating to Clara ("For heaven's sake relax, Gabriel"), and aroused pity in Ann ("Hush, Clara, I think he's fine considering all we've put him through").

The person who took the most interest in me was our landlady. On afternoons when he was alone in the garden in summer or the library in winter Gabriel would nap. And just as he was drifting into dream, it seemed to him that a great silence fell on the Wester Wemys house. Indeed it had. Mme. L.'s brisk footsteps had ceased; concealed by a shutter or a windowshade, she was watching. Not for anything in the world, not even the most pressing of household duties, would she have missed this sight—a little man, elderly, happy.

"You haven't asked for news of Louis. Aren't you curious?" Ann would ask during Sunday lunch.

"Of course I am, but I didn't want to be tiresome. How is Louis?"

"Well, one thing's certain: your father is no businessman. You don't mind my saying that, do you, Gabriel? I thought bicycles would sell themselves in Asia. Anyway, apart from that, all is well. Or so it seems."

Now don't get the idea that we were at a loss for a subject of conversation, that we spent our time gazing mutely at each other under the peerless Riviera sun. Not at all. We hadn't lost our tongue;

we often (for example) discussed the international situation, and we spoke a great deal of you—of you, our son, so late in coming.

"Is there still hope at our age?" asked Ann, asked Clara.

Gabriel reassured them as best he could, spent his leisure time consulting books on medical matters—or rather, on physiological rarities—and thus learned that a certain Ruth Kistler of Portland (Oregon) had been delivered at fifty-eight of a daughter, Susan.

"Is it really true, Gabriel, do you swear it?"

Gabriel showed them the book. The two sisters pored over it and launched into further endless questioning. "Would a baby conceived standing up be normal?" "And how would a child of mine turn out? Using the flash so much could cause a birth defect."

All this to impress one thing on you: you are not one of those children brought into the world by accident. Most likely there has never been a son more ardently hoped for than you. Most likely. Until they invent a machine for measuring hope, Gabriel prefers not to make extravagant claims.

Every now and then, when this sense of a miracle at work, of blue summer sky, when this sense of the frailty of all things became overwhelming and too much to bear, Gabriel assumed a brisk and casual air and suggested, What about a trip?

Not a chance.

Unvarying response from one or the other of the two sisters: "My dear Gabriel, short men like you are always inviting tall women like us to go to the beach with them. As if we were less intimidating on the beach! But my poor Gabriel, just look up Cannes-la-Bocca in an atlas. We're already on the beach! No point in leaving, we're already there!"

Proof (if proof were needed) that they had not been tamed, that they had shed none of their regal ways.

You know Cannes, my son, so there is little need for Gabriel to refresh your memory: a large retirement home complete with everything retired people might ever need—cardiologists, poodle groomers, shoe menders skilled at stretching painfully tight shoes, lying headwaiters who swear on their mother's bones that the Madeira sauce is not at all rich, travel agencies under the winter sun. . . . A cream-colored town, rather dull, too quiet, with no real ships in port.

But in springtime everything changes. The crew of the good ship *Hollywood* disembarks on the Croisette, takes over the rue d'Antibes, and spreads all the way to Suquet's: low-cut dresses, cigars, photographers, convertibles, foreign languages.

And the retired people of Cannes toss and turn in their beds at night at the thought of all those young faces, those roars of laughter. With something like sadness rising inside them they murmur, Is a festival really necessary in a retirement home?

So.

Avenue Wester Wemys was no exception. Every year our landlord the papermaker rented out his wing. Not for the money, he explained, but because old houses (old houses belonging to old people) need to be rejuvenated. And what better to rejuvenate an old house than a movie crew? Be nice to them, Gabriel, let them have a bit of the garden while the festival is on; it won't be for long. . . .

So for the fortnight, until the prizes were handed out, Gabriel, Ann, and Clara stayed indoors. Mme. L. discreetly dropped off provisions. And through our shutters, from dawn till dusk, we watched the tenants, different ones every year. The Italians of *Miracle in Milan* were nothing like their successors, the fake Mexicans of *Viva Zapata!* And each year the spectacle was different; each new tenant had his own way of rejuvenating the old house.

Gabriel is no tattletale. He will name no names, describe none of the scenes he witnessed from his side of the courtyard. But in the interests of truth and for the sake of the director's biography he will merely say that the party given by Alf Sjöberg was wild, very wild. Against a Gobelin tapestry in the wee hours of the night, it's extraordinary what a threesome can get up to in celebration of winning the Palme d'Or. Two years later we had Gisèle Pascal, apparently rather involved with Gary Cooper—ask her what made her blush so furiously that night. The film crew of *The Wages of Fear,* how shall I put it, were not exactly overdressed as they pursued Anne Baxter round and round a tub of nasturtiums. Like me, Ann and Clara also spied. I sensed them quivering and pawing the ground beside me. They longed to change wings, would have loved to wander into the garden and get invited to join the party. Luckily the festival lasted less than two weeks and the serious merrymaking didn't begin till the end!

But that's it, Gabriel will say no more. The silver screen must not be tarnished.

The papermaker (Gabriel's increasingly dear friend) would telephone from Paris: "Whatever you do, don't clean up."

And the moment his business permitted, he came down to Cannes and knocked on my door.

"How did it go? Want to make a tour of the premises?"

Together, Gabriel and the papermaker would stroll through the disordered rooms, sniff the air, comment in whispers, "Over there, that mirror by the bidet; what could those movie people have been up to?"

The papermaker was jubilant. "So you too like wild parties? Granted my house is a bit battered, but look how rejuvenated it is! Don't you find it rejuvenated, Gabriel?"

# 18

# *The Bicycles of Ho Chi Minh*

Bicycles from the Peugeot and Saint-Étienne factories were our taxis of the Marne.

—General Giap

This time Ann did not wait for Sunday. She returned from Monaco in midafternoon and called out while she was still outside in the street. "Louis has disappeared, really disappeared. Probably the Communists. . . ."

Clara had stayed at home with me. She lay flat on the low stone wall, busily photographing some detail of Creation (an insect? an acacia bud?). She did not rise, went on caressing her lens, every so often pressing the silver button, and said, "This means you are leaving, doesn't it, Gabriel? I understand. But it's a pity. I was beginning to get used to real life. The houses here in Cannes-la-Bocca abhor a vacuum, have you noticed? Pleasant journey, Gabriel."

## I

### Saigon

Tropical dinners had not changed: the whiteness of table linen, of evening gowns, dinner jackets, flowers and garden furniture. Foie gras from France, lettuce from France, duck from China, cheeses from France, strawberry charlotte as if you were in France (have you noticed we have excellent strawberries here?). And conversation of that very special overseas blend: global ideas and local gossip, communism and jock itch, decline of the West and amoebic dysentery. . . . The moment he arrived, the planters took Gabriel under their wing.

"You're one of us, old fellow."

"Rubber is one big happy family, isn't it?"

"Would you like to visit the Terres Rouges?"

"Do you remember our old quarrel with Brazil?"

"A tire expert at long last, a genuine one!"

"A welcome change from beardless diplomats!"

He was invited everywhere.

"Is this really your first visit to Saigon, even though you spent your whole life in rubber?"

The ladies couldn't get over it. They clucked their astonishment, called their friends over.

"Can you believe it's his first time!"

Who wouldn't blush at such remarks? Gabriel smiled awkwardly. Forgotten anxieties surged up to gnaw at him: the pimply skin and moist palms of adolescence.

Besides, Saigon recalled childhood days. A perpetual holiday, an endless August, a summer that goes on forever. When would they be closing the shutters? Winter never came, and the monsoon was no substitute for autumn. In every vacation resort in the world there are always people determined to stick it out to the bitter end of September, people who believe something might still happen, people who live on memories of the good old days: in a word, colonials.

Gabriel, little Gabriel, was the darling of Saigon in January of the year 1954. This is no boast. He is simply stating the facts: they fought over him. A newcomer is even better than an up-to-date newspaper. His schedule is arranged for him.

"So, are you coming over tomorrow night?"

"I'm sorry, but he's already taken!"

"You're going to need an appointment book."

Gabriel noted his engagements, rather haphazardly, on pieces of paper they gave him, seating plans and the like. It always strikes me as a little absurd to pull out appointment books unless one is wearing a dark business suit.

By the end of his first evening he knew everyone. Guest lists never varied. Always the same ones, a sort of closed group, like vacationers. The same. Only the hostesses changed places. One day they would be on his left, the next on his right. In the colonies you learn to appreciate the slightest novelty.

"I hope you looked at me closely last evening. Because tonight you're on my left and that's my bad side."

Tropical life had three other major features:

1. One spoke loudly, because of the fans and also because when native servants cannot understand what you're saying to them, it helps to raise one's voice.

2. The Parisian wit of Guitry and Achard was highly prized. Always that nostalgia for the dear old Third Republic (See, here in Saigon we can appreciate wit, too!).

3. Bitterness. "So how's France, not feeling guilty about leaving us in the lurch, I trust? Did you enjoy yourself this evening? Good! We still know how to be hospitable here: we don't bear grudges."

Hostesses sighed as they showed me the sturdy wire mesh covering their windows. "I'm afraid that's how things are, Monsieur Orsenna, every now and then one of these charming Vietnamese lobs a grenade in from the street."

Late at night, the hour for cigars, the planters took me by the arm and steered me into a quiet corner, in other words somewhere free of women and away from their subordinates.

"Tell us the truth, you're seeing all this with fresh eyes. How do you see the situation?"

"Edmond's right. We have to face the facts. Is it time for us to sell out, do you think?"

I did my best to answer. The planters nodded.

"In your view, my friend, why are the Communists so interested in Indochina?"

"Edmond's right, that's the crux of the matter. Might it be because they need tires? An enormous number of tires to help them overrun the free world? That's why we should make a stand right here. We are the free world's last line of defense."

The planters warmed to their subject.

It was at this point, in the midst of these bluish clouds, Havana smoke, and geostrategy, that Gabriel inserted his question, a humble question, a child's question, very politely, apologizing to the gentlemen for taking their time.

"You haven't seen my father, by any chance?"

"Your father, my dear fellow? When do you mean exactly?"

"A month or two ago."

They frowned, they thought hard, they wondered just what a tire expert's father might look like. Would he be the sort of fellow that planters such as they would want to spend time with?

"No, old boy, I've racked my brains but he doesn't ring a bell. Now, about tomorrow night: will we be seeing you at the Franchinis'?"

Saigon has its own tides, its own high and low water.

Every day at the two cocktail hours (noon and sundown), high-ranking officials, merchants, financiers, planters, plus a bevy of women of all types, came down from the cathedral area or drifted up from the port to converge on rue Catinat where the Hotel Continental sits enthroned, with its terrace and its French smells, anisette and sweet vermouth.

This twice-daily gathering was a time-saver. One glance at the tables sufficed to tell you who was in Saigon. And, in consequence, that M. Louis Orsenna was not honoring the capital of Cochin China with his presence.

It was on that terrace that Gabriel met an assistant police commissioner, a bald man with bushy coal-black eyebrows. He studied his glass with something like gloom.

"Look at the color of this stuff I'm drinking. Like a rice paddy. Pernod is exactly the same color as rice paddies, the mud of a rice paddy. . . . We have a file on your father, of course, as we do on everyone. At least on every white man. No white man can remain a secret in the colonies. Incidentally, that's one of the problems of my so-called Secret Service. Anyway, drop round to my office. You have connections in the upper echelons of banking, I believe? Very useful."

Overwhelmed.

A government official.

A French government official.

A conscientious French government official.

A conscientious French government official in the tropics.

No living being is more overwhelmed by the spectacle of daily life than a conscientious government official in the tropics.

From his vantage point, from his poop deck topped with the blue, white, and red flag, this representative of the Republic showed Gabriel the boulevard Bonnard.

"It teems every hour of every day, it never lets up. How can one possibly maintain files on such a faceless mass? Can you think of a way? No addresses, no numbers on the houses, no license plates on their four-horsepower Renaults, no distinguishing features. . . . These people don't have moles, hardly any of them ever go bald. . . . No chance of sexual blackmail, no regular habits, no dominoes with their pals after work, no walking the dog, no fishing off the railway bridge on Saturdays. . . . How can one possibly run an intelligence service among Asiatics?"

The conscientious French government official spoke sadly, almost tenderly.

"Why don't we sit down. But I warn you in advance, it's just as hot sitting as standing."

It was on this occasion that Gabriel first learned the true color of the Republic. Not blue, white, and red but dark green, the gloomy color of metal desks and regulation chairs, fake leather for the backs and behinds of visitors, fake stainless steel for their arms.

The fan was not working. Or else there was a power failure. The assistant commissioner's shirt clung damply to his skin in large patches, moist transparent zones. You could see the black hair through them.

"I'm wearing nylon. A mistake. Cotton is best. Take my word for it. Cotton and linen."

He stared at his desktop, then at his file-stuffed storage bins. René Coty, his hand resting on a big leatherbound book, looked down at us.

"Well, now, your father."

Without getting up he stretched out an arm, opened a drawer, pulled out a long folder, and resumed his defeated posture behind his glass-covered blotter.

"As I was telling you yesterday, we have files on all the whites, which is of little use to my operations here. All I have on the chinks are useless photos, either fake or just alike, much too much alike, looking like any old chinks. . . . Anyway. Arrival of Louis Orsenna December 1, 1950, aboard the *Pasteur*. Stayed at the Continental like everyone else, number seventeen, a very noisy room if I remember correctly. Does your father sleep well? Good! Two months later he opened a bicycle business financed by someone in the upper echelons of banking. Aha, so both Orsennas have banking connections, splendid, splendid. Associate: Élie Dekaerkove, alias Izoard, former organizer of the Tour de France. Shared a cabin on the ship. You know Dekaerkove? Good, that'll save us some time. I ordered surveillance, not on your father but on that character Dekaerkove, for a good long time. Using utmost precaution. He's a former reporter. In fact he's still official representative of *L'Équipe* in Indochina. Which doesn't exactly snow him under with work. Since the beginning of the war nothing has happened here, I mean in the way of sports: no bike races, no marathons. But Dekaerkove was chomping at the bit. He tried to get *L'Équipe* to broaden its conception of athletic activity. In his view war is a sport, the most terrible but the most fascinating of sports. Why not announce the results in *L'Équipe*? he wanted to know. This was one of his two obsessions; he expounded on them endlessly after he'd downed a few Suze apéritifs."

"Why Suze?"

"You obviously know nothing about cycling. Suze equals tonic equals mountains equals Tour de France. Suze is the choice of climbers, or so they claim. One Suze, straight up!"

"That's very funny."

"Yes."

He leaned across the desk, his tone low and confiding but with an occasional inflection of excitement. Lacking hard intelligence data, Assistant Commissioner Calet was now about to try his hand at biography.

"There's more. Or rather, there may be more. Sometimes, after a number of Suzes, our chum claimed that the Vietminh would win this war with bicycles. 'Shut up,' your father said, 'for God's sake shut up.' But Dekaerkove wouldn't stop. This was his second obsession. In his view the yellow race understood the advantages of the bicycle much better than the white man. They knew each bicycle could carry four hundred pounds of arms and move under cover of the trees without attracting attention. . . . And perhaps Dekaerkove was right. I mentioned it to our military geniuses. They roared with laughter. You know how they are, good-natured, manly; they slapped me on the back: 'Come on, François, old boy, intelligence has gone to your head. . . .' But if I could go all the way with this, I would draw up a list of all our bicycle imports (Manufrance, Peugeot) and then make a tally of all the bikes visibly in circulation in Indochina. Subtract the two, and that number is how many have ended up in rebel hands. Then I'd arrest the person known as Izoard for flagrant collaboration with the enemy. Incidentally, he wasn't motivated by politics. No. Just the greater glory of the bicycle. He would drink Suze and go on and on about the Winter Velodrome. He longed to wipe out the stain of the Winter Velodrome. Typical Suze thinking. . . . Mind you, I'm accusing no one. I'm suggesting possibilities, that's all. You need proof before you can bring charges. So you need staff. No staff, no investigation. No investigation, no proof."

"And my father?"

"Louis Orsenna is a different matter. And more complex. A Communist, is he not, or close cousin? But according to my sources he is also very interested in sects, and sects are our allies against the Vietminh, and Saigon is the world capital of sects. A veritable Manufrance catalogue of beliefs

"Manufrance again?"

"Always. Manufrance is our Noah's ark. Don't make me lose the thread. Where was I? Oh, yes, sects. We have hundreds of them. For every possible taste. Privateers, pirates, the underworld, Chinese, Annamite, some concentrated in the Mekong Delta, like the Hoa-Hao, others in the Plain of Reeds, like the Binh-Xuyen. Laymen, nationalists, Buddhists, Confucians. I'd need a whole storage bin just for the names of the sects. By the way, when you go back to France, would you do me a favor?"

"Gladly."

"Ask anyone, Colonial Ministry, Collège de France, School of Mines, to send me a scientist, the patient, dogged kind, you know what I mean, someone who's disenchanted with Trotskyism, to help me make head or tails of this morass of cults. Your father chose the craziest of them all: the Cao Dai. They combine everything. For them Buddha, Mohammed, Jesus, and Confucius are all prophets with Cao Dai as the supreme being. They massacred us in the summer of 'forty-five. Since then, we managed to enlist them on our side. Now they massacre the Reds. When your father discovered the Cao Dai sect, he was in raptures. He and Izoard kicked up their heels at the Continental to celebrate. I had a man at the next table. He took everything down. Thanks to the Suze they spoke in loud voices, no problem recording them. I have it all here. Want to take a look? After all, he's your father, and you do come with a recommendation from the upper echelons of banking—"

"I'd rather not."

"I understand. Friendships between old people are depressing. They were both raving about their obsessions; for one it was bicycles, for the other it was death-which-is-not-so-terrible. One monologue after another. They didn't listen to each other. 'Alexander's horses, Foch's taxis, Mao's march, Patton's tanks are all in the past. Now the hour of the bicycle is at hand,' declared our man Izoard. 'Exactly!' said your father. 'In Catholicism you have to wait around until the end of the world before you can be born again. At least in Buddhism there's hope for fairly prompt reincarnation.' 'Exactly!' said his pal. 'On a bicycle, balance comes from the movement.' 'Exactly what I was thinking! The Great Vehicle of faith. . . .' Et cetera. Exactly, exactly, exactly! If you don't mind my saying so, it's pathetic. Pathetic. They had to carry your father back to Room Seventeen. Old people are like oysters: no interaction, every man for himself."

"I believe I have noticed the same tendency in the young," Gabriel ventured timidly.

"Quite right. They're in training for later on."

The assistant commissioner stopped talking. The terrace curtains had rustled. For the first time since early morning the air seemed to stir and come alive again, becoming something more than invisible, motionless humidity.

"The good thing about nylon," said the commissioner, "is that it dries fast."

He showed me his shirt. As yellow-gray as ever, but the black hairs had disappeared.

"I'm going to have to cut this short. We have a security check every evening at five. But think this one over: there are not very many of us white men, and when we die we die for keeps. The yellow races breed like rabbits, and on top of that they are reincarnated. Don't you find that a little bit—what's the word—unfair? Disturbing? As for your father and his pal Dekaerkove, let me sum up. They shut up shop a month ago and left for the north. I don't know where they were headed. With my skeleton staff, how could I? I can't keep an ear in every glass of Suze. But from what I know of Izoard, I'd say Hanoi. Governor Giao loves cycling; he's built a velodrome and takes part himself in team competitions. Fixed, of course. He always wins. Dekaerkove loves that. It must remind him of the Winter Velodrome. He duly cables the results to the rue du Faubourg-Montmartre. But *L'Équipe* never prints them. Never."

The assistant commissioner winced. It was as if the rue du Faubourg-Montmartre had stuck in his throat like a bone, the bone of homesickness.

"Are you all right?" asked Gabriel. "Is there anything I can do?"

"Goodbye, Monsieur Orsenna Junior. Goodbye. . . ."

And he turned back to his big green storage bins, the color of the French Republic.

## II

### Tay-Ninh

The road to the north was lined with bamboo churches. Bamboo porches, bamboo transepts, even bamboo attempts at Gothic and Romanesque features, resulting in embryos of spires, rose windows still lacking stained glass, altars open to the sky with blue and white statues of Mary surrounded by yellow flowers planted in yogurt containers and candles stuck in bottles bearing the label of the local brewery. In front of every Virgin a crowd stood singing psalms. The commissioner was right. The road to the north was clearly the one Louis would take. A little Catholic, perhaps, but deeply confident in the Beyond, which is the main thing both for a road and for a terrified father. Vietnam was the ideal place to die. Like Switzerland for making money or Italy for falling in love.

The jam-packed bus, overflowing not only with human beings but with livestock, moved bumpily from rut to pothole. And Gabriel was receiving an education, thanks to the learned gentleman who seated himself on Gabriel's left knee just as the bus was leaving.

"Permit me to introduce myself, Le Than Binh, teacher and Cao Dai disciple. Please forgive me, there was nowhere else to sit. I never eat the day before a journey; I hope I am not too heavy for you. Do you know Cao Dai?"

"No," answered Gabriel, so compressed and constricted he didn't think he'd be able to open his mouth. (Luckily the Vietnamese were small, like him. How horrible if the Asiatic masses were made up of giants, of Swedes, of Finns!)

M. Le Thanh Binh, the lodger on his left knee, began the lesson.

Between 1914 and 1918 all intelligent Spirits focused on Indochina. Europe was hacking itself to pieces and Spirits, being of nervous disposition, do not like the sound of guns. . . . The Americas North and South had killed off their Indians, and the Spirits (ever mindful of human rights) cannot forgive them. China and Russia were preparing their revolutions, and the Spirits are conservative. Japan had plunged into modernization, which nauseates the Spirits. As for Africa, well, Africa has Spirits of its own, but civilized Spirits hold them in very low esteem.

In short, all the Spirits that amounted to anything took up residence in Indochina; you had only to walk past a table for it to start turning. The most sociable Spirits were Ly Thai Bach, the eighth-century Taoist poet; Quan An, the Buddhist goddess; Joan of Arc, Camille Flammarion, and Victor Hugo.

Instead of contenting himself with this favorable state of affairs, the district commissioner for Phu Quoc Island (Gulf of Siam), Ngo Van Chieu, decided to strive for a spiritual concentrate: he wanted to attain the Absolute Spirit. He surrounded himself with young mediums whose souls, fanned by fasting, relayed ever clearer echoes of the divine. And suddenly, in 1919, with the signing of the Armistice, the Absolute Spirit made his appearance: Cao Dai, the Supreme Palace.

Ngo Van Chieu left his island and brought the good news to Saigon and its legions of table-turners.

"The spirits communicating with you," he told them, "your table companions, are the prophets of Cao Dai."

But Ngo Van Chieu was unable to hold on to the Supreme Palace. He was divested of divinity and sent packing by a certain Le Van Trung.

"Would you mind speaking a little more slowly, monsieur?" asked Gabriel. "All these names are getting me confused."

"Of course."

And my teacher rattled on without the slightest break in speed.

Well then, Le Van Trung, the colonial administrator who had masterminded the coup, took the title of supreme pontiff. It was he who built the holy city of Tay-Ninh, where we are heading, and its towering 353-foot-high cathedral where all the prophets are worshiped. You will even see your own Victor Hugo there in his academician's robes.

From this point, it must be confessed, Gabriel's attention wandered, and he retained only the essential facts: it was Cao Dai who created the five branches of the Great Way—Confucianism, the cult of Spirits, Christianity, Taoism, and Buddhism. One made contact with Cao Dai and his prophets through a spouted basket which was upside down and covered with paper. A rod ending in a phoenix head went through the basket. When held by mediums, this rod transcribed messages from the Beyond.

My teacher's voice became very gentle, almost languid, suddenly free of the choppiness of the Vietnamese accent.

"One day, God willing, you will be converted. Then you will be given flowers, alcohol, and tea, for flowers symbolize human semen, alcohol is the breath of life, tea is the image of the spirit, and the sperm must become tea by passing through alcohol. . . ."

Whereupon Gabriel fell well and truly asleep, his last waking thought being the realization that religions, like rubber, grow best in the tropics. Catholicism is still a little bit too temperate.

The bus came to a halt in a square not far from a towering (353-foot?) building. A crowd gathered around us, a threatening crowd, made up of Vietnamese who (to a non-Vietnamese) looked like all the other Vietnamese, except they were clad in white albs or deep-blue capes embroidered with dragons, birds, and tortoises. A dozen Foreign Legionnaires held them at bay. A sergeant pointed north: Keep moving, don't stop.

"What's going on?" asked the white passenger sitting beside the driver, the only one on the bus with a seat to himself, with nobody on his knees.

"The Cao Dai are furious. Someone insulted one of their prophets a few days ago. They found graffiti in their cathedral, and now no one knows what's going to happen. Come on, get out of here, this is no place to hang around."

I'm on the right track, said Gabriel to himself as the bus departed, coughing painfully. Louis has been on this road. Louis, Dekaerkove, and maybe Suze.

Louis had always hated Victor Hugo. Undoubtedly the jealousy of a bookseller toward a writer. "How is it that Victor Hugo, less handsome than me, screwed so much more?"*

Gabriel is of course condensing. Condensing and simplifying. But he suspects that the reason for this fierce, childish hatred of Hugo is to be found somewhere under the skirts of Léonie Biard d'Aunet, of Alice Ozy, of Sylvanie Plessy, of Joséphine Faville, of Mme. Roger des Genettes, of Hélène Gaussin, of Louise Colet, of Laure Guimont, et al. I believe Louis knew the list of Victor Hugo's mistresses by heart and ran through it every now and then in order to whip himself into a fury.

The teacher had disappeared, extracted from the compact mass of passengers by who knows what Cao Dai miracle.

And Gabriel went back to sleep. With the shadow of a smile on his lips, a strained smile, a loser's smile (Louis is having a good time; Louis did not choose me as his last traveling companion), but still a smile. All is well. With the help of Suze and Dekaerkove, my father is managing to stay young.

*Is such vulgarity really necessary? *(note from Clara)*.

## III

### HUÉ

The Friends of Old Hué (an association authorized by the law of 1901) must forgive Gabriel, but when he reached the city his first objective was the velodrome. If you wanted to see the Governor in action your best chance was around sunset on Saturdays.

It was a small track, poorly lit by eight overhead lamps, and banked dangerously high at the turns. The crowd applauded constantly, although nothing in particular was going on. A multicolored pack rode around and around without ever picking up the pace. A rider in a red silk jersey was having trouble keeping up. The Governor, no doubt. He wore an enormous No. 1 on his back.

Gabriel pushed through to the press section, a small almost luxurious enclosure, chairs with backs, a small lamp for every two seats.

A policeman grunted, "What paper are you with?"

"*France-Soir,*" Gabriel replied, instinctively adding, "rue Réaumur."

The policeman was impressed, his eyes opening wide as he stammered, "This way, please, monsieur, follow me"—he evicted two natives with ballpoint pens—"you'll be right on top of the finish line here." He used his cap to dust off the concrete ledge that served as a writing desk, checked the lamps, wished him a splendid evening. "And if you don't mind, monsieur, give him a good write-up; the Governor loves good write-ups."

By now the Governor had outstripped the pack but was flagging badly. When he went past us we heard him puffing like a harpooned whale. His teammate called out, "Governor, Governor, let me spell you for the lead." But the Governor ignored him and forged ahead. In the stands across the track a group of Legionnaires could hardly sit still. Howling with laughter, they tossed their white kepis into the air: Ha, ha, ha! when you pound the bedsprings all night long it's hard to pound the pedals. The Governor seemed at the end of his tether. The other riders tried to hang back, not always successfully, for racing bikes have no brakes. To slow down they rode up the banked slopes of the track or actually grabbed the handrail.

"Yet I warned him to shorten these races. . . . May I introduce myself: Jean-Christian Bérard, president of the Cycling Club."

Gabriel turned. The voice was a Frenchman's. Or rather an official's, for sports officials are of the same race whatever their country of origin: blazer and badge, flannel trousers, Rolex watch, brilliantined hair parted in the middle, not a hint of perspiration despite the heat.

"Delighted."

"Excuse me, are you a special correspondent or a new permanent representative?"

The bell rang. Last lap. A sluggish sprint stirred the pack into a semblance of activity. The Governor threw his arms triumphantly skyward. The increase in applause was almost imperceptible. The Legionnaires were on their feet, hurling beer bottles onto the track and whistling the way real men whistle, half their fingers stuffed in their mouth.

"Worth a glowing write-up, wouldn't you say?" said the official.

"Indeed."

"In my opinion, the French sporting press is wrong to ignore Governor Giao. After all, Giao the racing cyclist is worth Chaban-Delmas the rugby player or Chaban-Delmas the mixed doubles player any day of the week."

The Governor was cycling back in our direction. Dismounting. They wrapped him in a dark purple robe with GOVERNOR GIAO on the back in glittering letters, boxing style. The official had risen: Bravo, Governor, yet another triumph!

"Off you go, Jean-Christian, they're all waiting for you!"

"Yes, please excuse me, I must go. Please do the right thing by Governor Giao. I'm not a politician, but *L'Équipe* let him down badly, and we need to keep the Governor happy. France doesn't have too many allies in this country."

The escutcheoned blazer ran down the steps. "I'm coming, I'll be right there!"

The Governor and his teammate climbed the podium.

"To the winner of the Francis Garnier memorial race of twenty-five laps I present the cup donated by the Bien Hoa Industrial and Logging Corporation."

And over the loudspeakers came first crackling and the scraping of the needle and then the strains of *La Marseillaise.*

Next day, with the sun high in the sky, Gabriel was aroused from slumber by the sound of someone softly scratching at his door. The Indochinese way of knocking.

"Monsieur, excuse me, the manager, Monsieur Amaury, begs pardon for disturbing you, but Monsieur Jean-Christian Bérard is waiting for you in the breakfast room."

The official wore sportsman's gear: white ducks, white shirt, an autumnal scarf at his throat.

"Forgive me for interrupting your ablutions, but I wanted to draw your attention to something. I am here on behalf of the French community of Hué. Governor Giao is a good-natured man, but there are limits to his patience. Look, this is the only result *L'Équipe* has ever published. In six years:

" 'April 3, 1952. In Hué (Annam) yesterday, at the Governor of Annam's Velodrome, the Governor of Annam was awarded the Governor of Annam's Cup, a twenty-five-lap pursuit race.' "

"A bit skimpy, I have to admit."

"So we're counting on you."

"I'll do my best. But we'll have to wait until Monday; that's when the results get a double-page spread."

"The Governor is perfectly willing to wait till Monday. But proper coverage is essential. What a welcome we gave *L'Équipe*'s correspondent when he arrived! A hero's welcome. For nothing. For those three lines. We're beginning to wonder if he didn't muddy relations between France and the Governor on purpose. That would explain everything. A Moscow hireling. Whose side is *L'Équipe* on, would you say? Believe me, when he came back through here a few days ago he didn't stay long. Nor did his shady accomplice, the one so interested in tombs. *Personae non gratae!* Escorted to the station, chop-chop! Destination Hanoi." The official was getting excited; red blotches had appeared on his fair skin. "Sport is a family, and that family is the only thing still standing up to communism. If Baron Coubertin were still alive he would have kept Indochina for us. Have a good day. And again, I apologize for the intrusion."

He strode off, muttering, "Damned shame, it's a damned shame." He threw his racket to the ground. It bounced back. Like a ball.

Gabriel was left alone in the breakfast room. Waiters waited for customers behind a screen of rubber plants. He saw the movement of their white tunics through the leaves, the big glossy leaves. He heard their whispers and their stifled laughter, like that of schoolchildren lining up after the bell. Through the French windows came garden noises: rakes on gravel, water sprinklers, the dry click of pruning shears.

The Grand Hotel must have bought its cups from the Wagon-Lits: same heaviness, same round contour, same blue lettering. Except that HUÉ had replaced COOK. The last swallows at the bottom of a cup of café au lait are like drinking syrup. Our hero added more milk, never a good idea because morning milk has a strong smell, and besides that, stirring it in revives the taste of sugar and, worse, often creates long shreds of skin that turn your stomach for the rest of the day.

Gabriel went to the hotel reception desk.

"Could you tell me the times of trains for Hanoi?"

Since Louis wasn't in Hué, he might as well take the shortest route to him.

The girl behind the desk looked horrified. "One moment, monsieur, one moment, please, I'll get Monsieur Amaury." The door (MANAGER—PRIVATE) opened and M. Amaury stood before me, a congenial-looking character (my height and just as roly-poly), wringing his hands and batting his lashes as if about to weep.

"What's this I hear? Forgive me for interfering, but were you planning to leave us without seeing Old Hué? Of course it's none of my business, you have your reasons, but all the same, Old Hué—"

"What's so special about Old Hué?"

"Why, the purple Forbidden City, the Gate of Resplendent Beauty, the Golden Pond, not to mention the Citadel, the Imperial Palace, and all the tombs, the finest tombs in the world."

No son of Louis could resist this last argument.

"Right, I'll see the tombs."

"Splendid! Please forgive my persistence, but you will not regret it. Since the war nobody takes the time to visit Old Hué any more, much less the tombs. They are wrong. The tombs are very safe. I myself on Sunday afternoons often—"

"Fine. Go ahead and make the arrangements. But I must be back for the train."

"At once." He clapped his hands.

From a group of a half-dozen Vietnamese seated near the door leafing through back copies of *Paris-Match,* a very young man* got up.

M. Amaury, manager of the Grand Hotel, beamed approval.

"What a splendid idea! You must take a guide. Asia is complex. Particularly tombs. It would be a pity to visit them and understand nothing. This is Nguyen.† You can have complete confidence in him. Historical accuracy guaranteed. I have had world-famous experts here, even university professors. No one has ever caught him in the slightest error. In fact, all my guides belong to the Friends of Old Hué . . ."

Gabriel was unable to get away. M. Amaury had come out from behind the counter and seized my arm.

". . . and they selected my hotel as headquarters of their association, a world-renowned association which is very legally constituted. Scrupulously conforming to every slightest clause in the Law of 1901. I made it my business to check in person. I could not risk a lawsuit . . ."

A Citroën 11 pulled up outside. It was black in front and black behind but bore advertising slogans on both sides: *Indochina Cinema and Films, 32 rue Boissy d'Anglas, Paris* and *French Small Arms and Bicycle Factory, Saint-Étienne (Loire), meeting all your overseas needs.*

"Yes, I know. A little inappropriate for tombs. But I have permission, the express permission, of the Friends of Old Hué. Part of the receipts go toward restoration, and restoration is expensive in this climate. Off you go, then, and have a nice excursion to Old Hué. I'll

*"A young man? I'll bet!" *(note from Clara).* "Why not, Clara? I believe he's been telling the truth up to now" *(note from Ann).*

†"Well, naturally, with all these exotic names he can get away with murder" *(grumble from Clara).*

"Let's wait and see. There's nothing funnier than a liar tripping himself up" *(note from Ann).*

hold your room, no extra charge, just in case you decide to stay an extra night.

Thank you, Louis. Once again I have learned from you.

Thanks to you I visited tombs that do us mortals honor.

And I was ashamed when my Nguyen* asked me what tombs we have in France. I mentioned the Panthéon, the Cathedral of Saint-Denis. But he pulled a face: Those are communal tombs, aren't they? Yes, communal. Death needs a little privacy, he told me in his staccato accent. And who would disagree? Only the Invalides found favor in his eyes. Wounded veterans all around, museum next door, golden dome above: Napoleon had not been ill served. Nguyen was keen to visit it. I promised I would do my best. If France weren't so shortsighted and stingy she would offer free trips to these young scholars. Instead of thrusting them into the arms of the Communists by ignoring them.†

Thank you, Louis. You were right.

Our funerary customs are so impoverished. All we have to show as an example of French funerary art is old Père-Lachaise cemetery. Now there's a noble cause, esteemed counselor: to develop a French burial culture. And high time, it seems to me, for a country in decline. Might as well prepare for the worst while there's yet time. No, no, I'm joking! Naturally I won't hold forth on these ideas on the witness stand. Relax. Besides, France isn't going downhill. The gross (as they call it) national product climbed another 5 percent last year. Long live life. Long live France. Another glass of Château Cheval Blanc?

The smiling young scholar disappeared for a second and came back laden with satchels.

"Why carry all this stuff?" asked Gabriel, always concerned for his subordinates' welfare.

*"There he goes again! Does he take me for a moron?" *(Clara).*

"Please! Don't be ridiculous!" *(Ann).*

†"And if he, or rather she, ever comes to France, I'll kill her" *(promise from Clara).* What a comforting display of jealousy in a woman over sixty. They are in the living room, next to my room. I lie here fascinated, listening to them read this passage aloud. And judging by Ann's tone, I picture her standing, laughing, puffing on her Dunhill cigarette holder.

"Some clients like to check the facts with the textbooks."

And our publicity-blazoned Citroën rattled into motion.

Not much farther on, at a fork in the road, the young scholar called a halt. Before us a stream known as the River of Perfumes spilled its languid blue waters between clumps of flame-of-the-forest and Japanese lilac. On the far bank the Royal Palace beckoned. "Monsieur hasn't changed his mind? He doesn't want to visit it?" Gabriel guessed at what it would offer: lacquer, mother-of-pearl, priceless vases. He shook his head.

The youthful scholar looked relieved.

I learned later that the Friends of Old Hué offered two kinds of guide, experts on the old city and experts specializing in tombs. The former shuddered when tourists dragged them among the graves, the latter were bored in palaces.

The road climbed gently. It was a mountain after my own heart, no precipice on the right, no snow on the left. A modest mountain, a relief after the arrogance of the Alps, and planted with varied species of trees instead of our inevitable evergreens. This multitude of unfamiliar species was as restful to the soul as opening a new book at the start of a vacation. Streams flowed downhill as one might expect, but silently, whereas even the least of our so-called temperate-zone torrents feels obliged to make the racket of an express train. As a result of this slow-paced trickling, the earth was carpeted with moss. There were tall trees to give shelter from the sky, clearings to give light.* We had not seen a soul since Hué. We were alone. A rare privilege in Asia.

At last we reached the top. Beside me, the young scholar had spilled out the contents of his satchels and was feverishly consulting the textbooks. Gabriel felt light. Floating. Freed from all earthly tensions. Thank you, Louis, for leading me to this magic place in our Empire.

With a vigor and agility worthy of youth, our Gabriel sprang from the car. But scarcely had he raised his eyes to the splendid view than he was obliged to lower them again: the scholar was showing him an open book.

*"Never have I known our Gabriel so lyrical. It's disgusting, old men drooling over their loves!" *(Clara).*

"Please!" *(Ann).*

Reverend Father Cadière, the most authoritative source on the tomb area.

"Here all conspires to quicken the imagination: sublime setting, harmoniously ordered foreground, untamed grandeur of the background, huge trunks mirrored in crystalline waters, old patinaed walls, temples breathing mystery, elegant pavilions, ideally situated belvederes. Hovering over it all are great memories, the majesty of death."

And Gabriel was obliged to compare. A look at the text. A look at the appropriate view. Exhausting visual calisthenics. It reminded me of those school exercises I couldn't stand, where under Monet you had to pin a photo of the "real" Seine, and, under Cézanne, a "real" Mont Saint-Victoire. But Father Cadière was right, we were indeed surrounded by the majesty of death.

"Thank you very much; you may put away your books. All your books. I won't need them."

He closed his eyes and didn't open them again until he heard the satchel fasteners click shut.

Then Gabriel Orsenna, accustomed to many sensations, particularly botanic ones, and (one might have supposed) a little jaded by now, had to fight back his tears. For the first time since Brazil he was experiencing *geographic emotion.*

Like a green ray of sunlight, just as rare but less fugitive, a lazy, unhurried ray. Like a kiss on the eyes. Like someone in the schoolyard saying "Will-you-be-my-best-friend?" The snug shelter of welcoming arms. An immense unmoving ocean swell of leaves and of clouds.

Countless minutes went by in this way, in perfect silence. For the driver was not chewing gum, the Citroën 11's engine was not dripping oil onto the road, and the scholar respected geographic emotion.

"Monsieur," he ventured at long last, "be careful of the heat. And I believe it is time we visited our first tomb if we are to see them all before dark."

"Let's go," said Gabriel aloud. And then, in a low voice, "Louis, here we come."

Yes, shame on Père-Lachaise!

A tomb of consequence comprises five elements:

1. Outer enclosure, where statues of generals and mandarins are

placed in conversational groups, surrounded by horses and elephants.

2. The stela pavilion.
3. Temple of the soul's tablet.
4. Pleasure dome.
5. The tomb itself, invisible, hidden within a secret walled enclosure and concealed by woods.

Not to mention the fortifications and deep moats protecting the deceased, the lotus-strewn ponds lulling him, and the visitors' footpaths, threading between mango trees and frangipani.

I searched for Louis all day. The tomb of Tu-Duc. Nothing. The tomb of Dong-Khanh. Nothing. On the right, Prince Kien-Thai-Vuong. Nothing. Farther on, Thieu-Tri, Minh-Mang the Great, Gia-Long the Strict, Khai-Dinh the Modern, which Louis might easily have picked. Still nothing. Behind me the youthful scholar was panting. I plied him with questions.

"Yes, monsieur, yes, it was the custom to live in one's tomb prior to death."

We returned to the car without Louis. I cast one last look around. I no longer understood my father. Where better than in Hué could one wait for death?

"If you want to catch your train, we must leave now," the scholar said to me.

It was getting dark.*

*Picture an elderly man emerging from sleep at about five in the afternoon: emerging painfully, for his afternoon nap has become his night. Daylight reassures him, heat soothes him. Whereas in the other night, real night, black night, he is too afraid. He cannot sleep.*

*Picture him lying there awake with his eyes shut and hearing the stifled laughter, the whispers, the opened doors, the books being moved, keys clicking in locks, snatches of conversation.*

*"Where do you think he's hidden them?"*

*"Could he have sent them directly to his attorney?"*

*"Obviously the old pervert isn't proud of what happened next" *(Clara)*.
"Yes, at least two pages have been removed" *(Ann)*.

*"Well, he's going to pay for it sooner or later."*

*"Perhaps in a bank in Cannes? They rent safe-deposit boxes."*

*It is very hot. Old Gabriel would love to go back upstream, back to his dream where, as far as he can recall, the air although Vietnamese was much cooler. Too late. Too far from sleep. Nothing for it but to open the eyes a slit or two.*

*Ann, Clara, and the papermaker are searching. Frantically. With scant respect for order. It will take me hours to straighten up, put things back where I had them. Well, since the landlord is in on it. . . . Now the group has left my study, the room where I sometimes address my son, sometimes get ready for the trial, two occupations that seem increasingly similar to me. The trio is still empty-handed. Well, naturally; Gabriel's not that stupid. But they've left. I can no longer see them. They must be climbing the spiral staircase to the library. Careful, now. They were cold, like my dream. Now they're getting warmer.*

*A moment of intense pleasure: I picture them groping vainly for a piece of me. I come very close to feeling their hands on my skin. The papermaker who loves the theater (I now know his secret passion, the passion that fills his oversized clothes) is not devoting the requisite zeal to the undertaking. He is embarrassed. That's understandable; he is my friend. "Do you think we should?" he keeps asking. "Don't you think he has the right to keep his secrets?"*

*"Not from us," said Ann.*

*"He knows all ours," added Clara.*

*"Tit for tat, tit for tat, our love is tit for tat," chanted Ann.*

*"Well, in that case . . ."*

*My friend gives in. I don't really blame him.*

*But they find nothing and would not have found anything without enlisting the help of Mme. Hélène, the handwriting expert. Because of her training, details leap out at her. She asks for silence. Within two minutes she has spotted the faintest of traces in the dust on a bookshelf. I have not been careful enough. You can never be careful enough with dust. I didn't think anyone would ever take it into their head to ferret around up there. It's my favorite spot in the library, the place I run to when I find myself alone. Three feet of shelf space packed with treasures, the most forgotten books and documents in the whole house, our only tangible souvenirs of the past: menus, concert programs, monographs published at the authors' expense,* Vive Schiaparelli *by Alain de Rède, five drawings by Drian entitled* In Praise of Lady Mendl, *publishing costs generously contributed by Paul-Louis Weiler.*

*There I had hidden the account of a rather spicy episode of my journey. A few vignettes from Old Hué. And there the handwriting expert found it. Without undue excitement. With scientific detachment. Three sheets folded in four inside* Nos Bals Masqués, *by M. and Mme. Fauchier-Magnan.*

*My four friends run downstairs to the garden. They are probably seated around the stone table. All I hear is the ring of Ann's voice; she must be reading. Every now and then my friend the papermaker exclaims, "Who would've believed it! That old rascal Gabriel."*

*"Shhh!" whispers the handwriting expert. "If you're not careful you're going to wake him."*

## IV

### Hué (continued)

The manager of the Grand Hotel stood in the lobby greeting returning guests.

"How was our trip to the coast, Monsieur Magny? And Madame Dunan, did we enjoy Dalat? Well, well, Monsieur Orsenna, you're the last to come back. Off at eight, back at eight! I was almost beginning to worry. A complete turn of the clock! So far so good, may I assume? Splendid, splendid. Luckily I held your room for you, because it's too late for the train. Once Old Hué has you in its spell . . . ! The Friends have a branch in Paris, I must give you the address: near the Opéra, I believe. May I offer you a drink? Yes, I remember now, rue de Vaugirard. An ice-cold Cinzano to celebrate the event?

Splendid, splendid. Don't worry. There are trains every day. Tomorrow and the day after tomorrow. There's no telling with Old Hué, I've known people to stay for months. Loc, call upstairs and tell them to run Monsieur Orsenna's bath. After twelve hours at the tombs it's the least we can do for him. Oh, excuse me. Good evening, Monsieur Charret. Happy with your room? Well, you're just like me, Number 17 also happens to be my favorite. I sleep there myself once in a while. Hotelkeeper's privilege in the off season. A change of scenery. Splendid, splendid. . . ."

Later on, after my bath, I dressed (I swear it) for only one reason: they expect it of you in the colonies. I had hardly sat down in the dining room and glanced at the menu (I felt like having fish) when the headwaiter (the manager's pride and joy, formerly assistant chef at Flo's, now living overseas for personal reasons) leaned over me: "There are some ladies and gentlemen at the bar who would like you to join them."

How could I refuse the offer of conversation with fellow Frenchmen far from home in the heart of a country at war?

*"What a hypocrite," said Clara.*

*"Be quiet," said Ann. "Let me go on."*

Besides, there was nothing sinister about the group. Unfeignedly warm introductions. Five handshakes. Not one moist palm: a statistical rarity, particularly in the tropics. Three men, two of whom were like peas in a pod, Victor and Max, fiftyish, prosperous businessmen. Bob, younger and balder. And two women, Irène, an intense-looking blonde, rather tall and thin, with pointed breasts. The other, Jacqueline—"I mean Nina"—the redhead, very plump and jolly, and all of them bright-eyed and most reassuringly fond of life in the midst of all these tombs.

"Well," said Victor, the oldest (brilliantined black hair, jacket lapel somewhat puckered at the spot where decorations are worn, clearly removed for the occasion; I should have known something was up), "we've organized a night excursion. Care to join us?"

"Oh, yes, please say yes!" giggled the redhead.

The manager came over. "Forgive me for intruding. But if I were you . . . at night the monuments of Old Hué are utterly transformed."

"Bravo, manager!"

"Hué has the best hotel manager in the world."

"Do come with us," said the tall bald man. "The more the merrier!"

"And we won't be going by ourselves. Our guides are authentic scholars. They'll explain everything."

"He has his faults, good old Georges—I mean Victor; I'm getting confused—but he's certainly a first-rate organizer."

"So, is it yes?"

Thus it was that gullible Gabriel left in the men's car. The women followed, escorted by two lady guides, guaranteed scholars.

"It's better this way," said Victor from his seat beside the Vietnamese driver, another of the so-called scholars. "Yes, much better, they'll get into the spirit much quicker on their own."

One after another, tree limbs swept by. Fleetingly caught in the headlights, then swallowed by the night.

"Where are we going?"

"It's a surprise."

"They have high expectations," said Bob, the bald-headed one, sitting next to me.

"Who does?"

"Our lady friends, who else? Yes, I have the feeling they expect a great deal. But let's be grateful. It's because of those high hopes that we're here."

Gabriel still did not understand.

"See my nose?" said Bob. "A good size, wouldn't you say? And a good indication for the rest, according to the ladies. That's what I call expectation. As for you, please don't take offense but you're not very big. Which suggests that the rest of you makes up for it. Even at your age. They liked you at first sight. Believe me, old man, they're anticipating miracles. We mustn't disappoint them."

Victor said nothing. He was watching the road.

"We're there," he said.

Our headlights had lit up a structure. A great red façade with no door, no window, and no building behind it.

"You've already been here, I believe?"

It was the entrance to the first tomb.

"Let's set up base in the royal baths, the pavilion over the lake. No objections, I hope? We're going to need your help. If you don't mind

I'll ask you to take one of these picnic hampers. Ah, here come the ladies! About time."

Seeing the direction in which events were leading, Gabriel should have refused. Refused to go any farther. Insisted that he be taken back to Hué. But wasn't this excursion his last improbable chance of finding Louis?

*"Improbable, all right," said Clara's voice.*

*"If you keep on interrupting I'll stop," said Ann's voice.*

And we walked into the compound along a side path, as was fitting, leaving the central path to the dead king. Suddenly silent, we walked in single file. The wicker of the picnic hampers creaked, so did the branches above. A gentle wind had risen since afternoon.

"Don't forget we're close to the sea," said a woman, in all likelihood Irène.

Her diction was very refined, I recall. Or at least she tried to make it so, distinctly enunciating all her *t*'s and *d*'s.

Just before we arrived I felt a hand. Light. On my shoulder.

"Believe me, my friend, a man needs a hobby in the colonies."

It was the voice of someone who had not yet spoken. Max the other businessman, Victor's almost-twin. Victor was already taking dinner orders. "Is everyone hungry? Good. Let's get started."

"Well, here we are, ladies," said Victor. "Don't be afraid. You can relax. The tombs are safe."

The women quickly forgot all about us.

It was as if they were meeting again after a long separation. The tall blonde was the thirsty one; her mouth roamed everywhere. The other was content to be lapped, and indeed her skin was like milk. The thirsty one kept her clothes on. You can drink fully dressed. The other was already naked. She opened herself, she spread herself, she tossed her hair back. It was the only work she did. She did not cry out, beverages are voiceless, did not even whimper; why should she, since the waves were flowing into her, into all her places? Every now and then the thirsty one, Irène, resurfaced, came up for air, seeking some source of oxygen, some anchorage. "Nina, Nina, are you there?" she called, not very hopefully, eyes wild; then she submerged again. In short, it all looked very much like love. Real love. A great one-way-street love. And we were forgotten.

Victor had perched the two lady scholars on his knees and was stroking their hair and murmuring "My children, my two pretty children, can you read?" or something of the sort.

The silent twin stared into his glass.

The scholar-driver-headwaiter knotted a thread around the champagne bottles and lowered them slowly into the lotus-strewn lake.

As for Bob (the bald-headed cousin) and me, we dared not exchange a word, our anonymity did not permit it. We smiled politely at each other. We felt useless.

It happened later.

Nina, the redhead with the milky skin, suddenly sat upright again. She stood. She ran her hands through her hair, over her body. She patted herself. Small brushing taps with the back of her hand. As if dusting herself off. "Nina," the other woman said. "Nina."

They went off together, heels clacking. "Georges—or rather Victor, excuse me!—can't stand bare feet," Irène explained. They went and leaned on the guardrail over the lake. We could hear their voices. Words echo across water, even lotus-strewn words. They discussed suntans. Nina preferred to remain white. Utterly and entirely white. Not Irène. She loved the sun on Cap Saint-Jacques so much. But I had guessed her reasons. Touching reasons. Trying to make the most of her looks but not a natural beauty, she hoped her tan would highlight her most useful assets. Now and then Nina turned toward us, laughing, saying nothing.

"I believe it's time," said the bald cousin.

We went over to them.

Of what followed (commonplace enough for most human beings, they say, and usually on Saturday nights), of what followed Gabriel has retained two memories.

Nina was a taker, absorbing delicate touches, moistness, passionate thrusts, assaults. She stored it all up like provisions for an endless winter.

And she recognized us right off, "Hello there, Bob!" or "Here you are again": she addressed me by the formal *vous,* the *vous* of Old Hué; she never mistook one of us for the other.

The other one, Irène, faked it. She really tried. She arched her back, changed her tactics, varied her rhythm, but all the while she was faking.

I wanted to express my sympathies to her.

Tricky, under the circumstances.

It was the two lady scholars who first raised the alarm. They pointed at the jungle: "Over there, oh no, over there, Lord in heaven!" and many native words as well, terrified words.

Our little group froze for perhaps a second. And it is this tableau vivant that has remained in the memory of the daily-older Gabriel, one of the last rays still reaching him from a youth already dead.

*"Well, that puts us in our place!"*

*"Clara, I swear I'll stop."*

The so-called Victor, arms outstretched toward the so-called lady scholars. His twin, motionless with his glass, phony Irène, phony Nina, leaning out over the lotus-strewn lake, and two men, one of them me, stooping close behind them, bodies hunched but heads up in the air, looking questioningly about. A few feet away a young Vietnamese patiently waiting, seated on a leather suitcase.

Gabriel admits it. It was an inglorious retreat. Tugging clothes back on, fumbling vainly at fly buttons. Sobs, shattered crockery; liar, I warned you. Orders: leave the picnic hampers. Counterorders: take the picnic hampers. Flight. Shortness of breath. Tumbles. Get rid of your high heels. Oaths. Disorderly scramble through the sacred gateway. Piling into the cars. Luckily they started.

Inside the Citroën, tearing along at a speedy and most reassuring pace, the little band of Friends of Hué gradually collected themselves. One grumbled. One pulled up his socks. One sought the tenuous connection between buttons and buttonholes. Only the twin, virtually mute since the beginning of the escapade, started to talk. Talked and talked. Described in minute detail the tortures we had just escaped. The Hundred Cuts, for example. Ba-Dao in Vietnamese. "Shut up, Maxime!" Not a chance. He went right on. "The first torturer extracts your entrails. The second cuts. The third counts the cuts. The fourth notes the numbers down. No doubt about it, France chooses her colonies well."

Our lady companions, just beginning to calm down, were again seized by violent shudders.

"Well, thank you so much, Maxime, now look what you've done," said the so-called Victor.

But the one who should have thanked Maxime was Gabriel.

Until that very moment our angelic hero had believed that the way to arouse the desired response in a woman was to reassure her. Reassure her and never stop reassuring her.

And now the opposite course was proving its effectiveness.

The phony Irène had thrown herself upon the aforementioned Maxime and was covering him with kisses. Be quiet, oh, do be quiet!

A tactic that was perhaps spontaneous, perhaps deliberate. But how to be certain, now that all the players in that evening's performance have scattered to the winds? In any case, Irène was forced to lean to the right in order to kiss, thus exposing a vista of undefended slopes to her neighbor on the left, Gabriel.

Gabriel sought to resist. I swear it, Gabriel made himself small, squeezed himself up against the door. But the more Irène yawed to starboard the more she bore down on him to port.

And thoughts he had believed dead, killed by their recent fright, adolescent thoughts, suddenly raised their heads . . . well, when I say heads . . . in short, brought me back to life.

Gabriel closed his eyes. His intentions were laudable: he was seeking to fight off temptation.

A fatal mistake.

Every confessor can confirm this: it is behind closed lids that the most unmentionable ideas flourish.

And Gabriel will attest to it. No sooner were his eyes shut than he saw, as stark and as clear as a slide on a screen, those untanned twin spheres that had already moved him so.

You can work out the rest.

As well as Gabriel's maneuver. Successful.

And Irène's reaction. Hospitable.

A quarter hour later, glancing into the back seat as we entered Hué, the so-called Victor was unable to stifle a cry.

He ordered the driver to slow down.

"So that we can all regain our composure," he added considerately.

There were no real goodbyes. Just whispers. The night watchman did not wake. We all crept back to our rooms in darkness. A pity. Gabriel would have liked to embrace them all: Bob my accomplice, silent Max the torture expert, Irène and Nina, the one who believed in tanning and the one who didn't. . . .

Our hero merely heard behind him in the night, just as he entered his room, Victor's fine sonorous voice.

"Bravo, old fellow. At your age! They can say what they like. Living in France must keep people young."

Gabriel took a long time, a very long time, to go to sleep. The physiological miracle had exhausted him. He had lost all strength, even the strength to slip into slumber.

He was awakened at dawn next morning by the sound of voices on the terrace outside.

"Geneviève, please! Get a move on. We have a long road ahead of us."

"Coming, Georges, I'm just going to say goodbye to Nicole and then I'll be ready."

The group was breaking up. They had dropped their cover names.

When it was time for Gabriel to leave, the manager embraced him ("I hope you don't mind; we are fellow countrymen after all, and in times like these!"). He gave him a present, a painted ashtray. "I know you don't smoke, so you won't burn the map of the city. Look. It's all there: the Citadel, the Imperial Palace, Decapitation Bridge, the French concession. Even a few tombs, the closest ones. . . . No doubt about it, you truly deserve such a souvenir. You most certainly have a rapport with Old Hué. Well, goodbye. Come back soon. Old Hué and its tombs could easily disappear. War is no respecter of tombs. Farewell then. And my respects to your father."

He waved. He grew smaller in the rear window, even smaller than Gabriel. Then he disappeared behind a clump of flame-of-the-forest.

What has become of him, of M. Amaury, the most zealous supporter of the Friends of Old Hué? Grand Hotels are at their most vulnerable in wartime.

And it was thus—old and imperial, old and victorious, as proud as he was exhausted, looking nonchalant, whistling, believing everyone was staring at him and applauding—it was thus, smug and whistling, that our old hero took war's sad train to Hanoi.

*After Ann's last words the garden falls silent. The silence of gardens. Bees buzzing. Sounds of a spade nearby. Children shouting in the distance. A flag flapping, whipped for no reason by the solar wind.*

*The papermaker is the first to find his tongue.*

*"My, he's a secretive one. And what stamina!"*

*"Of course it's obvious right away from his writing," says the handwriting expert. "If I had seen it earlier—"*

*"The filthy swine," says Clara.*

*"You're forgetting your past," says Ann. "That lovely cruise ship, for instance—"*

*"Hush!"*

*"I think he was in his rights. After all the tricks we've played on him."*

*"So what? I can't stand people who keep score and feel they have to retaliate."*

*Thus arguing, the two sisters leave the garden. I barely have time to scuttle to my bedroom and leap soundlessly into bed. (By this time I am familiar with its individual springs and can leap without creaking them.)*

*Yawning mightily, I feign the most convincing of awakenings.*

*And that night Gabriel dresses for dinner with extreme care. Even risks a red silk scarf of the sort that in broad daylight makes you look shorter since it (unnecessarily, God knows) emphasizes the area where the upper abdomen ends. But at night people notice waistlines less. He comes downstairs looking carefree, humming, exactly the same look as at Hué station. An average-looking old man who happens to be in good spirits. The looks he gets have changed. Intrigued. Brotherly. Infuriated. Baffled. Depending on who is looking. What a splendid evening! What a fabulous joyful feast! Oh, how heartily I wish the same to all my aging colleagues!*

# V

## HANOI

He pushed a bell. There was no sound. But a boy materialized. He said something to the boy. The boy vanished. The boy reappeared. Would the gentleman follow me? Everyone's door was open to Gabriel, practically everyone's. Because of the letter of introduction. Written on the typewriter of G. Franchini, Hotel Continental, Saigon, and signed by the president of the Cochin China Planters' Association. *Dear Friend, one of our colleagues, Gabriel Orsenna* . . . The all-powerful brotherhood of rubber. More secretive, closer-knit than the Rotary. From frequent perusal, the letter was no longer very fresh. There were thumbprints on it, in fact it was nothing but thumbprints, on both sides of the *Dear Friend* and lower down, around the signature. But the letter retained its power to open doors.

"Unfortunately I don't have much time," said the dear friend, "with things as they are. I apologize for all the noise."

Noises that sounded as though very heavy things were being dragged across tiles. Then the rustle of tissue paper, then a woman's voice. "Be careful, Binh, I'll die if you break that vase." Perhaps not an outright move, but preparations for it. A preliminary sorting, things to be taken, things to be left behind, a choice already proving painful. Occasionally dear friend left the room to bellow angrily, "Silence!" Then he'd come back and say, "And what do they think of all this back home?"

Gabriel launched into explanations whose incoherence was only increased by his efforts to keep them short. Then he told his story, all about a certain old gentleman named Louis, but spry for his years, you understand, a sportsman. . . .

Dear friend understood: "Thanks to sports, particularly cycling, age comes on more gradually, but how can one be expected to exercise in the colonies, in this climate? What were we talking about? Oh, yes, this lost gentleman. Well, no, unfortunately, I haven't seen any sign of this Louis, although God knows I see a lot of people. The way things are, the most bizarre creatures are crawling out from under stones. I don't mean the gentleman you're looking for. Of course not. Of course not." The friendlier of the dear friends added a few remarks about motor racing. "Do you know Fangio? Ah, no! That's right, you were prewar, weren't you?" There was no chance of a misunderstanding; the interview was over. Gabriel rose. Did not turn back to say goodbye, or thank you again. For as a rule dear friend shrugged as he watched the intruder withdraw. And this shrugging was a fatal blow to days already seriously afflicted by the absence of a father and by that icy drizzle that often makes Hanoi very like Breton communes such as Saint-Brieuc or Lannion.

Or else he knocked at office doors. The secretary inside never responded, even though he could hear her moving about and chattering on the phone. He went in and at once brandished the famous letter under her nose signature first, Planters' Association, fingermarks. "I'll go and see," she said. Then: "I'm going to go crazy if people keep bothering me. It's through there."

Cardboard boxes were heaped all around the office, and next to a pencil sharpener fashioned like a terrestrial globe sat a pile of white labels with buff borders, the same color as the boxes.

"Unfortunately, dear friend, with things as they are . . ."

Breton weather then, gray, misty, with a constant piercing drizzle that sometimes let up around 10 A.M. Then you heard the planes and remembered you were in Hanoi. Gabriel was at the Bay of Along Hotel, not far from the center of town, a modest two-story hotel to which a third floor had recently been added and christened the penthouse (or *pantouze,* as the French pronounced it), where Gabriel was staying.

The owners scarcely concerned themselves with looking after the hotel anymore. They listened to the radio, packed their bags, listened to the radio, packed their bags a little faster. Little by little the hotel was being drained of its contents. One morning the pictures in the corridor, the Japanese prints from Formosa, were missing. Next day the curtains. The owners, fine people, gave the newcomer a warm welcome. Gabriel was accustomed to it; ever since his youth he had moved hotelkeepers' hearts. They must have sensed in him the lack of a mother and the particularly footloose nature of his father. When they saw him return exhausted, ice-cold and of course empty-handed, the owners of the Bay of Along invited him to dinner. Lukewarm rice, fish cooked in a kind of white sauce, *blanquette*-style, and vinegary Rennes wine, "A very sturdy red, wouldn't you agree? As if Brittany can't grow grapes!" They told Gabriel their woes.

"At least we now have suitcases, thanks to the Chinese. Did you know that since the start of the siege of Dien Bien Phu, junks from Hong Kong have been unloading empty suitcases every day? Not exactly an encouraging sign, but thank God for the Chinese anyway! What would you do in our shoes? Twenty beds, two sets of sheets per bed, eighty sheets in all. Would you ship them to France right away? The problem is, a hotel without sheets automatically drops a category, and we don't like riffraff, do we, Annette?"

"No, we might as well leave when the sheets do."

"In any case, we're stuck here for another week. The honeymoon suite on the first floor."

"That's right. I'd forgotten them. A honeymoon has to have sheets. Do you mind (with things as they are) if I call you Gabriel?"

"I think Gabriel will like the couple. They're from Saigon. Working for the post office. Both of them middle-aged. Clearly a question of legalizing their former relationship, but they seem to be very nice all the same. . . ."

The hotelkeeper drew on his pipe as he spoke. A sucking in. A burst of words. A sucking in. The smoke never came back out. "For some strange reason these newlyweds have decided to visit us up here in the north," he said. "Apparently for our geological curiosities, in particular the limestone caverns in the bay. They're crazy about geography. Par for the course with post office employees. You should get along with them very well. After all, rubber too is geography."

Such were evenings in Hanoi: deadly. Glass after glass of Rennes wine. Gabriel climbed rather unsteadily to his room. He dreamed he came across Louis on the Paul-Doumer bridge.

Louis suggested a game of hide-and-seek. Gabriel counted to one hundred against the rusting struts of the bridge, then searched for Louis in the Bay of Along. In vain. So he called for help from the captains of the aircraft carriers *Arromanches* and *Bois-Belleau* (naturally, he offered a reward). The two captains flew into a rage. As if they had time to look for Louis with that naval battle raging to the west, aircraft carriers against bicycles! Toward the end of the dream the two commanders had Gabriel arrested. Attempted bribery of government officers. Then the two princesses appeared, fair-haired Ann and dark Clara, dressed Chinese style in long black tunics. They nodded their approval: the conviction was well deserved. With very uppity English accents. And with no trace of a smile. The firing squad lined up. Tiny little warriors with Siamese-cat heads. Gabriel cried out. Woke himself. The hotelkeepers slept on the ground floor. So heard nothing. Fortunately.

Chance brought him to Bach Mai.

Because he was in a bus. And because that bus had been hijacked by soldiers anxious to reach the nearest air force base as quickly as possible. And because the only way to get off a commandeered bus going top speed was to jump. Too risky a maneuver and irresponsible when, like Gabriel, you support a large family: Louis, Ann, Clara, and so many memories of Markus, of Elisabeth, of American Marguerite.

Bach Mai.

Today, just a few months later, people pretend they have forgotten. Some even swear they have never heard the name. Even though last March, April, and early May it was the most popular spot in Hanoi. Overrun by crowds, like a cemetery on All Saints' Day. Families seeking news. Reporters tracking rumors. Parachutists wanting to jump. Exhausted pilots trying to sleep. Distinguished lieutenants of the late Marshal Jean de Lattre saying, What a disaster. Weathermen scanning the sky. American mercenaries flying in French planes. Foreign Legionnaires speaking German. Inventors who had discovered a new defoliant (or whatever) that was sure to win the war against communism in one week. Who consequently wished to see the commander-in-chief at once. Who, when turned away, took the bus back to Hanoi muttering: At least the Communists recognize inventors. Traders paying dearly for hot tips. Street vendors of all kinds, the ones who live off rush-hour crowds. Even civilian travelers who had come here by mistake and were now frantically asking about flights to Saigon or, better yet, Paris, Salzburg, San Francisco, coach fare with excess baggage. . . .

Not to mention that peculiarly Asian phenomenon: space, any vacant space, immediately spawns multitudes.

And bear in mind that military airfields are not lavish with waiting rooms. So we were packed in tight. But Gabriel isn't here to talk about his personal comfort. The most salient characteristic of Bach Mai was something else—its boomerang quality: all these planes taking off from Bach Mai and, after two or three hours' flight, returning to land at Bach Mai. But don't take this to imply superstition or force of habit on the part of the airmen. It was simply that hostile artillery had destroyed the landing strip at their base.

Which was known in Vietnamese as Dien Bien Phu.

And in French as the "headquarters of the frontier district administration."

Since the end of March no plane had been able to land there: airstrip annihilated.

I am proud of myself. Gabriel is proud of himself. He acted methodically.

He looked inside himself. He drew upon his Grand Prix experiences. At Monaco, the only person who knew everything at all times (for instance, where to find Chiron's lucky polka-dot scarf and whether Nuvolari's American girlfriend Gladys had come down from her room with or without luggage), the only one who knew all the answers was M. Christophe (a Jew of Dutch extraction like Spinoza, just as human but much less abstract)—the bartender at the Hôtel de Paris.

Without a second's hesitation, Gabriel headed for the three canteen tables perched on ammunition boxes that did service as a bar. Behind it two small young men officiated, probably enlisted men waiting to be assigned to mopping-up operations in the rice paddies. They were openers of beer bottles rather than true bartenders (bartender: a sleepwalking alchemist in quest of the philosopher's cocktail, the one that will transform life into real life), but the man grows with the job, and bartending has its own states of grace.

No sooner did Gabriel mention Dekaerkove, the former Tour de France organizer, than the two substitute bartenders dropped their beer.

"That guy has total recall! We quizzed him all night, but could we trip him up? Not on your nelly! And I'm a charter member of the Twelfth *Arrondissement* Cycling Club. He's a genius, he is!"

"And believe me, Pops, it was a pleasure for us to run into an expert. A real breath of Paris air! Because these jokers here pretend to be cycling fans just to butter us up, but they don't know their ass from their elbow!"

"You're forgetting big Georges, the one who's so smitten with Madame Stern."

"That's true, he knows his stuff. Not bad at all for a man from Clermont-Ferrand!"

For a moment Gabriel wondered about this spellbinding Mme. Stern. Stranded in Vietnam? Or a lady left behind in Paris? And since he had only the planet Orsenna in his head he murmured, Could this be Louis's last lady-love, his very very last?

The bartender on the left was clearly moved. Dekaerkove . . . the Twelfth *Arrondissement* Cycling Club. . . . All he could do was shake his head and smile, his expression one of admiration, even hero worship.

"Yes, take my word for it, that Dekaerkove was unbeatable. He wanted to go to Dien Bien Phu. Like everyone else. Right now it's the place to be if you want to see action. So we gave him a good tip. Minister Pléven had just arrived. You should have seen his getup, just right for a seaside resort: panama, white suit, basket-weave sandals. . . . The Viets must have laughed themselves silly behind their binoculars when he arrived. Anyway. I know what visiting politicians are like. Just mention their home constituencies and they'll do anything for you . . . And what city do you think Pléven's constituency includes? Saint-Meen, the great champion Bobet's home town. . . . So Dekaerkove only had to say the word and presto! the minister would have taken him with him to visit the bowl."

Gabriel didn't understand. "The bowl?" "Dien Bien Phu is down in a valley, you know, with mountains on all sides. Everybody calls it the bowl."

The bartenders had returned to their rinsing and mopping, both of them, their expressions still registering their admiration of Dekaerkove.

"In any case they turned down the invitation, him and his pal, an old guy well on in years. They wanted to make their own way to the bowl. All they needed was a map. . . . Lean a little closer, Pops, lean a little closer, it's not a secret, but I slipped them a military reconnaissance map of Tonkin, and with things the way they are I'd just as soon you didn't spread it around. So you're a relative of theirs? You a cyclist too?"

The Cycling Club member abandoned his colleague and his dishrag and came over to me.

"I'll show you which way they went, I don't know about you, but the only politics I care about is cycling."

We walked for some time without saying anything. We heard the screech of aircraft engines and, farther away, a muffled sound like a crowd at an airport exit. The bartender pointed to a road leading off to the right.

"They set off in that direction, westward. Dekaerkove in front, the other behind. Which one are you related to? I saw at once that they were OK. Not armchair athletes, real calves despite their age, and believe me I know what I'm talking about: typical Longchamp muscles. And they used their heads, you know: they were riding Manufrance bikes, a bit heavy in the frame but solid, just right for local conditions. Know what Dekaerkove called Dien Bien Phu? The Summer Velodrome. Pretty good, eh? A bowl, Viet bikes all around it, the only thing missing is the banked turns. . . . I wonder what kind of welcome they got from the Vietminh. So it worries you too, eh? Do the Viets truly love bikes? That's the question."

We returned to his makeshift bar. He was anxious to get back to it; he didn't want to be detailed to a rice paddy for being absent without leave. He talked and talked, his Paris accent went on and on. If you closed your eyes you were back in Grenelle on race night, near the enclosures or else at the turns, favorite vantage point for Paris bike-racing fans.

I tried to get news of you, Louis. Without success. He always came back to Dekaerkove, who struck him as so knowledgeable and such a friendly fellow. Apparently you seemed a bit standoffish. I told him that Dekaerkove was my father, just to please him, you understand. I'm not sure he believed me; he gave me a funny look every now and then.

"Something tells me he was a Communist, the organizer's pal. I wonder if it was wise to give them that map."

"A Communist? No, he's not. I know him pretty well."

"All the same I wonder. He made a count of the races trapped at Dien Bien Phu, thirty-seven of them: Moroccan, Senegalese, Thai, Cambodian, Malagasy. . . . All those colors, I can't tell one from another, but I remember that figure, thirty-seven. He said Dien Bien Phu was the last colonial exposition. 'Colonial exposition,' that's Communist talk. And as far as I'm concerned, the Communists—"

He raised sudsy arms from the sink and *boom, boom,* lavishly sprinkled everybody within reach.

"Take it easy," his chum protested.

You recognized them right away, without looking, just by ear. From their conversation. There were no verses. Just a chorus: I want to parachute into Dien Bien Phu.

They arrived in droves every morning. And not just servicemen. Even a few women, small bags in their hands, strictly essentials, you mustn't carry too much on a jump.

The military authorities set up a reception desk. Candidates lined up in twos. Prefabricated hut. Wooden table, sergeant seated behind it. Portrait of Vincent Auriol on the wall, Indochina must have run out of Coty.

"Yes?"

"I want to jump into Dien Bien Phu."

"Why?"

"To be with the others."

"Are you a parachutist?"

"No."

"Thank you. Next!"

But the candidates remained standing there, smiling at the sergeant. For the press had misguidedly published statistics (allegedly an American study) showing that in parachute jumping a total neophyte, a virgin, does not run much more risk of injury than veteran jumpers. The advantage of innocence. Things get sticky only on the second jump. But at Dien Bien Phu you jump only once, isn't that so, sergeant? So why don't you put my name down?

The sergeant had been ordered to show willingness. He doled out false hope.

"Very well. I'll make a note of your name. Leave me an address.

We're building new units. We'll contact you about training. Next!"

Only then did they leave the line. But stayed on to prowl around Bach Mai.

Gabriel returned only three times to the Bay of Along Hotel. To sleep and take a shower. The hotelkeepers were disappointed.

"You missed the honeymooners. Charming couple. And so discreet. Like you. It must have to do with loving geography. What about the room? And the sheets?"

"Hold them for me."

"You'll have dinner with us, surely."

"Impossible. If my father were to return—"

"Well, he's certainly a lucky parent. Not like us with our children."

Gabriel pictured their children, hardware clerk in Pommery-le-Vicomte, assistant auto mechanic in Lanvollon. Earlier generations of Bretons had joined the navy in search of warm seas. But China and Indochina no longer held any magic for the residents of the chilly North Coast.

Gabriel left for the air force base, pockets stuffed with Traou Mad cookies. According to his hosts, the butter in them was a substitute for meat and gave you energy.

From time to time a form black with grease and oil came through the door and gently nudged a sleeping form, using his foot, so as not to make stains.

"Cab's waiting, lieutenant."

The lieutenant shook himself into wakefulness.

"Are you sure? Really sure?"

At the bar the ground crews boasted about their exploits, how they repaired everything with wire and hairpins: "Miriam made me promise to put three of her own hairpins in the Morane. So I did, they're holding the port flap in place. Miriam wanted a little of herself in there, see?"

Others sent locks of hair, photos, lipstick, earrings, dried flowers. Please stick these on the instrument panel. Gradually the aircraft were turning into reliquaries.

Suddenly a fight would break out, always the same one, between the air force on one side and navy pilots on the other, and routinely refereed by American mercenaries. Before fists flew, quite esoteric arguments were exchanged.

"It's well known that Privateers have trouble breathing below eight thousand feet."

"Ever see a Bearcat anywhere but in the clouds?"

There were revolts, too. The volunteers who (like Gabriel) didn't understand why they were being denied a chance to jump while the beleaguered heroes out there were outnumbered five to one. They shouted their qualifications: I'm an amateur radio operator, I'm a doctor, I'm a mechanic. . . . I want to give the boys a hand!

The NCOs didn't have a satisfactory answer, except to sound like Air France at the height of the vacation season: you applied too late, there are no more places. Oh, come on, the volunteers protested, planes in Indochina are never too full for one more; there's always room to squeeze a coolie or a pig on board in place of the fire extinguisher. . . .

"Not so loud, not so loud!" bawled the two NCOs.

And they pointed across the barriers to where airmen lay huddled on benches or sprawled on the ground, arms flung out, heads back, mouths open. Pilots back from a run didn't even try to return to Hanoi anymore: rotations were too rapid. And alerts were permanent. One of them would suddenly sit bolt upright, eyes wild, tortured by lack of sleep.

"Already? Are you sure?"

French troops defending Dien Bien Phu were trapped and under siege. The only way to get supplies to them was by parachute. The pilots of Bach Mai were responsible for keeping the heroes of Dien Bien Phu alive.

When the pilots were in the bar, I heard them talk about the wind.

"How can we make accurate drops with the wind shifting the way it does?"

"And the camp steadily shrinking."

"No more Jeannette, no more Béatrice, no more Anne-Marie. . . ." Each of the hills surrounding Dien Bien Phu had a woman's name, and many had been captured. The new base commander, De Castries, had just been promoted and was expecting two stars. The wind blew the parachute with the general's stars straight into enemy hands. Vietminh loudspeakers were said to be blaring thanks all day long for the manna falling from the skies in the form of scores of Legions of Honor. Nevertheless, they let it be known they would prefer food.

"We have to have the Bomb," said the pilots.

"The Americans are taking care of it for us."

Still more candidates for the jump came in. By train. By car. From all over Indochina. The unbelievable need to be part of something. Friendship, heroism, a lost cause. The terrible need for a little more fear. For certain death. This need to belong. You felt you were going backstage in the human psyche, opening locked rooms, dissecting darkness, wombs, dead-of-night anguish—all those things that surface only rarely, nakedness, that echo of childhood. . . .

And suddenly the uproar died.

All at once.

Whenever departures were announced, a shock ran through the pale troop of true volunteers, those who were really going to jump. They hugged white parachute packs to themselves like fat pillows.

It was the only moment of silence.

All you heard was fading footsteps, and then, from the hut next door, a very slow game of Ping-Pong, like a dripping faucet.

Parachute jumping is a form of bouncing, Gabriel told himself. With my red ball I too am a parachutist. A parachuting dreamer, head in the clouds, very cowardly, a parachutist subject to vertigo, but a parachutist all the same.

Twice a day the reporters swarmed in. Erupted from taxis as if from jeeps. Mentally rehearsed their articles. Pretended to belong. Were therefore dirty, coarse, drunken, desperate.

"What's happening?"

That was their eternal question.

They nudged the sleeping men.

"What's happening?"

No one could answer: military secret. It didn't matter. The reporters already knew the answer.

"The battle for Huguette, how's it going? Fallen, right?"

The reporters roused other forms crouched in corners. These were correspondents' correspondents, Vietnamese special envoys permanently assigned to the waiting rooms at Bach Mai.

"What's happening?"

"Nothing."

"You haven't given me anything for a week. So I'm giving you nothing. That makes us even."

And they left to nose around elsewhere for stories to help keep the planet informed.

Gabriel learned of the end by chance, as he was out strolling near the planes. A mechanic had his head buried in the instrument panel of an Invader. My shoes rang out on the asphalt. He must have taken me for a colleague. Everyone takes me for a colleague.

I heard a grunt.

"Can't you give me a hand instead of wandering around? Here, grab this wire."

I hoisted myself into the cockpit. My ears contacted earphones.

That's how Gabriel intercepted the historic exchange.

He had assumed generals spoke to each other in code. Not at all. They used our own language, everyday words. "What you have achieved up to now is magnificent. We must not ruin it by hoisting the white flag. You have been overrun, but no surrender. No white flag."

The mechanic straightened up, bumping into the control stick. Our heads touched.

After a long silence, a second voice came in.

"Oh. Very well, General. I was hoping to save the wounded."

"Yes, I know. Do the best you can for them. Your effort has been too heroic for things to end like this. You understand, my friend?"

"Yes, General."

"Goodbye, old man, see you soon."

The mechanic laid down his wrench.

"No need to bother with this anymore, eh, Pops? Hey, wait a minute, who the hell are you?"

Gabriel's story enters the final stretch and picks up speed.

In Hanoi he found the door of the Bay of Along closed. To the enamel plate on the door—

All modern conveniences
Weekly rates
Home cooking
Seafood specialties

—a message had been taped with sticking plaster. Addressed to me. "For Gabriel." Written in elaborate, painstaking script:

> With things as they are, we have decided to leave. We wish you and your father good health. Our best wishes. Signed M. and Mme. Le Guillou.
>
> P.S. We will incur so many expenses in getting resettled that we have taken the liberty of attaching your bill.
> M. and Mme. Le Guillou, 7-bis place de Martray, Paimpol.

At the station everyone was fighting for a spot.

The Trans-Indochina Express bulged at the seams. Overflowed with human beings, like every train in Asia: standing on the roofs, clinging to doors and windows, crouched between cars. And entire families still kept surging forward, fathers in hats, mothers in suits, children in tears. The father in a hat waved his tickets, pointed to the already packed compartment, "That's it," he yelled, "those are our reserved seats." "Do something, tell them who you are," whimpered the lady in a suit. He brandished his umbrella.

The baggage of a whole city on the move was heaped on the platform: ice-cream makers, Lorraine peasant furniture, bookshelves, rocking horses, planispheres, steamer trunks, rolled mattresses, a motorbike. . . . Four railway employees walked around and around this mountain, rolling their eyes and lifting their arms to the sky: "There's nothing we can do; this kind of cargo should go by ship." A prewar Citroën van appeared. The driver and his passenger, a dapper young man with a goatee, called for help in unloading.

"And what the hell is this?" yelled the stationmaster.

"The Geographic Society. Our records."

Heavy records. The porters could move them only an inch at a time. One crate escaped them and burst open on the cement floor in a crash of shattering glass. The geographer jumped into the debris and rummaged through it, tears in his eyes. "Do you know what this is?" he babbled. "This is the whole of nineteenth-century Indochina!" Soon his hands were bleeding. Photographs from that era were glass plates. He became a madman, running beside the train as it finally lurched into motion, handing the passengers intact plates. "Take care of these, I'd rather you took them. . . . Please, rue Saint-Jacques in Paris, take them to rue Saint-Jacques. . . ."

Gabriel spent the two days and nights of that journey in the company of a touching snapshot (Mme. de Verneville and Inspector General Verrier seated on their elephants ready for the tiger hunt). The picture's sharp lower right-hand corner drilled a hole in his chest. He still bears the scar today. (You liar, a woman did that, Clara roars, just to please him when he explains for the tenth time how he got this strange wound.)

The convoy stopped at every station. The local authorities had assembled more crates, more mountains.

"This is all ready to go. Read the orders from the ministry. Everything to be transferred to Saigon. So here are portions of the land registry, the tax rolls, overseas personnel records, reference books—"

"Impossible, impossible."

"—the budget department's files, land-reapportionment plans. Read the orders. . . ."

With a blast of his whistle, the chief engineer attempted to make his getaway, pursued by the local authorities, getting more furious and more threatening the more speed our convoy picked up, if you can call it speed, while still more human forms came scrambling aboard.

By the end of the journey there was nothing to be seen of the train, not even the locomotive. The Trans-Indochina Express was nothing but a dense mass of heads, arms, legs, and suitcases advancing on the rails, pulled along by its own steam.

# VI

## SAIGON (CONTINUED)

When he thinks back to his stay in Cochin China, Gabriel can't help cursing his positivist education. Posivitism with its three barely subdivided states (theological, metaphysical, scientific) was inadequate preparation for Asia and its depths. Even Catholicism, in spite of the Holy Trinity, the four Evangelists, and the Twelve Apostles, remains a simple religion, altogether sketchy when compared to the dizzying complexities of reincarnation.

Emerging molded and misshapen from the train, Gabriel addressed himself in the following Cartesian terms:

a. In all likelihood Louis is dead.

b. But his vital principle survives and is floating about in search of a new dwelling place.

c. What kind of environment do vital principles prefer? Answer: Decaying ones, where metamorphosis would be accelerated (just as we talk nowadays of the acceleration of particles). A place where death (if only because of the climate) immediately triggers the mechanism of rot and therefore of rebirth.

d. And what on this earth and in this late spring of 1954 is the capital of decay? Answer: Saigon, rue Catinat, terrace of the Continental Hotel.

It was therefore on this terrace that he sat for several weeks waiting for his father to return.

In this former shrine he swiftly acquired the status of a regular. The staff fussed over him, held him up as an example to other customers.

"Well, ladies and gentlemen," the manager of the Continental would say, "everyone else is planning to leave Indochina, but Gabriel Orsenna intends to stick it out come what may."

Despite his gloomy expression, men and women rose and came over to shake his hand.

"Thank you, monsieur! We need men like you south of the seventeenth parallel."

Noble words. Hypocritical words, uttered by the very people who were seeking to sell out but (with things as they were) finding no takers: Catinat department stores, Brewers and Bottlers of Indochina, the Randon Corporation, Descours & Cabaud, Portail Bookstores, Charnier Galleries. . . . (Selling? Slashed-price liquidation might be more accurate.)

Even the hotel manager, on certain evenings, had his moments of doubt. He approached Gabriel.

"It's a heavy load, the Continental. If you only knew, Monsieur Orsenna. After all these years. And its annex, La Perruche—all these rooms, all these tables weighing on one man's shoulders."

All around him they picked up the refrain.

"Yes, it's time someone else took over the burden; we've done more than our share for the free world."

Gabriel ignored them all. He was still searching. Like a Wimbledon fan he looked right and left, right and left. His neighbors at other tables mistook his vigilance for fear.

"Don't be alarmed, monsieur, they haven't thrown grenades onto café terraces since 1949. And don't forget the Geneva Treaty. Dien Bien Phu did have its positive aspects after all."

But Gabriel wasn't frightened. He was lonely and looking for his father. He studied every face, scanned every living thing, every passerby whether human, dog, or cat, birds on boughs, vultures on the wing.

He was waiting for a sign. Reproaching himself for having lived almost all his life without preparing for this exercise, this crucial exercise: learning to recognize—in someone passing by—the presence of a person who has passed away.

One night, tortured as usual by thoughts of Ann and Clara (what are they doing at this very minute?), unable to sleep, Gabriel heard sounds, noise, singing, laughter. He dressed and went downstairs. To get a glimpse of the grand old Saigon he had never known. And then, who could say? Might Louis have singled out some partygoer as a temporary abode?

In the lobby the manager was biting his nails.

"It's not that I approve, Monsieur Orsenna—my word, no!—but I do understand them."

"What's going on?"

"Those ladies and gentlemen"—he pointed to the closed door of a private reception room—"are celebrating the sale of the Charnier Galleries. To an American. I shall tell them to make a little less noise. Some of my guests are trying to sleep."

The following morning people stopped at the lucky sellers' table to congratulate them. The happy couple made no attempt to contain their joy. They were sailing next day.

"And you know what the Americans are going to make of our galleries? A university! To build tomorrow's Indochina. Yes, it warms our hearts, my wife and me, to be leaving on such an optimistic note!"

Which didn't prevent those still trying to sell from gnashing their teeth: celebrating the event so noisily would simply drive prices even lower.

From that day onward Gabriel studied American tourists more closely; there were more of them every week, and soon they were bold enough to frequent the terrace of the Continental. You had to scoot over for them, give way to their unwavering smiles, put up with their Hawaiian shirts.

And what if my father . . . ? Gabriel wondered.

But this notion remained outside him, like a wasp, a small permanent presence, irritating and dangerous.

Yet there were many arguments in support of an American incarnation for Louis: had not Marguerite blazed the trail? Whoever still had a true taste for Empire in this second half of the twentieth century must surely want to be adopted by the United States. And so, shaking off the usual restraint of a stranger, Gabriel approached these larger-than-life folk, came close enough to step on their toes. He inspected them, sniffed them, looked desperately for a wink, the slightest sign, something like: "Yes, Gabriel, it's me. Don't worry. I'm just storing up a little American vitality but soon I'll be back in France."

These overtures, these first steps, bought him a few rude remarks (although his age was some protection). But most of the time he endured endless evenings, appalling hotel conversations, the lethal boredom of male discussions, which for hours on end and detail by detail centered on all-encompassing plans to reform the tropics.

"Do you know Thomas Joseph Corcoran?"

"No."

"He's our new consul in Hanoi. Just you wait, he'll soon have Indochina back in shape."

And the more days went by, the more the Hawaiian shirts settled in, the farther Louis retreated. "Well, too bad, Gabriel. You didn't try hard enough. In the long run, you didn't love me. I'm off for good, Gabriel. . . ."

The plane lifted off uneventfully from Tan Son Nhut. I took with me: Traou Mad butter-cookie crumbs, two photographic plates from the French National Geographic Society, an unpaid bill from the Bay of Along Hotel, a map of Old Hué, the smell of pastis on the terrace of the Continental, a joke that had made M. Franchini roar with laughter ("I prefer nice behinds to great beyonds"), images when I closed my eyes of Hawaiian shirts, the swarming hum of a squad of Manufrance bicycles on the move in the jungle, the ludicrous sight of a French cabinet minister all dressed up for shrimp fishing, a governor who was partial to American women, a foolish need for colonial expositions, a problem of bedsheets airmailed to Saint-Brieuc, a man's first name, Louis: none of this can fairly be called excess baggage.

## 19

# *My Country's Justice*

AFTER THE END, the story gallops.

Back in Paris, Gabriel stopped by the auction gallery on the rue Drouot before traveling on to Cannes.

Something told him he might find his father there, or some trace of his father, because sooner or later everything turns up at the Drouot auction.

But it was an off day, offering enamelwork, Spanish peasant furniture, British stamps, nothing that might have belonged to Louis even in a secret life. No resemblance either between Louis and these collectors, with their noses pointed alternately at the coveted object and the catalogue.

But Gabriel did not lose hope. Gabriel would be back.

He had only to wait. Like the Drouot auction house, which casts its nets and then patiently waits.

After the Lyon stop our hero began to tremble, knowing that at his age there are no second chances: after a reunion that fails to click each party goes his separate way and lives the rest of his life alone. He therefore resolved to be the last passenger to get off, and he would exit from the last car of the train, so that Ann and Clara, seeing him from a distance and being unable to compare him with other travelers, might the more easily reaccustom themselves to his short stature.

He followed this strategy to the letter. It obliged him to change seats a number of times en route, for part of the train stayed in the station at Valence, and at Marseille they added sleeping cars (not real ones; the kind you convert into seats in the daytime) but he had learned to be constantly on the alert against such mishaps.

Only the handsome can afford to relax.

At Cannes, as planned, he got out last, from the last car.

Soldiers scrambled for the exits; families embracing one another vanished down underground passageways. Then the platform was empty.

They were not there.

But beneath the clock a solitary and imposing figure stood waiting. Pale flannel trousers, a rather loose blazer. The look of a yachtsman on vacation, minus the drinks at the Yacht Club. Minus any inclination whatsoever to weigh anchor. A dry-land yachtsman. As you drew nearer you saw that his face was deeply lined (comforting proof that tall people too have worries) and lit by a smile wide enough to swallow Cannes station.

The blazer thrust out a hand.

"Gabriel Orsenna, isn't it? Don't worry. I've been divorced myself many times. And I promise that they're waiting for you at home."

"But how did you recognize me?"

"Ah. They warned me."

"What about?"

"Guess."

And we didn't stop laughing until we reached number 13 avenue Wester Wemys (an alarmingly steep and narrow lane despite its grand name).

"Do you trust hand brakes?" asked the yachtsman. "Neither do I."

And as we wedged large stones beneath the rear wheels (not with an idle kick, as so many hill dwellers do, but carefully, our hands working out the best angles, our noses almost in the tail pipe): "Yes, it's obvious we've been through many divorces," said Gabriel.

The vacationing yachtsman pushed through a gate.

The air smelled of laurel, of hot stones, of nasturtium, that smell which keeps me company as I tell of it, as I remember and tell, sitting at this desk overlooking the garden: it has become the smell of my life.

They were there.

The three of us dined in the library. The yachtsman had disappeared.

"Your yachtsman is a papermaker," said Clara.

"And he has a wife," said Ann. "They live in Paris and come here only rarely, when the paper business permits."

I looked at them. Clara. Ann. Clara and Ann.

I blinked my eyes.

"What's the matter? Are you ill?" Clara asked anxiously. "Did you get grit in your eye from the locomotive? Do you want me to get it out?"

Gabriel shook his head several times: No Ann, no Clara. He simply felt the urgent need to pay tribute to two tiny parts of his body he had hitherto disregarded, unjustly disregarded. Eyelids have a most important role to play. They are like doors that never stop opening. Their function is to usher women in, usher women in, usher them endlessly into a man's life.

The sequel arrived in the mail.

Next morning, bright and early, two ordinary letters and a light brown envelope.

Ordinary, that is, if you discount the long list of addresses crossed out one by one.

~~Île de la Jatte, Levallois~~
~~Hotel Continental, Saigon~~
~~Grand Hotel, Hué~~
~~Bay of Along Hotel, Hanoi~~
~~Île de la Jatte, Levallois~~
Avenue Wester-Wemys, Cannes-la-Bocca

So many addresses seemed excessive, like row after row of decorations on a hero's chest, extending right down to his belt.

Ann was warning me. In a businesslike manner. Without wasting time, without literary frills. No-nonsense format:

CALLER'S NAME: Knight, Ann
DATE OF CALL: April 10, 1954
TIME OF CALL: 9:17 A.M.
OBJECT OF MESSAGE: Clara. Red alert.
Festival here. *Monsieur Ripois* crew renting house. Atmosphere very Dolce Vita. Head cameraman most attractive discusses light constantly with my sister. In short, Red Alert.
WILL CALL BACK:

PLEASE CALL:
CANCEL APPOINTMENT:
OTHER: Come back quick.

Before opening the second message I raised my head and a gentle breeze bore Louis over to greet me, Louis's ghost. "No, don't get up, Gabriel, I'm just passing through." The Cannes Festival was still something of a regret with him, one of his last: "We should have given it some thought, Gabriel; perhaps the Film Festival is the modern form of the universal exposition. You're young, Gabriel; couldn't you get a job with the festival?"

CALLER'S NAME: Ann
DATE OF CALL: May 2, 1954
TIME OF CALL: 8:05 P.M.
OBJECT OF MESSAGE: Clara. Bed empty this morning. Left with head cameraman *Monsieur Ripois*. As expected. Too bad for you. More than fathers in life.
WILL CALL BACK:
PLEASE CALL:
CANCEL APPOINTMENT:
OTHER: Come back anyway. Sister and tire expert objective allies.

Gabriel looked through the window. The sun had just appeared over the rooftops. Clara had gone downstairs and was already taking pictures. Bent over the flowers in a pale blue robe. He told himself he was very lucky. The head cameraman on the *Monsieur Ripois* crew must smoke in bed, or something, anathema to Clara. For as far as his own powers were concerned, Gabriel had no more illusions. Clara seduced. Went on seducing. Would seduce to the end. Gabriel would never be free of it.

The last envelope (brown) contained a summons from the Nice police:

> Your presence required tomorrow June 1, 1954, 10 A.M. In case of absence, report as soon as you return.

## *City of Nice*

I took the boulevard Gambetta from the station. People seemed to be strolling. Perhaps I was wrong. You look as if you are on vacation when you wear light-colored clothes. It was the delivery hour. There were smells of onions, of cut flowers, of new cardboard boxes. Someone was unloading an enormous bouquet from a van. All you could see was plump arms embracing the stems and a bald dome peeping above the red mass of carnations. A line had already formed outside the welfare office. A policeman, seated on a bench, was pulling on white sleeve covers.

Farther down, on the Promenade des Anglais, a group of window washers gazed at the façade of the Négresco. They leaned their long-handled swabs and special padded ladders against a bench between two tubs of flowers. They were counting the windows and were dismayed at the result.

## *Police Station*

No point in dawdling. Identity declared. Referral to a superior. Introduction into an off-white, very off-white, office. Smell of Gauloise tobacco smoke. Eight-by-eleven sheet of paper inserted with some difficulty into a typewriter. Two hours of questions and answers. Giving up. ("This is all very complicated.") Signing of brief statement. "Sergeant, take him to the judge." End of police-station sequence.

## *Judge*

Madame Judge. In fact, Mademoiselle Judge. Mlle. Lublin. Gray hair, bowl haircut. Smoker. Not unpleasant. But a smoker. And Gabriel, taking his seat before her, reflected that defendants should have the right to choose between smoking and nonsmoking judges. A prisoner, once proven guilty, can be fined or sent to prison or even condemned to death. But there is no article in the Penal Code pertaining to chronic bronchitis or lung cancer. This thought (I shall write to the Chief Justice about it) bolstered his spirits before the preliminary hearing.

*Attorney*

On leaving the Palais de Justice, a brandy in a café of the same name (Palais). Naïve Gabriel realizes today that the sympathetic young man who approached him ("You look so pale, are you ill?") was not there by chance.

Funeral parlors stand next to hospitals. Plaster expressions of eternal regret can be bought at cemetery gates. Félix A. was on the lookout for clients in the Café du Palais.

*Night*

Often in the middle of the night (I believe I've already mentioned this), when one of the three, Clara, Ann, or I, is overcome with fear, the other two come to the rescue. We turn on all the lights.

Clara takes pictures of things. Lots of things, a table leg, a burned-out bulb, a shoe. Develops them on the spot. And finally day dawns.

"You—sweet little Gabriel—charged with a crime; it's too funny!"

"In a trial does everything come out, Gabriel?"

"Will you be talking about us?"

"We're going to be young again, thanks to you, Gabriel, thanks to your trial."

"Now don't tell lies, Gabriel. Ann and Clara will do their best to further their country's justice."

And that is how they were when the handwriting expert saw them on opening her window that morning, the three of them chatting in the big bed. She tried to recall Gabriel's writing. She wondered if a man's writing might reveal his taste for sisters.

*Letter from Louis*

Bach Mai airport, Hanoi

Gabriel,

Would you do me one last favor?

Would you allow me to burden you a little?

For you see a dying man must make himself light, light, without baggage, if he is to have a chance of catching another existence.

Read the Buddhists, Gabriel. They'll tell you the fate of heavy people. They are not reincarnated, Gabriel. They stay on the earth, in the earth.

Is that really what you want for your father, Gabriel? Maggots, bones? Do you want to deprive him of further travels?

I know you.

You agree? Thank you.

I shall be frank, Gabriel. Your old Louis is going to cause you a few more headaches. But they will be the last, I swear. I was forced to tell them you were responsible for the things they accused me of, do you understand? My bicycle business with Dekaerkove, for example. They're going to question you for sure. You'll be obliged to tell your story. It will do you good, Gabriel. People should lay their lives bare, Gabriel, not hug them to themselves the way you do. Every life is special. The minutest detail is worth describing. We should make universal expositions of our lives. One day you will finally have a son, Gabriel, and sons like to know who their father was. Take my word for it: I know nothing of mine, except that he was Mexican. Thanks to me, your story will swell the records of justice. One day there will be an Orsenna file in the judicial archives, as good a way as any of achieving immortality.

Nor will your audience let you down: a woman never listens as attentively as a jury. Not Clara, who just goes on taking photos. Not Ann, who never listens at all.

And if it all gets too painful, if things go badly, then show them this letter. I admit I am still suffering from the disease of hope. I admit I helped the Vietnamese Communists. You too, if you hadn't met two sisters, would have joined me in the disease of hope. Damn these two sisters for stripping you of your sense of History! I don't reproach you. It is not your fault. How can you believe in Progress when you are maddened by an impossible love (love of sisters)? My son Gabriel has no great project for the human race, my son Gabriel has only two ambitions (two sisters) and only one philosophy (bounciness, not dialectics). *My son is gentle, botanical, cowardly, democratic.*

But please keep this confession secret for as long as you can. Don't disclose it until the very last moment. Give me time to move into my new existence. The dynamics of reincarnation have nothing in common with the class struggle. Once I've settled in, perhaps I'll return to communism. But let me travel light on the way there. Relieve me of my ideas. I don't want policemen trampling on my grave or rummaging through my papers. I authorize you to deal with them. Thank you for doing this. And I'll see you in Jerusalem, as our Jewish friends say.

Your light father Louis embraces you, Gabriel.

Lightly, Gabriel, thanks to you.

An imaginary letter.

Never written by Louis.

Or at any rate, never received by Gabriel.

So who could have denounced me? The Saigon police inspector, perhaps, once it became known that bicycles were instrumental in the fall of Dien Bien Phu? Or Ann, or Clara, for a lark, just to recapture their past?

Gabriel had not waited for Louis's advice: his whole life was there, told in full, a fat file 800 pages long, a true and meticulously told tale. An impossible love (two sisters) leaves plenty of free time for work. It is ready then, this life, for whoever might like to read it, written for a son's eyes, but, since this son is slow in coming, ready for the judge, why not? What would you like to know about me, Mademoiselle Judge?

The judge and Gabriel were not interested in the same things. As soon as our hero mentioned Levallois, Auguste Comte, time standing still in Belém (Brazil), or the Washington and Albany, Mlle. Lublin impatiently flapped her hand.

"No red herrings, please, Monsieur Orsenna. We are in Indochina. How did the Vietminh pay you for their bicycles?"

Red herrings indeed; what an expression! So talking about oneself was introducing red herrings? Could I be a herring, could my life have been red?

I swear I did my best, Louis. I began slowly. Then, little by little, just to please them, I invented plots, dreamed up deeds of derring-do, perhaps I told it like it was, Louis, but you should have given me more information, you know, how the bicycles got to the jungle in Vietnam—through China, wasn't it, through Canton and Yunnan and then Lao Kay, the Red River Valley? I'm right, aren't I, Louis, aren't I? Well, they didn't believe me, neither the judge nor handsome Félix. They stared more and more pityingly at me. Why is this harmless little man going to so much trouble? He could never pass himself off as a Communist collaborator.

A dreadful feeling to disappoint people, especially for Gabriel, who is so anxious to be loved.

To think I believed this would be a famous case! That's what the judge was thinking. She sighed between drags on her cigarette.

Here I was dreaming of a genuine political trial! thought my attorney, stealing desperate glances at his watch.

Then Gabriel stopped dead. Politely said goodbye. Rose. Was not stopped by the police. Ultimate humiliation.

"My fee? Fee for what?" the attorney shouted a little later on the sidewalk outside the Café du Palais (its customers had turned to stare). "You actually wanted to be indicted, didn't you? You wanted me to help you take a dive, yes, that's it! Well, let me tell you, my fine friend, I have no wish to be disbarred because of you. An attorney helps keep people out of jail, not throw them in. Ask the President of the Bar Association if you don't believe me. Yes, that's it; write to him!"

And he charged off without another word, without a handshake, head thrust forward as if he wanted to butt something. But what? The Nice air?

Forgive me, Louis, I wasn't up to the part; forgive me, I hope this failure won't ruin your plans, that you will still be reincarnated. It is terrible, you know, not to feel anything, at the end of a life, I mean not to feel anything, *anything*, not even guilty.

Gabriel often thinks of Mlle. Lublin. It was with great regret that she dismissed (in a manner of speaking) my case. Her wistfulness that day was obvious: rather nervous gestures, staring off into space, more cigarettes than usual. An understandable wistfulness.

A magistrate's life is not cheerful: gray offices, gray dossiers. So many gray offenders charged with misdemeanors, so few public enemies Number One. So when a promising case comes along, botanical and Marxist, incestuous and filial, it's only human, you seize hold of it. You close the book on it most reluctantly, and only because you have no choice, because this little botanical man, Gabriel Orsenna, has nothing—nothing!—of the terrorist about him, no matter what he says. Oh, why do the most interesting cases turn out to be innocent? I should never have chosen this career, Mlle. Lublin must say to herself.

Gabriel often toys with the idea of sending her roses. They would have a reconciliation. They would lunch together from time to time in the Vieux Port. They would talk about life. They would exchange points of view: a magistrate's point of view for a tire expert's point of view. She would protest—"Oh, I don't usually"—but would let him pour her some more wine. . . .

Gabriel never carried out his plan. He is angry with Mlle. Lublin. In fact he is getting angrier and angrier with her as the years go by and time becomes harder to kill. He has it on reliable authority that some magistrates, true friends of the human race, make a point of letting the trials of old people drag on and on. They know that a very embroiled, very complicated lawsuit is the most welcome of occupations for retired people. Better still: a second youth.

Mlle. Lublin was not so obliging.

# *Epilogue*

WELL.

Here we are sitting together with evening approaching.

Clara and Gabriel.

Louis has disappeared. Elisabeth has disappeared. Markus has disappeared. Marguerite has left for America.

Ann will be back soon from her business trip to Monaco.

We are the three survivors.

The chief peculiarity of the Orsenna and Knight families, apart from overweening ambition, is their faculty for disappearing. We leave no bodies. That is why Gabriel never takes his eyes off Ann, off Clara. He finds them beautiful; they might easily disappear, like the others.

We are sitting on the café terrace at the end of rue d'Antibes. An impossible place during the festival, but so quiet and welcoming now.

Soon we'll order a drink and watch the fishing boats come in.

It is the hour when Bao Dai usually takes the air. His two bodyguards are his best guarantee of anonymity. You notice only them. They talk loudly, fling racing odds and horses' names at each other. They go to Cagnes-sur-Mer every day during the former emperor's afternoon nap. It would be the ideal time for an assassin. But what purpose would it serve to assassinate a former emperor?

There are days when I think the Côte d'Azur looks like Indochina. Hardly surprising. Most of the piasters reaped over there have been invested in this area. And everyone is waiting for death. In the sun, just like over there.

Well.

The dossier sits in front of us. Gabriel never lets it out of his sight. He carries it everywhere in a schoolboy's satchel. He hopes the case will be reopened one day, that he will be able to tell a jury about his life, about himself, since Ann and Clara don't listen to him as attentively as he would like. An inattentiveness Louis mentioned, you may recall, in his imaginary letter.

Sailors—they must be sailors—are repainting their boats for summer.

How much white paint do they use in preparation for summer every year? Such essential questions still leap to my mind. By the time I have found the answer, a new question pops up. . . . That's why women find me taciturn.

Clara looks at the schoolboy satchel, the one containing the 800 pages; Clara looks at me.

A small fair-haired boy is playing soccer between the plane trees. He races after a ball, he kicks. He puts all his heart into it. But it is obvious at a glance that his skin is wrong for this game. A too-fair skin that turns too red. Gabriel can foresee the inevitable outcome. The small fair-haired boy's huge disappointment when the trainer one Thursday evening puts a hand on his shoulder, takes him aside, and tells him that for the position of right wing on the first team it-would-be-better-to-leave-it-to-someone-else-but-promise-me-you'll-keep-up-sport-won't-you-kid-sport's-good-for-your-health.

"It could be him," says Clara.

"Yes."

His parents call him from a white Ford Vedette.

"We could give him our name. Orsenna's a beautiful name," says Clara.

"And our life too; perhaps he could be happy in it," says Gabriel.

"Yes," says Clara, "it's often convenient to have another name."

"And the life that goes with it."

We could not see the parents. But we could tell from the sound of their voices that they were worriers. They were worried that "something" might happen to him. They were the sort of people to tell him over and over: Never accept anything from a stranger, do you hear? Never.

"But you should try," said Clara. "Take him our dossier, you never know. Want me to come with you? People are less suspicious when there are two."

* * *

Usually after our evening drink we return to avenue Wester Wemys by the lower road between the wall and the railway line. It is my favorite route; I feel protected there. We hold hands, with me walking in the middle: Ann on the left, Mediterranean side, Clara on the right, railroad side. Gabriel looks from one to the other with joy. There they are, so tall, a good head taller than he is. From time to time they decide to play; they lift him and swing him by his arms as if he were a child beneath the gray hair. They both laugh. Our group fills passersby with delight.

Gabriel hates these moments. But he says nothing. He knows women do not like spoilsports. So he patiently weathers the storm, shouting "Vive la France!" at each swing, which sends Ann and Clara into further gales of laughter. He tries to land as smoothly as possible, then takes a deep breath before bouncing up again and shouting "Vive la France—please stop—Vive la France, Vive la France!"

## ABOUT THE AUTHOR

ERIK ORSENNA is the pseudonym for a Counselor to President François Mitterrand. He is currently in the Ministry of Foreign Affairs, specializing in relations with the Arab World.

His life has always been divided between the "serious" and the imaginary. On the one side, he is a novelist and book publisher, on the other a professor of economics.

*Love and Empire* (called *L'Exposition coloniale* in French) is his fourth novel. It won the Prix Goncourt and gathered enormous critical and public acclaim in France and the rest of Europe.

## ABOUT THE TRANSLATOR

JEREMY LEGGATT was born in India, educated in Paris and Oxford, and now lives in the United States. He is a broadcaster, journalist, editor, and translator.